DO DRUMS BEAT THERE

Doe Tabor

New Victoria Publishers

Norwich, Vermont

Published by New Victoria Publishers Inc., PO Box 27 Norwich, VT 05055
A Feminist Literary and Cultural Organization founded in 1976

Cover Design Claudia McKay

Printed and bound in Canada
1   2   3   4   5   2004   2003   2002   2001   2000

Library of Congress Cataloging-in-Publication Data

Tabor, Doe.
   Do drums beat there : a novel / by Doe Tabor.
      p. cm.
ISBN 1-892281-09-0
   1. Indian activists--Fiction. 2. Indian women--Fiction.
   3. Feminists--Fiction.   I. Title.

PS3570.A235 D6 2000
813'.6--dc21
                              00-025377
                                CIP

Acknowledgements

In addition to Wes Hoskins I wish to thank Barbara Shaw, Beverly Allen, Deanna Mather Larson and Elaine Knighton for their good ears and strong hearts. I also want to express my gratitude to Elizabeth Engstrom, whose class brought us together; to Morgan Smith, Derry Malsh and Carol Monroe for the encouragement necessary to get me enrolled in the University. At the University of Oregon, I wish to thank Wally Slocum for his early library assistance, Lynn Raughley, Peter Ho Davies, Marie Carvalho, Corrina Wycoff and especially Sidner Larson. Special thanks also to Scylla Earls.

For invaluable assistance on and about Alcatraz I want to acknowledge Libby Schaaf of the Golden Gate National Recreation Area, Adam Fortunate Eagle and Joe Morris. My thanks also goes to Thom Chambliss, Jenny Root and everybody at Tsunami Books.

For their help with things Lakota, I thank Dr. A.C. Ross, Dr. Twila Souers, and Robert Owens. For reading rough drafts and giving invaluable feedback my gratitude goes to Kirk Haviland Shultz, Jeffery Mailer for his mechanical expertise, Russell Morton, Jeffrey Burch, Sandy Enos, Jennifer Lampe and my mother, Jean Ewing. For their patience and loving support I thank my children, Matti and Andy. For inspiration, I thank Ferron, whose music has enriched me as a writer and as a woman.

Jill and Mark Wisnovsky, thanks for the first Mac. And to everyone at Sawtooth Writer's Conference; especially Virginia Finkelnburg, the very hospitable Coles, Jeff Metcalf, David Cranes and Barbara Smith—my appreciation for the wonderful opportunity.

A special debt of gratitude to Literary Arts, Inc. for their Emerging Writer Fellowship.

Leaving the Grassland

Lying awake in the soft grey light before dawn, Agnes told herself the *wasicu* have no memory. Unlike the Lakota, Agnes remembered her mother's memories, and through them, her grandmother's, so that her memory reached far back and held many sad times. Some of her mother's people were killed at Wounded Knee. Agnes felt her mother's grief whenever the story was told. She remembered Custer's regiments at Greasy Grass. A great victory. The last victory in the fight with the *wasicu,* "those who eat the fat." Agnes remembered all this, even though she was born in the first year of the new century.

She rolled her old tired bones over and closed her eyes, recalling in detail the day the man came to their land, the land where her babies were born. The place she had buried two of them before they were a year old. The man came to tell them they had to leave, this place is going to be used by the War Department to drop bombs, for practice. She told him no, this was their land, the allotment papers her husband kept in the wooden box beneath their bed said so. He said the Germans and the Japanese could be over these hills soon. The Army needed to be ready and she had to do her part for the War effort. They had to give up their land, must leave in ten days. Ten days! How does one move everything in ten days? And where will we go? This is our home. He promised they could have it back when the War was over. What was left of it. And they would get money for using it. A lease, like leasing grassland to the white ranchers to run their cattle, but this money was for bombing. To pay for damages.

She asked him why the government would want to bomb this land, it was good land. Our river never dries up in summer, unlike most water on the reservation. And the grass is better here than anywhere. The horses and cattle grow fat here. Why not bomb some land where people don't live? The man shook his head and said again it had been decided. They had ten days to move.

She tried to stop crying when Will and Henry came home that night, bone tired from riding all day, moving cattle. They told her she must have misunderstood. Who would bomb Sheep Mountain, the most beautiful place on the reservation? Move all the families that lived there? She must have heard wrong.

The next day the man came back and talked to Will. His name was Ben and he told Will how sorry he was they had to move. The War Department had ordered him to tell everyone around Sheep Mountain their land was going to be a gunnery range. They had to do their part for the war.

The War. Already her only son, Henry, had signed the papers that said he would go fight, like so many of the young men. He was to leave in five days. She asked Ben since they were giving up their land if her son couldn't stay and help them move. How else could they get their cattle off, even if they didn't know where they would go? He said he would ask the government man if her son could be deferred. Henry was angry, he wanted to go fight, but she told him he was needed here.

Five days later they took Henry anyway. He never came home.

She felt again the sorrow of those days and of the years that followed, renewed by the meeting she had attended yesterday. Angry words had flowed like the creeks swollen with the spring rains. Many people like herself were wanting the government to make good on their promise to return Sheep Mountain to those people whose homes had been there. But the Tribal Council told them the government had already paid them, twice, for that land. Agnes stood up and announced the little bit of money they had received six months after being forced to leave, what was left after the seed loan Will had taken out on account of the drought was deducted, that money was only for damages done by the Army and their bombs. She had not accepted the check in '59 and did not want to be "rehabilitated." Everyone in the room got quiet when Agnes asked the Tribal Council just what was under Sheep Mountain that the government wanted so bad. No one on the council answered her. Finally one of them suggested she apply for some of the rehab money. The meeting fell apart when she walked out.

She, and many of the others who left with her, just wanted their land back. It was still good land. Most of the craters left from the bombs had grass growing back in and held the snow melt till summer. The last time she went out there the house was still standing, though the barn had fallen down a long time ago. She was an old woman now but she still wanted to move out there, leave the little cabin on her mother's allotment. The water still tasted good on Sheep Mountain, the sweetgrass and herbs still plentiful. She had buried Will there, next to their children, nine years after they were forced to leave. She promised him she would get his land back.

Agnes pulled herself upright and tightened her curled fingers into fists, then tried to straighten them. The red hot ache that filled her joints matched the brilliance of the sunrise in her east window. She poured herself some willow tea from the cold kettle on the back of the wood stove before she went outside to pray.

* * *

Ritta lifted her bedroom window with a hand on the glass to still its rattle. She sat on the sill, swung her legs outside and dropped into blooming thistle. Shards from an old pane crunched beneath her shoes. Needled leaves poked through the soft denim of her jeans before she pushed the weeds to the ground with her foot. After glancing inside to be certain her sister still slept, she left.

At the edge of the hill the early morning sun touched her face with the promise of another hot day. Prisms sparkled on the lashes of her closed eyes as she breathed the sweet air still damp from the night.

She glanced back at the dust colored houses, clustered on top of the hill. From this distance they all looked the same, been built that way. Cheaper, she supposed, to make them from identical parts. Then no one could say their gov'ment house was better than anybody else's.

Below her, grass rippled in the wind, down the long rolling slope and beyond. No fences. No roads. Just waves of green, tasseling heads on sparse, slender stalks. She never grew tired of looking at it, and knew the colors the grass turned with the seasons: the yellows and golds then burnished brown, until snow filled the gullies and the land looked flat, deep with white. Sometimes, cows had free range and she pretended they were a great herd of buffalo.

She let the slope pull her along, brushing the feathery plumes with her fingertips. At the bottom, she stopped to blow away the pollen and tiny golden petals stuck to the fine hairs of her arm.

Today she would gather more *tinpsila*. She bet Agnes had the bunch from yesterday already peeled and braided. In winter, it was good to pull the hard, white turnips from the tightly twisted leaves and add them to stews.

She remembered the spring three years ago, when she was twelve and Uncle Lawrence first took her out to Agnes' cabin. Ritta was so proud when the grandmother asked her to stay and help gather. This spring, Ritta went alone to dig the roots and brought them to Agnes who waited, rocking on the porch, for her to return.

She checked the laces on her new sneakers. For once her younger brother, Jake, had outgrown a pair before he destroyed them playing basketball. She nabbed the shoes when he complained they were too small for him. Her toes snuggled comfortably beneath the scuffed rubber tips.

A warming breeze blew back her hair. The soft shhh of rustling grass whispered in her ear. She knew as soon as she got to the cabin Agnes would be pulling her hair into tight snake braids, combing out the snarls with stiff fingers. A morning dove coo-coo-cooed. Ritta took a deep breath and began to run.

Three miles later, near the slight rise above Agnes' cabin, Ritta heard a scream. She pushed to the top of the hill, stopped to wipe the sweat from her eyes and looked at the commotion below.

Two men dragged Agnes from her porch. They shoved her at the feet of another man. Agnes shook her fist at him, shouting angry words in Lakota too fast for Ritta to comprehend them.

The man laughed. "You sold the land, old woman. There's not a damn thing you can do about it now."

Agnes pulled herself up. He struck her with the back of his hand. The slap rang out sharply before her muffled whimper.

Without a thought of how she would stop him, only that she must, Ritta hurtled towards him. From behind, she grabbed the arm poised to strike her grandmother again. "Leave her alone!"

He flung her off like one would sling a kitten. She landed hard. All the air left her lungs.

With a fearful look, Agnes shouted, "Ritta, run," before the man hit her again and she slumped to the ground.

Ritta pulled herself up to her elbows and tried to breathe against the sharpness in her chest. With a mighty gasp, her lungs filled. A sharp pull on her hair jerked her backwards. Anger turned to cold fear as somebody pinned her shoulder down.

A dark, pock-marked face sneered above her. "Got a wild one, Frank." His breath smelled sour. She turned away and tried to wrench free, then felt the pop, pop, pop of her shirt snaps. A rough hand shoved beneath her bra, clawed at her breast. Tears filled her eyes as he squeezed hard. Through them she saw Frank Lopate, the man who'd hit Agnes, fumble with the zipper of his jeans. "Hold her, boys."

"Let me go!" She kicked wildly at his groin. The smooth rubber toe of her shoe glanced off his thigh. He caught it and held her foot.

His slap filled her head with a red flood. She felt him yank off her pants. His hands spread open her legs. She pulled her arm free and clawed her ragged nails across his face.

He swiped his cheek and snarled. "Now you did it, bitch." The handle of his gun loomed above her.

A loud crack echoed between her ears. Everything went dark.

Slowly, from some black, still place, she started to rise. Something hard struck her body. Again, then again. Bright, pain-filled flashes split the darkness with every jolt, each bringing her closer to the surface. The side of her face pulsed. She ached deep inside.

One eye opened, focused on nearby bits of hay golden in the sun. Long white corrugated troughs led eventually to a man in a Levi jacket. He sat on the open tailgate, gripping the side of the bouncing truck with one hand, a rifle with the other. His cowboy hat jumped around on his head.

Her body lifted a few inches off the bed and slammed down again. Wincing, she turned over and found Agnes. She looked bad. Her cheeks were the color of ashes, a small trickle of blood dried on her chin.

Ritta waited for the next large bump to roll closer, whispering in her smallest voice, "*Unci*. Grandmother. Can you hear me? We got to get outta here."

Agnes' body flopped about limply, her scarf twisted half off. A small humming moan escaped from her mouth.

Ritta's heart beat so loud she was afraid he would hear it. How could they get away? A *wanblee* screamed. Squinting at the sky she found the hawk's tiny arched silhouette circling between billows of clouds.

The truck stopped. Gears cluncked beneath her before they started uphill, pitching side to side in the ruts. Her body slammed again into the bed. She wondered how Agnes' brittle bones would stand it.

Ritta started to slide and grabbed the side wall. She took a quick look around. They were between Agnes' house and the main road.

The guard bounced on the tailgate. His loose rifle popped up and down between them. He turned to grab it and looked right at her.

Braced against the wheel well, she bent her knees and slammed her feet into his twisted backside as hard as she could. His face froze in surprise. The truck went airborne over another deep rut as he flew off the tailgate. She grabbed for the gun and landed next to it in the chalky dirt. The white truck kept going, sun glinting off the chrome of the siren lights on top of the cab. Agnes, alone in the back, curled into a fetal ball.

Ritta knelt in the tall sparse grass, peering up at cautious intervals. The breeze carried her whisper. "Hold on, Agnes. I'll get Lawrence."

Rubbing her side where it stung bad from meeting the ground she noticed the cool, wet stain on her jeans. Touched it. Stared at the tinge of blood on her fingers.

With the truck's drone growing fainter in the distance she knelt to pick up the rifle, and had to hold the side of her head before she could stand up. Her fingers explored her puffy, hurting cheek as she walked to the guard's sprawled body.

She recognized him, too. Didn't know his name, but she had seen him in town driving one of the police trucks. She wondered why they would hurt Agnes, and what they had done to her. A red trickle spilled over the rock behind his head and soaked into the chalky clay. She kicked him in the side of his soft belly. He didn't move. She hacked up as much as she could from her dry throat and spit on his face before starting downhill. It was miles to Uncle Lawrence's. Miles she knew well.

She left the ruts to run through the waist-high grass, hobbled by the ache in her gut. Something sticky pulled the hairs between her legs. At the bottom, she stopped and listened through the pounding in her chest for the truck's engine, still faint in the distance. Under the cover of cottonwoods along the creek she leaned against a tree until she caught her wind, then undid her pants and squatted to pee. It burned so badly she had to stop and let it go in little squirts. Her blood-stained underwear were ripped to the elastic. She tore them free and cleaned herself with a dry corner before burying them in a heap of last winter's snapped branches.

The grass she had run through was beaten down like an arrow, pointing straight at her. Praying they weren't looking for her yet, she followed the creek bank and went through the water at the shady, low spot she and Agnes always crossed on their way to Lawrence's. Using the rifle like a walking stick, she climbed up the steep slope on the other side, then cradled the gun and tried to run.

Ritta pushed to the top of the first hill, then felt a wave of nausea. She spit a mouthful of bitter bile into the grass and started to cry, but remembered Agnes was still with those men. She picked up the rifle and started down the hill.

Pushing her pain away, she concentrated on each burning breath. Across the flat. Up another hill and down the other side. Picking up her feet. Trying to land on them as she flew down the long slopes.

Her uncle was in the corral, rubbing a blanket over the filly's legs and chest. The young appaloosa whinnied and flung her head in the air. Ritta knew the young horse smelled her fear.

Lawrence looked her way, shielding his eyes against the bright sun. She waved at him and tried to keep going, but stumbled and fell. He climbed through the rails and ran to her on bowed legs.

Kneeling beside her, he gently took her shoulders. "Ritta, what happened?"

"It's Agnes. They have Agnes." She tried to get the words out between raw gulps of air. "I tried to wake her, then I ran away."

His callused hands lifted her until his familiar, weathered face was near her own. "Who? Who has Agnes?"

She had to tell him so they could go. No time to cry. "Frank Lopate and two others. I think they were policemen, too. They hurt her. We got to find her, Uncle."

When Lawrence helped her stand, Ritta saw him notice her dark stained jeans. He pulled the hair away from her swollen cheek. "Let's get you inside."

She nodded. He started her towards the cabin and caught her as she faltered, still clutching the rifle. He gently took it and pulled her arm over his shoulder. "Where did they take her?"

"I don't know. I jumped out at the big hill, on the shortcut to Agnes'."
She grabbed his shirtsleeve. "We got to find her."

"Whoa, girl. We got to take care of you first. Tell me what happened."

"They hit her. I don't know why. I woke up in the back of their truck, me and Agnes. She wouldn't wake up. I pushed one of them off. He hit his head on a rock. Then I ran. They hurt her so bad, Uncle. We gotta find her."

Inside, after putting the gun behind the door, he pumped some water into a basin and handed her a sliver of yellow soap. "Here, wash up. I'll get you some clothes." He ducked behind the tattered curtain that separated the room where he slept.

She looked around. I'm safe here. If they come, I'll hide. It was all so familiar. The slab walls, the hand-made table beneath the basin. Many times she'd sat here with Lawrence and Agnes, listening to their stories.

Agnes. Why?

She tucked her snarled loose hair into the back of her shirt and lathered her hands. Lightly, she rubbed her wound. It broke open again and bled, tinting the water. She tried to clench her teeth against the pain, but that just made it worse. Blotting her skin with a towel, she struggled not to cry as she peered into the cracked mirror that hung on the wall.

From her cheekbone to her jaw looked like raw meat and seeped fresh blood, the whole right side of her face swollen and purplish. She touched beside her ear and opened her mouth a few times, relieved it still worked. A blood vessel near her hairline quivered in time with the throbbing inside her head. She ran her finger along her teeth and felt a cracked molar, maybe two.

Lawrence lifted the curtain, carrying a blanket and a pair of his faded jeans. "These may hang on you some, do you have a belt?" He looked again at her stained pants. She shook her head, shame sharp on her cheeks.

The old man covered her hands, his fingers so gnarled they reminded her of short, twisted branches. "Look, honey. You did real good getting here. Saved your own skin and maybe Agnes', too. I'm going to find her as soon as we get you on your way."

"Uncle, he…they…"

Lawrence put his crooked finger on her lips. "I know." He pulled a leather thong from his pocket. Attached to it was a small, beaded pouch. Ritta knew it was Agnes' work, the medicine wheel in the four sacred colors was one of her favorite designs. Agnes talked a lot about the way things came in fours; roots, stems, leaves and fruit; sun, moon, stars and sky; infancy, childhood, adulthood and old age. "Like where I am now," she'd said, laughing.

Lawrence picked up a small round stone from the window sill and put it in the palm of Ritta's hand. "This will bring you home again, when you make the circle of where you need to go."

Her eyes were full of tears as Lawrence opened the leather folds. She poured the stone into the medicine bag, then tied it closed and draped it around her neck. "Now wash the spit of that man off you and get dressed. Come out to the barn when you're done."

When he closed the door behind him, Ritta took off her dirty clothes and used a corner of the towel as a washcloth. She felt better after she gingerly cleaned between her legs, filling the basin twice from the red-handled pump at the sink. When she was done, she stuffed her bloody jeans into the firebox and lit them with a wooden match, watching long enough to see the denim start to smolder before closing the cast metal door.

Lawrence's pants were baggy but fit all right after she rolled up the cuffs. It was strange being in his clothes. He had always seemed so big.

She finished dressing, found a comb and worked out the snarls. As she parted her hair down the back of her head she thought of Agnes' arthritic but strong fingers and the tight braids the grandmother loved to do. Ritta put her hands over her heart as it threatened to burst with the thought of the dear old woman. *Tunkasila, Wakan Tanka,* watch over her. She tied her flat plaits with strips of soft leather that were beside the comb.

* * *

In a corner of the barn, a shaft of light from a gap in the rusty siding shone on Lawrence's short-cropped steel grey hair. He brushed years of hay dust off an old metal trunk and opened the creaking lid. Inside was the uniform he wore home from the war in Europe, and the army canteen with the hole shot through it. He picked up a framed newspaper clipping with a picture of him and several other men from Pine Ridge sitting at a table with a bunch of old white men in Washington. They had been guests of honor of the Order of Indian Wars, the night before he shipped out. He had found it so ironic, still did; his sitting there with some of the very men who had opened fire on his people at Wounded Knee. But they were fighting on the same side now. He was now the soldier, taking orders to kill. He had hoped to have more honor than these old men had when they wore a young man's uniform.

In the bold print beneath the headline the paper quoted Collier, then director of the BIA, "The fact that the Indians were specially honored guests provides a measure of the transformation that time has brought."

Lawrence had come home from the war proud, but that pride had withered away with each new desecration of the places he held sacred. Nothing had really changed, no matter how many Lakota died.

He knew why they had Agnes. He had told her last night when he drove her out to her place after the meeting that she had angered the New Dealers. She said, "Just because they run for office they don't speak for everybody."

"If you and the rest of the traditionals would vote maybe we could get some changes made."

"It's not my government." Then she scoffed and looked out the window into darkness. She and many other elders had boycotted tribal elections for years.

It made him feel bad, like he should have done more to back her up in the meeting. He knew Agnes had to believe she could get her land back. It kept her going. But Lawrence knew better. He knew the 400,000 acres around Sheep Mountain the military had taken would never be returned. He'd seen the world and knew the power of the United States government. Agnes had seldom been off the reservation.

He took down an olive drab canvas backpack from a nail on the wall and stripped dusty cobwebs from the metal frame. From the trunk, he took the coat, cut the stitching from the embroidered name tag off the front and the gunner emblem off the sleeve with his knife, and stuffed the coat in the bottom of the pack. Digging deeper, past more newspaper clippings and black and white photos of serious young Indian men in the Fourth Infantry, he found the pants and put them in the pack, too. Headlines caught his eye and he remembered clearly the exhilaration of liberating Paris, how proud they were to be fighting. Indians make good soldiers. His was one of the first divisions into Germany, after chasing the Nazis across northern France and Belgium. Served the Nazis right. He was still angry the Germans had declared the Sioux people to be Aryans before the war. It had made him fight them harder.

On the earthen floor he spread the wool blanket he'd taken from his bed and rolled it into a tight bundle, tying it with strands of used baling twine. Peering again into the trunk, his eyes caught the letter Amos Follows Water sent him after the war. Amos was a Blackfoot from Montana. They'd fought side by side many times and had become buddies, even though they hadn't seen each other since. He tucked the letter in the pack.

Ritta walked up and returned his smile, but her eyes were dull.

He pointed to the corner. "Bring me a piece of that tarp over there, and some more twine."

She followed his directions, and watched as he wrapped the bedroll in the canvas and tied it on the frame. "It's about her land, isn't it?"

"*Han*."

"I don't want to leave, Uncle."

"I know. But they'll be looking for you here and you can't go home. I'll find Agnes, but first I'm takin' you to the road to Montana. In the pack there's a letter from an old friend of mine. He'll help you if you can find him. Show him the letter. Tell him what is happening to our people." He closed the trunk and led Ritta back to the cabin, carrying the pack.

Inside, Lawrence pulled coffee cans from the wooden apple crate nailed to the wall beside the stove. He took thin, brown strips of jerky from one and a few handfuls of dried chokecherries from another, putting them in bread sacks he tied with string and dropped in the pack. He took a tin cup with a bent handle and a towel and stuffed them in, then filled a glass jar with coffee. What else, what else?

From a Prince Albert can on the table he shook the small remaining amount of tobacco into a pile on the faded, red plaid oilcloth, then half-filled the can with matches. He snapped the lid shut and put it in the middle of the pack. From his shirt pocket he took several, inch-square pieces of red cloth and tied a pinch of tobacco and a prayer inside each with a length of string, which he attached to the frame of the pack.

He grinned at her as he pulled a tattered curtain away from another cupboard and removed a new package of Oreos. He'd been saving them.

She looked back at him, the hint of a smile on her face. Finally, he took out his small saucepan, placed a can of Campbell's chicken noodle soup in it, and dropped it in the pack, too.

As Lawrence tried to start his pickup, Ritta walked up to the corral, let the filly sniff her outstretched hand, muzzle her braids. Horse lips smacked on her neck and she laughed.

"Good-bye, High Tail." Ritta buried her face in the red mane. The thought of leaving hurt so bad she thought she would break in two, right down the middle. The filly nodded her head in exaggerated agreement.

The old truck pulled up and Lawrence opened the passenger door from the inside. As they drove away, Ritta looked back at the cabin, the barn, the horse in the corral. She knew it would be a long time before she saw this place again.

* * *

Black clouds boiled in from the west, drawing a shadow across the land. Ritta heard, but didn't heed, a distant rumble. The darkness above her split with a crash of lightning that spread to each horizon the instant before it disappeared. A thunderclap immediately followed. She ducked and held her ears.

A gust of warm, pollen-laden air brushed heavily against her cheek. Cleaved only by the road, the vast green sea of grass rolled wildly in the wind. Heavy droplets splattered against the worn gray asphalt.

Ritta pulled the pack from her shoulders and groaned as the weight left her back. Hair whipped across her face. The dusty wind invaded her eyes and stung her skin as she stood to face the storm. Raising her hands at the thunderhead, she shouted, "I am here, *Wakinyan!* I have survived."

The wind blew her screams back. Tears bathed her wounded soul as the rain washed the dried blood from the gash on her face. Her hand touched the bruised places between her thighs.

"Never again. Nobody will ever do that to me again." The wind picked up her vow and carried it away. She thought of the man she had pushed from the truck, his blood spilling onto the ground, and wondered if he died. For a moment she hoped he had, then realized she alone had killed him if he was dead. She knew his friends would want to get even with her for that, even though they had hurt Agnes, and raped her. She remembered what Agnes had said the last time they were together. "Our people fight each other so much there is nothing left to fight the government."

The clouds above burst, as if a hole had opened and let fall a wall of water. She tilted her head back and let herself be drenched. Soon the droplets lightened, the storm passed.

Through the gray curtain of rain, beyond where the road disappeared, glowed a pair of headlights. Thank God, a ride. She wiped the rain from her face, lightly pressing the injured side with her cool hand. What if it's them? They'll kill me. What am I going to do?

She heard a soft cooing behind her. A small brown owl, perched on a lichen-covered post, swiveled and glided over the prairie on silent wings. Ritta shuddered, owls being *Wakan*. Ritta looked at the encroaching headlights, then threw her pack over the fence. Lifting the middle strand of barb-wire, she slipped through and followed the bird.

Before she hit her stride the soft, wet earth crumbled beneath her shoes. She slid, then hunkered down in the slate mud of the draw. Her fingers clutched the pouch that hung from her neck as the mud streaked police truck slowly drove by. She lifted her head in time to see the passenger's face. And the scratches where her fingernails had raked him. She half expected to see Agnes still in the back, but it was empty. She laid her head in her arms and cried long after the truck was gone.

When she looked up again, the sun broke through the end of the fleeting storm. Minute sparkles of light shimmered from water droplets dangling on bent grasses. The air filled with the warm aroma of rain-bruised sage. In front of her a small, brown mottled feather drifted down from the sky. Looking up, she thanked the owl, wiped her muddy hands on her jeans, then took the feather and stroked it flat before she put it in the beaded pouch. The sharp quill end stuck out just a little.

She shook the rain from the canvas pack and leaned it on the fence post, then removed a damp t-shirt, tattered around the v-neck. Drier than the one I got on. Thank you, Uncle Lawrence. The memory of him gathering supplies and stuffing them into the backpack made her chest hurt before she brushed the thought away.

The bra strap broke when she pulled apart the snaps of her wet shirt. "Damn it. That's my only bra." Her fingers fumbled with the hooks then peeled the soaked, quilted cups off. She noticed a sting along her ribs and lifted her left arm. When her fingers touched the raised, red marks she remembered the man who'd grabbed her. Damn him.

She rubbed the material over her cold and clammy breasts before pulling the dry shirt on. Leaning to each side she squeezed the rain from her braids, then wrung out the wet shirt and torn brassiere and placed them on top of the post.

She dug around in the pack until she found the coat and a pair of baggy green pants. They had lots of pockets and buttons along the top that she couldn't find any reason for. After taking off her wet jeans, she slipped the green ones on. These would be okay if I had a belt. She untied one of the lengths of bailing twine from the bedroll and pulled two of the buttons together with a loop.

The coat hung to her knees, its sleeves covering her fingers until she rolled the cuffs up twice. Ritta smiled and buried her nose in the crook of her arm, breathing in the warm scent of grass hay and horse manure. She wrapped the coat tight around her, surrounded by pleasant memories of Lawrence's barn. Then she remembered the Oreos.

She found the package, carefully opened the cellophane wrapper just wide enough to extract the first cookie, which she put whole in her mouth. It dissolved while she tied her bundle of wet clothes on the pack frame and slung it over her shoulders.

The last heat from the setting sun warmed the sodden ground. Like ghostly apparitions, mists of steamy vapors rose off the pavement and low mounds of rock. The road's crumbling shoulders, overcome with tufts of grass and stunted sunflowers, crunched beneath her feet. She looked towards home, far in the distance and shrouded by the veil of rain. She stood tall and tossed her braids over her shoulders, each thumping on the backpack in turn. Her shadow stretched out long and flat on the ground. Slowly, she lifted an arm and waved good-bye. The shadow waved back.

Resolutely, she turned around and walked the faded center line. Taking another cookie from the package, she twisted it apart and scraped the sweet filling on her lower front teeth. She sucked on the hard part, until it turned to chocolate mush in her mouth. Eating one Oreo after another, she walked towards the sun as it sank lower into the prairie.

When the sky's rosy hue dimmed to purple dusk, Ritta found a trail that intersected the road. As she climbed through the fence, tufts of gray hair caught in the barbs lightly touched her face. Wolf. She took the fur and put it into her pouch before following the winding path that led to a narrow stream swollen with the downpour. Along its bank grew chokecherries and pussy willows, some of the bark ragged where deer had gnawed. She knelt, scooped water into her hands and let the debris settle before she drank.

Ritta pulled dry grass from under the shrubs and snapped off the dead tips of branches. In a patch of barren earth she piled the tinder and struck a match on the metal zipper of her coat. She touched the dancing flame to the smallest of twigs. When the fire was strong enough she left to search the creek bank, dragging back part of an old fence post and several dead sagebrush. Soon, she sat on the blanket near the blazing end of the post, eating jerky and dried fruit.

She loved sleeping in the open. Every summer, when the rains quit, she and her sister, Janey, hauled their bed outside. The mattress filled up with so much dust they had to beat it with sticks before they put it back in their room in the fall.

Lying here miles from home, wrapped in the Army coat and watching the stars get brighter, she felt safe enough. Until her eyes closed.

No matter how hard she tried she couldn't stop the scenes that played on the back of her eyelids, so she gave up and stared at the countless stars that sparkled above her, picking out the few constellations she knew. When the half moon rose over the hillside, she was still lying on her bedroll, staring at the Milky Way. An occasional tear stung her wound. Finally, she threw off the blanket and knelt by the dying fire, stoking it back to flames.

The creek sang in the moonlight, its shimmer danced on the surface of the water. She stood on the bank, aware of the ache in her heart and the soreness between her legs, wishing she could wash the pain away.

Her clothes came off quickly. The water was warmer than she expected as she knelt in the stream. She scooped some into her cupped hands, held it and offered her gratitude, then drank. After splashing her face to cool her burning cheek she poured some over her breasts to soothe her heart. Her body glistened in the moonlight, a woman's round body, newly formed from the pudginess of childhood. She still hadn't gotten used to it.

When her pain was replaced with chilling numbness, she rose and shook like a dog, spraying droplets and swinging her braids. It made her cheek hurt again, and she held the side of her face, burning hot in her cool palm as she left the water. She broke off a few branches of sagebrush to put on the glowing coals. As the flames consumed the sage, she stood in the fragrant smoke and let the heat dry her body. This time, when she crawled into the protective folds of her blanket, she fell asleep.

As the first light of dawn reached over the horizon and birds began to sing Ritta rolled over, her arm searching for her sister. She woke, realizing there was no one lying next to her. Janey, where are you? She sat up, stiff and sore, and watched the sun creep over the edge of the earth. I'm all alone. What am I going to do?

She had enough food for a day, and the twenty-three dollars Lawrence had stuffed into her hand before he drove away. And, someone out there, somewhere, who would help her if she could find him. She reached for the pack, pulled out the rest of the Oreos and popped a whole one in her mouth before searching for the letter, which had slipped to the bottom. As she chewed, she read the return postmark. San Diego, CA May 5, 1949.

My God, that's twenty years ago. How am I going to find this man? She opened the yellowed envelope and read the words on the brittle page, written in a careful script:

Lawrence, I am leaving the hospital soon and going back to Montana to work on a ranch near Absorakee. My cousin is married to the foreman. He is looking for cowboys that can really gentle horses. I told him I know an Indian that can break horses so gentle babies ride them. He said come if you need a job. I am thankful to you for saving my skin in France and will always owe you a great debt. I hope all is good back home. Your friend, Amos Follows Water.

Ritta carefully folded the paper and put it back in the envelope. Now, at least, she had a place to start. Fear crept slowly into her heart. She had only been off the reservation three times. Last summer, Lawrence took her and Agnes to Bear Butte, then to *Paha Sapa,* the beautiful Black Hills, for ceremonies, held secretly since they could be jailed for praying with the sacred pipe that had been handed down from their ancestors. And she'd been to Rapid City, twice. Once for the county fair. Then she had been with Mom, Janey and the boys, and that awful man her mother was seeing, who kissed her and tried to put his tongue in her mouth.

She pulled open the pouch and poured the contents into her palm. She stroked the owl feather. The wolf fur she pinched between her fingers and thought of the story Agnes told her about a woman who lived with the wolves, how they brought her meat every night. And another story where the wolves hid in the day, never being noticed. They too were very *Wakan,* sacred.

Ritta rolled the round rock between her palms, then noticed the scratches on it. Looking closely, she recognized the shape of Bear Butte. Lawrence must have drawn it with his knife, etching the smooth surface of stone.

She began to put them back in the medicine bag when a splashing noise in the creek startled her, making her heart jump against her ribs. The river otter, surprised by the unexpected human, dashed away.

The carved stone rolled into the dirt.

Ritta laughed at her jitters and tied the bag shut. She tucked the letter in the pack and took out the pan and jar of coffee. After grabbing two cookies she walked along the creek bank in the opposite direction than the evening before, playing an old childhood game of pretending to be the only person alive. All this is my home. She looked out over the prairie, ignoring the farmhouse in the distance. And everything I need is here.

She broke several small, dead limbs from the shrubs downstream and returned to her camp. After reviving the fire, she placed a few large rocks around the flames to hold a pan of water, threw in a small palm full of coffee into the pot to simmer and went to wash her face in the stream. When she came back she poured the black liquid into the tin cup which she held with the towel wrapped around its handle. The bitter brew tasted better after dunking several cookies in it.

She packed her few possessions and poured water over the coals with the pan, stirring them until she was certain no heat was left in the sodden ashes. Sorry the deer would be frightened by her scent, she silently thanked them for the use of their refuge.

*　*　*

Thirty miles away, Lawrence buried Agnes.

He'd found her, barely alive and reeking of whiskey, near where Ritta said she'd escaped. Lawrence knew what the Tribal Police had done; beaten the poor old woman unconscious then doused her to make it look like she was drunk and had died in the hot sun. As carefully as he could, he hoisted her into the truck. On the way back to his place, with Agnes slumped on the seat next to him, he stopped at Thomas Running Deer's. Thomas agreed to drive to Kyle and ask an elder there for help.

Through the long hours of night Lawrence tended Agnes, wetting her parched mouth, washing the alcohol from her wrinkled skin, carefully binding her broken ribs with strips of sheets. She became lucid only once. Her eyes opened wide, her raspy voice screamed, "Ritta, run!" before she receded back into the deep sleeping place.

Through the night he lit sage and sang what songs he knew. He had promised Agnes many years ago that he would not let her body be embalmed, that he would bury her himself if he could. She was dead when Thomas arrived with the elder. The old, bent woman wrapped Agnes in moth-eaten buckskin. She began the death song so Agnes could find her way to their people, sprinkling the body with herbs from the tattered suitcase that held her sacred things.

At dawn, Lawrence began to dig the grave behind the barn. The sun was nearly overhead as he carried her body from the cabin.

When the earth was back in place he pounded a piece of galvanized pipe into the ground for a marker and attached a long strand of tobacco ties to it. Then he joined in the ancient burial song. A *wanblee*, high overhead, screamed in her spiral ascent.

*　*　*

By mid-morning the sun was hot on Ritta's shoulders as she trudged slowly along the narrow road that severed the undulating prairie. She longed to go back. She wanted to run the miles to Agnes' house, wanted to know that Agnes was all right, but with a sharp swing of her head, her braids whipping over the pack on her back, she walked away from all that she loved.

By noon her feet were blistered where the heels of her socks wore thin.

Sweat dripped into her eyes, stung her cheek, staining the sleeve of her t-shirt where she wiped it away. She was so thirsty she picked up a small pebble from the roadside and rubbed the dust off before putting it in her mouth to suck on. She considered opening the can of chicken noodle soup in her pack, but the thought of the concentrated, salty broth wasn't appealing.

She kept on walking, and tried to forget her discomfort, tried hard not to think of Janey and the boys. What's going to happen next time Mom goes away? Janey was only twelve and couldn't keep their brothers in line like she could. Being older made a lot of difference, the boys looked up to her. Hard telling what kind of trouble they would get into now that she was gone.

The road forked. She stood at the divide and slid the straps off her shoulders. The pack dropped with a soft thud on the hot pavement. Her back cooled in the breeze she made by flapping the hem of her sweaty t-shirt. She looked one way, then the other, at the immense expanse of rolling grassland, divided by the grid lines of asphalt and endless miles of barb wire fence. If she turned, she would stay on the reservation. By continuing north she would soon be off.

She could find someone she knew in Pierre. She had some relatives there. But that might be more dangerous than doing the unexpected. She grasped the beaded bag around her neck. Lawrence told me to find his friend, Amos. And that is what I am going to do. She put one blistered foot in front of another, turning her back on the reservation.

The long, gradual slope seemed to stretch on forever. Her shoulders ached. The pack's weight pulled her backwards until she put her hands beneath it and leaned uphill. The sky darkened. The air became thick and humid. Soon a cool wind began to blow, kicking up a dust devil that danced along the side of the road. Dirt stuck to her skin. On top of the hill, she saw the storm extended to the far western horizon, blowing the fields of knee-high corn and sunflowers planted in tight, even rows. Prosperous *wasicu* farms and green pastures dotted with fat cows stretched beneath the blackening sky. Behind her lay the sparse, alkaline reservation land, glowing amber in the remnant of sunlight.

A clap of thunder caboomed a split second after the brilliant crack of lightning lit the sky. As the echo died away, a mechanical rumble lingered, sputtering in the distance behind her.

Near the junction at the bottom of the hill was a school bus. Instead of the familiar regulation yellow, this bus glowed purple and orange in the premature dusk of the storm.

The light must be playing tricks on me, she thought. Amazed, she rubbed her eyes and looked again. Like a fluorescent, mechanized caterpillar, the bus crawled up the hill. As it came nearer, she saw huge flowers and round-lettered words painted on the top and sides in bright colors. Every inch of the bus seemed to be adorned. No doubt about it, this wasn't a reservation rig. She hoped they had some water.

She slid the straps off her shoulders and stood trembling in the middle of the road, praying this strange vehicle would stop. Its brakes squealed, a horrible grinding metal sound that made her wince. Finally it slowed, lurching side to side. The wide, chromed front bumper stopped less than an arm's length from her. On the grill over the radiator, written in fat, red letters, was "Hell no, we won't go! Fuck the war!" As she dragged her pack to the door, she noticed a rainbow painted on the side of the long hood, with a golden pot labeled "Kool-aid" at the end of it. She thought it was very pretty.

Through the dirty glass she saw a young, white man grip and pull the lever that opened the door. His short uneven beard and long straight ponytail were coppery gold. Curls the same color lightly covered his tanned bare chest. When he grinned at her, his eyes smiled, too. "Where you headed?"

"Montana." She tried not to sound scared.

"Do you know where we are?"

She nodded. "The big highway is north a ways."

"Glad to hear it. We've been lost for hours. Hop in."

She lugged her pack up the two steep steps, grabbing the metal pole on her left as the bus lurched forward. Her head nearly hit the ceiling.

Between second and third gear, the young man reached to shake her hand, clasping his fingers around her thumb. After fumbling a little, she did the same to his.

"Name's River."

"Hi, I'm Ritta. Thanks for stopping." She smiled. I was right. Nobody from the reservation.

"Well, Rita, I wasn't going to run you over and it looked like you might grab the bumper if I passed you by."

"It's Ritta, short i. And I might have. I really need out of here." She looked down to escape the scrutiny of his bright blue eyes and noticed he wore shoes made from straps of leather. Sandals, like Jesus wore.

"We all needed to get out of somewhere, too. Everyone here's just rolling stoned." He looked into the round mirror above his head. "Hey, Willie, you want to drive soon?"

An arm appeared from behind a huge pillow. A thin arm, covered with the darkest skin Ritta had ever seen. Graceful, long, pink-palmed fingers offered a skinny cigarette to a heavy-set man with a scraggly blond beard and round glasses. A guitar rested in his lap. He reached for the cigarette and took a long, airy drag before handing it back to the waiting hand. He held his breath and said in a odd, little voice, "Sure thing, River." After he exhaled, his fingers strummed the guitar once, then started picking a melody more complicated and beautiful than anything Ritta had ever heard on the radio.

"Go make yourself comfortable," River told her through the music. "You look like you've had a rough time."

Ritta nodded, took a deep breath and headed for the back. Most of the windows were covered with long, orange curtains. In the dimness, she could barely make out a path between the bedding and belongings scattered on the floor. Swaying with the bus, she put a hand on the ceiling just above her head for balance and made her way to an empty, large pillow. Ritta dropped her pack and sat down across from the woman the arm belonged to; who sat half buried in the other large pillow, her long fingers holding out the hand-rolled cigarette as she asked, with a sparkle in her black eyes, "Maryjane?"

Ritta put her hand on her chest. "No, I'm Ritta."

The woman grinned and looked down. Ritta was more bewildered than ever.

The woman sat back in her beanbag, contemplating the tarry smoke. "This is marijuana. Some of the finest blow in South Dakota, I would imagine." She leaned towards Ritta again. "Would you like a toke?"

"No, thank you. But I sure could use some water."

The woman pointed to a fur-covered bag shaped like a large kidney bean and decorated with ric-rac and bright strings on the floor between them. Ritta picked it up and felt the water sloshing inside. She tried to figure out just where to unscrew the strange lid. The woman held out her hand for the bag and pulled it open with a pop. "Like this." She lifted it and poured a stream between her large, even teeth, swishing it around noisily in her mouth before swallowing. "It's a bota bag."

Ritta took it back and squeezed a long cool stream down her parched throat. When she had her fill, she closed the top and thanked the woman.

"Hey, it's only water. I'm Mazie." She offered her hand. Ritta wiped her chin on her shirt and clasped Mazie's slender fingers like River had hers. Mazie seemed pleased. "Right on!"

"That's a beautiful dress." It was unlike any garment Ritta had ever seen; brightly patterned material seemed to wrap seamlessly around the woman's torso, leaving her arms free.

"It's batik." Mazie stood and did a quick pirouette, weaving with the motion of the bus. As the material swirled in front of her, Ritta thought Mazie must be the most beautiful person in the world.

"Part of my heritage, you know. Like my afro." Mazie patted the densely curled cap of blue-black hair that surrounded her head and sat back down with a plop. "Want to feel it?"

"Sure." Ritta rubbed Mazie's down-turned head. "It's soft."

Mazie laughed.

A large, golden yellow dog rose up from a heap of dirty clothes stuffed between some boxes in the back corner. Long fringes of hair along his torso swayed as he limped over to Ritta. "And who are you?" she asked.

He sniffed her outstretched palm. She stroked his soft, graying muzzle. His earnest brown eyes searched hers.

Mazie told her, "That's Patch. He's River's dog."

"Patch?"

He wagged his tail and moved closer, letting Ritta run her hand down his thin, muscular sides.

"Yeah, he was broken and River got him patched. He only has three legs."

"What happened to you?" Ritta asked the dog as she felt the stump off his left hip.

"He gets around surprisingly well. Hello, I'm Dora." A round woman rose up from some pillows on the mattress and reached out a plump, freckled hand. When Ritta took it, Dora looked at her face. "You're hurt."

Ritta nodded. Dora leaned closer and pressed lightly on a spot that made Ritta wince. "When we stop, may I have a good look at that?"

Ritta nodded again. She reclined her heavy head on the over-sized pillow and nestled comfortably into it.

Dora took a short drag off the cigarette and handed it back to Mazie before lying back on the bare mattress. Raindrops began to bombard the metal roof. A flash of sheet lightning illuminated the entire sky and exploded into thunder. Mazie hurried to open a side window. "Holy cow! Did you see that? Incredibly far out!"

Ritta no longer cared. She pulled off her socks and shoes, peeled the blistered skin from her heels, then elbowed more of the beanbag's crunchy sounding stuffing under her head. The rumbling drone of mechanical parts vibrated through the floor and soothed her raw nerves like a balm. She breathed deep the sweet smoke and let Willie's twelve-string melody and the rocking of the bus lull her to sleep.

Mazie sat next to Dora on the mattress, their backs on the pillow-lined wall, and watched the sleeping hitchhiker. River's dog lay by her side, his muzzle close to her hand.

Dora whispered, "What do you think happened to her, Maze?"

"I bet she's been pistol-whipped. It happened to my brother, before he left for L.A. Looked just like that, sort of bruised and smashed open."

"Poor thing. I hope it doesn't scar. She's so cute, even with her face like that." Dora rolled off the bed to cover Ritta with a thin, cotton blanket.

"She's beautiful," Mazie said under her breath.

Willie drove most the night, hoping to make it to the next sizable town. The brakes were getting worse, and the shocks were so far gone every slight curve in the road felt dangerous. Never was he more thankful for the long monotonous stretches when he could get out of second gear. After passing the sign that welcomed them to Hayes, he circled around a few blocks before he found an empty lot. When he got the bus to stop he staggered towards the mattress to find some sleep.

"Shit!"

River's shout, followed by the shrill scream of the train's whistle, startled Ritta awake. She covered her ears. River ducked. A deep, loud rumble shook the bus. Rusty metal rushed by the windows as boxcars sped past on the other side of the glass.

Willie and Dora bolted upright. Willie laughed hysterically. Dora held her chest with both hands.

River patted Willie on the back. "Park close enough to the tracks, Bro?"

"Hey, like I said, man. The brakes don't work so good."

"Where are we?" Ritta peered out the back window. Across the large, graveled lot were two rows of well-kept houses, divided by the tracks like an alleyway between them.

Dora stood beside her. "It's not a campground, that's for sure."

"Hayes, Wyoming. 'Home of the Real Cowboys'." Willie rubbed his belly where it hung over the drawstring of his pants. "And, hopefully, a parts store. We need shocks as well as brakes. We'll be here a day or two."

River nodded at the empty sleeping bag by the door. "Anyone seen Mazie?"

Ritta looked out the back window. "Here she comes."

Mazie walked stiffly and very quickly down the street, glancing over her shoulder. Before she even jumped up the steps she shouted, "Quick, close the door."

River looked out the opening before pulling the lever. "What's chasing you, Mazie?"

"Fucking bigot bastards! I couldn't even drink my coffee."

Dora leaned into Willie's arms. "Ah, so that's what this is about. Had to have your fix." She turned to Ritta. "We ran out of coffee in Minnesota."

Mazie turned towards the mattress and glared at Dora. "No. It's about my right to be treated like a person. In Chicago or Bumfuck, Wyoming."

"You're right, Hon. I'm sorry."

"I should have expected it. This place even looks like 'Middle America'. Look at it."

They peered out the back window at the homes with deep green lawns and bloom-laden lilac bushes planted in hedgerows.

Ritta turned to Mazie. "I got coffee."

"You do? Far fucking out. I'll get the Coleman."

Mazie dug around in the back of the bus and returned with a camp stove, tin percolator, and a jug of water. Ritta picked up her pack and followed Mazie outside. They set up the stove in the shade of a few aspen trees growing between the edge of the gravel and the tracks. Ritta took a match from the Prince Albert can and handed it to Mazie.

Waiting silently for the water to boil, Ritta heard Mazie's stomach growl and offered her some dried fruit.

Mazie grumbled as she ate. "No breakfast, no fricken coffee." "Hey, these aren't bad. What are they?"

"*Canpa.* Chokecherries. Uncle Lawrence gave them to me. Have some more."

Brown liquid popped lightly into the glass knob of the percolator. Mazie leaned over the stove and inhaled so hard the sides of her nose caved in. "Yeah, that's coffee. Maxwell House?"

"No. Lawrence House."

Mazie looked at her like she was strange before they both laughed.

After they poured their cups full, Willie came over, bleary-eyed. Ritta pointed to the coffee pot. "Want some?"

He smiled, holding out his empty mug. She filled it and he left to scout for parts.

Ritta leaned against the mottled white and black bark of the aspen, basking in the morning sun. She sipped from her cup, spit out a stray ground, then cocked her head to one side. "Mazie, what's it like where you come from?"

"Chicago? Girl, it's as different from around here as you can get. There ain't no wide open spaces unless it's across the lake. And crowded? Man, is it crowded. People live on top of each other stacked up high as the sky. But the music is fine, and there's lots of Brothers and Sisters."

"You got a big family?"

Mazie laughed. "No, no. I just have one brother. I meant Black men and women. Lots of Brothers and Sisters in Chicago."

"Oh, I see. There's lots of people like me back home, too. But I'm *iyeska*."

"What do you mean?"

"A breed. My granny married a white man. I seen his picture. I think he was Swedish or something, blond."

"So do the full-blood Indians treat you differently?"

"When I was a little girl the other kids teased me and beat me up. Now they don't say nothing. But they don't have to. Know what I mean?"

"Oh, honey, do I know what you mean. Back home we have the black as night Blacks, the brown Blacks and the barely Blacks. I'm brown, honey." Mazie held her arm next to Ritta's and smiled. "But I'm still darker than you. Back home, the lighter you are, the closer to being white, the better everyone treats you. Even your own people. 'Cept now the Brothers and Sisters are trying to change that. We're taking back our heritage and we're proud to be Black. But the po-leece, they don't like it. Honky sons-of-bitches."

Ritta put her hand up to the tender area of her face.

Mazie asked softly, "Did a po-leece-man do that to you."

"Yeah, the honky son-of-a-bitch."

Mazie shook her head. "Come on, I bet Dora has some super-dooper hippie salve for that."

Dora dug around in one of the boxes and returned with hydrogen peroxide and a small jar, hand-labeled Calendula Cream with Thyme.

Mazie laughed. "See, Ritta. I told you."

"Say, would that stuff help my blisters?"

Dora nodded. "I got some Band-Aids, too." She sat Ritta down in the driver's seat and carefully dabbed at the wound with a saturated cotton ball.

Mazie patted Ritta's leg. "You're in good hands. Dora's a midwife, you know. She's the only one of us that learned anything practical in school."

"Come on, Mazie. Social work isn't practical?"

"I got two more years before I can be a social worker. And I ain't too sure how much good I'm going to be to anyone by then." Mazie turned to Ritta. "My mama died last winter. I'm going to L.A. to live with my brother and finish school out there."

"Willie got his degree in Psychology," Dora said, proudly.

Mazie scoffed. "Yeah, and a whole hell of a lot of good it's done him, too. He sits around all day playing his gee-tar, trying to forget everything they taught him. How many different ways can you say somebody is just fucked up?"

Ritta looked up at Dora. "How about River? What did he study?"

Dora's sweet smile lit up her round, freckled face. "River studies life."

"And Papa's money pays for it," Mazie hissed under her breath.

"Mazie, be nice. You know River only asks for money when he needs it."

Ritta winced and tried to hold still as Dora spread the thick salve on her cheek.

"There, I've been wanting to do that since you stepped on the bus."

Ritta started to thank her but was interrupted by the roar of a loud engine and the skid of tires through the gravel beside the bus. Patch's low, throaty growl made her neck hairs stand up even before she heard the man's voice demanding, "Where's the nigger?"

Ritta grabbed Mazie's arm. Mazie's nostrils flared as she glanced around. Dora asked, "Where's River?"

River answered from outside the open door, his grip firm on Patch's leather collar. "Right here. Do you know these yahoos, Maze?"

"Oh, yeah. All my friends call me 'nigger'."

"Keep Patch in the bus." River looked at Mazie. "You, too."

Ritta put an arm around Patch and pulled back an edge of the curtain. Three young *wasicu* got out of a blue and white pick-up. Cowboys with all the trimmin's, as Uncle Lawrence would say.

River walked over to them, his hands out, palms open. "Hey, man. We don't want a hassle or anything, so just leave and it will be all right."

One of the cowboys stepped into River's path and shoved a hand between River's, hitting his chest with a thud.

Ritta gasped as River reeled back a few steps then straightened, yelling at the cowboys, "No reason to do that, now. Just get into your truck and get outta here. We aren't hurting you any."

Dora grabbed her fry pan, Ritta gave Patch to Mazie and they headed out the door to help River, just as an old truck, shiny red with big, round fenders, drove into the lot and pulled up in front of the bus. Willie sat on the passenger side. The driver was a big, burly man in overalls; the two of them filled the whole seat. The cowboys backed off.

Ritta and Dora met River at Willie's open window.

River slapped Willie's shoulder. "Good to see you, man. We got trouble. These dudes just pulled up and started yelling 'Where's the nigger'."

"Ritta, Dora, River. This here's Mr. Swanson, from the parts store."

Swanson nodded solemnly. "I had these boys in shop when I taught over at the high school. I'll talk to 'em." He got out and walked over to the cowboys, their white shirts and straw hats gleaming in the sun. "Rick, Charlie, Matt. I'm surprised to see you boys in town during the day. What brings you down this way?"

One of them put his hands in his tight jeans pocket and scuffed his boot in the gravel. "Just wanted to see the nigger girl, Mr. Swanson. I ain't never seen a real one before. Heard she was here."

"You boys don't need to cause any trouble. Just go on about your business now." Swanson stood with his hands crossed over his belly until they got into the pickup and started to leave. When he turned his back, the driver spun the wheels, peppering the side of the bus with gravel. Tires squealed onto the pavement.

"Sorry about that, folks. Just some boys off the ranch with too much time on their hands." Mr. Swanson looked straight at Mazie as he spoke, then pulled himself onto the red leather seat of his Dodge.

Willie unloaded the parts from the back. "Thank you, Mr. Swanson."

"Sure thing." Swanson waved his beefy, freckled arm and drove away.

Willie started the bus and moved it a few yards further from the track. "Let's get this baby fixed and get out of here. River, see if you can find something to block the tires. Mazie, you all right?"

Mazie slowly shook her head.

"Stay with her," Willie whispered to Ritta. She nodded and sat next to Mazie on the mattress.

Soon, a loud metallic clang sounded from beneath them, followed by Willie's cursing. River came in through the back door of the bus and moved the beanbags away from a trap door in the floor. He pulled it open and started to dig through one of the greasy wooden boxes inside. "Liquid Wrench. That's great. Hey, Mazie, did you know there's really something called Liquid Wrench?"

"Yeah, it's for guys with tight nuts."

The brakes were shot, metal ground fast onto metal. Willie made another trip to the parts store, but the binders he needed weren't in stock. A few phone calls later and Mr. Swanson promised they'd be along on the morning run.

"Tell you what," Swanson told Willie. "I'll drop the dang things off to you in the morning, fresh off the truck."

* * *

Lawrence wasn't surprised when the white Ford pickup came down the lane, its siren lights flashing. By the time it pulled up outside his cabin he was sitting on the porch, in the chair he'd built long ago of pine limbs, rolling a cigarette. Lopate and one of his officers piled out of the cab. Two more stood up in the bed; all of them out of uniform. Lopate motioned the two in the truck towards the barn with his chin. The men jumped out, their rifles ready.

Their boss sauntered to the porch, tipped his sweat-soaked Stetson towards the back of his head, then rested his hand above the grip of his pistol. "Got a warrant here for a Ritta Baker," he said, though he obviously didn't have any papers with him. "Thought you might know her whereabouts."

The scratch marks on Lopate's face confirmed all of Lawrence's suspicions. He took a wooden match from his shirt pocket, struck it with a thumbnail and lit the tobacco with short bursts of smoke. "What'd she do?"

"Almost killed one of my officers. Bashed his head in."

Lawrence knew Lopate was lying, but for Ritta's sake was relieved to hear the man hadn't died. "How did a little slip of a girl manage that?"

Lopate slammed his boot onto the first step of the rickety porch and leaned on his knee. "Don't matter how she done it." With his eyes locked onto Lawrence's he said to the man standing behind him, "Search the house." He smiled coldly. "We also want to ask the girl about the disappearance of Agnes Thunder Dog."

"What makes you think Agnes is missing? It's summer. The old woman is up Sheep Mountain, gathering her plants."

"The Tribal Council says she's missing."

"Ah, and the Council was so concerned about her they asked you to look for her."

"She was last seen with the little *iyeska* bitch."

"Was that before or after Ritta beat up your flunky?" Lawrence relaxed back in his chair, as if he were talking about the weather.

"Look, old man. I've had enough of this. Where did you send her?"

"Haven't seen either one of them." Lawrence struck another match to re-light his cigarette. He smoked and watched the veins in Lopate's neck bulge above his grimy collar. Lopate's hand twitched as he grasped the pistol butt. Lawrence was ready to duck when one of the men came through the doorway. He held up Ritta's jeans, covered with soot and dotted with blackened holes where the flames had almost caught.

Lawrence mentally kicked himself for not wondering what she had done with them. Outwardly, he didn't move a muscle.

Lopate took off his hat and rubbed his hand over the flat top of his crew cut. "Haven't seen her, huh. Old man, you're a goner now. Let's take him in, boys."

After his arms were handcuffed behind him, Lawrence shook off the policeman's grip and walked to the pickup. As he put a knee on the tailgate one of them pushed him face down on the bed. Quickly, he righted himself, put his back against the cab and sat in a crouch. Two men leveled their guns at him as they sat on the side walls.

The officer stuffing Ritta's pants into a plastic garbage bag pulled them back out. He spread the legs to show the blood-stained crotch. "She must have had an accident." He laughed before dropping them back into the bag. Only then did Lawrence's rage show on his face.

As the truck pulled away the filly began neighing, frantically circling the corral. Near the top of the hill, Lawrence watched as the young horse leapt over the poles and flailed the top rung before she tumbled into the dust. He saw her stand up as they went over the rise.

* * *

After sundown, while Willie and River tried to get the grease off their hands, Ritta spread the tapestries under the aspen trees beside the tracks. Mazie brought out a bottle of wine and tapered candles. Dora followed, balancing an assortment of glasses and utensils on a stack of unmatched plates. Mazie uncorked the bottle and poured the Chianti. Dora dished the lentils over rice. Cumin and garlic competed with the stench of brake fluid and grease that permeated Willie's clothes. Dora held her jelly jar glass in the air. "To the fine mechanics."

Willie smiled. "Thanks, dear. But we're not out of the woods yet. Still need some parts."

As they ate, Ritta watched the sky darken and flicker with faint stars. Mazie lit the tapered candles and stuck them around in the gravel. The soft glow isolated them from the strange world they had stumbled into.

After dinner, Dora took their dishes to the bus and returned with Willie's guitar. "Sweetie, could I make a request? Play Abraham, Martin, and John."

He wiped his hands on his pants before he took the instrument. His arm wrapped lovingly around it and he strummed a few tuning chords. "It's so sad, though."

"Please."

As Willie played, Mazie and Dora's voices rang clear and beautiful in the warm night air. Silence hung after the last refrain, until the rumble of another train sounded in the distance.

The single headlight of the engine blinded them. Their ears, filled with the iron cadence of the train, didn't hear the police car pulling up behind the bus. The candles flickered, then blew out, from the rush of the locomotive. The rest of the train roared by in darkness. After it was gone, Mazie fumbled to relight the candles. A flashlight suddenly illuminated her actions.

The intruding beam shone on one surprised face after another. Before the light got to her Ritta ducked between the trees, pulling Patch with her. She knelt down and curled over the dog, gently gripping his muzzle to stifle his growl.

Willie stood up. "Who the hell are you?"

The policeman's light shined briefly on his badge. "The law. I got a complaint about some disturbance of the peace over here."

Mazie snorted. "Us or the train?"

He pointed his light into Mazie's face, blinding her into a grimace. "Pack it up and get out of Hayes."

Dora told him, with a bit of exaggerated Southern twang in her voice, "We would love to, Officer. But we can't fix the bus until our parts come in the morning."

"Well then, stay in your rig there until you're gone. We got ordinances against loitering in city limits. This is a decent town here and we don't hold to no hippies camping out."

Dora shielded her eyes from the glare. "Sorry, Officer. We didn't mean to cause any trouble."

The man swept the area with light. He reached down for one of the nearly empty glasses and sniffed the contents. "I need to see your IDs."

Ritta waited in the darkness and listened to the shuffle of boxes inside the bus. She could see just the outline of the policeman as he stood beside the door, carefully checking each I.D before handing them back. "I could run you in for drinking on the street. Consider yourself warned."

Willie thanked him curtly, then closed the door while the officer still stood in front of it. A moment later he walked away.

After the car drove off, River came out and whispered hoarsely, "Ritta, it's all right. You can come out now."

She stepped from between the trees, the dog beside her. She was shaking and couldn't stop, even when River put his arm around her. He kept it there until they stepped into the bus.

Dora gathered the tapestries from outside and hung them back over the windows. "Hayes, Wyoming. Home of the real cowboy."

Mazie sulked in her corner by the door. "Real assholes."

River took a wooden box from its hiding spot. "I don't know about you guys, but I need a joint." He rolled a big cigarette from the contents and licked the paper with a flourish. Then he held it by the tip, placed the whole thing in his mouth, and drew it out through his pursed lips before handing it to Willie. With a chuckle, Willie struck a farmers match on the metal wall. After a long inhalation, he held the joint near Dora's head in his lap. She stretched out her neck and took a drag without touching it. Then Willie held it out to Ritta.

"Are you sure he won't be back?"

Willie grinned. "I think he's done his duty for the night."

Ritta looked in all their faces before she took the offering. Cautiously, she put the end to her lips.

"Take a little air in with it," River explained, pressing his fingers to his mouth and sucking in. She imitated him. "Good," he said, "Now hold it for as long as you can."

The smoke expanded in her lungs and burst out in a harsh cough. She thrust the joint at Mazie. Her head felt a little lighter. When the joint came back around to her she tried it again, and managed to keep the smoke in a little longer. After exhaling, she sat on the beanbag and watched Mazie unroll a flannel-lined sleeping bag near the steps in slow motion.

River touched her arm. "Where do you want to sleep?"

His hand was warm. His eyebrows glistened in the candlelight like spun gold arches. Never had she seen such beautiful eyes. She watched the candle's flickering reflection on his huge pupils.

He smiled and asked again, "Where would you like to sleep, Ritta?"

"What? Oh, sleep?" She looked around like she was lost. Patch nudged her hand with his wet nose. Then she remembered. "Here, where we did last night. Isn't that right, Patch?" She took off her shoes and arranged her blanket. River put his foam pad next to her beanbag and blew out the candle.

She couldn't sleep. Her mind wandered back to those pools of blue. No wonder his name is River. She hugged herself and pretended it was his arms that were around her, like he held her when the policeman went away. I think he likes me. I don't know why, with my face all messed up, but he likes me. When sleep did come, so did dreams of swimming in deep, warm water.

Another train's whistle split the night's silence. Its rumbling passage was followed by a soft moan from the mattress. Soon a wet, licking sound filled the darkness, followed by a stifled giggle and more moaning. Ritta had heard similar noises before, at home when Mom had a man over. She had a good idea what caused them. Then came the rhythmic stirring. She felt it through the floor.

"Jesus Christ," Mazie grumbled, wrestling a pillow over her head.

Ritta curled into a ball. Her heart pounded, remembering the ugly men forcing her open. I'm safe, River is here. River. The thought of him dispelled the evil memories, but replaced them with a longing she found nearly as frightening. She bit her finger and cried softly, aching and confused.

River took her hand and gently pulled her to him. "Please, Ritta, come here. Let me hold you." Patch settled down at their feet. River stroked her hair.

She whispered, "Every time I promise myself I'm not going to cry anymore, the tears just fall inside me."

When dawn came, she awoke to River's sleepy smile and morning-breath kiss soft on her forehead. She snuggled a little closer, not wanting to lose the safety of his embrace.

He tugged at the leather strip around her neck. "What's this."

She pulled the beaded pouch out from beneath her shirt and held it in her hand. "My uncle gave it to me before I left."

"Groovy. What's in it?"

"Just things." She was afraid he would laugh at her if he knew what it held.

They dozed, entwined, until Willie emerged from the cocoon of his blankets. "Let's get out of this hell hole today."

Dora stretched herself awake beside him. "What, you tired of being Hazed?"

"That's good, Dora. Hazed. Hey, Mazie, did you hear that?" Willie tried to waken the lump by the door but got only a grumble in return.

Dora smiled. "I'll make some coffee. That will get her going,"

"Make some for me, too, please Dora." River spoke quietly.

"Me, too," Ritta murmured with her eyes closed.

"Looks like a coffee morning." Dora pushed her auburn curls from her face and looked at Willie as he stood above her, tying his pants. He smiled, then gently pushed her back on the mattress, lying on top of her. She squealed as he playfully bit her neck.

"For God's sake, would you two knock it off." Mazie rolled from her sleeping bag. "You kept me up half the night and gave me wet dreams for the rest of it." She pulled the tapestry from the corner of the window. "Great, here comes another goddamn train."

By the time Dora had coffee made, River and Willie were back under the bus. She placed their cups nearby and promised, "We'll have some breakfast soon."

"Thanks, sweetie." Willie gave her a wink before she left.

32

Shortly after nine, Mr. Swanson pulled up. Patch barked at him until the man reached down to pat his head.

"He likes you," River told him. "He only barks at good folks."

"Glad to hear it. So how's the work going, boys?" Swanson squatted down by the dismantled wheel.

Willie wiped his fingers on a grease rag and shook the man's hand. "Your timing is perfect. We got the shocks on last night, and we're ready for the binders. Then it's down the road we go,"

"None to soon, either." River informed him. "Your local law enforcement wants us out of Dodge, ASAP."

Swanson laughed.

Dora walked up and handed breakfast to Willie and River. "Do you have time to join us, Mr. Swanson? There's plenty of food."

He looked at the plate of eggs and potatoes all scrambled together. "What are those little plants there? They look like they just got started growing."

Dora handed a bottle of catsup to Willie. "Alfalfa sprouts."

"Alfalfa sprouts?" He took off his cap and scratched his head, then looked closely at the plate. "By God, so they are. Thanks, anyway, Missy. I had my breakfast earlier. But I'd like a cup of that coffee I'm smell'n. If you got some to spare?"

"Sure. Take anything in it?"

"A little sugar."

"How about honey?"

"Honey?" He shook his head in wonder. "Black will be fine, Missy. Thanks."

"Coming up." She walked away humming softly to herself, swinging the catsup bottle by her side.

"She's sure happy this morning," River teased. The redness creeping up Willie's cheeks showed through his beard.

Mr. Swanson sat on a crate and sipped his coffee, watching them work until the brakes were together. Willie carried a large box of unused parts back to the truck. Swanson insisted Willie keep half of them. "For spares. I'll make you a good deal. You never know when you might need them."

"Thanks, Mr. Swanson. We could be sitting in jail if it weren't for your help."

"Glad to be of use. Hope you have a good trip to wherever it is you're head'n."

When the wheels were back on the axles and the bus packed, Willie asked Ritta where she needed to go.

"Absorakee, Montana. But I'm not sure where it is."

River took the road map from the little glove box and spread it out on the mattress. They all knelt around it. Willie looked up the town in the index and traced the coordinates with his fingers. "Here's Absorakee, just north of Red Lodge."

Ritta looked at the paper. It seemed like such a long way to go. She tried to sound brave when she told River, "You don't have to take me all the way. I can hitchhike from here."

River smiled. "We'll take you. It will be good karma."

"What's 'karma'?"

"You know, like, your destiny. You did something before, maybe in a previous life, that lets good things, or bad, happen to you now. That's your karma."

Willie pumped the gas pedal, then depressed the starter button on the floor with his toe. "Come on, Baby, come on." When the engine turned over he patted the dashboard. "The bus runs on good karma."

Back on the open road, River took the stash box from its hiding place. As he rolled the day's supply, sweat trickled down his brow. "Goddamn, feels like an oven in here." He stood and touched his hand to the metal ceiling, pulling it back after a brief instant. "No wonder."

Dora peeled off her shirt and dried the sweat beneath the folds of her large breasts with a corner of it. She rummaged through her wicker bag, took out a printed scarf and tied it around herself for a bra.

"Hey, Dora, where's your turban?" Mazie asked from her spot beside the steps. Dora dug a little deeper into her bag and pulled out another scarf with silver threads through it and long purple fringe around the edges. She wrapped it around her head, and stuffed the ends under. The fringe covered her forehead. Locks of red curls escaped at her temples and the back of her neck.

Willie, looking into the round mirror above his head, blew her a kiss. "My hippie Bedouin."

Dora stood and shimmied like a belly dancer, then laughed heartily. "So, who wants a sandwich?"

Everyone said yes. Ritta offered to help. The bus rolled steadily down the road as they slapped sandwiches together on a piece of clean cardboard. Dora served Willie, then set the makeshift tray on the mattress for the rest of them.

River took a bite. "This is delicious, Dora. What's the spread?"

"Peach butter. I've been saving it. A dear old friend of mine, Sarah Thompson, made it. I stayed with her for awhile up in the Shenandoah Mountains when I went to midwifery school in Roanoke. She taught me about herbs and growing things. She's about eighty now."

"I have a friend like that." Ritta spoke quietly from the beanbag, barely able to get the bite past the lump in her throat. "I hope they didn't kill her."

Dora dropped her sandwich. "Who, Ritta. Who would kill an old lady?"

Ritta looked down. "The Tribal Police."

Mazie slammed a fist into her other hand. "Fuckin' pigs."

Dora shook her head. "Why would the police kill your friend?"

"She was trying to get her land back from the government. They took it to drop bombs on for World War Two and promised to give it back after the war."

Mazie asked, "How much land did they take?"

"Three hundred thousand acres."

River whistled. "That's a big piece of land. How many people got kicked off?"

"Agnes told me over a hundred families had to leave, or they would be shot and have bombs drop on them. She was trying to get together all the people who lost land."

"Why would that make the police hurt her?" Dora asked again.

Ritta knew this was going to be hard to explain. She didn't really understand herself. "Because they aren't traditional people like Agnes. They want Indians to be more like white men."

River asked, "The Tribal Police are Indians?"

Ritta nodded her head. *"Han."*

Dora sounded exasperated, "But why would they hurt an old lady, Ritta? Just for trying to get her land back. I don't understand."

"Agnes told me once she dreamed there was something about her land that was very special, something *Wakan,* that made the government keep it. She didn't know what it was, but it made her want more than anything to live on her land again. I think they were trying to make her go away."

"But why would Indians hurt other Indians?"

Willie took his eyes from the freeway long enough to say, "My dear, Blacks hurt Blacks. White people hurt other white people. Greed knows no color."

Mazie sat down next to Dora. "I had a professor last year that called reservations 'third-world countries in the middle of America'. It's because of all the screwed-up treaties. The Feds got jurisdiction over some things but each tribe has their own government. Besides, policemen all over the country are hurting good people. Look what happened to the Freedom Marchers in the south, or the protesters at Kent State. Pigs are pigs, man."

Dora asked quietly, "Is that how you got hurt?"

"I tried to stop them from hitting Agnes." Ritta dropped her head and pulled a dog hair off her sandwich. "A man hit me with his gun."

"What happened then?"

She couldn't bear to tell them, not everything. "I woke up in the back of their truck, next to Agnes." Her sandwich blurred from the tears in her eyes. "I left her there, with those men. I jumped out and ran to Uncle Lawrence's. He told me to go to Montana and took me to the main road before he went to find her."

She took another bite of her sandwich, broke the remainder into several pieces and put them in front of Patch. He smacked noisily at the sticky bread, working the peach butter off the roof of his mouth. Ritta knelt on the mattress and rested her head on her hands over the open window sill, staring at endless miles of buffalo grass and silver sage that reminded her of home. The fresh asphalt still smelled of hot tar and left a bitter taste in her mouth.

Dora knelt beside her. "You didn't want to leave, did you?"

"Not like this. Not knowing if Agnes—"

"Sometimes we have to go where our karma leads us. You know, like a rolling stone."

Remembering her carved rock, Ritta pulled the medicine bag from beneath her shirt. She poured the contents into her hand, then frantically shook the pouch. Searching her lap, she cried, "Oh, no. It's not here!"

"What?" Dora shook her head. "What's not here?"

"My rock. My round rock. It was to get me home again. I've lost it."

"I don't understand, Ritta. How can a rock get you home again?"

Ritta stared at the scrap of fur and owl feather in her hand. "Lawrence gave me a round rock. It was supposed to see me home." Ritta shuddered as she held back her tears.

Dora embraced her and whispered in her ear. "The bus can be your home. Like it is for us. We'll be your family now."

"Thanks, Dora." An emptiness settled inside her. "I guess this karma wants me to be a rolling stone, too."

Montana

On the outskirts of Billings, a labyrinth of electrical cables hanging on lofty concrete poles marred the sun's burning descent behind distant blue mountains. Refinery smokestacks spewed stinking billows of white fumes. Gas-blue flames ignited hellishly against the darkening sky. A noxious smell forced them to shut the windows as they pulled off the freeway, into a Standard station.

In the 'Ladies' restroom, amid crumpled paper litter and dirty walls, Mazie, Dora, and Ritta took turns behind the stall door. Mazie struggled to get her fingers through her afro. "God, I'll be glad for a real bath. I hope River's serious about getting a motel room tonight." When she opened the door to leave, the stench of the refineries overtook the smell of the bathroom. "Damn. This place stinks worse than Chicago." The door banged shut behind her.

Ritta started to wash her hands and caught Dora looking at her in the mirror. Dora wasn't smiling. "I kind of read between your lines when you were talking. I'm going to be blunt, so tell me to mind my own business if you want to, Ritta. Did those men rape you?"

Ritta recognized the kindness in Dora's blue eyes, so she nodded. "I think so. I was knocked out."

Dora said quietly. "Did a doctor or anyone examine you?"

Ritta looked down at her hands under the running water and shook her head. Tears dripped off her nose. She wiped them away and stared at the long marks on the lower wall where water droplets had left a trail through the dirt. Dora handed her a paper towel, then gently lifted her chin until Ritta had to look at the redheaded woman's soft, round face.

"Does it still hurt?"

"It burns like crazy when I pee."

"When we get to Red Lodge, you should go see a doctor."

The thought of another man touching her there made Ritta adamantly shake her head.

"Then would you let me look? Maybe I can help. But if I think that you need a doctor you have to promise to see one. I'll go with you, if you want."

Ritta nodded reluctantly. Dora squeezed her hand for a moment before they opened the door to the reeking world outside. River and Patch walked towards them from a weedy vacant lot next to the station. The three-legged dog ran with a comical gait to Ritta's side. She knelt down to rub his chest and ears, and allowed him to lick her face.

River laughed. "He's like a puppy when he's with you, Ritta. I've never seen him act like this."

"I like him, too. He's a good dog. Where did you get him?"

"I found him limping down a country road last year. He must have fallen out of a pickup or been a farm dog that got hit. He had lots of skinned up places. The vet called them 'road burns'. And a badly broken leg, the one they took off."

"He has a good spirit. Don't you, boy?" The dog followed Ritta into the bus and plopped down at her feet as she nestled into the beanbag. When everyone was aboard, Willie pulled the bus back onto the road.

River lit a candle inside a large, perforated tin can. Its light danced on his face as he removed another joint from his shirt pocket and held the tip to the candle flame until the paper caught. After several deep tokes, he offered it to Ritta. She held the glowing tip upright and swept the smoke towards her face with a graceful motion of her other hand, then passed the joint to Dora.

River leaned on pillows along the wall of the bus in front of Ritta. "Why did you do that?"

Ritta shrugged her shoulders and smiled. "Easier than smokin' it." She knelt on the mattress and leaned her head out the open window. Twilight hung in the western sky, silhouetting the darker hills. Scattered stars winked at each other.

Mazie got up to close the windows. "Damn, it's cold. I hope all these honky towns aren't the same as the last place."

Ritta agreed and sat on the beanbag, spreading the blanket over her. A soft voice beside her asked, "May I join you?" She lifted the corner of the blanket. River settled in beside her. She shifted her weight to give him room and nestled into his arms. His body odor was strong, but not unpleasant. She sniffed his skin to pick up more of the scent.

"Pretty bad, huh. Too many days on the road."

"No. Just smells like River."

He kissed her head as it lay on his shoulder.

Willie opened his window. "Hey, River, do you hear that noise?" The engine roared as the bus chugged up the incline. A loud clunk-clink-clink-clunk-clunk reverberated off the hillside.

River sat up, startled. "What the fuck is it? Sounds awful."

"I'm thinking it's the universal joint."

"Where's that?"

"In the drive shaft." Willie closed the window. "Could hold for a long time."

"Or?"

"Could throw the whole shaft through the floor of the bus." Willie's concerned face reflected in the round mirror above the dashboard. River snuggled closer to Ritta and closed his eyes.

Willie whispered, "Hey, River. Wake up. We're almost to Red Lodge and I'm too tired to drive in town."

As the bus made its way down main street Ritta leaned out the open window, until she saw a policeman in his parked car. She ducked below as River smiled and waved at the cop.

"What do you say we go have a beer before we find a motel?" River turned the corner and parked the bus before anyone answered.

When they entered the crowded, smoky bar the jukebox was blaring a song about a bullfrog named Jeremiah. Four men leaned over a Foosball table, shouting and slamming goals. The clangor of pool balls rang sharply from the back. After the quiet of the road, it was deafening.

They found an empty booth. Ritta slid beside Mazie. Soon a barmaid appeared. "I need to see IDs."

Mazie cussed, then asked Ritta to let her out so she could go back to the bus for her student card. Dora fumbled through her bag for her wallet. River handed the barmaid his license. "I'd like a Millers."

"Okay. What about you?" The barmaid asked Ritta.

"I don't have one."

"How old are you?"

"Fifteen."

"Speak up, honey. It's loud in here."

"Fifteen." Ritta wanted to slink under the table.

"Well, you can have a Coke or something. Don't any of you give her a drink or I'll kick you all out. The cops have been coming down on us real hard for serving minors."

Mazie came back with her wallet. The barmaid looked at it closely. "Hey, Chicago. My brother goes to school in Chicago. He loves the Blues."

"Right on. I'll have a Michelob."

The barmaid laughed. "In Chicago you can have a Michelob. Here we got Coors."

"Okay, I'll have a Coors."

River pulled a chair to the end of the table and paid for the drinks when they came. As he, Dora and Willie reminisced about a bar back home, Ritta concentrated on wiping the condensation off her glass. Mazie nudged her. "Let's go for a walk and see what we can see."

Ritta downed her Coke and slid out of the seat after Mazie. When they started for the door, River called out to them, "Hey, where you two going?"

Mazie smiled impishly and said real slow, "We're going to see what kind of trouble two minority women can stir up in this honky town." She took Ritta's arm and the two strolled out the door; Mazie in her flowing caftan and afro, Ritta with her long, loose black hair, hightop basketball shoes, plaid western shirt and baggy Army pants.

Outside, the night air was cool and crisp. Mazie shivered. "Let's go back to the bus and get a jacket."

Ritta dug in her pack until she found the Army coat. It made her feel smaller, but she welcomed the warmth. Mazie pulled on a hooded sweatshirt that said 'Roosevelt University' in big white letters.

As they left the bus Patch looked pleadingly at Ritta. "Sure, you can come. Can't he, Mazie?"

"Shit, I don't care."

They passed the IGA and the Blue Ribbon bar, where polka music from the jukebox blared out the open door.

As they walked down the quiet street Ritta asked, "How did you get to be on the bus, Mazie?"

"Oh, Willie and I had some classes together. He's a decent dude. Helped us arrange a march on campus last winter. That's when he told me about his friend that had this old bus they were going to work on during spring break. Then they were headed to California. My momma died, you know, so I wanted to go see my brother in L.A. Willie asked River if I could travel with them. I sure didn't think we'd be in Bumfuck, Montana, though."

"You don't like River very much, do you?"

"I don't dislike him. I just don't trust anyone who's been rich their whole life. Especially those that say they can understand what it's like for me. Nobody can know what it's like to be poor, unless you been there."

Ritta thought of home and of the bed she and Janey shared, the nights they went to sleep hungry when Mom went to Whiteclay. She remembered when she became aware that other people didn't live like they did. Not everyone ate commodity food and picked out their clothes from boxes at the mission. She couldn't remember how old she'd been when she made this great discovery, old enough to know she didn't want to live like that anymore.

Then Uncle Lawrence convinced her mother she should go to a powwow. It was there she first met Agnes Thunder Dog. Agnes was proud to be *Lakota*. How she missed the feisty grandmother. The ache that lived in her heart since she'd left the reservation swelled until it threatened to choke her. She had to know if her *Unci* was all right. "Mazie, I need to make a phone call."

"Who you going to call?"

"My mom. It's Saturday night, she'll be at the bar."

"Got any money?"

Ritta dug into her pocket, pulled out the roll of dollar bills Lawrence had given her and held the wad out to Mazie. "I have this."

"God, girl. Don't go flashing that around in plain view. "

They both looked around at the deserted street. Ritta laughed. "I think we're safe, Mazie." She took a dollar from the roll and stuffed the rest back in her pocket.

They jaywalked across the street to a motel office. Inside, the woman behind the desk gave them a disdainful once over, then looked at the dog with his nose against the glass door. When her eyes came back to Ritta and Mazie, she asked coldly, "May I help you?"

Ritta gave her a dollar and asked for change, but when she picked the receiver off the pay phone in the lobby the woman said, "I'm sorry, but that phone is for guests only. You'll have to use the one down the street."

"How far?"

"Next block."

As they walked out, Ritta stared at her hand-me-down shoes and baggy drab pants gathered around her waist with a piece of twine. She pulled the Army coat a little tighter around herself.

Mazie took her by the shoulders and shook her slightly. "Look, don't you ever let some white woman make you feel unimportant. They only win when we give up. And we're too smart and too proud to let them win, aren't we?"

Ritta nodded and smiled into the fierce brown eyes of her new friend.

Mazie hugged her. "Come on, let's go call your mama."

The phone was attached to a gas station at the very edge of town. Nearby, a bridge spanned the river, loudly cresting with spring runoff. A sign read "Rock Creek Campground and Park."

The air off the water was even cooler. Ritta huddled into her coat after dialing O. "Information. For Whiteclay, Nebraska."

Mazie held her pocketknife over the painted surface of the phone booth.

"For the Pony Bar." She repeated the number to Mazie. "Thank you." Mazie finished etching the numbers on the wall.

Ritta dialed, then fumbled coins down the slots. "Hello? Hello? Is Mabel Baker there? Thank you." Honkey tonk music came through the phone as she turned to Mazie. "He's going to get her. I told you she'd be there." Then back into the receiver, she said, "Hello, Mom? It's Ritta. Yes, I'm all right... I did-n't run away, I had to leave... I can't tell you where I am. Only that I'm in Montana. Yeah, I'm okay. I'm with some real nice people. Tell me, is Agnes all right? ...Of course I miss you. Where is she? ...Now, you know Agnes never drinks. What do you mean she's on a binge? ...I love you too, Mom... No, I can't come home... Why? It's a long story. Tell Janey I miss her but don't tell anyone else I called. Please, listen to me, Mom… Listen. Don't tell anyone else but Janey and Uncle Lawrence that I called you. Tell Lawrence I'm all right and thank him for me."

The operator broke into the conversation, "Three minutes."

"Mom, I got to go. Tell Janey I miss her… Yes I love you, too. Don't cry, Mom. Remember, don't tell anyone else. Bye."

"So. Was it good news?"

Ritta knelt to hug the dog by her side. "She's missing. The rumor is she's on a drunk." She looked up at her Mazie. "But everyone knows Agnes doesn't drink."

* * *

At the Pony Bar, the bartender took the phone back. "Hey, Mabel. That sounded like long distance. Must be pretty important. Everything okay?"

Mabel's bleary eyes tried to focused on the table where her beer sat waiting, her companion slumped in the chair next to it. She stood and pulled the hem of her flowered polyester blouse over her ample hips, then motioned for the bartender to come closer. "Everything is just fine, Joe. That was my girl calling me. She's in Montana."

* * *

When Ritta and Mazie returned, the others were in the bus smoking a joint. River offered it to Ritta. She shook her head and sat in the driver's seat, worrying about Agnes.

Willie picked up his guitar, strummed a few chords and fiddled with the little pegs. Dora sat up and patted the mattress beside her. "Ritta, come join us. Aren't you cold? I'm freezing. Hard to believe it's the end of June."

Ritta slid under the blanket with Dora, glad for the warmth. Dora held her hand under the covers. "Where did you girls go?"

Mazie answered, "We went walking. Found a motel at the other end of town. There's a campground across the creek. We could park there."

Dora smiled. "That would work. Some of us could sleep in the bus and still use the shower in the motel."

River jumped up. "I'll drive. Show me where it is, Ritta."

She sat behind him on a crate and leaned on the back of the driver's seat. River kissed the top of her head before starting the bus. It coughed and sputtered.

Willie said, "It's the thin air. We might have to adjust the carburetor tomorrow."

"I hope that's all we have to do."

At the campground, River pulled the bus beneath the trees along the raging waters of Rock Creek. He and Willie left to see about the motel room.

Dora dug through the boxes in the back of the bus. "God, will I be glad to take a real shower. No wonder everyone in the bar looked at us when we came in. What a rag tag bunch we are."

Mazie stuffed her shampoo into a nylon bag. "Everyone looked because Ritta and I were there. Did anyone else notice that we were the only dark skins in the place? Christ, in this whole fucking town."

"Well, dear, since you are an emissary for your entire race, you best be nice to the locals."

River pushed open the door and dangled a motel key from his finger. "Willie's decided he'd shower first. Room 208." After he gathered his clean clothes he looked at Patch, who was eagerly wagging his tail. "Sorry, ol' boy. You got to stay here and guard the bus."

Ritta knelt to hug the dog. When she stood, she and River were alone. They walked out into the moonlight. He asked, "Are you all right?"

She looked at the ground and scuffed her shoe in the pine needles, raising a little cloud of dust.

His arms folded around her, his face nuzzled into the hair at her neck. She felt his heartbeat. Her head turned towards him and his mouth found hers, warm and soft. He parted her lips with his tongue and shifted his body. She felt something hard against her belly, and pulled away.

He caught her gently, brushed her fingers with his lips, then guided her hand down until it reached his pants, over the very thing she was so afraid of. It pulsed against her palm. She gasped when it jerked a little. River looked at her, his eyes liquid in the moonlight, then brought her fingers back to his lips. "We should go."

As they walked silently to the motel, River still held her hand. Room 208 was the only one with a light on. Dora met them at the door, opening it before River could use the key. "Thought you two might have gotten lost."

Ritta felt herself blush, like Dora knew what had just happened. River said, "Just a little moonlight stroll."

Dora put her hand on Ritta's arm and whispered, "Tonight would be a good time for me to examine you, after your shower. Okay?" Ritta nodded.

Dora turned to River. "Why don't you take a shower next? Then y'all can go back to the bus. Ritta and I need some time alone."

"Okay. Say, whose going to sleep in this real bed?"

"Well," Dora rolled the l's off her tongue. "I thought maybe Willie could come back and he and I could stay here."

River laughed. "Good idea. Maybe the rest of us could get a decent night's sleep without you two rocking the bus."

Willie pulled himself out of the chair. "Yeah, well it would be nice to have a little privacy. Besides, we were just warming up." He winked at Dora.

Mazie looked into the mirror over the sink, lifting her freshly washed afro with a wide-forked comb. "Just remember, motel walls are thin."

Willie laughed. "Look whose worried about upsetting the white folks."

"I just might want to take a shower in the morning, too. How long are we going to be here, anyway?"

Willie shrugged. "River?"

"Well, Ritta needs to track down her friend."

Ritta corrected him. "Uncle Lawrence's friend. I don't even know if he's still around here."

River smiled. "We aren't going to leave until you find him, whatever it takes. Mazie, do you have to be in L.A. any special time?"

"No, but I didn't plan on—"

"Dora, Willie, when do you have to be at the commune?"

Willie scoffed. "Time? On the farm? No such thing, just seasons. When we get there will be fine."

Dora took her toothbrush out of her mouth and talked through the bubbles. "Fern's friend is due in August. I need to be there before then."

Mazie screeched, "This is June! We can't hang out here until August. I'll go fucking crazy!"

Dora spit in the sink. "Mellow out, Maze. I was only kidding."

"Thank you, for staying," Ritta said quietly.

Dora gave her a hug. "I'm going back to the bus and get some things." Then she turned to Willie. "Why don't you come, too?"

Outside, Dora took Willie's arm as they walked across the empty street towards the campground. "Those policemen raped her, Willie."

"I wondered. Poor kid. Well, that explains her sudden disappearance last night when Deputy Dog showed up."

"That was amazing. I didn't even hear her move."

"She definitely has some tricks up her sleeve. I'd love to talk to her about growing up on the reservation. Must have been a real drag. What we drove through looked pretty tough."

"River seems taken with her." A shadow of a frown darkened Dora's face under the glow of the street lamp.

Willie held her closer. "Not near as taken as I am with you."

Her frown didn't disappear. "But you can't hurt me the way River could hurt that poor girl."

"Should I tell him?"

"I don't know. I'll ask Ritta."

"Try to get her to talk, if you can. She seems real strong, but I wouldn't be surprised if she's holding some guilt about being raped."

"Why should she feel guilty?"

"Victims often feel they are to blame for what's been done to them. That's why most rapes and beatings never get reported. Who knows what kind of perverse religious upbringing that girl had. Weren't the reservations doled out to churches?"

Dora hugged his arm as they walked across the wooden bridge. "That's what I love about you, Willie."

"What?"

"Your understanding of women."

At the bus she collected her thoughts, then her black bag, checking to be certain everything she might need was there. She kissed him. "You'll come to the room when Ritta gets back?"

"Couldn't stop me." She smiled at him from the top step as she was leaving, her face lit by a candle on the dashboard.

He whispered, "Bye, beautiful."

When she reached the motel, River and Mazie were walking down the metal and concrete steps from the room. River's wet hair dripped down his back. "Better put that towel on your head or you're going to catch cold," Dora admonished. River draped his towel over his shoulders.

Inside, Ritta sat stiffly on the bed. Dora sat beside her, and took one of her hands. "Have you ever had a vaginal exam?"

Ritta shook her head slightly.

"Well, first I'm going to feel all over your belly." Dora opened her bag and removed a gleaming metal spoonbill instrument. "Then I'm going to insert this into your vagina and carefully open it up, like this." She squeezed the handles together to make the rounded ends spread apart. "Then I can see if everything is all right. It shouldn't hurt, so if it does, you need to let me know." She patted Ritta's back. "Now, go take a shower and I'll be ready when you come out."

Ritta stood and unbuttoned her flannel shirt. Her dark brown eyes looked into Dora's. "Will you be able to tell if I'm pregnant?"

"'Fraid not, sweetie. But we'll cross that bridge if we get to it."

Ritta got into the shower. Dora shed an angry tear, then thought of the wonderful lovemaking she and Willie shared. Why can't all women be treated that way? She pulled the bedspread down to the floor, and placed the stand-up light from the corner of the room at the foot of the bed.

After her shower, Ritta came out wearing only her shirt that hung halfway to her knees. Dora patted the bed in front of her. Ritta reclined stiffly, pulling the shirttail around her straight legs.

"Tell me if it hurts."

Ritta shook her head each time Dora's fingers pressed into her abdomen.

"Had you ever made love with anyone?"

Ritta's cheeks glowed red. "No."

Dora took the speculum into the bathroom and washed it with hot, soapy water. "Slide to the edge of the bed, please."

Ritta scooted down and wrapped herself in her shirt again. Dora felt Ritta's legs tremble when she took the girl's feet and put them on the mattress beside her hips. She pulled on her gloves, squeezed some gel from a metal tube and rubbed it over her fingers. "Remember, tell me if it hurts."

Ritta nodded. Dora scooted the lamp closer with her foot and knelt at the end of the bed. She touched Ritta's legs with the back of her gloved hands, careful to avoid the bruises as she slid them down Ritta's thighs. As gently as she could, she inserted a finger.

"Ow."

"There's just a little tear here. I'll give you some cream that will help. I'm going to put the speculum in now. Try to relax. Take a few deep breaths."

Ritta inhaled sharply as the instrument entered her. Dora carefully opened the speculum, then shined her penlight on the area it exposed. The cervix was contused, as were the tender membranous walls. She could make out remnants of the torn hymen. "I don't see any lacerations inside. That's good."

"What are lacerations?"

"Cuts."

"Oh. It sure does hurt."

"You're really bruised. No sign of infection though. Looks better than the wound on your face did. And look how nicely that has started to heal.

"Thanks to your super-dooper hippie salve."

Dora laughed. "Well, I have some more super-dooper stuff that's going to help you here, too." She closed and removed the speculum. Ritta breathed deeply.

"Does it still hurt to pee?"

"A little. Seems to be getting better."

Dora sat down. "That's good. Ritta, do you want to talk about it?"

Ritta looked at her hands in her lap. "Not much to tell. When he hit me with his gun I guess he knocked me out. I don't remember what happened after that."

"What do you think happened?"

She started to cry. "I don't want to know."

Dora held and rocked her until the tears lessened, then said, "Ritta, listen to me. Sex can, and should be, a beautiful experience. What that man did to you wasn't about sex. It was power. That may be hard for you to understand now, but someday you will."

"Does it really feel good, I mean, when it's like it's supposed to be?"

Ritta looked so hopeful Dora was glad to tell her, "Yes, Ritta, it does. It's the best feeling in the world."

"But men are so big, and...their...thing...gets so hard. How can it feel good?

"When a woman is aroused, she gets wet. You've felt that, haven't you?"

Ritta nodded her head.

"Well, when that happens it all sort of works. And, it's not supposed to hurt. At least, not very much."

Ritta looked perplexed. Dora shrugged her shoulders. "There's a little pain in pleasure. Someday you'll find out for yourself. Does River know?"

Ritta shook her head. "Please, don't tell him."

"I won't. But you should. He needs to know."

Dora took a hairbrush from her wicker bag, sat behind Ritta on the bed and started to unsnarl the ends of her wet hair. "Do you need a toothbrush? I have an extra."

"Yes, I do. Thanks, Dora."

After she could run the brush all the way through the long, straight strands of Ritta's hair, Dora showered. By the time she finished, Ritta was asleep, curled up on top of the blanket. Dora smiled and covered her with the bedspread, then remembered Willie waiting at the bus. "Damn, there goes our night of privacy." She quietly went out the door to tell him, after sticking a toothbrush in the pocket of Ritta's pants.

Ritta stirred, her head flopped side to side on the pillow. In her dream a *wanblee* flew high above the clouds. Ritta flew with the hawk until she looked down on the whole reservation. The agency towns looked like dirty little rats' nests, strewn with piles of trash.

She looked to the west across the prairie and saw ghosts of buffalo, roaming freely, the barb wire meaningless to their spirits. The sun grew closer as the bird pulled her upwards. All the Lakota land spread out before her, as it was before the *wasicu* came with their roads and wagons. *Paha Sapa* called, the sacred Black Hills, inviting her to rest. The hawk screamed.

The shrill sound from inside her head woke Ritta. She sat up, startled to find herself confined in four unfamiliar walls. "Agnes, what does it mean?" She pulled the other pillow to her chest and rocked herself back to sleep, letting the dream fade into the mist of her memory.

In the morning, Mazie opened the motel door and smiled at the sleeping form sprawled half-covered on the bed. Ritta's plaid shirt twisted around her middle, one bare leg exposed where the bedspread wrapped underneath. Quietly, Mazie closed the door, tip-toed in, and knelt beside the bed. With her face near enough to feel the girl's soft breath, Mazie reached out to brush the hair away from Ritta's wounded cheek. *How I would love to kiss you and make you all better.* Her fingers lingered on the soft skin below the ear, stroking the downy hairs. Ritta stirred, then her breathing deepened as she fell back to sleep. Mazie rose from her knees and went into the bathroom. She was brushing her teeth when River came in.

"Hey, Maze, I thought you were going to wake her up?"

"I wanted to let her sleep just another few minutes. Besides, she looks so peaceful."

"She looks like a battered Sleeping Beauty." He tenderly kissed Ritta's lips. She smiled, her eyes still closed. "So it was you." River stretched out beside her, kissing her again.

Mazie filled her mouth with water and gargled hard, then spit.

Ritta pulled away from River's embrace to see who was there. "Good morning, Maze."

"Hey, there."

"Boy, do I need to brush my teeth. Dora said she had a toothbrush for me. Is it in there, Mazie?"

River rolled off the bed and walked to where Ritta's pants were folded over the chair. "Mother Dora strikes again." He tossed the toothbrush to Ritta.

***

Ritta and Mazie walked into camp as Dora hung the last edge of a tapestry on a low hanging branch beside the bus. Shafts of early morning sun filtered between the trees and glowed through the orange and yellow print, making the little curtained-off area seem warmer than it was. Ten feet away, the creek overflowed its bank; the air glistened with mist from spray off the rocks.

They followed Dora to the picnic table, where she stirred the contents of a chipped, blue-enameled pan over the Coleman stove. Coffee perked on the other burner with an inviting pop–pop-pop. She smiled cheerily. "Java's almost done. Who wants oatmeal?"

Ritta shivered. "I do." She stepped into the bus to grab her blanket from the beanbag. Outside, she took a corner of it and wiped minute droplets from the wooden bench before wrapping the wool around her legs and sitting down. Dora placed a dish of steaming oatmeal in front of her. "Thanks, Dora. This looks good. Where's River?"

"Oh, he's around. I think he and Willie went to wash up in the creek. Milk?"

"Please." The oatmeal warmed her insides. Dora was pouring her a second cup of coffee when River and Willie pulled the tapestry aside and entered their little sanctuary.

Willie hugged Dora from behind. Got any more of that coffee?"

Dora poured him a cup. "You, too, River?"

"Sure." He sat next to Ritta. "May I share your blanket?"

She nodded and covered his legs when he slid next to her. He placed the back of one hand on the unharmed side of her face. It felt like ice on the blush of her cheek. She took it and his other hand between hers, to warm them. "You're freezing. Here." She put his hands under the blanket.

He slipped them between her thighs. "Is this okay?"

She nodded. The cold from his fingers didn't last long. Dora set a cup of coffee in front of him. Ritta could feel his reluctance to remove his hands. River looked at the steaming coffee with clownish longing, stretching his lips towards the cup. Ritta laughed, her head flung back as his fingers retreated.

Willie looked up from his cereal. "What's so funny?"

River took the cup in his hands. "Oh, nothing. Just a personal dilemma."

It was a word Ritta hadn't heard before. "What's that?"

"Dilemma? It means, um, a difficult choice."

"Oh. Like when I had to leave Agnes."

Willie sat a little straighter. "Yeah. That was a dilemma. It must have been a real hard decision. How do you feel about it now?"

"Like I shouldn't have left her."

Willie's brow scrunched over his eyes. "Didn't you have to leave? Wouldn't those men have hurt you more if you'd stayed?"

Ritta's heart constricted with anger. She nodded.

"You had to leave and you couldn't take her with you. You're not Wonder Woman."

"Who?"

River leaned towards her. "A cartoon hero, like Superman."

"Right." Willie held his mug tightly between his hands. "I'm sure you did every thing in your power to help your friend. You couldn't just pick her up and fly away with her."

Ritta lowered her head, thinking hard. Was there something she missed, something she could have done. She wanted to go back and pick up Agnes and fly away, like this Wonder Woman. After thinking about it for a few moments, she said quietly, "No, Willie. I couldn't take her with me."

"I'm sure Agnes knows that, too, Ritta," Dora said with a kind smile.

"Hey, dudes. Take a look at this!" Mazie posed on the top step of the bus, one hand on the rail, the other on her hip. She wore a red, brown and yellow batik caftan with a deep red sweater over it. The colors complemented each other, and the hue of her brown skin, beautifully. Around her head was wrapped a strip of tawny muslin entwined with material similar to the caftan. She danced down the stairs.

Dora lifted the edge of Mazie's skirt and let the material flow. "Mazie, that's beautiful."

"I forgot I had this pair of long johns." Mazie picked up her skirt to reveal the waffle material covering her legs. "Found my favorite sweater, too. I'm tired of freezing. I thought it would be summer here, like it is in the rest of the country." Dora handed her a steaming mug.

Willie swirled his cup. "Hey, River. Before we leave to find a parts store let's measure the brake line. Probably should'a got another in Hayes." He swallowed the last of his coffee and set the empty cup down hard on the table. "So, what are you girls going to do today while we work on the bus?"

"Us girls?" Dora bristled. Willie just chuckled.

Ritta smiled as River's fingers entwined around hers under the table. "I thought I'd try to find Amos."

"I'll help you," Mazie told her. "We can go to the County Courthouse and look at their records. If he got married here they should have it. We can also look through the deeds, see if he bought land."

Dora put her hands on her hips and smiled. "Why, Mazie. I'm impressed."

Mazie grinned back. "What? I know how to do genealogical research."

***

The Chevrolet dealership, the only car lot in town, and the courthouse were on the same block of Broadway, on opposite corners separated by a two-story funeral home. Willie parked the bus on the side street near the parts department. "If they have what we need we'll be here working on the bus."

The brick courthouse, centered on a well-manicured lawn, looked more imposing the farther up the steps Ritta walked. She couldn't get herself to move through the foyer until Dora took her arm. Inside, they found Mazie looking at the directory on the wall.

Mazie whispered, "This building holds all these offices. Look, it even has the jail in the basement. In Chicago, the jail alone covers a city block, three stories high."

"Been in jail, Mazie?" Ritta whispered back.

"Yeah, for a social studies class, smart ass."

Dora pointed to Records—second floor. They headed up the wide staircase single file, each running a hand along the burnished oak banister. Near the beginning of a long, wainscoted hallway was a wooden door with 'Records' written in gold script on the window.

A large woman in a flowery print dress stood behind the counter. "May I help you?" She donned the glasses that had been resting on the shelf of her breasts and peered through the top half.

Mazie cleared her throat. "Yes. We're looking for information on Amos Follows Water. He lived near Absorakee last we know."

"Are you a relative?"

Ritta crossed her fingers behind her back. "Yes."

"Just a moment. I'll get someone to help you."

After a few minutes Dora slumped into a chair along the wall. Mazie leaned beside her and slid down to a crouch. Dora whispered, "Now what, Maze?"

"How the hell should I know?"

50

Ritta paced in front of them, chewing on a hangnail. "Do you think she forgot us?"

Mazie snorted. "Unlikely."

Finally, a younger woman walked up. Smiling, but not looking at them, she lifted a hinged part of the counter, stepped through and politely asked them to follow her. Tottering on high heels, she escorted them down the dark hallway to an unmarked wooden door. After fiddling with several keys, the clerk opened it into a large room, lined with a row of tall wooden shelves full of leather-bound books. A long, wooden library table surrounded by matching chairs filled the middle of the room. Light filtered in the windows through the drawn white shades. The stale air held a hint of lemon furniture polish.

The clerk's heels sounded hollow on the gleaming wooden floor as she walked into the room. "Now, who are we looking for?"

"Amos Follows Water. This is all I know about him." Ritta reached into her back pocket for the dog-eared envelope, spread it out on the table and read the loopy scrawl.

"Lawrence, I am leaving the hospital soon and going back to Montana to work on a ranch near Absorakee. My cousin is married to the foreman. He is looking for cowboys that can really gentle horses. I told him I know an Indian that can break horses so gentle babies ride them. He said come if you need a job. I am thankful to you for saving my skin in France and will always owe you a great debt. I hope all is good back at home. Your friend, Amos Follows Water."

She folded the paper back up and looked at the clerk. "Not much to go on, huh?"

"What's the postmark say?"

"May, 5, 1944. Mailed from San Diego."

The clerk turned to the shelves. "Let's find May, '44 and start from there. Do you know his cousin's name, or anything else?"

"Nope. That's it."

The clerk gave them each a book to search through as they sat around the big table.

After nearly an hour of looking, Dora shouted, "Here's something!" The others peered over her shoulder as she pointed at the line that marked his existence. "Look! 'October 23, 1947. Born to Amos and Gertrude Follows Water, a son named Joshua Lawrence Follows Water—Stillborn—weight 3 lbs 8 oz., and daughter named Josephine Elizabeth Follows Water—Live birth—weight 4 lbs 3 oz.'" Dora looked up, her lips pursed in a sorrowful pout. "Oh, how sad. They lost their baby boy. I wonder what happened?"

Silently, each went back to their task.

Soon Mazie looked up from the book she held and said flatly, "Come look at this."

She read it out loud, "'February 27, 1952 Deceased-Amos Follows Water, age twenty-nine. Accidental death. Survived by wife-Gertrude Follows Water and daughter, Josephine. Roscoe, Montana.'"

Ritta's heart fell. Now what am I going to do?

Dora closed her book and straightened out the others, piling them neatly on the edge of the table. The clerk thanked her and locked the door behind them.

When they were alone in the hallway, Mazie stood on her toes and walked with her buttocks turned up, mimicking the young clerk wobbling on her high heels. It made Ritta giggle as they started down the stairs. Suddenly, she froze. Her bowels churned. Standing on the landing below them was a sheriff.

His khaki uniform was so well-pressed the creases on his pants had shadows. The badge on his chest seemed to glow in the hall light. His sizable belly, snugged tight against his shirt, hung over a wide, black leather belt, matching the tooled, shiny holster snapped shut over his revolver, its pearl handle exposed.

He looked up and tipped the brim of his tan cowboy hat at them. "Afternoon, girls,"

Ritta felt his eyes like a heat wave, flushing her with fear. Dora gripped her hand; it was the only thing that kept her from fleeing.

Mazie bounced down the stairs and said pleasantly as she walked by, "Afternoon, Sheriff."

Ritta didn't look at him as Dora pulled her stiffly down the steps. When they reached the landing, Dora's arm looped around hers. She gripped Dora's hand and kept her eyes on his shiny black boots as they walked beside him, close enough to smell the leather of his holster and his sweet after-shave lotion. She felt him turn as they passed. Felt him watch her walk away.

Mazie waited for them in the foyer, a perplexed look on her face. Dora whispered harshly, "Let's get out of here."

Ritta pulled the door open. It was all she could do not to run down the outside steps. At the sidewalk, they nearly turned right, but between them and the dealership, in front of the mortuary, stood another man in a tan uniform with a gun in his holster, talking to a someone in a dark suit.

They veered in unison to the left, speed-walked to the corner where they quickly turned left again. Ritta kept telling herself it's okay, it's okay. When they were parallel with the middle of the courthouse, she noticed a small walkway that led down to a basement door made of bars. The Sheriff stood on the other side. He twisted a key in the lock then shut a solid metal door behind it with an echoing clang.

She made a run for it. Mazie followed right behind her as Dora struggled to keep up. They didn't stop until they were surrounded by tidy homes and bright sunshine. Ritta leaned against a telephone pole, breathless.

"I just want to know one thing, Ritta," Mazie gasped. "Why are you so paranoid?"

"What's that, Maze?"

"Bein' scared shitless somebody's goin' to get ya."

Ritta looked away. "Can't help it."

"You're gonna see pigs your whole life and each one of them is thinking you did something bad when you freeze like that."

"But I can't help it." Ritta's eyes stung with tears.

"You gotta believe you have as much right as anyone else to be here. You believe it and they can't take it away from you."

"I think I killed a policeman, Mazie. Back home. I pushed him out of the truck and his head hit a rock. I killed him."

Mazie's arms flew into the air. "Jesus H. Christ. Now she tells me."

Dora hugged Ritta. "Back off, Mazie. You aren't helping her any."

"We were in the cop shop. Talking to the fucking Sheriff. Now she tells me she killed a pig?"

Dora asked quietly, "Was this one of the men that raped you?"

Ritta nodded.

Mazie took hold of Ritta's arm. "They raped you? Then it was self-defense."

Ritta looked up from Dora's shoulder. "Who would believe me, Maze?" She tapped her chest. "Who's gonna believe *me*?"

"I see what you mean. I do, sugar. But, for Christ sake, let's be more careful."

* * *

When Willie walked into the parts department the blond teenager behind the counter seemed surprised. He asked, "What can I do for you?"

Willie leaned on the counter. "How 'bout some three/sixteenths brake line for a start."

"Can do. How long?" The kid grabbed a pad and started to write.

"Thirty-five feet."

"What else can I do ya for?"

Willie laughed. "Can you get us a carrier bearing for a '47 International school bus?"

The kid's face lit up. "No wonder you need all that brake hose." He looked behind Willie, out the window. "Is it here?"

Willie smiled and, with a toss of his head, indicated it was outside.

"Is that the front carrier bearing?" The kid thumbed through the pages of the big book on the counter.

Willie liked his efficiency, this kid knew the parts business. "Sure is."

"Do you need the seals, too?"

"I'll take 'em if you got 'em."

"My old man's in Billings at the auto auction," he told Willie while he looked up the numbers. "He'll have 'em here tomorrow, 'bout noon."

Willie stuck out his hand. "That's cool, dude. My friends call me Willie. Come on out and see the bus."

The kid's fresh face grinned. "Hey, dude. Call me Jeff."

Later, on his lunch break, Jeff sat on the curb with River and Patch as Willie changed the brake line, telling them about his '55 Belair. "It's the hottest car in town. Nobody can touch me on the straight stretch by the cemetery."

Willie slid out from under the bus in time to see Jeff's jaw drop. He turned to see what the kid was looking at. Dora, Ritta and Mazie walked towards them.

Jeff stood up so fast he nearly fell backwards.

River put his arm around Ritta. "Any luck?"

"Yes and no."

Dora kissed Willie on his head before he stood up.

Mazie said, "Found him, but he's dead."

Jeff stared at her. Willie chuckled a little, sure Mazie was the first Black person this hick kid had ever seen. "Jeff, meet Mazie, Ritta, and my darling Dora."

Mazie put out her hand. Jeff stared at the dark fingers wrapping around his.

"Jeff's the parts man around here. Damn good one, too. He's gettin' us everything we need."

Dora smiled. "Nice to meet you, Jeff."

He took his eyes away from Mazie long enough to say, "You, too."

Mazie asked, "Want to touch it?"

"What?"

"My afro? You keep staring at it. Go ahead. It feels good." She gently took his hand and placed it on her head.

He rubbed it lightly. "Hey, neat. Feels like a little lamb."

Mazie laughed.

Willie lowered his bulky frame back down on the sheet of oil-stained cardboard he used to cushion the asphalt, to check the clamps on the brake line one more time. After he slid back out and folded his cardboard next to his tools, he stretched backwards with a groan and asked Jeff, "How much do we owe you?"

"Sixteen, even. You can pay for the parts you ordered when you pick them up tomorrow, just in case my old man can't get them in Billings."

"I bet he can. Our parts karma seems to be holding."

"I could deliver them, if that would help."

Willie thoughtfully scratched his scruffy beard. "That would be far out.

We'll be parked in the campground just west of town. Do you know where it is?"

"Sure, across from the A&W."

"That's the one."

River handed him the money and said with mock formality, "It's been a real pleasure doing business with you."

"You too. Need a receipt?"

"What for?"

Jeff shrugged and waved as they pulled away.

* * *

A new Silver Stream trailer was in their spot when they returned to the campground. A man with a graying crew-cut peered out a curtained window, giving them a snide look as they drove by. His clipped Schnauzer wore the same expression as it chased the bus, yipping at the tires. Patch barked back through the glass of the door.

Willie drove the road that circled around the grounds, searching for a new campsite. When it led back to the entrance and they hadn't found a suitable place, he asked the others for suggestions. Ritta saw tire tracks and pointed towards an overgrown driveway beyond the edge of the campground. "Over there."

Willie followed the barely discernible two-lane path to a clearing. A small stream flowed down the steep hillside in front of them, swelling over its grassy bank. A wall of trees sheltered them from the rest of the campground, making the little spot very private.

Willie stopped the bus in the middle of the clearing, near a circle of blackened rocks. "Looks like home to me."

Dora began to clean the foil and burnt beer cans from the ashes. "It's beautiful. Perfect. You can't hear anything but water." The meandering tributary met the charging flow of Rock Creek near the road. The din rose above the spray, acoustically separating them from the rest of the world.

Ritta walked upstream a short ways, stepping on clumps of grass between boggy spots. After listening to the birds in a nest above her, she turned into the woods and started gathering fallen limbs. When her arms were full, she went back to camp.

Mazie looked up from chopping vegetables on a makeshift table.

River knelt before a small fire, pulling dried grass away from the rocks. Ritta dropped her load. "Hey, you guys have been busy. What can I do?"

Willie was hanging the printed bedspreads on some bushes a short distance from the bus. "Looks like you done it."

"Then I think I'll find a phone book and look for Gertrude Follows Water." Ritta checked the deep side-pocket of her pants for a pencil and the information from the courthouse before walking down the road.

When she turned around, River was standing beside her. "Want some company?"

"Sure."

In the booth where she had called her mother, the chain hung empty where the phone book should have been.

River grabbed her hand. "Come on. Let's use the phone at the motel."

Praying the woman that was there last night would be off duty, Ritta followed him across the street. The lobby was deserted, but she could hear half a conversation from the little room behind the desk. They squeezed into the wooden phone booth and closed the squeaky door. A soft light came on above them. She opened the book to find Roscoe and finally found it listed with Absorakee and Columbus. All three towns didn't fill two pages. No Follows Water were listed, under F or W. She had to look twice because it was hard to concentrate with River so close. He played with her hair as she looked through the Red Lodge listings.

"Find anything?"

"No."

"Let's ask the clerk if she knows her."

Ritta tried but couldn't stop him before he called to the woman hanging up the phone behind the desk. It was her. Ritta gulped.

"Excuse me." River smiled at the older woman. "We're looking for someone named Follows Water. What's the first name, Ritta?"

"Gertrude. She married Amos Follows Water."

"What do you want with Gert?"

"Amos was a friend of my Uncle. He asked me to find him."

"He's dead."

"I know. I just want to talk to his wife."

River looked amazed. "You know this woman? Man, this is some small town."

"I went to school with her. She's my husband's second cousin, but we haven't seen her in ages," the clerk told him.

"Please, can you help my friend find her. It's very important."

She looked at him over her glasses. "Gertrude's crazy as a loon and probably won't even talk to this girl. Still lives in the old cabin her and Amos built above Roscoe. Your friend will have to go find her. Gert won't put in a telephone, even though the lines go out that far now. Afraid the family would try to keep in touch, I suppose. Nobody's seen her since Jody left."

River asked, "Will you draw us a map?"

When the clerk looked hard at her Ritta prayed, Please, *Tunkasila*. Make her say yes. She tried her most pleasant smile on the woman. "Please."

"I don't suppose it would hurt." The clerk pulled a notepad from under the counter and began to explain to River the directions as she drew.

Hungry and happy, they returned to the bus. Dora handed Ritta some dinner. She sat on the blanket next to Mazie and told her the good news. Ritta started to take a bite, then noticed something very strange mixed in with the vegetables over rice. She picked up one of the spongy white squares. "Uh, Maze, what is this stuff?"

"Toad food."

"No toads I know." Ritta moved the piece back and forth, watching it flop against her fingers.

Mazie looked at Dora. Ritta noticed River and Willie had quit eating, their gaze also on the cook. Dora started to laugh so hard she had to stop serving. Finally, she dried her eyes on her sleeve and explained to Ritta, "Tofu, soybean curd. It's good for you. Very high in protein."

Ritta wrinkled up her nose as she brought the piece to her teeth and bit off a corner. "It doesn't taste like anything, just kind of squeaky."

"Here, put some tamari on it." Dora handed her a glass bottle filled with dark brown liquid.

"What's tamari?"

"Soy sauce."

"That makes sense. Soy sauce for soybean curd, whatever that is." Ritta doused the white pieces with the sauce.

River warned her, "Careful, it's pretty salty."

Everyone watched as she took the brown, dripping forkful into her mouth. She crinkled her nose again. "Now it tastes like something anyway."

Dora laughed. "Well, you're in luck, that's the last of what I brought with me. And I doubt any stores out here will carry it."

Mazie looked to the sky and joined her palms together. "Thank you, God." She nudged Ritta's arm. "You don't know how lucky you are. We've had tofu in beans, tofu in sandwiches, tofu in God knows what." She looked at Dora. "But it was all good. I'm not complaining. And you were right, I do feel better now than I did when I ate my Momma's cookin'. But it won't ever take the place of barbecued ribs or beans and ham hocks."

"Or pastrami and sauerkraut," said River, wistfully.

"Or fried chicken," Willie added. "But it is very good, darlin'."

Dora put a hand on her hip. "Uh-huh. Well, we're running low on all our supplies. And we're almost out of Ritta's coffee. What's the plan, gang. If we stay here we got to stock up."

Willie looked at Ritta. "What did you find out?"

Ritta chewed fast and swallowed. "Gertrude still lives in the place her and Amos built in Roscoe. We even got a map."

River laughed. "Talk about a small town. The motel clerk is a cousin or something. So let's go find her tomorrow."

"Can't. Jeff's bringing us parts," Willie reminded him.

River scratched the sparse whiskers along his jaw. "Will the bus make it a little further like it is?"

"Probably, now that the brake line is good. The drive shaft should be okay for a little longer."

"Let's stop by the shop in the morning and tell Jeff to hold the parts. We could pick them up on the way back."

The last light of evening faded. Ritta sat on her blanket next to River and watched the fire burn while he rolled and lit a joint. She fanned the marijuana smoke towards her face, liking what she inhaled, before she passed it on.

When the last of it had been smoked, Dora stood and pulled Willie up by his hands. "Shall we make our bed under the stars?"

River heard something. Through his slumber the sound reached him, waking first that part which understood it best. The utterances that followed left no doubt to the cause. By the time Dora's orgasmic cry pierced the air, River was out of the bus and headed for the creek.

He knelt on the rocks, gathered the icy water in his hands and splashed his face. The mountain stream was so cold it constricted the vessels in his head until he thought it would burst. When that agony subsided, the only feeling left was the ache in his groin.

He headed back for the bus, until the low muttering of Willie's voice answered by Dora's soft laughter stopped him.

I can't. I can't go back in there and listen to them ball another night.

He ran to the middle of the street, wildly turning in each direction. Not back to the bus, not downtown, where can I go?

He raced hard for more than a mile along the highway that followed the bank of Rock Creek. When the adrenaline that surged through his veins was exhausted, leaving him panting and weary, he dropped on the grassy stretch along the road. By the time his sides quit heaving and he could focus on the stars overhead, he was ready to walk back, grateful it was downhill.

Everything was quiet at the campground. In the light from the lop-sided moon, he could just make out the curtained room Willie and Dora shared beneath the trees. When he pushed the door of the bus open, Mazie stirred. He whispered apologies. After stumbling in the darkness, he closed his eyes for a moment so they would adjust. He heard Ritta's soft breath and the thud of Patch's tail. When he opened his eyes, he was surprised to see the beanbag empty.

Faint light came in through the side windows, illuminating Ritta on the mattress, her back along the wall of the bus. He stood over her a long few moments, then quietly removed his sweaty shirt, socks and shoes. Carefully, he stretched out beside her, pulling the blanket over his back. When she didn't stir, he slid a little closer, feeling the rise and fall of her breath. He matched his own to her rhythm. Soon his eyes closed and he drifted off to sleep.

In the morning, River woke when he felt Mazie's angry stare. She shook her head at him, then walked outside.

He furtively removed his arm from over Ritta's shoulder and rose from the bed. Patch followed him out of the bus.

"Morning, River. Coffee?"

"Thanks, Dora. In a bit." River walked barefoot around the bend in the creek. As he relieved himself in the bushes he looked down at his penis. "Soon, real soon."

The sun's bright rays cut through the pine boughs and broke into shafts of light. By the time they finished breakfast and had the bus packed, the sky was so blue it turned to indigo if one looked up for long.

The bus chugged up the hill north of town, past the stone mausoleum surrounded by marble headstones and withered flower arrangements. The nearest mountain loomed above the cemetery, an awesome sentinel for one's final resting place. The road curved around foothills and rolling pastures, lush from spring run-off.

"Look, baby sheep." Mazie pointed to two lambs cavorting around a newly shorn ewe.

Ritta pulled the window down and leaned her elbows on the metal sill. "Lots of them. Look how many twins there are."

"How can you tell they're twins? They all look alike."

"I can tell. Can't you?"

Mazie laughed and pointed at a small boy standing in a field with his dog, scratching his head as he stared at the bus. Dora pulled a window down and reached her hand out to wave at him. Ritta stuck her head out her window. Standing with her back arched, she felt like one of those figureheads on old sailing ships. Mazie popped out between them and shouted to Ritta. "Did you see those little white crosses along the road?"

Ritta looked back, the wind whipping her hair. She pulled it out of her eyes and yelled over the erratic knocking of the failing u-joint, "That's where people died in car wrecks."

Dora pulled herself out of the window and shouted to Mazie. "What are those little white crosses?"

"Leprechaun churches."

Beaver Creek Road was once a wide swath cut into the foothills by Conestoga wagons veering off the Oregon Trail. Now it was connected to the secondary highway by a county road. They made good time down the freshly-graded gravel.

Ritta noticed a small, weathered sign that pointed towards the mountains. "Pull over, Willie." He stopped and read it, then ground the gearshift into first and turned down the narrow road.

The bus crept through a sheltered valley. A mountain ridge loomed beyond, bigger than anything Ritta had ever seen. She sat on the crate behind Willie as they jostled down the washboarded road. After a few miles they came to a homestead nestled in the trees. On the far side of the pasture, ponies raised their heads.

Ritta hoped the numbers on the mailbox would match those on the paper in her hand. She grinned. "This is it."

The lane continued between old but straight fences to a large, weathered barn with x's of white-painted wood on the doors. A small house stood off to the side, nestled under tall pines. Its siding, too, was aged to a silvery gray, its trim neatly painted. Lace curtains billowed out the open windows in the breeze. Chickens scratched around a large mound of tiger lilies, making chicken sounds, their copper-colored feathers burnished in the sunlight. The screen door slammed before the bus came to a stop. A woman stepped out, still drying her hands on a dishtowel. She wore a large, blue work shirt with pearl snaps over her ample bosom, loose tan pants and round-toed work boots. Her short, wavy gray hair framed a round and pleasantly wrinkled face. The chickens scattered as she walked past them.

Ritta stood at the open door of the bus, clutching Lawrence's letter in her hand.

The woman pointed in the direction they had just come. "The highway is back that way."

"Are you Gertrude Follows Water?"

The woman suddenly stopped. "I am. Who might you be?"

"My name is Ritta. My Uncle sent me to here to find Amos. They were friends in the Army." She handed the woman the letter.

"Amos died over seventeen years ago." Gertrude examined the postmark, then opened the envelope. Ritta saw the woman's weathered, speckled hands tremble as she pressed the letter to her chest.

"I know. I'm sorry."

"Not as sorry as I was. Come in, come in. All of you. Gracious. How many are there?"

They filed off the bus under her gray-eyed gaze. She smiled when Patch hobbled off and held out her empty hand for the dog to sniff. "Well, come on up to the porch. I need out of this hot sun."

She led them to the house and up the steps, shooing a tawny rabbit off the porch swing. Patch started to chase the rabbit until River told him, "Leave it." The dog reluctantly stopped.

"That's a good dog. Have a seat, I'll get us some tea." With her eyes on the letter, Gert opened the door into the house. After several minutes Dora called through the screen, "Can we help, Mrs. Follows Water?"

A faint sob answered, then Gertrude blew her nose. "Please."

Dora looked at Ritta and nodded. They both entered the dim kitchen. Gertrude sat at the table, the letter spread out in front of her. "I'm sorry. Just seeing his handwriting again after all this time. Remembering how he spoke when I first met him. You'd think after all these years I wouldn't miss him so, but I do. Every single day."

Ritta knelt beside her. Gertrude took her hand. "And what happened to you that your uncle would send you to Amos?" She brushed the hair from Ritta's face, then tipped her cheek to the light from the window.

Ritta looked into the woman's sad eyes. "It's a long story."

Outside, someone shrieked. Mazie's laughter filtered through the screen. Hooves clattered on the wooden deck. A tiny horse pushed open the door and ran to Gertrude, neighing.

"Dopple, what did you do?" The gray speckled, knee high pony nuzzled her pants pocket, leaving a damp print.

Mazie peered in, framing her face with her hands on the screen. "You should have seen River jump. This tiny little horse came up and started sucking on his neck. It was great!"

Gertrude shooed Dopple away, then reached into a high cupboard for glasses. She wiped each one off with the damp dishtowel and set them on a tray along with a tall pitcher of ice tea from the refrigerator. Dora picked it up and they went outside.

Gertrude looked where River was rubbing his neck. "Are you all right, young man? Dopple didn't break the skin, did he?"

"Oh, no. Just scared me, that's all."

"Well, you should be scared. Look at what he done to me when he was just a colt." She pulled at her earlobe. The fleshy tip where an earring would hang was gone, a crescent shaped piece neatly cut out. "He was orphaned. His mama was a stunt horse for a rodeo clown and they were goin' on the road again. Couldn't have a baby slowin' 'em down. So I bottle-fed him milk from my cow. One day he mistook my earlobe for a tit. I felt sorry for the poor bugger so I let him suck on it. I'm guessin' he got mad when it didn't do nothin' for him, 'cause he bit it off. Spit it out, too. Jody said I shoulda gone to town and had one of them doctors sew it back on but I didn't want the bother." She took a long drink of tea, the ice cubes rattled down her glass. "Now he's my stud horse. Throws some good ones, too. Real smart."

Dora perched on the railing. "He's cute as could be. How many do you have, Mrs. Follows Water?"

"You kids call me Gert. I got around twenty of the little beggars. You saw them in the pasture comin' down the driveway."

"Those ponies were all his size?" River laughed. "I thought they were just far away."

They spent the rest of the morning on the shaded porch. Gert brought out an old photo album with pictures of her and Amos, young and strong, building the barn. She showed them a mahogany framed photograph taken at their wedding. "We went to Billings to get hitched at the Justice of the Peace. That way, none of my family could stop me. It's what I wanted to do."

Amos's hair was sleeked back, a starched white collar tight around his neck. His angular, handsome face contrasted with her plumpness, her white dress against his black suit. Even in this stern formal portrait the happiness of their wedding day was captured.

She told them Amos worked as a guide for an outfitter every autumn, taking hunters up the mountain. "That's how I met him. He'd come into my Daddy's store to buy grain for the string before they packed out. He was so quiet and shy, 'til I got to know him. But I liked him from the first time I laid my eyes on him. So it was up to me to start the sparkin'.

"When Daddy died we sold the store. My share was the down payment for this ranch. Amos still worked the pack string in the fall and we kept buildin' our herd. He had a good eye for cattle. We always worked real hard, and were close to havin' the stock we needed to make this place go when he was killed." Gert touched the image of him on the photograph she held in her lap.

"Killed? I thought he died in an accident," Dora said.

"Weren't no accident." Gert's voice was flat and held no emotion. "There's folks 'round here still that don't believe an Indian should own land. Thinks they should all be on reservations. And one of them 'upstanding citizens' shot my husband's horse out from under him as he was making his way down the canyon. We found his body at the bottom." Gert sighed as she turned the picture face down.

"I kept the ranch, even though there was a lot of pushin' to get me to sell. Every time someone made me an offer I wondered if he was the murderin' bastard that killed Amos."

Gert looked out over the pasture. "It's good land, got good water. Makes a whole lot of difference in this country if you can keep it green. So I hired a hand and we worked it, sunup to sundown. My girl, Jody, was just four when her daddy died. She grew up on the back of a horse."

Ritta asked quietly, "What's she like?"

Gert smiled. "She's smart as a whip, just like her daddy. Real stubborn like him, too. Come inside here and see what she done." Gert led them into the front room. Along one of the walls, hung over yellowed floral paper, were dozens of photographs in a variety of frames. All had a dark-haired girl as the subject, maturing from pre-adolescence to adulthood sequentially along the wall. In many, she wore a blue and gold track uniform, running ahead of everyone else or receiving trophies. Jody had grown up to be a striking woman with piercing dark eyes under a thick brow. She had her father's high cheekbones and her mother's wide smile.

Ritta looked carefully at the pictures of the long-legged runner. In one, the photographer had captured Jody's stride at full length, feet barely touching the ground. Her short damp hair was blown back by the wind as she ran, both exhilaration and anguish apparent on her face. Ritta felt like that when she ran across the hills at home.

Mazie asked, "Where is she now?"

"She got a scholarship at the University of California."

Willie looked incredulous. "Track scholarship?"

"Only part. She got some grants, too, for her grades." Gert laughed. "That girl loves to run. Sometimes she'd get off her pony and they'd race across the field together. She was always running with the dogs. You should'a seen 'em.

"She was a good hand, too. Her and me and one hired man did all the brandin' and castratin'. It was quite a sight. She didn't want to leave but with her coach gettin' her this scholarship and all, I knew she'd be a fool not to take it. It only pays for her classes though. I sold most of our cows, and she waits tables so she can get by. She's a real hard worker, that girl. She's goin' to be a lawyer. Wants to change the world."

Around noon, Willie announced they had parts waiting for them.

Gert was walking them to the bus when she asked Ritta to stay. "For the night, if you want. Your friends could come for you tomorrow in the afternoon. I'll fry us up a chicken and we'll all have supper."

Ritta wanted to stay, more than anything. She looked at Dora. "Would that be all right?"

"Okay with me."

Willie rubbed his belly. "Fried chicken. I was just wishing for fried chicken. We'll be back. It may be late though if we're still twistin' wrenches."

"That's all right. Fried chicken's best when it's set for awhile. Ritta and I'll wait supper on you. We'll have us a late picnic."

As Ritta got her backpack from the bus, Mazie came in. "Hey, sister. She's a pretty cool old lady. Not what I expected."

"She kind of reminds me of Agnes. I guess that's why I like her so much."

"Maybe you remind her of Jody. She seems pretty lonely, out here all by herself."

"But grandmothers like her and Agnes would die if they had to live in town." Ritta hugged Mazie good-bye. "Make sure you come back to get me."

"Sure thing, sugar."

Ritta stepped into the bright sunshine. Patch stood between her and Gert as they watched the others board. River called him. Patch looked at Ritta, then back to River, but didn't move.

Gert looked at the dog. "You can stay, too."

Ritta's heart leapt for joy. "Is it all right, River?"

River shrugged. "Sure. Looks like he'd rather stay."

When they pulled away, Ritta waved. She knelt to stroke the dog, watching until the bus was lost in the dust.

Near evening, Gert dumped leftover ham and beans into a cast iron pot on the stove, wrapped some leftover cornbread in a clean dishtowel and put it on the flat lid of the pot, covering it with a used piece of tin foil. "Saves on propane," Gert grumbled. "You wouldn't believe what they charge to come out and fill my tank."

Ritta crumbled the cornbread into her bowl, like Gert did. After they washed the dishes at the chipped porcelain sink and put the pan over the pilot light on the stove to dry, Gert led Ritta out the screen door.

"Let's sit a spell, where it's cool." From one end of the swinging bench, the old woman picked up the lazy brown rabbit, so docile it could have been stuffed, and plopped it down in her lap as she sat. She patted the cushion beside her. Ritta sat down, near enough to Gert to hear her breathe. "Amos took me to his reservation once. Wanted me to see how his people lived, and why he left. What's it like for you, Ritta? At home."

"I hated it when I was there. But I miss it now." She remembered a field trip with Sister Margaret. "When I was little, I thought everyone lived like we did. Then my fourth grade class went to Rapid City with the nuns and I saw these nice houses, and playgrounds, and parks with little children in them. Then I knew we were different. We went to see this museum. Some white kids spit on us. Called us 'red niggers'. Here we were, looking at the things my ancestors made that were important enough to be in a museum and we couldn't even be proud of who we are because some stupid little boys were calling us names."

"Do you live with your folks?"

"My dad died when I was little. Mom works sometimes. But mostly, she's at the bar. My sister and I try to keep our brothers home when she's gone, but they like to go hang around with the other boys."

Ritta looked at the sky and wondered, do they miss me? Mom will when she's sober. The boys probably don't care. But Janey will be lonely.

Then Ritta told Gert everything; about Janey and the Mission where they had to go to school, how fed up she had been with the whole place. That there was never enough food for all of them, even with the Spam and long blocks of commodity cheese Mom brought home. She told Gert how she met Agnes.

Ritta stood up, the pain in her chest suddenly to big to hold still.

Gert asked quietly, "What happened, Ritta? What happened to you and Agnes?"

She paced the porch's length, remembering. "I tried to stop these men that were hurting her. I think I killed one of them." She clutched the rail and let all the raw memories spill out of her mouth. Gert sat very still, and listened. When Ritta was through, it felt like a burden had been taken from her. "How could anyone hurt Agnes? She was the kindest person I ever knew."

Gert took her hand. "It's hard when you're so young, knowin' how brutal men can be. Meaner 'n any animal. Not all men. Some are good, like my Amos. He wouldn't hurt nobody, 'cept in self defense. I wish I could tell you how to protect yourself in this world, Sis. I wish I could've told my Jody before she moved to the big city. I guess the best thing is to stay away from 'em and watch your back. And if that don't work, fight like hell. Just like you did.

"I admire people like Agnes for hangin' onto their beliefs. We all got a right to our religion, and the Indian way of prayin' is as good as any, I say."

Ritta looked at the last rays of sun shooting up from behind the mountain. "Agnes might be dead. But she's with me. I don't know how to explain it."

"Oh, Sis. You don't be needin' to explain. I feel my Amos here with me, sometimes so strong." The old woman patted her chest. "But don't tell no one. That's why I'm a crazy old bat to these folks 'round here. I won't sell 'cause Amos tells me not to. And he's right. Here is where I belong, till the day I join him. I carry him in my heart and in my head 'til then. I don't know how, either. Maybe that's what love is."

They sat in the twilight, wrapped in their own memories. Finally, Gert stood up. "Let's git you fixed up with a bed. You can sleep in Jody's room. You too, ol' dog."

Ritta and Patch followed her up the stairs at the back of the kitchen to a sleeping loft. A low bed took up most the floor, the walls covered with a collage of horse posters and ribboned medals.

"How far is Jody from L.A.?"

"She's in a place called Berkeley. I don't know 'xactly. It's north some." Gert rolled down the quilt. "Won't be needin' this tonight."

"The bus is going to Los Angeles to take Mazie to her brother's. Maybe we could stop there and meet Jody."

Gert's eyes twinkled. "I think that's a fine idea, Sis. Or you could stay here, I'd be glad for it. Just think on it awhile. Now, to bed with you." Gert showed her how the light turned off, then pulled an old, neatly folded blanket from under the bed. "Jody always wanted her dog, Ginger, to sleep with her and I wouldn't let him on the bed, neither." Patch crept over to the blanket to lay down.

"What happened to Jody's dog? Did he go with her?"

"No, poor old thing. Died of a broken heart. I told her that takin' him to the city would have killed him, too. He just pined away for a couple of weeks. Me and him would cry in the barn together." Gert headed down the stairs, then stopped. "But don't you be tellin' Jody that."

Ritta switched off the light and fell back on the bed, trying to imagine what it would be like to have your own room, and a mother like Gert.

She awoke to the clanging of pans, the sizzle and smell of bacon frying. It took her a moment to remember where she was. The room looked different in the daylight, unfamiliar. When her feet touched the floor, Gert called up to her, "Mornin', sleepyhead."

"Good morning." She noticed the empty blanket on the floor. "Is Patch down there?"

"Yep. He and I already got the chores done. Didn't we, ol' boy?"

Ritta heard the toenail click of Patch's uneven gait up the stairs as she pulled her pants on. He came over to her in his side-winder walk, tail wagging. She nuzzled her face into his neck and smelled the fresh scent of hay mingled with horse manure. "Yeah, you even smell like a barn, dog."

At the open window, dappled sunlight on her face, she looked out over the pasture. The miniature horses cavorted in the field. A young colt reared up and strutted his stuff to the fillies who pranced away, unimpressed. An early morning concert of bird song emanated from the trees. She watched a tiny, drab brown bird, its melodious warble added to the choir like a featured soprano.

"Flapjacks are ready whenever you are, Sis."

Ritta put on her shirt and headed down the stairs.

Gert had a tall stack of plate-sized pancakes on the table, along with two steaming cups of coffee. "Sit down. Eat." She heaped three stiff strips of bacon on Ritta's plate.

"It smells delicious, Gert. Thank you."

"It's good to have someone to cook for. I'm tired of throwin' flapjacks out to old Doppler, there." She pointed to the locked screen door where the pony stood with his nose pressed tight against the mesh.

Laughing, Ritta piled pancakes on her plate, then reached for a bottle of burgundy red syrup and held it to the sunlight where it glowed as if aflame.

"Chokecherry. My last bottle. Hope the berries are good this year." Gert heaped a few cakes on her plate.

"I love chokecherries, we call them *canpa*. But I never had them in syrup." Ritta poured some over her pancakes, careful not to take too much since it was Gert's last bottle. The familiar tartness couldn't be tamed by sugar. Accentuated by the tang of the sourdough batter, it was delicious.

"Eat hardy, girl. I'm going to put you to work today, if'n you don't mind. Got some fences to mend along the creek. Can't have the little horses muddying up the banks."

"I don't mind at all. Glad to help. I'll need something to do to work off this big breakfast."

"Good. I got my bread dough about ready to sit. Then we can go before it gets too dang hot."

"What time did you get up this morning, Gert?"

"Oh, I slept in some. Got up after 6."

Before Ritta put the last bite in her mouth, Gert had the table cleared and the dishes under hot soapy water. When Ritta started to help, the older woman refused. "Shoo, go wash up and tie that pretty hair of yours out of the way. We got work to do, Sis."

Ritta returned, face scrubbed and hair neatly braided. She watched Gert push a large ball of light-brown dough down onto the floured table and fold it over, roll it around and do it again, until she was mesmerized with the easy rhythm. She remembered making frybread with Agnes, watching the lumps get big and brown in the hot grease.

Gert patted the dough like it was a baby's bottom, then rolled it into an oiled bowl and covered it with a clean damp cloth. She placed the bowl on a wide board nailed to the ledge of the window sill. "There, the sun will hit it soon and it'll be done raisin' when we get back." She took off her apron and draped it over the back of a chair. "Let's git to work."

Ritta followed her to the front of the barn, still in the shadow of trees. Chickens flocked around as they entered the barn which was abuzz with flies. Gert made a sweeping gesture at the chickens, saying, "Now, git!" The birds receded then flowed back around her boots. "Sis, would you get some grain out of that barrel there in the tack room and throw it in the yard for these pesky hens?"

Ritta pulled the door open into a long, low room. The ghostly shape of a cat scurried away, barely visible in the dim light coming through a square foot hole beside the door, screened with dusty cobwebs and chicken wire. The smell of old leather, stale horse sweat and saddle soap filled the dimness. As her eyes adjusted, she made out a wooden barrel, a curved piece of tree limb for a handle on the cover. She lifted it open and scooped up the mixture of grains with the coffee can inside. The chickens immediately surrounded her, moving en masse to the yard where she flung the grain, a fistful at a time. The hens clucked frantically as they started to feed.

When Ritta returned, Dopple was looking into a metal bucket as Gert filled it with tools. Gert pointed behind Ritta. "Can you handle that wire, there?"

Ritta lifted the thick coil of smooth wire enough to put both arms through the middle and managed to stand up with it. Walking stiffly, so the heavy load wouldn't bang into her, she followed Gert to a stall in the side of the big, open barn. An old Willys jeep station wagon, standard issue green, filled the paddock. Gert opened the back doors, swung the bucket up and tucked it into a corner. She took the wire from Ritta, and tossed it near the bucket. Then she stood aside and held the door open for Doppler. Like a goat, the little horse leapt onto the rubber matting in the back of the Willys. Patch wobbled over, tail wagging. Gert closed the doors, then looked at the dog at her side. "You ride up front with us, ol' man." She opened her door then turned to Ritta. "You might want to get in this side. I have to park real close or she won't fit."

Once Ritta was in, Gert lifted Patch up onto the blanket-covered bench seat before the dog could muster the jump. He sat in the middle. Gert turned the key, depressed the gas peddle deliberately, then reached the toe of her right foot to the starter button on the floorboard. The jeep sputtered, then sparked to life as Gert pulled the little knob marked "choke."

She slowly backed into a narrow spot on the other side of the aisle way. "Do you know how to drive?"

"Uncle Lawrence was teaching me, but we hadn't gotten very far."

Gert put it in first gear, turned the wheel sharply and let the vehicle creep out of the barn. "Well, old Willamina here, that's what Jody called her, she's an easy rig to learn on. Wanna try?"

"Sure!"

Gert stopped the jeep in front of the fence. "You jump out and open that gate there, then git in this side."

The gate was still swinging as Ritta grasped the steering wheel and pulled herself up into the driver's seat. She sat behind the large wheel and adjusted the mirrors, feeling important. She slowly depressed the clutch, then grabbed the worn gearshift handle. "Is first left and up?"

"That's right, but don't forget the hand brake."

Ritta looked around nervously. Gert pointed to the gray handle below the dashboard. "Squeeze it first, then it will release."

Ritta did, then stood on the brake pedal as the Willys started to slide backwards down the slight incline. Taking a deep breath, she put it into first gear and quickly placed her foot on the gas, easing the clutch out like Lawrence had taught her.

It had been a frustrating lesson. He had parked his truck on a hill and had her practice working the clutch and gas until she could get it to go up the slope without killing the engine or rolling backwards. He'd sat silently beside her, smoking one cigarette after another as she struggled to get it right.

She thanked him silently as the jeep went smoothly up the incline. Gert seemed impressed. They bounced along the open pasture. Ritta put it in second. The pony stood splay-legged in the back.

Gert held onto the padded door handle, her other arm around Patch. "See the break in the bushes along the creek there? That's where we want to git to."

Ritta turned the wheel, a big smile on her face. The sun warmed her arm as she leaned her elbow pseudo-nonchalantly out the open window. She looked over the smooth green field, to the forest in the distance. Closer, flowers danced among the blades of grass, blurs of muted blues and yellows.

Ritta slowed to turn into the clearing cut in the dense brush surrounding the creek. She saw a narrow wooden bridge and stopped. Rough cut planks were nailed across two log beams that spanned the creek and continued up the bank for a few feet. The road sloped down slightly, then continued beyond the bridge and up a steep, rutted incline. Sure enough, she thought, those are tire tracks on the other side, but this rig isn't going to fit across that bridge.

"What are you waiting for?" Gert asked.

"Oh, no. I can't drive across that."

"Sure you can. Put it into low 4-wheel." Gert indicated the shorter stick on the floor between them.

"With the clutch in?"

"You're shiftin', ain't you? Now look out your window and line up the wheels with the edge of the bridge. Keep in mind, you've about six inches to spare on the sides. Don't give her any gas until you git across't."

"Oh my God." Ritta sat up very straight in the seat, clutching the steering wheel with sweaty hands. Peering out the side, she steered as Willamina crawled towards the bridge.

Gert stuck her head out the passenger window. "That's it! Good. A little more your way. There, now you got it." The jeep bounced as the tires met the planks, then pulled its way in low gear slowly onto the bridge. Ritta shuddered as she looked down at the creek. She had a strange sensation of being airborne. Halfway over, the timbers groaned under the weight. Ritta blanched and looked at Gert with terror in her eyes.

Gert laughed. "It always does that. Don't worry, this bridge is as solid as the day me and Amos built it."

When the front wheels dropped off the other end of the bridge, Gert shouted, "Give her some gas. Now!"

Ritta gunned it. The Willys roared up the incline. After stopping at the top she wiped the sweat from her brow on the bandanna Gert handed her.

"Well done, Sis. First time Jody drove across't she ran off at the end there and we had to git the winch to pull us out. You did great!"

"Really? Thanks, Gert. That was fun. Can I drive back?"

"Sure. It's kind of nice being ferried around again. Head over there. That's where the horses been gittin' out."

It was obvious once she saw it. The rusty wires had been pulled away from the posts and trampled into the ground. Doppler walked right over to the spot after Gert opened the back to let him out. She shooed him to the other side of the creek. "Damn little horses. Don't know why I bother."

"I do."

The old woman looked sharply at Ritta. Then her face softened, "Why?"

"You like having someone underfoot."

Gert laughed. "I s'pose you're right. Actually, the cows did most of this damage. The little horses tain't much of a bother at all."

After the new wire was strung, Gert asked Ritta if she was up for a walk. "I'll show you my spread."

They crossed the bridge on foot and headed further up the brush line. Patch and the pony followed, each stopping to eat tasty clumps of grass along the way. Ritta picked a sample of each new blossom she came across.

When they reached the top more new wire barred the way up the mountain. Gert turned and proudly pointed to her home. It lay below them, small and unreal, like an oil painting, the house barely visible between the sentinel trees. The barn's new aluminum roof gleamed silver in the sunlight. Cross-fenced pastures, quilted in hues of green, were tucked around the buildings.

"Those fields there," Gert pointed to the fenced-off areas east of the creek, "I got leased to a neighbor. It's good hay." She turned the other direction. "Over there, I still own half that herd. Don't got to work 'em, just supply the pasture. And in the middle there, 'round home, is just for me and the little horses."

"It's a beautiful place, Gert. Amos would be proud of you."

A shadowy smile came to Gert's lips as she looked over the valley.

Ritta held out a flower with five blue petals topped with five more rounded white ones and touched the slender spurs that hung below. "Would you tell me what this one is?"

"It's a columbine, Jody's favorite." The old woman took the blossom and stroked the colored petals. "What else you got there?"

Ritta held out her bouquet. "Some tansy, a paintbrush, at least I think it's paintbrush. The ones back home are yellow and not this pretty.

"Yep. We have the yellow, too. But the red, that's my favorite. What else?"

"And these. Agnes used to call these 'butter and eggs'." She held out a yellow and cream-colored wild snapdragon.

"That's what they are, all right. I got the perfect little vase to put them in at the house."

They made their way back. Before she climbed in the passenger door Gert peered down the fence line.

Ritta followed her gaze. "What'cha looking for?"

"Oh, yesterday morning, when Doppler and I were on our walk, I saw an owl just sittin' on the post over there. Then I saw the fence was down and forgot all about it. Strangest thing though. Never seen an owl in broad daylight 'round here before."

* * *

Earlier that morning, the Sheriff had sat at his oak desk, going over the APB's. Not that he had ever apprehended any of the criminals who warranted an all-points bulletin, but he always looked them over real careful. It was his job.

He bolted upright in his chair when he read the description of the fugitive from South Dakota: Female, Indian, 15 years of age, 5'6", 135 lbs. May have contusion on right side of face.

"Hot damn! I knew she looked suspicious." His hand dropped to the smooth leather of his holster, stroking it with his palm. How was he going to find her now? How far could she have gotten in a day? And what was she doing hanging around his courthouse when she was a wanted criminal? Before long, he was climbing the stairs to talk to Mildred in Records.

* * *

Gert saw the Sheriff's car drive up to the barn just as Ritta pulled Willamina through the trees. Ritta shifted into reverse and quickly backed up.

Gert sat up straight on the bench seat. "What in blue blazes is he wantin'?"

"Probably me."

"Hmm. Well, he can't have you. Why don't you and Patch stay up here for awhile. I'll go see what Sheriff Holecomb thinks he's lookin' for."

Ritta got out and sat beneath the pines with Patch. Gert smiled at the scared girl. "Don't that pitch smell good?" She took a deep breath of the woody tang and was glad to see Ritta did, too. "Don't worry, Sis, I won't let on you're here."

Back at the barn, Gert took her time parking the Willys in the paddock. She opened the back to let the pony out and was grabbing her bucket of tools when the Sheriff found her.

"Afternoon, Gert."

She thought he sounded overly friendly for a man who had been snooping around her house. "Howdy, Sheriff. Find anything of interest?"

"Now, Gert. I was just looking for you. Figured you might be out working the back forty. Fixing some fence?"

"Yep. These little horses are harder on fences than my cattle were."

"I don't mean to tell you your business there, Gert, but if you'd use barbed wire they wouldn't do it."

"Sure, and I'd be doctorin' up ponies night and day from wire cuts. No thanks, Sheriff. I'd rather mend fence than horseflesh." She swung the bucket out of the jeep. The Sheriff grabbed the handle from her, and she let him carry the load into the tool room.

"What brings you out this way, Sheriff?"

"Looking for someone who was looking for you."

"You mean them kids that was here yesterday? Strange lot. Chased 'em out of here. Don't need no hippies hangin' around." She watched the Sheriff's face fall in disappointment.

"Do you know where they might have gone?"

"I didn't ask 'em where they was headin'. What did they do, Sheriff? Must have been something real bad to get you all the way out here."

"Was there an Indian girl with them? Maybe had a nasty bruise on her face? And another girl black as coal?"

"Yeah. What'd they do, Sheriff?"

"The Indian's wanted by the reservation police. Had an APB out on her this morning."

"That so? Anything else I can do for you, Sheriff?"

He took out a notebook from his shirt pocket, flipped it open and poised a pen over the paper. "What did they look like, Gertie?"

"Just a bunch of unkept kids. One Negro girl, like you said. Not sure how many there were. Didn't let 'em get off the bus."

"I already got a description of the vehicle. Shouldn't be hard to find a big old school bus all painted up like that. Looks like two long-haired Caucasian males and three females, one white, one black and one red. All about twenty years old, except for this Injun. Can you add anything to that?"

Gert tried hard to contain her irritation. What she really wanted to do was punch the man in his fat belly and tell him to get the hell off her land. Instead, she said, "No, I didn't see them very good. Gittin' old, you know, and I didn't have my glasses. Is that all, Sheriff? I got bread risin' and it needs to be gittin' in the oven."

"What business did they have here? What made them look you up at the courthouse?"

"Ah, something about my Amos knowing a relative of the Indian girl. Told 'em I weren't in anybody's debt. Probably just a flimflam. Anything else?"

"No, thanks, Gert. You be sure to call my office if they come back to bother you again. But we should apprehend them soon. Can't get very far in a rig like that."

He started to leave but suddenly stopped, eyeing the sun-splashed ground at the entrance to the barn. "Did you get yourself another dog, Gertie?"

"No, Sheriff. Why do you ask?"

"Got a lot of paw prints here. Big dog."

"Them kids had a dog. Got out and chased my chickens all over. Told 'em I was going to shoot the damn thing if they didn't git it out a'here."

"What kind of dog?"

"Oh, just a mutt. Mangy lookin' thing. Not well cared for." Gert laughed to herself, thinking how much Ritta loved that dog.

"Hmm. Well, anything else you remember, call and let me know."

"Sure will, Sheriff."

After she watched him leave, Gert went into the house and washed her hands. Not being accustomed to lying, especially to law officials, she told herself in this case it was all right. She believed Ritta and knew that as much of an idiot as Cliff Holecomb was, the Tribal Police could be a whole lot worse. The world is ruled by ignorant men. She punched down the bread dough that had risen to an airy, rounded mound in the bowl. Her greasy fists disappeared time and time again into the warm dough. It soothed her riled nerves. By the time she felt it was safe to walk over the field to find Ritta, she was calm again.

Patch met her on the bridge, his tail wagging so fast it threw his already unsteady gait into a buffoonish shuffle. Gert laughed and greeted the canine with similar affection. "Where's Ritta?"

"Right here." The girl stepped out of the woods. "Is it clear?"

"Well, we have some work to do when your friends git back. He was looking for you, all right. He knows you're with the kids in the bus. I don't think he'll be back, but you can't stay here, much as I would love to have you. Any chance you can go back to the reservation and git this mess straightened out once and fer all?"

The terror in Ritta's eyes answered the question before she adamantly shook her head.

"I didn't really think so. Let's get you down to Berkeley where you can blend in a little better. You'll have to be real careful, but Jody can help you once you're there. Come on, let's git dinner cookin'."

* * *

At the campground, River stepped from the bus, a freshly rolled joint between his fingers. "Hey, Maze. What time are we supposed to be at Gert's for dinner?"

"She didn't say. What time is it?"

"About quarter to five. Think we should wake up the love machines?" River lit the joint and handed it to her. "Wait a minute," he said in a creaky, breathless voice. He tore off a top flap from one of the kitchen boxes, produced a black Marks-a-lot from his pocket, and carefully drew large letters on the piece of cardboard. "What do you think?"

Mazie snickered "'Den of Fucking Iniquity'. That's great. It sure is obvious you and Willie grew up Catholic."

"Now we just need a way to hang it up."

"I know." Mazie disappeared into the bus, returning with two large safety pins and helped River hang the sign on the tapestry. She called sweetly to the occupants, "Wake up."

When Willie stepped out between the curtains, Mazie and River tried to keep their cool, but they were too stoned and thought the joke too funny.

Willie took the joint from River. "Okay, what did you two do that is so hilarious?"

Dora came out and immediately saw the sign. "Yes! I always wanted to live in a den of iniquity." She whooped loudly and shimmied her breasts at Willie. He took her hands and swung her around, only stopping when the well-tuned, white and red Belair pulled down the lane towards them.

"Hey! Our number one parts man. Good to see you again, dude." Willie walked over and shook Jeff's hand as he got out of the car. "What's wrong, man?"

"The sheriff came into the dealership today, asking about you guys. Wanted to know about the girls, er, ladies." He blushed at Dora.

"Did he ask you about Ritta, specifically?"

"No. Just wanted to know if she was with you."

"Did you tell him where we are?"

"No, no!"

Dora took Jeff's hand. "Thanks for the warning."

"Sure. I suppose this means you'll be leaving soon." Jeff kicked the dirt.

River looked at Willie and they both nodded. River pulled another doobie from his shirt pocket and handed it to Jeff. "This one's for you."

Jeff's face lit up with his delight. "Thanks, River. That stuff last night was sure some kick-ass weed."

"This one's Colombian. Just a little 'toke in' of our appreciation for all your help. I don't think we could have gotten done without your expert assistance."

Jeff blushed. "Ah. Willie could do it, no sweat."

Willie laughed. "You kidding? I'd still be sweating under the bus."

* * *

Gert was pulverizing potatoes with a hand masher when she noticed the bus pull up the lane. "Ritta, go open the barn door and have the boys park inside. There should be room by the hay."

Ritta put the last plate on the table and headed out the screen door with Patch close behind. Gert put the cold fried chicken on the table, shook the green Jello salad with cottage cheese and chopped onions out of the mold onto a pretty plate. She stirred the gravy one last time before taking off the apron that covered her new tan trousers and pressed blue shirt. Meeting her guests at the screen door, she welcomed them into her home.

Willie walked in last. He stopped, filling the doorway, and inhaled deeply. "Fried chicken. And gravy. And fresh baked bread. Gert, you're the greatest!" He took the surprised woman in his arms and waltzed her smoothly around the kitchen. She glided with him in the dance of her generation, laughing like a schoolgirl.

"Come now," she said after Willie stopped dancing. "Go wash up there at the basin and let's eat before the gravy sets up."

They gathered around the big sink on the back porch. River nudged Ritta. "Jeff came by and said the Sheriff's looking for us."

"Yeah, he came out here, too. We were on the hill when he pulled up. Gert came down to talk to him. She has a plan."

"What is it?"

Gert stood in the doorway. "After dinner, young man, I'll tell you all about it. Sis and I didn't cook all afternoon so you can stand out here and chitchat."

When they were seated at the table, Gert bowed her head for a short, silent prayer before passing around the serving dishes.

Mazie bit into a thigh. "Mmmm. Gert, this chicken is as good as my Momma's, and I thought that would be impossible."

"Thanks, Mazie. My momma taught me how to cook it, maybe that's why." Gert relaxed back in her chair and watched them clean their plates. She noticed the Jello salad wasn't a big hit, but there would be no leftovers of anything else. It had been a long time since her house had been filled with young people, and she was enjoying it. The only thing missin' is my Jody.

When Dora and Mazie rose to clear the table she told them, "Just stack the dishes in the sink, girls. We got us some discussin' to do.

"The Sheriff knows that Ritta is with you, that you're drivin' a painted up school bus, and he has descriptions of all of you. There's two things we could do. One—you could take my Jeep. She's a good rig, probably make it just fine to where you're going. It'll be crowded, what with Patch and all your belongin's. Or, you could paint the bus. I have a five gallon can of new barn paint. It's kinda red, but it would be less conspicuous than the pedulas and hoolaras you have all over it now."

River looked incredulous. "Paint the bus? But it's taken us years to get it this way!"

Willie looked solemnly at Gert. "What would happen to the bus here?"

"I'd keep it in the barn. It would be all right, 'til you could come back and git it, when things cool down some."

"What would you drive if we took your Willys?"

"Oh, I'd find something. Don't worry 'bout that. What's important is that you git Ritta safely down to Jody in Berkeley."

River looked at Ritta. "Is that what you want?"

She nodded.

"Okay." River leaned back in his chair. "We paint the bus."

Willie asked, "What makes a red bus any less conspicuous than a flow-ered one?"

Mazie said, "Back home, lots of churches have buses. Some of them are painted different colors."

River brightened. "Yeah, we could paint 'Praise the Lord' on the back."

"And Hallelujah across the front," Dora added.

River sat up, excited. "And a big white cross on the top so the airplanes could see it."

Ritta laughed. "So that's how the bus got to look like it does."

Willie nodded, "You got it. May I suggest we don't defeat the purpose here. We are after subtlety, at least as subtle as a red school bus can be."

"So it's settled? That's what you want to do?" Gert looked at each one of them. When she looked at Mazie, the girl just shrugged. "Hey, I just want to get to L.A. in one piece and stay out of trouble. Red bus, rainbow bus, makes no difference to me."

Willie scratched his beard, "It's going to be a hell of a lot of work to get it painted. We'll have to sand it down some and primer it if we can, that would help. What do you have in the way of paint supplies, Gert?"

"We'll have to go look. My old neighbor gave me the paint and a bunch of other things when he sold out last year. He thought I should paint the barn and the house, but I like the bare weathered wood, don't you? I decided to paint the trim and that's all."

In the barn, Gert and Willie scouted around for things they might need. She piled several extension cords into his arms. "Somewhere 'round here I got some of those trouble lights. We can hang 'em off the rafters." She opened a drawer in the workbench to find the sandpaper had been nibbled by mice and cussed her barn cats.

They dropped the supplies near the bus, then she led Willie to a small locked room off the back of the barn. As she fiddled with the rusty padlock, Gert told him, "This here's my 'poison room.' Nearly lost old Ginger, Jody's dog, when he was a pup 'cause he got into some bug killer. Since then I lock all that chemical stuff in here."

She pointed to the five gallon bucket of paint and Willie carried it away as she gathered brushes and rollers, trays and turpentine, and set them out the door.

Willie opened the paint, carefully prying up the tabs that locked down the metal lid. A layer of oil mixed with specks of red pigment floated on top. He took a clean piece of wood and stirred it gently, mixing the thick paste color with the oil until he was satisfied. He held the stick up into the light, wiped it off with a rag and said, "Not bad, man. Kind of a rust brown instead of fire-engine red. Dark enough it should cover at least most of the stuff."

River had been watching and agreed, though he didn't seem too thrilled.

Gert nudged him with her elbow. "Cheer up, son. You can always paint it again."

"Oh, it's not that."

Willie asked, "What is it, man? You've been bummed out all evening."

"How are we going to disguise us? We're obvious too, not just the bus."

Gert laughed. "You want a haircut, boy?"

River's hand flew up to his ponytail. "No! I don't. But I would if it'll keep us from getting busted."

Willie looked at his friend. "Well, I'll cut mine. I don't care. And shave my beard, too. That should help. I can do the driving and the rest of you can sit where no one can see you. We'll keep Mazie from hanging out the window. It'll be okay, you'll see."

"You can't drive all the way, man."

Gert asked River, "Don't you have a hat you can tuck that pretty hair into when you drive?" When he shook his head no, she added, "Well, I might have just the thing." She went into the tack room and came out brushing the dust off a light brown felt hat, something of a cross between a cowboy hat and a bowler; with a short brim, squared top, and pleated satin hat band. River smiled at Gert as she piled his hair on top of his head and plopped the hat over it. "There, now you look like a real dandy."

River checked it out in the bus' side mirror. "Thanks, Gert. It's really far out."

"Far out, huh? Well, you're welcome. We better get crackin' here if we're going to get this beast of yours painted before dawn. I'll get my work clothes on."

Gert headed back to the house and turned at the side door of the barn. "You boys drink coffee?"

"Sure do. Thanks."

The kitchen brigade had finished the dishes and were just heading out the door when Gert stepped on the porch. Ritta told her, "We put some water on the stove for coffee."

"Good girl. It's going to be a late night. I'm going to get some work clothes on. Do any of you need grubbies?"

Dora laughed. "No thanks, Gert."

Mazie shook her head. "I'm fine."

Ritta looked at her pants, unsure she wanted to get paint on them. Gert took her hand. "Come with me." She led Ritta into the upstairs room. "I'm sure Jody won't mind if I give you some of her clothes. She didn't want to take 'em with her, anyway."

Gert opened the drawers and pulled out jeans and t-shirts, sweaters and socks. Ritta pulled off the army pants she had worn for days and tried on the faded Levis Gert threw on the bed. They fit except the length. Gert knelt down

77

and rolled the cuff up once. "Perfect. That's how Jimmy Dean wore 'em, you know."

Ritta helped Gert onto her feet and gave her a big hug. "Thanks, Gert, for everything."

"You're welcome, Sis. Just be safe." Gert rummaged through the drawers a little longer until she found a tattered pair of sweatpants. "Here, these'll do to paint in."

Ritta dressed and walked alone to the barn in the near dark. When she opened the door she could just make out the scent of marijuana smoke mingling with the warm hay.

River's head poked out of an open bus window. She could tell how stoned he was by the way he smiled and motioned for her to join them. Back inside the familiar surroundings she sat beside him on the beanbag, but refused the joint he offered her. After he passed it on, he put his arm around her. "So how are you doing, sweetie?"

"Good. I like it here. We had a great time until the Sheriff came." She looked down to the floor. "I'm sorry we have to paint your bus, River."

"Hey, this old thing was due for a new look. Besides, Willie and I have it all figured out. When we get to Bezerkeley, we'll paint it again. Only more far out."

"Thanks." She turned to the others as they headed out the door. "You guys, too."

Dora looked back and smiled at her. "Well, you sure know how to stir up an adventure."

"That you do." River put his arm around her. When the others left he kissed Ritta on the lips.

She kissed him back, but felt awkward. Gert could find them like this. And his breath smelled from smoking. When she stopped him, he looked hurt. She said, "Sorry."

"That's okay. Don't do something your not groovin' with. Come on, Patch. Let's get to work."

The dog glanced up at Ritta for a brief second before following River out of the bus. Ritta clenched her fists and eyelids shut. Damn. Why did I do that? He's done so much for me. Where would I be without him? She looked around the familiar mess and decided she would do whatever made River happy.

When she went out, Willie showed her and Mazie a palm-sized block of wood with sandpaper taped around it. "Take this and smooth out where the designs are." He demonstrated on a purple flower adorning the rear fender. "Try not to get past the original yellow paint, though."

Ritta started sanding by the door, rubbing peace signs into dust that made her sneeze. River handed her a few sheets of new sandpaper he'd torn into pieces the right length to wrap around her block of wood. She smiled, a little sheepishly, but felt better when he smiled back before turning away.

He returned a few minutes later with a handkerchief to tie around her face. "There, now you look like a real bandito." He tucked a stray lock of her hair under the knot. "Does that hurt your cheek, there?"

She adjusted the material over her ears. "No. It's just fine. Thanks."

Mazie sanded on the same side of the bus as Ritta, starting at the back and working her way towards the front. Nearly an hour later, they met under the windows. Mazie swatted Ritta on the hip with the sanding block, leaving a mark like a chalkboard eraser.

Ritta twisted around to look at the rectangle of mud-colored paint dust on her new sweatpants. "Hey, you can't do that."

"I just did." Mazie walked off, wriggling her hips tauntingly. Before she was five feet away, Ritta threw the block of wood in her hand. It smacked flat on Mazie's high round buttocks and fell.

Mazie turned and looked at the dusty imprint on her hind side. She wiggled it again, then headed for the enameled blue coffee pot and assortment of cups set on a hay bale by the door. "Anybody else ready for some java?"

River, working on the hood, stopped the circular motion of his arm in mid-stoke and jumped down. "Good idea. Let's take a break."

Ritta slyly picked up her sanding block from the dirt floor as she walked towards the coffee. Mazie handed her a steaming tan mug decorated with rows of common cattle brands. Ritta held the mug up to look at them and noticed a hairline fissure where the handle had been repaired. She tasted the sweet black brew. "Thanks, Maze, you fixed it just right."

"You're welcome. What are those marks on your cup?"

"Brands. You know, for branding cattle." Ritta set the mug on the ground beside a hay bale. As she was rising, she smacked Mazie's unsuspecting rump with the dusty block. "Here's the B Bar B." She slapped her again. "And the Flying Circle." Whack. "And the Double square T."

Mazie swung her hips to avoid the last swipe. Ritta laughed at Mazie's astonishment, and barely had time to run when Mazie chased her. Both squealed as they ran around the posts and bales of hay. Ritta dodged through the door into the dimly lit tack room and hid behind one of the rough hewn posts. Mazie snuck up behind and caught her by the hand. Ritta squirmed and laughed as Mazie pushed her until her backside butted up against a saddle on a sawhorse. Both were breathless.

Ritta looked into her captor's smiling eyes and felt the inhaled lift of Mazie's ribs, the roundness of Mazie's breast against her own. She slapped the block on Mazie's rump with her free hand, raising a cloud of dust. "Got you good, didn't I?"

"You don't know how good." Mazie caught Ritta's free hand by the wrist and held it gently. Mazie's lips softly touched Ritta's, brushing them more than kissing, before she released her grip. She hurriedly walked away, but turned towards Ritta for a moment as she went through the door.

The flustered look in Mazie's brown eyes confused Ritta even more. Ritta didn't move, trying to understand what had just happened. When she finally went back, everyone but Mazie stood around the side of the bus, sipping their coffee. She sat down with Dora on a hay bale that Willie brought over for them. Dora smiled gratefully at him.

Willie kissed the top of her head. "We're almost ready, man. That didn't take long at all. A little more sanding and we can wet down the dirt on the floor so we don't raise a lot of dust when we paint. After we wipe the bus down with turpentine."

Dora groaned.

River stared fixedly at the mottled metal body. "It was so beautiful."

Willie shook his head. "Hey, man. Don't freak. We can do it again and it'll be more far out than the first time. She still has soul and that's what counts."

"You're right. We got to camouflage all of us until we get to Bezerkeley. Then we can do anything we want with it. How 'bout paintin' something on the side, you know, like where it said…shit. What did it used to say?"

Willie scratched his head. "'Something School'. I don't remember either."

When the sanding was done and the dust removed with turpentined rags, Willie ladled red paint into small plastic pails. He gave everyone a brush and a position on the bus. Then he walked around constantly while they painted, making certain everyone did the best job they could. Even Gert, painting around the grill and the headlights, received Willie's gentle admonishment to keep her strokes long and even. Shortly before three a.m. they were finished.

Gert placed clean towels on the basin in the back porch and wished the kids good night. She laid her bone-weary body in her bed and said her nightly litany of blessings, including a new one for safe passage and Godspeed for the freshly-painted bus.

She woke up late, six-thirty, to the sounds of her chickens clucking their concern over her whereabouts. She didn't expect anyone else to be up and was startled to see a someone standing over her stove as she walked into the kitchen. "You're up early, Mazie. Or did you sleep at all?"

"No. May I get you some coffee?"

"Please, dear."

Mazie carefully lifted a cup from a mug tree and poured the warmed-over remains from the night before. "I watched the sunrise from the field out there. One of your ponies came and stood over me, like a guardian angel. It was beautiful."

"A little brown one with a flaxen mane?"

"Yeah, what's its name?"

"That's Butternut. Isn't she a sweet thing?" After a few sips Gert asked, "Want to talk 'bout what's troublin' you?"

Mazie laughed. "You're pretty intuitive."

"My Jody used to sit in the pasture and watch the sun come up when something was eatin' away at her."

"Well, Dora's going to cut Willie's hair, and River's got that bitchin hat you gave him to hide his ponytail. Dora can just dress straight and blend in anywhere. But me, there's not much I can do. What if we get busted because I'm sticking out like a sore black thumb."

"You and Ritta should just hide till you get to California."

"I don't want to hide, Gert. I haven't done anything wrong! And neither has Ritta. We shouldn't have to hide."

"I know, I know. But the time's not right and this ain't the place to fight. You'll know when it is. When you get there and it's right, fight like hell, girl. But let Ritta get her feet under her before she has to defend herself again. Hide."

"Where?"

"Have the boys make a place so it looks like it's part of the bus, or full of boxes or something. They can do that."

"We have the cargo holds under the bus," Willie told them when they gathered for breakfast and Gert brought it up. "One has most my tools in it and the other is full of Dora's midwife books and medical equipment. We'll just clean hers out and make it cozy. With the bed over the hatch on the floor, no one ever knows it's there. But it could get uncomfortable if you were in it for long."

After breakfast, Willie and Dora removed her collection from the compartment. Some of her boxes stacked in the other hold. The rest crowded the interior even more. When they were done, everyone gathered for a trial run.

With the others standing over them, Mazie and Ritta lowered themselves into the plywood and metal-framed compartment. It was cramped and hard, but they fit if they sat crouched with their knees bent.

Gert took Willie by the hand. "Come with me. I got just the ticket."

When they returned, Willie carried the thin mattress from Jody's bed, its ticking patched in several places with sack cloth. He plopped it down into the compartment.

Ritta pulled it around until the mattress rolled a little ways up each side. When she and Mazie went back down in the hole again it was all right, until Willie lowered the trap door over their heads. The padding made them crouch even more. Ritta shifted around but couldn't get comfortable until Mazie suggested they both lie in the same direction, with their knees bent. It felt good being close to Mazie, to touch and smell her skin.

The top edges of the compartment had half-inch gaps open to the underneath of the bus, letting in long slits of dim light. Mazie twisted her head around until her right eye was lined up with the gap. "I feel like Anne Frank."

Ritta heard heavy footsteps above her. "Who's Anne Frank?" she asked.

"This young girl whose family hid for years from the Nazis. During the Holocaust.

"Holo-what?"

"Holocaust. Didn't they teach you that in school?"

"I didn't go very much."

"Oh. Well, during World War Two the Nazis rounded up nearly every Jew in Europe, put them in concentration camps, and killed most of them."

"Sounds like what happened to my people. How much can you see?"

"Not much, but enough to keep me from going crazy." Mazie gasped and jumped back. "Jesus Christ, you scared me."

Through the crack, River's blue eyes peered at them from under the bus. "Sorry. How you two doing in there?"

"I'm okay." Mazie turned to Ritta. "How about you? Think you can handle it down here if we have to hide?"

"Sure," she said, but was very relieved when the trap door opened.

"That should work just dandy." Gert extended her arm to pull Ritta, then Mazie, out. "Let's go on up to the house and get you some provisions."

Dora put her arm around the older woman. "Gert, you don't have to do that. You've done so much for us already."

Gert patted the hand on her shoulder. "And just where are you going to go shoppin', Missy? It would be safer if you didn't stop near here. Which direction you headin', anyway?"

Dora looked at Willie, who shrugged his shoulders. He nudged River. "Hey, man. Do you know where we're going?"

"LA, via Oregon."

"What route?"

"Good question."

Gert said, "Well, now, you could go north over to Columbus, get on that big freeway road they built. Keep you out of town. If you went south at Livingston you'd go through Yellowstone Park. That would be good this time of year, lot's of tourists, better chance of blending in. Real pretty place, too. Got a big herd of buffalo."

"What do you think, Mazie?" Dora asked.

"I don't care, as long as we're on the road. Ritta, what do you want to do?"

Ritta knew what she wanted. "I want to see the buffalo."

Dora smiled at her. "The Park it is then."

When she was satisfied the kids had enough food to get them on their way, Gert packed a box of things she wished Jody had taken with her, like the wool letterman's jacket she used to wear all the time. Then she wrote a letter telling her daughter about Ritta. She knew her girl; Jody would be suspicious. She also had a hunch that, in time, Jody and Ritta would be real good friends. She tied the box with twine and went to find someone to give it to.

She found Willie and Dora on the porch. Willie sat on a stool, a towel draped over his shoulders. Dora stood over him, scissors in hand. She had cut his hair straight across the back, even with his collar. Dora dunked the comb in the glass of water and once more wet his hair down. "I just can't get it to look right."

Gert looked at Willie. "Mind if I try."

"Shoot."

Gert took the scissors and cut the hair up the back of his head. Ignoring Willie's wincing, she quickly tapered it around, in the standard barber cut. Parting the hair in the middle on top of his head, she evened out the side to match the back, leaving the top only slightly longer. She left and came back with a mirror, a straight razor with its leather strap, and a bar of soap. When she held the mirror up for Willie to look, he smiled. "That's how my dad used to cut it when I was a kid."

Gert took his face in her hands. "Trust me?"

"Implicitly."

"Fool." She laughed, snipping his beard short and ragged. "Dora, get me the kettle from the stove." When Dora returned, Gert poured hot water over the towel and wrapped Willie's face in the steaming cloth. She hooked the leather strap on the railing and stropped the blade in a nearly forgotten rhythm until the metal shined, then lathered up the bar of soap in her hands. After nodding to Dora to remove the towel from Willie's face, she lathered his remaining beard, wiped her hands on the wet towel and took up her razor. Willie's eyes grew large as she came at him with the straight blade. "Relax. I used to shave my father all the time. 'Course, that was forty years ago." Willie squirmed. Gert held his head in the crook of her arm and began to scrape his whiskers off. She extended his neck to get under his chin. He winced when the blade nicked his Adam's apple.

"Sorry. I used to wing Papa there, too."

When she finished wiping off the remaining soap with the towel, Willie rubbed his face and turned towards Dora sitting on the railing.

"Oh thank God, you do have a chin." She felt his smooth cheeks and kissed his exposed lips. "Hmm. This might be all right."

Gert left them in their embrace after she gathered up the things strewn about the porch. She had an idea.

The Bible was nothing special to her now. She had found her own brand of religion and you couldn't get it in a book. But the Bible had been in her family for a long time, so she asked Willie to leave it with Jody. The suit belonged to Amos, the one he bought when Jody was christened, the last time any of them went to the big Lutheran church in Red Lodge. It barely fit Willie. He couldn't get the jacket buttoned. She told him, "But it still make's ya look real dignified, Willie. What with the short hair and all."

Mazie teased, "Hey, Preacher man, it's a long way from Sodom and Gomorra."

He winked at Dora. "Not as far as you might think."

Ritta, Doppler, and Patch were chasing each other around the middle pasture when Ritta heard the engine. From up the hillside she saw the bus pull out of the barn and had a moment of panic, thinking they were leaving her behind. It passed quickly when the bus turned away from the lane and parked in the pasture behind the barn. When she was close she imagined she could see the paint drying in the bright sunshine. River joined her and shook his head as he looked at the brick red color of the bus in the noonday light. The wide, low front bumper with its chipped chrome was the only bright spot. "I can't stand it being so unadorned. Want to help me paint just a little more?"

"Sure."

Ritta watched as he penciled out the straight lines, puzzled over the letters. He went to Gert's unlocked poison room and found a small can of white paint that he and Ritta brushed over the slightly tacky red. Standing back when they had finished, River seemed pleased. He pulled a joint from his shirt pocket and lit up, offering it to her. She looked at it carefully, then took a deep inhalation, trying to fight back the cough that burst from her lungs.

"Smaller tokes. Remember to take in some air with the smoke."

She tried it again, this time it was easier. She felt warm all over, her head began to swim a little before she exhaled. River took two more hits and didn't offer her any more before he rubbed it out on a rock and carefully placed the remainder back in his pocket.

Ritta turned to look out over the pasture where the little ponies were standing placidly in pairs to swat each other's flies, their heads hung low nibbling the short grass. The clean smell of horse manure and summer sweetness filled the air. Taking a deep breath, she reached her arms towards the fluffy clouds and twirled around and around until River caught her. She reeled dizzily in his arms. Before the world held still, she was kissing his lips, his mustache tickling her nose.

They were interrupted by Willie's booming laughter from the other side of the bus. "You did it, man. I don't fucking believe it."

River took her hand and winked. They walked around to the other side. Ritta stopped in her tracks when she saw him. That can't be Willie.

River said, "I had to. I knew you'd look like a fucking preacher and it seemed the thing to do."

"It's great. Church of the Reverent Brethren. That should get us to Berkeley." Willie clasped River around the shoulders and the two went off to finish the roach in River's pocket.

Ritta wandered up to the house. Something cooking smelled very good, the aroma wafted down the slope towards the barn. The scent pulled her into the kitchen like she was hooked and reeled. Dora stood over the white enameled range, stirring a pan of sizzling onions that made Ritta's mouth water. Ritta asked, "What'cha makin'?"

"It's going to be vegetable stew, want to help?"

"Sure, want me to cut these up?" She pointed to the scrubbed potatoes on the table.

"Yeah, and the carrots there, too."

Mazie stumbled in from her nap in the living room. "She slices, she dices. It's the vegetable slaying Indian from the Badlands."

Ritta extended her left arm over her head, held the kitchen knife in her right and lunged at the nearest potato, stabbing it and bringing it up like a trophy. She opened her mouth, trilling her tongue in a high pitched ululation.

Dora looked at her disapprovingly. "Gert is lying down, Ritta."

Ritta pulled the potato off her blade. "I'm sorry, I didn't know." Behind Dora's back, she and Mazie snickered before they went to work on the vegetables.

The afternoon's light dimmed behind the mountain. Gert carried to the bus the still-warm leftover soup the girls had cooked and a loaf of bread baked the day before. Supper had been solemn. Gert felt edgy, twice she had gotten up from the table to peer out the window.

Her eyes stayed dry as she hugged them all good-bye, until she knelt down to rub Patch behind his ears. "Take good care of Sis, ol' man."

The dog's brown eyes seemed to reflect her own sadness. He licked her, then followed his people into the bus. Ritta came back and pressed into Gert's hand the letter Amos had written so long ago. "Here. I want you to keep this. Thank you, Gert. For everything. Goodbye. *Ake waciyankin kte.*" Ritta jumped into the bus and held onto the rail, waving with her free hand as the bus lolled down the lane.

"For God's sake, be careful," Gert shouted back before they turned down the gravel road. Standing there, staring at their dusty wake, she realized two days ago she hadn't known any of them. Now they were gone, and a big part of her heart was gone, too.

She walked the familiar path to her silent little house. Without giving it much thought, she went straight to the cupboard where the bottle had sat untouched for days. It kept her company for the rest of the evening.

Yellowstone Park

Ritta woke with dawn's first light, sat up and drew back the curtain. Outside, the narrow road and gravel shoulder where they were parked seemed to be the only solid ground. Between mounds of tall spiny grass, countless pools of water reflected the sky's steely hue. She pulled her jeans out from under her bedding, tugged them on, and wrapped the blanket around her shoulders. Quietly, she stepped over Mazie, opened the door and let the dog go out first.

The light crunch of her bare feet on gravel was the only sound except early birds' warbling and the soft whispering breeze. She dropped her jeans and squatted, glad it no longer hurt to pee as she pulled up the edges of her blanket and watched the dark rivulet spread, then disappear in the small round stones. As she buttoned her pants, the peacefulness was shattered by a flat trumpet sound. Her heart jumped.

The call echoed off the mountain walls that hemmed in the marshy plateau. She swirled around, trying to determine which direction the bellow had come from. It sounded again, closer. She ran around the front of the bus and stopped Patch before he could give chase.

Across the road and forty feet away stood a massive, long-legged animal, black in the faint light. He dropped his wide-horned head to feed.

Mazie's head poked out the driver's window. "What the hell is that?"

The moose lifted his prodigious head. Long strands of marsh grass draped from the shield of his antlers, raining down his dark velvet neck.

Mazie ducked inside. Soon the others popped their heads through the windows, gawking at the creature as he loped majestically through the hummocks of grass. Ritta leaned against the bus, her gaze locked on the forest where the moose disappeared.

Dora fired up the Coleman beside the bus and had water in the pot before everyone had relieved their bladders. "Do we want breakfast here or later down the road?"

"It's going to take a while to get water to boil at this elevation, sweetie. Let's eat here." Willie looked around to see if anyone agreed with him.

Dora shrugged. "Fine with me. How 'bout you, Maze?"

Mazie stretched her arms in front of her like a sleepwalker. "Coffeeee."

River put his arm around Ritta. "You hungry?" Her stomach rumbled and she laughed.

Dora pulled the first of Gert's fresh eggs from the cooler. "Over easy or scrambled?"

* * *

"Well, old man. You're in luck. We're not going to hold you any longer." The grinning policeman turned the key, pulled open the metal door and stood aside.

Lawrence slowly rose past the pain of broken ribs, held his head high and walked out. Half-expecting to be shot in the back for attempting escape, he ducked out into the bright sunlight on the dirt street, looking for a ride.

The first car going by slowed down, its engine racing louder as it stopped. Lawrence peered in the windows. Mabel, his sister-in-law, was in the back seat of the Rambler station wagon, propped up by two guys he didn't know. Lawrence looked at her puffy face and remembered a time when she was as pretty as Ritta. She slurred, "*Hau*, Larry, wanna ride?"

Ray Big Bull was driving. He nodded as Lawrence opened the door. The stench of stale beer almost sickened him as he carefully got in, but he knew he didn't smell much better after four nights in jail. Ray's lips pointed to the engine. "Choke's stuck. Glad they let you out."

Lawrence tried to adjust his ribs. "Me too."

Before they got to Whiteclay Lawrence turned carefully around. One of the men beside Mabel had his hand up her flowered blouse, pinching a nipple she half-heartedly defended, lightly slapping his arm until he removed it. "Larry, did you hear? Ritta's in Montana." Mabel's voice held a bit of pride.

Lawrence's heart dropped. "How do you know that?"

"She told me so. Called me at the Pony, long distance. 'Call for Mabel Baker.'" She laughed at her imitation of the bartender.

Lawrence wanted to slap the woman. Instead he quietly asked her, "What else did she say?"

Mabel squinted back tears and rocked between the men. "She misses me. My girl misses me."

Lawrence waited in the car while the others went into the liquor store at Whiteclay's. He hated this filthy little town. Just beyond the reservation border, its only purpose was selling booze to Indians. He understood though, how so many of his people lived between alcohol and sadness. He had been there himself.

The others came back, already cracking the seal to their bottle of Four Roses. The Rambler started with a roar and Ray turned it around and headed back to Pine Ridge. He offered the cheap whiskey to Lawrence. "You're a hurtin' unit. It's good medicine for that."

Lawrence took a long swallow, glad for the burn down his throat; and knew he had to stop or it would swallow him. Two miles on the other side of town Ray started to turn off onto another dirt road, headed for the powwow grounds to do some serious drinking.

"Let me out here," Lawrence said.

Outside, with the sun burning high in the blue sky, he started walking the long road, and recalled the first time his brother brought Mabel home. She had just returned from the boarding school and was thin as a sapling, her eyelids red and oozing with the sore eye disease. Their mother cooked up something to clean them with. His brother had the girl pregnant before summer ended, and every year after that until he wrapped his car around a telephone pole and died.

A pickup pulled over to the side of the road in front of him. Lawrence eased himself onto the seat next to his friend, John McAdam, whose allotment was about twenty miles from his.

John slid a pouch of tobacco across the pickup seat. "Bill's got your filly. He told me they had you locked up. Some on the Tribal Council was damn mad about it, too. What does Lopate think he's doin', throwing good folks in jail?"

Lawrence looked out the open window, smoked his cigarette and wondered how Ritta was doing. He couldn't blame her for calling her mother. He just hoped it wasn't a big mistake.

When John turned off the main highway and onto the road that led home, Lawrence woke from his fitful sleep and rolled another from John's tobacco. He couldn't remember ever being so tired, now that he felt safe enough to rest. When he dozed off again the cigarette dangled dryly from his lips.

The pickup topped the hill that overlooked Lawrence's place and came to an abrupt halt. Lawrence startled as John's grasp shook him awake. "*Wan*. What is it?"

When he got his bearings, Lawrence looked down the familiar hillside to the pile of smoldering ashes. Only the rock of the chimney still stood where his cabin had been.

* * *

Sheriff Holecomb woke with a dull headache. Then he remembered the officer from South Dakota was due around noon and his head started to throb.

He pulled himself out of bed and asked the white Persian cat nestling down on his wife's recently vacated pillow, "Where the hell did that girl get to?"

The night before, he'd driven through the campground where Ruby, the desk clerk at the Yodeler, was sure the hippies were staying. He even posted a deputy there, had him sit in his own truck with a CB radio. Around midnight, and again at three, he called the man to see if there had been any sign of them. None at all.

He stumbled into the bathroom, took a piss, and swallowed some aspirin. He looked in the mirror and asked his reflection, "Just what is Jeff not telling me?" As he pulled up on his heavy jowls to shave the whiskers under his chin, it occurred to him. That boy is trying to protect those hippies. Why? Jeff's a good kid, but he sure started to sweat when he saw me yesterday. Maybe I should go talk to him alone, without his daddy around. Before this Officer Lopate from the reservation gets here. And talk to Gert again, too. Something just isn't making sense 'bout all this.

By the time he walked through the gate in the picket fence that surrounded his wife's flower garden he was all the more determined to find that girl. Before noon.

* * *

Ritta sat on the railing by the open door of the bus, her feet propped on the dash. Mazie leaned beside her. Around each corner was another beautiful vista and they both went "oooh" and "ahhh" shamelessly. Ritta was the first to see the herd of thirty or more buffalo grazing in the meadow beside the road. She jumped from her perch. "Stop, Willie!" Anxiously, she watched the edge of the pavement as the bus slowed but didn't come to a standstill. She turned to the driver.

Willie shrugged. "The shoulder's not wide enough. I can't park here."

Ritta held onto the edges of the door and leaned out, keeping her eyes on the placidly grazing herd. She felt like she was watching them from another time; the present running faster, leaving the past behind.

She vaulted and hit the ground running.

Willie stopped in the middle of the lane. Mazie called after Ritta, "What are you doing?"

Ritta turned around, still running towards the herd. "Wait for me. I'll be back."

A stone's throw from the nearest buffalo, she stopped and hunkered down, glad for the fresh breeze on her cheeks that carried her scent away from the slowly meandering herd. Most of those closest to her were cows and calves. The biggest bull rolled in the dust far on the other side. An old male, too feeble to travel with the other bulls, took up the rear.

An adventurous youngster bounded close by. He stopped abruptly when he saw her, took a cautious step closer, then another. Slowly, Ritta straightened her legs, standing by the time the calf was three feet away. She could smell his musky animal odor. He sniffed the air, then snorted at her with flaring nostrils. She laughed. The sound sent him scampering back to the safety of numbers.

His running started the herd to veer away from her. When they were gone she ran back to the bus parked a short distance down the road. Inside, she said, "Weren't they great! Did you see that calf? He came this close to me." She extended her arms.

Dora scolded, "Ritta, those are wild animals. What would you have done if that buffalo charged at you?"

"Probably run like hell. But he was just a calf."

"He was bigger than a horse."

"I was all right, really, Dora." Ritta leaned on the chrome rail. Dora shook her head and walked towards the back, weaving as the bus started down the road again.

Mazie joined Ritta and whispered, "That was great. Mother Dora sure had a tizzy-fit. River literally had to hold her back."

"Yeah, well I don't need a mother."

"I hear you, sister. I hear you."

An hour later, on Grand Loop Road, a front tire blew out. Willie managed to get the bus down a little side road and parked on a fairly level spot. Ritta grew restless when River pulled out a joint and it became obvious they weren't in any hurry to fix it. She told them she was going for a walk, but she ran down the road for the sheer joy of it, ignoring the passing carloads of tourists.

When the muscles in her thighs burned with exertion, she slowed. The warm afternoon sun on her back quickly dried her damp shirt, but her feet still sweated in the shoes. She pulled them off, stuffed the damp socks inside, and slipped her index fingers in the loops on top. She swung the sneakers in rhythm with her lengthy stride along the edge of the road. Cool mud squished between her toes.

Surrounded by the ever present mountains, another lush green marsh lay before her. The empty road curved through it, hidden by tall grass. A piercing cry far above made her stop and search the clear blue sky until she could make out a soaring silhouette. When she whistled an answer the bird circled high overhead. Ritta spread her arms and spun, the basketball shoes flung at the end of her fingers, her eyes on the descending bird as it spiraled in the air above her. Her heart seemed to soar with the bird as she whispered, "I'm free, I'm free." A car sped by. The eagle flew off.

When the bus finally reached her, River slowed it to a crawl and opened the door. A car behind him honked its horn and passed when oncoming traffic allowed.

"Hey, there, good-lookin'. Want a ride?"

"Depends on where you're goin'," she replied, mockingly coy.

"To the big city, bright lights, millions of people. Far away from this." He gestured out the windshield.

"Sounds great." She jumped into the bus. Her muddy feet slipped on the step before she caught the handrail, laughing.

At dusk, they pulled into a campground. No spaces were vacant but they parked anyway, near the restrooms and a water pump painted shiny red. After everyone washed up, River suggested they try to find a less congested area to spend the night.

Ritta sat on the crate behind him as he drove. Together they watched the round moon ascend from the craggy black outline of mountain top. Snow in the deep crevices shadowed during the day, glistened in the silvery light. Each pool of water in the bogs reflected the orb. When they entered the woodland, a large wooden sign proclaimed this to be *Grizzly Country—Tent camping prohibited, sleep in hard-shelled vehicles only. Do not feed the bears.* The moon cast down ethereal, luminous pillars through the forest.

Ritta leaned her head down on the back of the driver's seat as the road twisted around the mountain. The others had fallen asleep, leaving her alone in the moonlight with River.

He turned to her with a burning look that kindled the spark between them. She was still warm from it when River pulled the bus into a small campground. A secluded spot between the trees seemed to be waiting for them.

River pulled on the hand brake and opened the door. "Got to take a leak." Patch followed him out.

She was nestled into the beanbag when River came back. He spread his sleeping bag on the floor beside her. Suddenly, being so close to him made her want to cry. The empty places in her, places she had just begun to comprehend, longed to be filled. When she reached over and put her hand on his chest he pulled her down beside him. He stroked her hair. The long strands entangled his fingers. Her head tilted back as he tried to free his hand. Her eager mouth found his.

Trembling, she pressed her body next to him, this time not recoiling from his growing hardness. He leaned over, gently brushing his silken beard on her unhurt cheek. His arms around her, he slowly pulled her on top of him, kissing her mouth as he rolled her to the other side. She descended into a patch of moonlight so bright it cast shadows of his fingers as he unbuttoned her shirt.

He knelt over; his long, coppery hair adorning her naked breasts. She watched as her nipple disappear into his curly beard, watched him gently suck on it until she had to close her eyes. Even in the darkness, passion was a safer place than she had imagined.

She opened them again when he stopped. The cold air made her wet nipple harder. He pulled off his shirt and rubbed his naked chest lightly on hers. The curly golden hairs tickled at first, until the exquisite feeling of skin against skin filled her senses.

Gathering the blankets, he covered them both. She snuggled into him, her head on his shoulder and rubbed his chest with the open palm of her hand. He kissed her on the top of her head. Boldly, she moved to the tautness of his abdomen, her fingers making light circles around his navel.

He held absolutely still as her circles became larger, finally brushing what strained against the muslin of his pants. He caught her hand and gently pushed it down until her fingers folded over the part of him that seemed to get stiffer when she touched it. She stretched her body along his side and kissed him hard, bumping teeth.

She felt him search under the waistband of his drawstring pants for the tie. Then he slid her hand under the fabric. Her fingers met the wet, slippery tip and wrapped uncertainly around it. He moaned and moved her hand up and down the length of it in a steady rhythm. When he let go, she continued until he grasped her hand to stop it.

"What's wrong?" she whispered.

He rolled her on her back and leaned his weight on one elbow. "Nothing, I don't want to come yet." Stroking the hair from her cheek, he spoke barely loud enough for her to hear. "I want to make love to you."

His eyes never wavered from hers as he touched the wetness that seeped through her jeans and pressed his finger into her. He raised himself to his knees, undoing the buttons of her pants, then looked at her questioningly.

She nodded. Oh, God. I want to do this. I want to. She raised her hips and he slid her pants off. She gasped when his finger went inside her.

"Did I hurt you?"

"You didn't. Somebody else did. Please, River, don't stop."

His fingers touched her again, softer now and only pressing into her when she moved against them, harder and harder, until the pain of her defilement faded into the ache of longing.

She turned and took his quivering, hard penis in her hand. Sliding her palm up and down it, she matched his rhythm. Suddenly, he shuddered and arched his back, moaning. She pulled away, certain he was having one of those seizures, like her friend Betty used to have in grade school. "Oh, my God," she whispered. "Are you all right?"

He found her hand and put it in something warm and wet on his belly before he wiped it off with the edge of her blanket. Soon she heard his breath become deep and measured.

As her passion cooled it all started to make sense; the things Dora had told her, why her crotch was so sticky that day, why she hurt so bad. She tried not to think of those men putting their big, hard things in there. The only way to do that was by stroking herself, slowly so she wouldn't wake River, pretending he was touching her still.

93

When Mazie woke, the first thing she saw was Ritta and River entwined on the floor a few feet from her. She sat up, rubbed the tight curls on her head, and tried to determine why she felt the way she did. She couldn't even put a name on the emotions that welled up inside and threatened to explode. Near rage, staring at Ritta with her head on River's bare chest in sweet repose, Mazie pulled on her pants. Then she grabbed a sweater and slipped out of her warm sleeping bag. She found the Coleman stove and coffee pot in a kitchen box and opened the door. The air was damp and cold. Shivering, she placed the stove on a near-by picnic table and went to search for water.

When she returned, Dora appeared with the can of coffee Gert had given them and a few cups. They sat silently, waiting for the water to boil, while the birds sang and the sun peeked through the trees, heralding another beautiful day.

Mazie's heart grew colder as she chastised herself for the way she felt. I've no right to be jealous of River. He's a kind person, even if he is a little flaky. He can take care of Ritta. I don't even have a home to go to. River at least has his daddy's money.

Willie came out from the bus, a grin on his face. "Looks like River had a good night."

That was more than she could bear. As Mazie furiously walked away she heard Willie ask Dora, "What's her problem?"

River woke from a dream. It escaped him as his consciousness returned, leaving him wanting whatever the dream had promised. He turned towards Ritta, wrapped her in his arms. His morning hard-on tapped her belly. She moaned and snuggled deeper in his embrace. He kissed her cheek, then her closed eyelids, and had just found her lips when Willie's booming voice filled the bus. "Hey, none of that."

"Look whose talking," River chided, his eyes still on Ritta.

She smiled, then untangled herself from him and groped for her clothes in the heap of bedding. Holding the blanket over her breasts, she put Lawrence's undershirt on, then her cowboy shirt. Under the covers, she pulled up her pants then stood with her back to Willie to zip them. She padded out in bare feet.

When she left, River said to Willie, "No lectures, man. I know she's young."

"Just be careful. She's been through an awful lot."

"I know, Willie." River nodded his head pensively. "I know."

Over breakfast it was agreed that Old Faithful, fifty miles away, would be their next stop. They neared the geyser around ten.

It took half an hour to find a place to park. Cars lined up, crawling ahead at the direction of Park employees. A large wooden sign with removable numbers proclaimed the geyser's next eruption to be at ten-forty-five. "That explains the crowd," Dora said as they crept along. "Looks like we're just in time."

They joined the throng of people walking along the boardwalk passed the rustically beautiful lodge. Ritta marveled at all the different kinds of folks when it occurred to her, I'm a tourist! We're all tourists here.

Back home, when a car with out-of-state plates passed by, it was hard not to feel like one of the attractions people drove through the reservation for. South Dakota: Badlands, Indians, Mount Rushmore.

She eavesdropped on a small cluster of people walking next to her, straining to understand their foreign words. Then she noticed the cameras most of them had draped around their necks. One guy had three between his chin and big belly. A group of children ran off the boardwalk in a game of tag and a Park Ranger came over to tell them to stay on the pathway. When he turned around, Ritta glimpsed his young face. He looked to be about River's age.

Right on time, with the crowd gathered impatiently at the end of the boardwalk, steam began to rise from a mound some fifty feet from the audience. It sputtered, then amassed again, sending a stream of boiling water twenty feet in the air where it dissipated into the blue sky as clouds. A low roar filled the air.

Ritta heard a boy standing in front of her say to his father, "Big deal. We waited all morning for that?"

A handsome young man nearby told him, "Just wait. That's pre-play. The geyser's just building up steam for the real gush."

"Oh, yeah? How do you know?"

The young man replied, "I'm a geology major."

The boy kept his eyes on the rising plume. His father smiled thankfully at the student.

River stood close behind Ritta. His arms wrapped around her waist. "That was just pre-play," he whispered.

"Hmm." She snuggled against him. Suddenly, the geyser expanded, shooting its superheated plume fifty, eighty, then one hundred-twenty feet into the sky. She felt its moisture on her face, tasted the sulfur-laden air. A noise like a freight train rumbled deep in the earth.

In her ear, River said softly, "That's how I felt last night."

She felt her cheeks blush as she turned to look at him. He put his wet mouth over hers and filled it with his delicious tongue. The geyser shot its last gurgle of water and returned to steam, slowly lowering back into the earth.

The college student looked at the kid. "So. What did you think?"

"It was nifty, but they should leave it on longer." The boy headed for the gift shop.

When the crowd thinned, Willie tapped River on his shoulder, disrupting his and Ritta's embrace. "Show's over, man. Let's go."

As they started back, Ritta composed herself, then asked Dora, "Where's Mazie?"

Dora pointed ahead of them, "She could be back at the bus by now. She left as soon as the geyser quit." They walked through the crowd, four abreast, arm in arm, the dog near Ritta's heels.

Mazie sat on the steps of the bus, an open brochure on her lap. Ritta sat down beside her. "Hey, what'cha readin'?"

"Look at this." Mazie showed her a map detailing the other geysers. "There's more, just north of here. Not as big as Old Faithful, but maybe not so crowded, either." Patch put his nose on Mazie's lap.

"Can we go check it out?" Ritta looked up at River, who turned to Willie and Dora. With a round of shrugs and nods, it was decided. They inched their way to the highway, caught in the stream of traffic exiting the parking lot.

Ritta perched next to River on the beanbag. He leaned into her and started to lick the lobe of her ear. It tickled and she made him stop. Mazie and Dora sat on the mattress, still pouring over the geyser brochure.

Willie looked at them in the round mirror that hung above him. "Too bad we can't hike in someplace, spend some more time in the Park away from all these people."

River asked, "Why can't we?"

"Camp?"

"Yeah. Why not? We're camouflaged now. I sure would like to spend some more time here. Anyone else?"

Dora nodded emphatically. "What do you think, Mazie. Good for one more night in the wild?"

Mazie smiled. "Can we still go to some other geysers?"

"Sure. That's where we're headed. Look on the map there for a hike a few miles in, but not too difficult."

Dora brought up the brochure to show him a few likely spots and laughed. "Willie, you look like the cat that ate the canary."

Willie stopped the bus at every roadside attraction. They ate lunch sitting on the boardwalk over a sulfurous field of mineral hot springs, feeding bits of bread to chipmunks that pestered them for more.

After a short walk around the sapphirine pools, they were back on the winding, narrow road. Around a corner, Mazie pointed to a sign for another geyser. "Hey, Willie."

"Okay, Maze. Last one, though, if we're going to hike in somewhere before dark."

This geyser field was smaller, set closer to the trees instead of the barren moonscape terrain of the others. As Willie maneuvered the bus into two adjoining parking spaces, Ritta noticed a small gathering of people at the end of the half-empty lot, away from the geyser. They all faced the edge of forest. A few pointed into the tall pines. One man removed his camera from its case and positioned himself slightly away from the group.

As he moved, Ritta saw a woman pick up a little dark-haired girl and put her on the other side of a low split rail fence. More people pointed. Ritta's eyes followed their gestures, squinting for a few moments until she saw the bear saunter out from the trees. She watched in disbelief as the woman handed the girl a yellow plastic tub and gave her a small shove towards the bear.

"Oh my God!" Ritta pushed on the door but it wouldn't open. She reached behind her, grabbed the knob and jerked it. As the glass doors parted she ran through them. The air seemed thick and heavy, slowing her every motion.

The bear stretched up to her full height. Her torso seemed to grow longer as she lifted her head in the air, swaying. She grumbled, fell again to all fours, following her nose.

The little girl clutched the honey container to her chest.

The click of cameras sounded behind her as Ritta finally reached the fence and vaulted over. The bear rose again, towering over the screaming child.

Ritta wrapped her arms around the girl as the bear reached for the honey. Claws cuffed Ritta's left shoulder. She spun from the blow and tumbled into the pine needles, the child beneath her. Ritta tried to wrench the bucket free, screaming, "Let go, let go!" The bear loomed over them, myopically searching for the sweets.

Ritta pried the girl's stiff fingers away and threw the honey behind the bear. Patch nipped at the sow, tearing fur, his hackles high. Growling formidably, the bear turned, taking empty swings at the frantically barking dog.

Ritta rolled the girl beneath the fence. The man with the camera gathered her to him as Ritta pulled herself under the rail. River grabbed her arm and shouted, "Patch. Come!"

The man and girl joined the others funneling into a station wagon, shouting accusingly at each other. Ritta couldn't run. Everything still seemed to be clicking slowly by, second by second. River half-dragged her to the bus, where he deposited her into Dora's waiting arms, then shut the door behind Patch. Ritta turned to look when Willie pointed to the bear with the yellow tub in her massive paws, licking drips of honey from the shredded plastic.

Dora guided Ritta to the beanbag, then began to remove her torn cowboy shirt. Mazie knelt beside her. "Whatever possessed you, girl. Christ, don't you know you could have been killed."

"Didn't you see what those stupid people were doing? Just to get some pictures!" Ritta winced as Dora pulled the undershirt off her shoulder and patted her skin with a square of gauze.

Dora shook her head. "I don't believe it. Look at this." She held up the tattered shirt so the five long rips showed through the cloth layers of the back yoke, then lifted the gauze from the scratches on Ritta's skin.

Everyone looked so amazed that Ritta stood and turned to the round mirror to look. From the back of her neck to her shoulder were three thin long lines. The middle one oozed tiny droplets of blood. The others were swelling into pink welts.

River stood in front of her. "Do you know how brave that was? You saved that kid's life."

When he touched her, Ritta turned to him and let him wrap his arms around her. His trembling seemed to match her own. She nodded, then looked at him with a sudden realization. "Patch saved us. Is he all right?" She dropped to her knees and kissed the dog on top of his head, then tenderly ran her hands over his torso, then limbs, watching carefully for any sign of pain. Finally convinced he had escaped unscathed, she buried her head in the dog's side.

River took her arm and pulled her up in time to see the station wagon pull out of its parking spot. When the car drove past the bus, the little girl looked up from the back seat, her brown eyes still wide with shock. Ritta smiled and waved. The girl waved back, then slowly turned her stunned gaze towards the bear.

River shook his head. "Poor little kid. She'll remember this day for a long time. Hope she grows up smarter than her folks. Willie, we should get out of here."

"Yeah, I've lost my taste for camping, too. Anyone else keen on getting out of the Park and back on the road?"

Mazie agreed. "I've had enough of the wildlife for a while."

Ritta slumped in the beanbag on her side, her scratched shoulder exposed. Dora knelt beside her with a small bowl filled with soapy water. "This might hurt a bit." Ritta grimaced as Dora lightly scrubbed the scratches.

As it dried, Dora fixed a dressing. Willie and River decided to continue to Madison and leave the Park by the West Entrance.

They had just passed the sign welcoming them to Idaho, 2.5 miles from the park boundary, when Willie shouted, "Oh, shit! Look behind us."

The light green Jeep Commando, official police lights swirling, was passing all the cars that hurriedly pulled over. When the siren sounded, a short blast of ear-piercing noise, River lifted the mattress and raised the trap door.

Shaking, Ritta followed Mazie into the hold. She wrapped her arms around her legs and lowered her head between her knees. Her shoulder stung like crazy. The metal trap door clanged shut above them.

River dropped the dusty mattress on top. Willie coasted to a stop on the side of the road.

A young man in a green uniform and a felt mountie hat stepped up to the door as it folded open. "Sorry to bother you folks, but we had a report of a bear mauling at the Lower Basin area. Witnesses said one of the victims got into this bus."

The Ranger walked up the steps. Dora moved around to the front of the box she had been using for a table and slid the bloody gauze and jar of salve behind her.

"We just want to make certain everyone is all right. The other folks said the young lady that interfered had been injured."

River couldn't believe his ears. "Interfered! They push that little girl out for bear bait then say we interfered? Of all the stupid—"

The ranger held up his hand. "That was the report over the radio. I heard they didn't speak English very well." The young man took off his hat and extended his hand. "My name is Tim, Tim Ewing."

"Call me River, man. This here's Willie and Dora." When he pointed to Dora, River noticed the edge of the mattress lift up off the floor.

Tim shook Willie's hand then nodded politely to Dora. "Are you the one that stopped the bear's attack?"

Dora held her hand to her chest. "Oh, no. Not me."

Tim looked confused. "Hey, look. I need to fill out a report. If the bear really attacked someone then she will have to be destroyed. If it was an STI, then we'll just tranquilize her and move her to safer ground."

Dora shook her head. "An STI?"

The Ranger's face reddened. "Stupid Tourist Incident. We get a lot of them, you know." His eyes searched the bus. "Is the woman involved here?"

River was trying to think of a good lie when Ritta pounded on the trap door and shouted, "Let me out!"

Dora held up the mattress as River lifted the door. He grasped Ritta's hand and pulled her, then Mazie, from under the floor.

The Ranger dropped his hat and stared at Ritta for a moment. "You must be the one. Are you all right?"

"You can't destroy her. It wasn't the bear's fault."

Dora laughed. "This girl's got heap good medicine. She barely got scratched."

"May I see?"

Ritta turned her shoulder towards him.

The Ranger shook his head. "Do you know how lucky you are?"

"Patch saved me." She patted the dog by her side. "And he didn't get hurt at all."

"Why don't you start at the beginning. Like, why were you hiding down there?"

Only then did Ritta look scared.

"Oh, the uniform. Hey, I'm not a cop, I'm not even a full Ranger, yet. I just got the job for the summer. But I do have to fill out a report to keep this bear alive." He looked around for his hat, then picked it up. "I don't really care why you were hiding down there, okay? I won't even use your real name if you don't want me to, but let's get the facts straight about the bear so no one else gets hurt." He looked around at the silent group. "Deal?"

Ritta smiled. "Deal."

Tim removed a small notebook and pen from his shirt pocket but didn't write anything down as Ritta explained to him what had happened, he just kept shaking his head and looking at her in awe. When she finished, he opened up the book. "Okay. Give me a name."

Ritta looked at her friends, and shrugged. Dora suggested, "Linda Doak."

Ritta nodded and looked at the Ranger. "Okay. Linda Doak."

"How do you spell that?"

Ritta turned to Dora once again.

"D O A K," Dora replied.

"Okay. Thank you very much, Miss Doak." He shook Ritta's hand. "You're a most courageous and fortunate young woman." He turned to River and Willie. "I suggest you leave the Park. Soon. Before this report is filed. Just in case one of my superiors want more questions answered. I'll put down I had no reason to detain you."

"Hey, man, that's where we're headed." Willie took the driver's seat. Tim moved to the door, put his hat on and adjusted the brim. He turned to Ritta before he left. "I'll make sure they don't do away with the bear."

She graced him with a big smile. "Thanks."

Idaho

The next morning, before the sun was hot, they stopped in Pocatello. Late the evening before, Dora had vomited. Twice. The first had been sudden; vile fluid spewed on the walls of the bus and her bedding before she found a suitable receptacle. Despite their attempts to clean the mess up in the dark, it continued to reek. Dora was still sleeping when Willie eased the bus next to the pump at the filling station on the outskirts of town.

Ritta's shoulder hurt. The gauze had dried to the scab and it pulled with every motion of her arm. She was hot and sticky and wanted to wash off the stale smell of fear. When the attendant came to watch Willie pump their gas she asked him for the key to the restroom.

"It ain't locked," he grunted. As he stared at her, his oil-stained cap crooked on his head, Ritta thought he looked like someone who always breathed through his mouth.

The bathroom's concrete walls were enameled the color of eggshells and dotted with dirt splatters. Sunshine overheated the small room through a window near the ceiling. The garbage can overflowed. A brown-crusted disposable diaper, rolled into a ball and fastened with its tapes, sat stuffed on top of the heap. Ritta propped open the door with a brick she found on the sidewalk, then tried to tuck her braids under the back of her shirt without tugging on her bandage.

Dora walked by the opening and sat down a plastic mop bucket. A splash of Pine-sol sloshed in the bottom. "Here, let me help you. God, it smells worse in here than it does in the bus." Dora pinched her nose shut with one hand and tucked Ritta's braids with the other. "Do you want to wash your shoulder?" she asked with an occluded nasal twang.

"Yeah. It really stings."

"Wait till we get back in the bus and I'll do it. This place is so dirty I wouldn't even trust the water to be sanitary." Dora hurried out and stuffed the bucket under a faucet outside the door.

Ritta leaned on the jamb, lathering a splinter of soap onto a washcloth. "Are you feeling better?"

"Yeah, just tired. I feel like I could sleep all the way to the commune.

Maybe I'll wake up and this will have been one long dream." Dora turned off the spigot.

"Are we close?"

"No, but we'll be there tomorrow or the next day. You could stay at the commune with us, you know. You'd like it. Lots of trees and good soil. It's really beautiful there, so close to the ocean."

"The ocean? You mean, we could go to the ocean?"

Dora nodded. "Sure."

Ritta rubbed the soapy cloth along her arms, then stopped. "You know, I hadn't really thought of where I'm going. Just what I left behind."

"Well, look to the future, sweetie. Your adventure is just beginning." Dora strolled away, leaving a hint of pine in her wake.

After Ritta rinsed, she looked in the mirror and told herself, "I'm really going to see the Pacific Ocean."

Mazie's reflection flashed behind her. "Don't count on it. I'm beginning to wonder if we're ever going to get to L.A. Goddamn, does it stink in here or what?"

Ritta tried to find an unused corner on the dirty cloth towel that hung limp from the dispenser. Mazie flushed the toilet. "Oh, God!"

"What's a matter, Maze?"

"It's not going down!"

Ritta peeked into the stall. Toilet paper floated in an upward spiral, then slithered over the side of the stained porcelain bowl. Mazie backed out just before the filthy tide spilled towards the drain in the middle of the floor. Her eyes rolled up so high the brown of her iris disappeared beneath her eyelids for a moment. "Let's get the fuck out of here." She grabbed Ritta's hand and pulled her out the door.

The attendant stared at them through the window in the station. Mazie shouted at him, "Hey, Dufus! Try cleaning your bathroom once in a while."

Linked arm in arm, Mazie and Ritta speed-walked to the bus. River was ready to roll. Leaving the station, he steered around the worst of the potholes.

The road out of Pocatello took them past a huge manufacturing plant. Towering chimneys spewed gray clouds towards the heavens. Soon, the noxious odor of fertilizer filled the bus. Before Mazie and Ritta got all the windows closed, Willie was holding Dora's forehead over the plastic bucket as her body retched with dry heaves.

Ritta observed, "Pocatello sure as hell stinks."

* * *

Lopate sat in the Carbon County Sheriff's office, his finger slowly moving down each line of the teletyped report as he read. Nothing. But he was close, he could feel it. That old *wasicu* woman, that married the Blackfoot,

102

she's lying. *She looked at me like she knows.* He touched the parallel lines of scabs on his cheek. *She knows, all right.*

Sheriff Holecomb stood in the doorway. "Might want to amend that APB of yours. Just talked to one of the city boys on duty Saturday night. Says he saw a hippie bus with Massachusetts plates."

Lopate pulled a rag smeared with dry, rusty brown paint from his pocket. "Think I'll make it a brown bus from Massachusetts."

Holecomb scratched his head. "Where did you get that?"

"Behind the old lady's barn. Setting next to an empty paint bucket. It's fresh. Did you see anything this color around the ranch?"

* * *

Dora rested on the mattress. Willie worried as he knelt by her side. He poured a glass of water from the jug, dribbling some on a cloth before offering it to her. When she refused the drink he took the cool, moistened rag and wiped the sweat from her forehead. "What else can I do for you, darling."

"Get your guitar," she replied with a weak smile. "Play something sweet for me."

Willie rolled his large body over and stretched to pull the guitar case from under a pile of dirty clothes. After a mile or so of tuning, the familiar refrain of 'Lay, Lady, Lay' rolled off the strings.

A pillow struck him, as hard as a pillow can, along side the head. He looked at Dora in disbelief. "What was that for?"

She started to cry.

"What's the matter, Dora? What's wrong?"

More tears brimmed over her lashes. She pulled Willie by her side and whispered in his ear, "I think I'm pregnant."

He knew her well enough to know she was watching him carefully for any clues as he digested the news. He wondered if her emotions had already run the gamut his were. Finally he whispered back, "Don't you want a baby?"

"Someday. Do you?"

"Dora, I love you. I always will, no matter what you decide. But this is your decision." He couldn't keep the grin off his face. "But I'd try to be the best dad in the whole world if you wanted to keep it."

Dora smiled and rubbed his cheeks that hadn't been shaved since they left Gert's. "I'm thinking about it."

Willie took her hand and held it close to his chest. "We were so careful. All those rubbers and foam."

"It happens. Remember that time in Minnesota when the condom slipped off? Or maybe we played a little too long before putting one on. Who knows? It's like eighty-five percent effective. We're in that fifteen percent that gets caught."

"Is that how you feel? Like you got caught?"

"Well, yeah. Especially when I'm throwing up all the time. It's no picnic."

"How long is that going to last?"

"Hard telling. Maybe it's just being in the bus with all the smells and motion that's making me sick, or it could last for the first trimester." She looked upwards. "God, I hope not."

Mentally calculating the miles, he said, "If we drove all night, we could be at the farm tomorrow morning. Would that be easier?"

Dora thought about it for a moment, then nodded her head.

"I'll talk to River, see if he's up for a marathon. Can I tell them?" He nodded towards River, driving with Ritta sitting behind him. Mazie was hunkered in her corner, reading a book.

"Not yet."

"Not even River?"

"No. Let's wait until we're really sure."

"Your call." Willie knew it was going to be hard not telling River.

"Maybe I have a flu."

"Uh huh."

"But I doubt it."

Willie kissed her on the cheek and held her while she fell asleep. He thought about how a child of theirs would look. He hoped it would have Dora's red curly hair and bright blue eyes. And her smile.

Several hours later, River shook him awake. "Hey, man. Your turn to drive. I'm beat."

"Where are we?" Willie asked before he even opened his eyes.

"Just east of Boise, on the Interstate."

Willie gently rolled Dora over and pulled himself from her sleepy embrace. Outside, at the edge of the rolling hills, the sun shone incandescent crimson on the last leg of its evening descent. Willie watched Boise twinkle faintly in the distance as he pissed on the gravel.

"Would you mind taking turns driving all night?" Willie asked River when he returned to the bus. "Dora wants to get to the commune as soon as possible."

"Is she all right?"

"I think she will be." Willie tried to suppress his grin as he looked at his darling, sleeping peacefully.

After stopping for gas and two quarts of oil in Boise, Willie drove till late into the night. Eastern Oregon passed by the windshield like a dream in the darkness. Lights tucked into the distance reminded him of the families that lived there, of children snug in their beds. Babies. He hadn't been around very many of them, but he had seen some that were cute.

A few miles outside of Pendleton, River sat down behind him in the darkness. "Do you want a break?"

"No. I'm doing okay. The bus sounds tired though."

River tilted his head. "Sounds okay to me, man."

"Hmm. We've headed uphill for miles now. It's just been a long trip. I'll be glad to be at the farm."

"Do you think you and Dora will stay there long?"

"Depends. Maybe we'll settle down a bit. Who knows?" Willie was ready to burst, he wanted to tell River so badly.

Patch rose from near the beanbag where Ritta was sleeping. He stretched, then walked to the steps above the door and whined.

"Okay, boy, we'll pull over," Willie said as he steered the bus to the side of the freeway.

Oregon

The stillness woke Ritta. She walked to the door and burst out laughing. In the waning moonlight stood River, Willie and Patch all in a row, all taking a leak.

Mazie stirred in her sleeping bag. "What's so funny?"

"You missed it. Just boys being boys. I'm going out. Wanna come?"

"Sure. Do you know where we're at?"

"I don't know." Outside, Ritta asked, "Hey, guys, where are we?"

"Oregon." Willie pointed to lights in the far distance. "That must be Pendleton."

River added, "Like the shirts."

Ritta looked at Mazie, puzzled. Mazie shrugged before walking down the fence line. They squatted in the tall grass beside the road.

"So. Do you think Dora's pregnant?" Mazie asked.

"You think so?"

"Bet she is." Mazie pulled up her pants. "My girlfriend Sally puked up like that for weeks before she got rid of it."

Ritta hoped again that she wasn't pregnant. At least she wasn't puking. She remembered her cousin who got 'in the family way' after some of the high school boys made her do 'it'. Now Ritta knew what 'it' was. They'd done 'it' to her.

River and Willie leaned on the side of the bus, smoking. Ritta took a toke. She was beginning to like the softness of it, the way things didn't seem so awful. She basked in the moonlight a few minutes before Willie said, "Time to hit the road."

"Want me to drive?" River asked.

"No, I'm good for a while longer."

"Okay, holler when you're tired."

River pulled Ritta into the beanbag. The stuffing crunched as her hips settled into a more comfortable position beside him. She placed her leg over his thigh and used her bare feet to kick off his leather sandals. His foot caught hers, holding her slender brown toes with his white hairy ones. She laughed as he tickled her sole, then his toes pinched her above the heel where the ligaments narrowed behind her ankle. "I like your feet," he whispered. "I like all of you."

She couldn't think of anything to say, so she kissed him lightly. He kissed her back, teasing her lips with his tongue. His mustache tickled and she stopped kissing him to rub under her nose. She snuggled, safe by his side, and fell asleep.

River lay awake for awhile, listening to the engine sounds. He felt her heartbeat through his side and stroked her hair before drifting off.

Willie shook him awake. "Your turn. Man, I got one hell of a headache. We're at The Dalles. Watch the wind."

River untangled himself from Ritta's limbs. He squinted at the bright lights illuminating the immense white structure that held back the Columbia River. Willie had pulled the bus off beside the intersection to the dam, under one of the concrete light poles that lined the thoroughfare. A semi-truck passed, its downshifting added minutely to the thunderous rumble of water over the spillway. The roar filled the empty space in River's head as he sat in the driver's seat and stared at the steady stream of traffic. Some of it turned to drive across the dam, probably workers for the graveyard shift at the huge plant lit up across the river. The noise and raw energy that seemed to fill the air jangled all his nerves. He turned the key. The bus sputtered to life.

The road down the gorge wound treacherously. High winds pushed against the bus then abruptly stopped, rocking it before River could compensate. During the long bleakness between the dams and corresponding small towns, he only sensed the river to his right and the canyon walls that paralleled the watery byway. Around the man-made obstructions, towering floodlights lit the road and massive concrete structures, as if the dams themselves emitted the glare.

The freeway led, finally, into Portland, transforming into long winding bridges suspended high over the city and the tamed river. By then, River was convinced of the unreality of it all, and wished he had dropped the acid in his pack, but settled for a foul-tasting roach he fished out of the ashtray. Soon, he was navigating his starship across the vast, glittering universe of Portland.

He landed on the straight stretch of freeway headed south, intent only on keeping between the white lines that marked his course. Finally, he spotted the Corvallis exit, veered off and parked on the side of Highway 20, as close as he could to a clump of trees. He knew which exit to take off the freeway, but Willie hadn't given him directions to the farm.

He didn't have the heart to wake Willie now. He knew they were close. The sun barely peeked over the misty, gray horizon. And from what he'd heard about the farm, he suspected no one would be up for hours. Pushing Patch from the blankets on his foam mat, River crawled in and was asleep before the dog curled into the crook of his bended knees.

He barely stirred when Ritta lifted the blanket and slid in beside him, just enough to wrap his arms around her and nestle between her back and the canine behind him. In his dream they were playing in a field of flowers. Ritta was happy, laughing, her face no longer bruised. She placed a garland of blossoms on his head and danced around him, joyous and alluring.

When he woke, his hand was resting over her cotton undershirt. He caressed her breast. She rolled against his groin. Still more than half asleep, he loosened the tie of his pants, pulled out his morning-stiff erection and slipped it between her legs. As he rubbed against her cotton-clad crotch her thighs tightened around him.

Ritta's eyes opened wide, surprised at how hard it was. Like a piece of smooth wood between her legs. It hurt and teased at the same time, and made her ache as if something had a hold of her insides and was pulling down. The fingers on her nipple tugged and pinched, making her squirm. Then his hand moved to the elastic surrounding her thigh and pulled it aside. She felt the tip, velvety smooth and wet, touch her, prodding. With his hand firm against her belly, the hard thing ripped into her.

She screamed.

River withdrew immediately and bent over her. "I'm sorry, Ritta. I'm so sorry." He touched her face, brushing a strand of hair from her cheek. "I didn't mean to hurt you. I'm so sorry." Pulling his pants up from his knees he covered the shrinking offender and tied the cord.

Tears welled in Ritta eyes, distorting the brown of her iris like pebbles under a stream's ripple. When River offered his arms to hold her she hesitated, then turned away. He looked at Willie and Dora, lifting his shoulders in a helpless shrug. Dora crawled over Willie's legs, wrapped her arms around the huddled girl and cooed soft sounds into her ear.

River turned to leave and met Mazie's cutting stare at the door. Willie followed him a safe distance from the bus before asking, "What happened?"

"I don't know. She felt so ready." River walked furiously down the two lane road, raking his fingers through his long hair. He turned to Willie and threw up his arms. "I was half asleep, man. She was just there, like a dream. I thought I was dreaming. Damn." River turned away so Willie wouldn't see the tears in his eyes and started running.

Soon he slowed to walking resolutely down the highway. He remembered her lying naked in the moonlight in the Park and the memory filled him with longing, the same wonderful feeling he thought she had felt for him. What happened?

Voices argued in his head. The loudest was chastising, condemning him for causing Ritta more anguish. But another argument demanded to be heard, alleviating some of his guilt. *She came to me last night. I couldn't have mis-*

read her completely, I know when a girl's hot.

You fool, the damning voice inside him said. You should have gone more slowly.

Reason countered, She wanted it. I know she did.

She's just a poor, sweet kid. And you took advantage of her.

I won't let it happen again.

When the bus coasted onto the road's shoulder beside him, River grabbed the railing through the open door and stepped up without breaking his stride. When Willie dropped it into second gear, River weaved above her as she sat in the beanbag. "Ritta." His voice sounded flat.

Both she and the dog turned their faces up to him. He noticed a hardness about her brown eyes that clinched his aching heart. "I'm sorry. It won't happen again."

"It's all right."

That was all he wanted to hear. He turned and crawled onto the foam pad a few feet away, facing the metal wall.

When they pulled into the commune Willie parked beneath a tree with the biggest leaves Ritta had ever seen, each one the size of a dinner plate. She stared at them, watching the dappling shadows play on the windows. Chickens scattered at her feet when she walked out of the bus. A few were the same burnished color as Gert's. Most were just white and walked on bowed legs. Among the tall trees were a few dwarfed outbuildings, constructed from weathered wood and adorned with rainbow hues. They left River asleep on his mat and walked over to the largest, most decorated shed, peering in where the door was missing from its hinges. A round-faced, young woman slept on a quilt-covered bed on the floor, the elastic neck of her embroidered peasant blouse tucked under a large breast. Her arm laid over a chubby baby napping beside her, its puckered mouth quivering dreamily.

Dora's laughter rippled through the trees as she led them down a well-worn path. Ritta could tell Dora was feeling better already. And why shouldn't she be? Ritta liked this place even before she rounded the corner and saw the farmhouse.

It stood in a small clearing, weedy with saplings and bramble. A garden filled the front yard, surrounded by a tall, crude fence of black netting hung on unbarked poles. Shrubs planted around the foundation reached the second story. The house was clabbered with additions painted bright yellow and sky blue. Most of the curtainless windows were open like toothless gaps in a sagging smile.

"Hey, Fern," Dora shouted at a woman in the garden pulling weeds. The woman looked up startled, then ran to greet them, her skirt gathered in her hands. Ritta noticed first the round breasts, sheathed in a lightly printed scarf that crossed between the mounds and tied behind her neck, then the woman's pretty heart-shaped face, her deep blue eyes.

"'Bout time you all got here." A large man came through the screen door and down the wide stairs of the porch, avoiding the rotten lower step. He looked to be ten years older than any of them and wore only coveralls; one strap hung loose, the other almost disappeared in the hair covering his shoulders. Wild, wiry, brown coils were tied back into a ponytail, his full beard just a tighter curled continuation of the hair that crept up his neck. Even his brown eyes were shaded by thick, loopy brows.

Soon Ritta was sitting with Dora in a swinging bench suspended from the rafters on the covered porch, a tall, sweating glass in her hand. "Dora, the color's back in your cheeks."

"I feel loads better. Must be all this good fresh Oregon air." She winked at Willie sitting nearby with his back against the rail. Fern came out with a few more glasses of tea and handed them to Mazie and Cal, the hairy man.

The bushes along the path rustled as River came towards the house.

Willie chuckled. "Hey man, you're up. Come meet our friends."

"I'm Cal." The man stuck out his meaty, woolly arm. The two gripped each other until River let go.

"Hi, River. I'm Fern." She extended her hand. Her breasts danced in the silky material as River shook her fingers. The gossamer folds did little to hide their shape, just colored them in a light floral pattern that her nipples blended into, like blushing posies.

He stared at them until Cal's booming baritone asked, "Want something to eat first or a shower?"

Mazie rattled the ice in her empty glass. "A shower would be great."

Fern asked, "How 'bout a dip in the river?"

It was as if Ritta's ears opened up at the mention of the word and the sound of rushing water filled the air. "How far away is it?"

Fern shook her head, her eyes locked on River's. "Not far. I'll take you down."

He matched her gaze. "Take us down?"

"To the river," she smiled, "River."

"Far out."

Mazie stood up. "You guys coming?" she asked Dora.

"No, thanks. Think I'll just sit here and enjoy the shade." Willie took Ritta's place on the swing when she followed Mazie, River, and Fern off the porch and down a path beside the garden. Through the mishmash of chicken wire and netting she could make out some corn stalks and a few flowers among the jungle inside the fence.

Past the garden, the trail divided a huge mound of thorned, leafy vines and headed slightly downhill. Fern held her long cotton skirt bunched in one hand in front of her, keeping it away from the stickers. She carefully pulled a long, stray vine out of her way and hooked it by the thorns to the wall of tangled brambles. The plants grew taller the farther down the path they went, until the growth met overhead, creating a tunnel they had to crouch slightly to get under. Fern continued to hook the new growth onto the sides and out of the path. Those that were too short to stay, she held until the next person could take it and walk past. One nasty tendril broke loose and snagged River's shoulder, leaving a bloody mark.

"Ouch. What is this awful stuff?"

Fern pointed to a cluster of small white blossoms tinged with purple. "Blackberries." She said it matter-of-factly, with her other hand on the bare inward curve of her waist.

The top of the tunnel became progressively lower, until they had to bend over to get through it. Abruptly, it ended. One by one they stood up, dazzled by the blue sky and the mixed evergreen and leafy color of the trees covering the steep surrounding hills. More amazing was the river below. Its shimmering water flowed gently between rifts. A dragon fly soared past Ritta's nose, iridescent in the summer-scented air. It flitted towards Fern as she made her way, stark naked, down the huge, black rocks along the bank. She hesitated only a moment on the river's edge, then dove into the darkest water. When she resurfaced, she motioned for them to come down. Then, like a mermaid, she rose half out of the water and dove again. Her tanned, round buttocks and the mystery that lay between them flashed for a moment before she disappeared.

Ritta didn't know what to do. She wanted to jump in the inviting water, would give anything to be able to dive in, like Fern. River quickly kicked off his sandals, untied his pants and stepped out of them onto a short piece of dried bramble hidden in the yellow grass. "Ow, shit! Ow, ow." He bounced on the other foot long enough to pull the thorn from his sole, then tenderly hobbled down to the river, jumping in and swimming towards Fern.

Mazie took Ritta's hand. "The path goes on. Want to take it and see if there is a more private spot to swim?"

"Sure. But Mazie?"

"Yeah, sugar."

"I don't know how to swim."

"Me neither, but I sure can wade good."

She followed Mazie downstream. River shouted, "Where you going?"

Ritta didn't want to turn around and see him and Fern naked. Mazie answered, "Lots of water here. What river is this anyway?"

Fern yelled back. "South fork of the Alsea. Isn't she beautiful?"

River climbed up a large piece of basalt on the far shore and dove into the hole again. Ritta heard his holler carry downstream between the walls of trees.

She followed Mazie down the narrow trail to a wide shallow bend and was soon lying naked in the ripples. Cradled by the water, Ritta felt insulated from the rest of the world. When she relaxed she realized how much her chest had ached since dawn, when River woke her up. She couldn't blame him, he didn't mean for it to hurt her. But it did.

She took a deep breath, trying to ease the ache again. Through squinted eyelids she watched the sun sparkle in her wet lashes until something blocked the sunlight. She opened her eyes as a large bird glided over them, near enough for her to see individual feathers and the crinkled skin of claws. "Maze, look!"

Mazie was slowly removing her pants, grinning at Ritta as the bird continued her slow flight upstream.

Ritta was on the porch when River returned to the farmhouse, his pants wrapped around his groin like a diaper. He didn't see her in the deep shadow of the bright afternoon. After a moment she followed him inside.

Dora turned from her pan of sautéing vegetables. "What happened to you?"

Mazie shrieked, "Good burn, white boy!"

"Fell asleep on a rock. See?" He turned around to show his light side.

Dora walked over to pick some moss from his snarled hair. "Lucky for you, Fern has an aloe."

"A what?" he called after her as she left the room.

She came back holding a plant with long, thick spines spilling out of a clay pot and broke one off. When she split it open with a fingernail it oozed clear gel which she wiped on his shoulder. He twitched every time the slime touched him.

"Hold still, this will help." She slathered his arm and chest with the sticky aloe, breaking off more as she needed them. He picked up the used pieces of plant and stuck them to his chest like medals of honor.

At dinner, Ritta sat across from him. He was still shirtless, the deep pink half of his chest glistening from the aloe. She stared at the chipped plate, heaped with brown rice and something Dora called rat-atooey, before her on the wooden table. The dining room was painted pastel purple with flat green trim. She thought it was kind of pretty, but a little weird. The sweet smell of blossoms from the shrubs outside the open window mingled with the aroma of dinner and the musky scent that permeated the house. Early evening light filled the room with half shadows.

Sunny, Cal's young girlfriend, bounced the baby on her lap and fed him small bites of mashed vegetables with her fingers. "It must be exciting to take a trip across the country, with your friends."

"We didn't all know each other before we started," Dora told her. "Willie knew Mazie from school and we found Ritta in the prairie land of South Dakota. But we're all good friends now." She smiled at Ritta.

Cal sat at the head of the table, between Fern and Sunny. "Did you live on a reservation, Ritta?"

The past tense of the question threw her. "Yeah. I guess I don't live there anymore, huh?"

"Is it as squalid on the reservations as I hear it is," Cal asked.

Ritta squirmed in the hard-back chair, not sure what the word "squalid" meant. It didn't sound good, like he was calling her a squaw. She looked at River. He answered for her. "Probably worse."

Nobody spoke for quite awhile until Cal said, "The Indians on the coast in Washington have been causing quite a ruckus over fishing rights. Looks like they're going to get them, too. Said it's in their treaty."

Ritta dropped her fork and looked at Mazie. "Maybe we can get *Paha Sapa* back. It's in our treaty."

"The Black Hills, you know, where Mount Rushmore is," Mazie explained to Cal and the others. "It's sacred ground for Ritta's people."

"Is that true, Ritta?" Dora asked.

"*Han*. Uncle Lawrence says 'It's easy to steal land from Indians. Just make a law and take it.' They took *Paha Sapa* because of the gold."

Dora shook her head. "Wait a minute. That's Black Hills gold. My mother has a ring out of it. Kind of a pink and green gold. I didn't know. God, that's awful."

"Then they carve faces in the rocks, of Great White Fathers." Mazie held up her long middle finger. "Like a big 'fuck you' to the indigenous people."

"How did you learn all this, Mazie?" Dora asked.

"From this groovy professor I had for American History. Remember Mr. Schnitzer, Willie? He gave us a very different version than we got in grade school. He got canned because of it, too. Said the Indians had lost the right to claim their history."

Cal pointed at Ritta with his fork. "Well, the Puyallup tribe and a whole lot of others in the Northwest are demanding their rights. Friend of mine took his bus up to a fish-in. Guess there was some big shot actors up there, too."

Ritta opened her mouth to ask Cal what a 'fish-in' was when Fern interjected. "Why does your bus say 'Church of the Reverent' whatever, River?"

"'Cause Willie looked like a fucking preacher when he cut his hair and shaved."

Ritta glanced at River, then at Fern. "Willie cut his hair and we painted the bus to keep me safe, so we could get out of Montana. It used to be the most beautiful bus in the whole world."

"Are you in some kind of trouble?" Fern asked.

Cal swallowed a bite quickly to say, "It's a great color now, that primer brown. Reminds me of tree trunks, Redwoods. I see a forest, green from the windows up. It'd be so heavy."

River perked up. "You could paint it like that?"

Sunny beamed with admiration. "Cal paints beautifully. You should go look at his mural in the pump house." The baby on her lap started to fuss until she pulled up her blouse and stuck a succulent teat in its grubbing little mouth.

"The pump house?" River asked.

"That's just where I got inspired." Cal explained. "I'll show you after dinner. If you want."

In the bus, River rolled a joint from his diminishing stash while Mazie dug through her suitcase. The sound of chalk rubbing on metal echoed eerily inside as Cal sketched a design on the vehicular canvas. River offered Mazie a hit, then stepped over the dog. Patch got up and followed him outside. River handed the doobie to Cal and looked at what the big man had drawn. Faint long lines were barely visible on the paint that seemed redder than River remembered. Perhaps it was the salmon-colored sunset that tinted even the air around them. "Trippy." He reached down to scratch between Patch's ears.

"Get some brown, man, like sienna, for the dark part of the bark. Tuck a few critters into the trees, you know, like a raccoon. Put some birds in the branches. Can you dig it, man?" Cal handed the joint back.

"I can dig it. How long would it take you?" River blew smoke in a long stream and watched it change hues in the light.

"To paint it? Hard tellin'. There's a lot of work to do around here. I got wood to chop for next winter. Got to keep it warmer now, for the rug rat. He'll be crawling around before long. Ain't he cute, though? Just as sweet as his mommy."

"How long?"

"I'm tellin' you, it depends. There's a lot of chores round here. Fern helps me as much as she can. She's a fine, strong woman." Cal bumped River suggestively with his elbow.

"But Willie and Dora will be here."

"Willie's damn good with his hands, from what I've seen."

"Best mechanic I know," River added.

"Good thing, too. Our van's about to blow. But there's two more mouths to feed. We need a greenhouse. I got lots of windows I been collecting. It would take about a week to build it with three men," Cal hinted. Then added, "and Fern."

"Ah, Fern." River remembered how she looked in the Alsea.

"She's hot for you. Damn fine lay, that one." Cal bumped him again with his elbow. "I told her I don't mind sharing."

"Ah, you and her?" River's finger moved back and forth. "And Sunny?"

"Sure. We're easy to get along with here."

River grinned. "I guess."

Mazie stuck her head out the window, startling him with her brusque, "River."

"Yeah, Maze?"

"I need to talk to you."

Cal cuffed him on the back. "See you inside."

Mazie lit a candle on the dash as River entered the bus. "I can't stay here. I'm going crazy as it is. I need to get my life going again, can you dig that?"

"Sure Mazie, I know. But doesn't it sound like a blast, building a greenhouse? You got to see the mural that dude painted. It's amazing. He could make this bus into a piece of art. Wouldn't you want to stay just for a few weeks?"

"Hell, no. We been on the road a whole lot longer than I thought it would take already. My brother's waiting for me, man. Can't you see, I got to be with him." She started to sob. "He's all the family I got."

"Okay, Mazie, okay. We'll head south in the morning. Then I'll come back."

On the porch, swinging in the dark, Willie agreed to go along. "We can make a fast trip out of it. It will be far out to have you here on the farm."

Later, River followed Fern to a clearing by a small stream that bordered the property. On a blanket beneath the stars, she slathered aloe on the places he had been burned by the sun, and a few he hadn't.

In the early morning, he woke alone beneath the blanket soaked with dew. Shivering, he carefully peeled the clammy material off his sunburn and caught a glimpse of Fern down by the creek. Pulling on his socks, he thought he saw her again, walking through the trees up the hillside.

His shirt and pants were under the bedding, dirty but dry. After putting them on, he followed the footpath through knee high grass, to a bend in the small stream. The water was shadowed by trees leaning over the bank, the hollows of their roots exposed. He knelt on the small pebbles and splashed his face with a double handful of cold, clear water. On the second scoop, a crimson streak of claws flashed near his fingers. He snatched his hands back. Fern laughed behind him.

"What was that?" he asked.

"Crawdads. Crayfish, you know, like filé gumbo. The birds come here and catch them." She pointed to fragments of lobster-red shells littering the bank that he had overlooked.

She was lovely in the soft morning light, her hair all tousled and tumbling down her shoulders. He watched her lips, still red and swollen from their lovemaking. "What are you doing?"

"Watering."

"Watering what?" The nearness of her was enough to excite him. Her full, India print skirt was tucked into the waistband in front, revealing strong, hairy calves. Her full breasts swung loose under a baggy sweatshirt. She looked at him with a promise of raw desire. He realized that must be how he was looking at her.

"Come." She lead him along the narrow path. Watching her walk up the hillside, he knew he would follow her anywhere.

* * *

The filly's nickering woke him for the third morning. Lawrence rose from the bunk made of hay bales and moth-eaten blankets in the stall next to the Appaloosa's. Still half asleep, he threw a flake from a broken bale over the shoulder-high wall that separated them. The Appie pawed at the partition with an insistent hoof, then flung her head up and down as she tore into the grass hay.

"Horse, you're worse than a woman." The old man scratched the spots on his back the hay mattress had irritated, despite layers of blankets. He placed his hands over his taped ribs, took a breath deep enough to know he was better than yesterday. The blood in his urine had cleared up the day before.

When he walked out into the morning light the anger welled up inside of him, as it did every time he looked at the rubble that once was his home. His mother had been born in that cabin. She died there, from tuberculosis, when he was nine and away at school. Mary had died there, too, along with the baby she bore that winter. The shack had contained most of what he had left in this world, reduced now to a pile of barely recognizable pieces that he sifted from the ashes. He stared at it a long time before the rumble in his stomach won out.

After walking down the hill to the creek and back with water, he fried a sausage and two eggs on the camp stove his neighbor, Bill Thomas, had loaned him. Bill had kept the filly while Lawrence was in jail. Other friends had supplied the cooler full of food, and blankets, even clothes. They were angry too, and scared. If this could happen to Lawrence and Grace, respected elders, then everyone was vulnerable. He told only a few how he found Grace, careful not to mention Ritta. He really trusted no one.

After he ate he wiped off the plate with a ragged piece of flour sacking which he then stretched over the skillet, tucking the ends underneath to keep the bugs out of the congealing grease. He poured another cup of coffee and went to the side of the barn where he had a workshop of sorts.

Today he was going to try to reassemble the water pump after days spent cleaning burnt parts, coating them with used motor oil. If he could make it work, then he would stay. But if there was no pump when the creek froze over he would try to winter somewhere else. He was too old to haul water up the hillside in the cold like they had when he was a boy.

He sat on the stool made from an old metal tractor seat welded onto a base of heavy iron and stared at the coffee he swirled in the cup, remembering Mary. She had been so pleased the day he brought the pump home. It took three more months before the well was dug and everything was hooked up, but Mary was patient. At first, she couldn't make any water come out, too weak to force the metal handle up and down fast enough to prime the pump. But she kept trying. He remembered how proud she was the day she worked a small stream from the faucet. The same day she told him she was pregnant.

* * *

Dora sat with Willie in the kitchen, finishing their breakfast of eggs over toast, sprinkled with kelp. Willie put a hand over her belly. "I don't want to go, but the sooner we get on the road, the sooner River and I can get back."

"I'm glad for the decision we made last night."

"Me, too. Tell River when he comes in from wherever he is, that I want to leave by ten. I'm going to check the bus."

Dora nodded and folded her hands over where Willie's had been. She made herself another cup of tea and found Ritta on the porch. "You could stay here if you wanted to. We'd—"

Ritta shook her head before Dora finished. "I couldn't, not with Fern and him."

"Fern's just like that."

"Yeah? Well, River is, too. It's okay. But I can't stay here."

"Well, I know you don't want a mother but if you ever need help, just call me. Willie and I would do anything for you."

Tears smarted in Ritta's eyes. "I know. Thanks." She took Dora's hand.

Dora squeezed. "Willie and I are going to have a baby."

"That's great. Oh, I bet Willie is so happy. You'll be the best mom."

Dora looked down at her lap. "Isn't Sunny's baby cute? Babies are so wonderful."

"Yeah, well you can have 'em. I'm thankful I started this morning, cramps and all."

"Yee haw!" Dora shouted. "Congratulations. I'll give you all my tampons."

After breakfast, Mazie started running hot water into the stained white sink. Dishes had been left from dinner, along with the breakfast ones, and she needed something to kill the time before they could leave. She reached for the dish soap, found a dirty sponge that she rinsed well as she looked around. This place is a filthy mess. After attacking the dishes she went on to the counters with such fervor her mother would have been proud.

When the kitchen was clean she went out to the bus and sat alone, fuming. Willie was still tinkering under the hood, mumbling something about the carburetor when she asked him when they would be leaving. Each time he started the engine her hopes would rise. Then he would shut it down again and bury himself under the hood for another half hour.

Dora brought Willie a sandwich, and suggested to Mazie she come up to the house to eat lunch with the rest of them. Mazie refused at first, afraid that if she left the bus she would somehow get sucked into the placid life here and not escape. But hunger won out over fear and she walked up the path. As Dora handed her a plate of food, Mazie asked, "Where's Ritta?" Dora shrugged.

Sunny shifted the nursing baby to her other breast. "I saw her walking towards the spring a little while ago."

Mazie looked down at Sunny. "Is that all you do is feed that kid?"

Sunny laughed. "Seems like it. That and change and wash diapers. At least I don't have to wash bottles and make formula. Yuk. Besides, I get off on it. Feels good."

"And look how healthy little Heron is. I think he's grown since yesterday." Dora tickled his chubby foot. Mazie took her plate onto the porch.

Ritta lay across the stump of a giant cedar, on a thick cushion of moss. Above her rose a full canopy of trees, taller than she had imagined trees could ever be. Huge ferns, as big as the oldest sagebrush, grew everywhere. Even high on the tree trunks, smaller fronds sprouted from moss covered branches. She spread out her arms and wondered how tall this grandfather tree must have been. Her fingertips hung over the sides of the stump and touched something slimy. Looking over the edge, she found a snail attached to the rotting wood, trailing silvery mucous, its little antenna waving. It was as cute as the ceramic one her aunt had hanging in her bathroom.

With a small stick, she turned over a piece of decaying bark. Beneath it were white grubs with funny brown heads, and small armored crawlers that rolled into tight little balls when she touched them. A moist, bug-eyed lizard scampered by. Picking it up, she marveled at its bright orange underbelly. The newt's legs paddled the air and didn't miss a stride when she put it back on the ground.

Leaving the path, she walked deeper into the woods, making her way between bramble and bracken. A fallen old tree, with lanky offshoots growing upright from its trunk, stretched out between the still standing giants. She put a foot in the rotten bark for a toe-hold, grabbed one of the small trees like it were a saddle horn, and pulled herself up. The old tree was as soft as a bed beneath her. She pushed on the moss and watched it spring back. Carefully, she tore a piece away, enough to see the fibrous tendrils reaching into the dark, peaty bark. She replaced it and the rip disappeared in the matted moss.

The giant cedar was still half-rooted in the slope. A spring trickled beneath it. She swung her leg over the far side, and dropped into ferns. Kneeling by the water she scooped a sweet handful to drink. Then she heard the yips. In a den scratched out between the cedar's roots, several fox kits tumbled over each other. Their hazy blue eyes hadn't seen her. Ritta looked around quickly for their absent mother, then took a few steps closer to watch the pups' play. The biggest one caught her scent and stood his ground, yipping at her. She laughed at his bravado. "Okay, little brother. I'm leaving."

She followed the trickle of water down the gully, until it disappeared in the spongy earth. She wondered if River was ready to leave yet and decided she should return to the farmhouse, when she realized she didn't know which direction to head. It all looked the same under the trees. Light fell through the branches in small, brilliant shafts. No horizon. No sun to guide her. Sitting on her heels, she clutched the leather pouch around her neck. "What am I going to do?" Her words fell to the dense forest floor.

A familiar bark answered her. Patch bounded between the trees, a piece of thorny vine tangled in his fur and trailed behind. She hugged him, and removed the bramble. "Patch. Hey boy, don't you love it here? What a magical place."

She followed the dog to the path and was surprised to see Cal a little way downhill. "Hey, there," she said softly.

He turned around. "Where did you come from?"

When she pointed into the underbrush he shook his head. "I came up to find you. Willie's almost ready to roll."

"Patch beat you to it." Together they started down the slope. Ritta looked around. "It's so pretty here, I almost hate to leave."

Cal stopped in his tracks. Ritta halted, too, looking at him questioningly.

"You don't have to go." He stepped a little closer. "Stay here. I'll protect you from whatever bad guys are after you."

Ritta pushed away his arm as he reached for her hair. He caught her hand and leaned towards her like he meant to kiss her. She slapped him across his bearded face.

He jerked her arm. Patch snarled a deep, throaty threat.

Cal let her go. He yelled after her as she ran down the path, "Go on, get the hell out of here. I don't need a cock teaser like you around."

She reached the bus, out of breath and angry, with Patch on her heels. Mazie asked, "What's wrong with you, girl?"

"I'll tell you later. Let's get out of this place."

"I hear ya, Sister."

Inside, she walked around Dora and Willie entwined in each other's arms. Dora looked ready to cry.

That's what love should be, Ritta thought. Something sweet, like they got.

Willie took Dora's face in his hands and kissed her. When he released her, Dora handed him a sack of goodies and walked over to Ritta. "Remember what we talked about. You're always welcome here."

At that moment, Cal appeared through the trees.

Ritta looked briefly at his scowling face then turned back to her friend. "I don't think so, Dora. Thanks anyway."

"Well, be careful, Ritta. Good luck. You too, Maze. I'm going to miss both of you. Keep in touch."

Ritta tried not to cry as Dora hugged her.

River ran from the little cabin when he heard the horn.

Willie told him as he jumped onto the steps, "You drive. I've been working all day."

He drove off, waving at Dora, Sunny with her baby on her hip, and Cal beside her. Then he saw Fern, standing naked in the cabin's window, waving back, her beautiful breasts swaying with the motion.

Before they reached the main road River lit one of the joints he had stashed in the new beaded bag tied on his belt loops.

Mazie took the joint and lifted the bag to take a closer look. "Hey, that's cool. Where did you get it?"

Slightly embarrassed, River said, "Fern. She makes 'em." In the mirror, his eyes caught Ritta's pained expression. What he had been dreading since last night was about to come down. "Ritta?"

She lowered her head a moment then lifted it to look back at him in the mirror. "Yes, River."

"I hope you understand."

"It's okay." Her voice sounded empty.

He nodded, relieved. "Thanks." He saw her sprawl on the mattress and close her eyes.

Mazie sighed, opened her pack and pulled out a deck of playing cards. She shuffled and laid out rows for solitaire. She was still at it when they stopped at a gas station. In the twilight, River took Patch for a walk in a nearby field. Ritta still slept, or seemed to.

Back on the road, River sat beside Mazie. He opened the sack of goodies and offered her a thick, chewy bar made of oatmeal and dates. She set it aside and took a bite only when she got to play a card. When it was too dark to see, River held his flashlight for her. The batteries were going dead as Willie pulled over to fill up in Yreka around midnight. Mazie had just won her first game.

River was ready to sleep. It had been a long day and he hadn't gotten a lot of shut-eye last night. A smile came to his lips as he recalled the sight of Fern perched on top of him, the stars behind her. Cal was right. She's some kind of woman. Some kind of gardener, too.

He replayed the events of the morning in his mind like a dream, recalling his surprise when she led him up the steep slope. Across the whole top of the mountain all the trees had been cut down. Huge stumps poked out of the ground like headstones in a graveyard. He was overwhelmed at the destruction and starkness of the clear-cut after coming through the dense forest. He remained there, in shock, for a few moments before Fern gently took his hand.

"Look at this." She lead him further along the edge where forest met pillage, then stopped and pointed towards a big stump.

At first he didn't see anything. "What?"

She laughed, took a step closer into the rubble of branches and pointed. Then he saw the circular chicken wire enclosure. It was about chest high and small enough to put his arms around, draped with strands of dead grass. He peered in at the healthy three foot tall plant with the familiar five-fingered lancelet leaves.

"Far out." He chuckled, then laughed heartily. "Far fucking out."

"Shhh. We try to be real quiet up here. Not that anybody ever comes up. Once they cut, they run. But it is BLM land, so we have to be careful."

"Are there more?"

She smiled, then led him around the perimeter of the clear-cut. He was amazed at how well the plants were hidden, often coming right up to them before he saw anything. "Why the cages?"

"Deer. They love to nibble on all this new growth."

Then he nibbled on her for a while, as though she was a tender shoot and he a creature of the woods.

California

Willie added two quarts of Valvoline to the engine and checked the tires, then steered south for what he hoped would be a long, peaceful night of driving. He enjoyed the open road, even on the freeway. It gave him time to think about him and Dora, and baby making three. His cut for delivering the mushrooms to Cal's connection in Santa Cruz would give them enough money to stay at the farm for awhile. Still, he was glad River would be there. Nobody ever went without when River was around, thanks to his trust fund and generous nature.

Just outside of Red Bluff, Willie heard the siren behind him, saw the lights in the rear-view mirror. "River! Goddamn it, River. Wake up. We got company."

Ritta was already on her feet. She shook River, then Mazie. "Quick, Maze. We gotta get in the hole. Come on."

Ritta pulled Mazie off the mattress. Mazie snatched her arm away from Ritta's grasp. "What are you trying to do to me, girl?"

"Get you down in the hole. We got company." Ritta pointed with her thumb at the red and blue lights bouncing off the walls.

River pulled up the trap door. "Stall them if you can, just another minute, Willie."

He slowly coasted down the shoulder until Mazie and Ritta vanished from the little round mirror, then pulled to a stop. River shoved his stash box into Ritta's hand, closed the door, and dropped the mattress. He slid to his sleeping bag.

As the flashlight through the glass door illuminated him, River raised his head from the pillow. Shielding his eyes from the glare, he stood up and pulled on his t-shirt. Another patrolman told Willie through the open window, "License and registration." Willie removed the paper from the visor and handed it down, then reached in the glove box for his wallet and waited for the officer to take his license.

He closely inspected both. "Massachusetts. You're a long way from home, William."

"Just traveling. Spreading the good word."

"That so." The patrolman held the flashlight over his head and trained his beam on River, nearly blinding him. "Name, please."

"Scott Fitzgerald Cochran, the third."

"This your vehicle?" The officer studied the registration.

"Yes, sir, it is."

"May I see your license?"

River dug through his bag until he found his wallet. He handed the paper card to Willie to forward out the window.

The other man walked around the front of the bus, checked the plates, took the papers and walked back to the squad car. Willie heard him muttering, "Church of the Reverent Brethren. Sounds like some kind of pinko organization."

"Where you boys headed?" the officer at Willie's window asked.

"South, wherever the Lord leads us."

"Hmm. Anyone else traveling with you there, Reverend."

"No, sir. Just me and Brother Fitz."

Patch nuzzled River's hand. River tried to ignore him. The dog became insistent, whining and bumping his hand again. "What, boy?"

Patch walked over to the mattress and pawed at the edge. River grabbed him. "No." He pulled the dog to the front of the bus.

The officer strained to see what the they were doing. River asked him, "Can I take my dog out to, uh, urinate?"

The man nodded his head, then walked to the squad car. River kept hold of Patch's scruff until they were well into the weedy area beside the freeway. When he let him go, the dog lifted his stump briefly on a clump of crabgrass then ran, in his three-legged lope, straight for the squad car. River ran after him, stumbling on the loose gravel. He caught the growling dog as Patch powered up to jump at the nearest patrolman.

"No! Bad dog." River caught Patch by his ears, forcing the dog to pivot on his back leg. Both officers turned, their hands over their weapons. River grinned nervously. "Sorry 'bout that. He's very protective."

They looked at River disdainfully, then went back to their muffled conversation. River dragged Patch back to the bus. He sat down on the beanbag and held the dog securely. "It's okay, boy." He tried to believe it himself. Patch's ears went up at the sounds coming from under the mattress. River heard them, too, and kicked his heel against the floor.

They felt more than heard the warning thump above them. Ritta didn't know if she wanted to laugh or cry.

Mazie whispered, "Shush, girl."

"I'm about ready to pee my pants."

"Well, don't get any on me."

They both giggled till Mazie put her hand over Ritta's mouth. "Shh."

Ritta shifted around, crossing her legs, and began swaying back and forth. Mazie held her, picking up the rocking motion, then began to stroke Ritta hair. She curled in Mazie's arms.

Ensconced in the darkness, her reality became just the two of them, hunkered together. Kissing Mazie seemed to be the most natural, wonderful thing in the world. They stopped when a big semi passed by, shaking the whole bus and filling their little enclave with the roar of its diesel engine.

"Mazie?" Ritta whispered softly.

"Yeah?"

"Kiss me again."

Willie held Gert's Bible on his lap. In the side mirror he watched the two men in uniform standing in front of their patrol car. It seemed the heavier one wanted to do something about them and the other was willing to let them go. They were almost arguing before one nodded and strode towards the bus again. Great, the one that wants to take us in. "Pig alert."

River sat up and gave Patch a stern look. "Stay. I mean it."

The officer walked up to the driver's side. "Step outside. Both of you."

Willie pulled the door handle and debated about taking the Bible with him, but decided that might be a little too much. He put it on the seat and shrugged at River before he walked outside. River looked at the anxious dog. "Stay."

Outside, the belligerent officer made them stand spread-eagle with their hands on the hood of the bus. He patted Willie's back and chest, along the inside of Willie's legs from the crotch down. After he did the same to River, he told them to turn around. The other officer trained his flashlight beam just below Willie's face. "Where were you boys before you headed into our territory?"

"Just left Seattle, been on the road for three days."

"Can anybody verify that?"

Willie looked at River, then turned back to his interrogator. "No, sir. We were ministering to the bums and runaways on the street."

The belligerent one asked, "Have you seen an Indian girl. Maybe gave her a ride?"

River shook his head, trying to look straight into the officer's eyes through the glare of his flashlight. "Saw lots of Indians in Seattle. Sad lot, mostly drunks. No girls though."

"How about a neegra girl, ever travel with a neegra?"

Willie looked at him calmly. "No, sir."

"You boys been with any girls at all?"

"No, sir," River said emphatically. "We've taken vows of celibacy."

Willie nearly choked on that one and was grateful the other officer had walked off. He heard Patch's low, throaty growl. The officer shined his light on Willie's face. "You. Hold your dog."

Willie sat on the mattress and held Patch. The patrolman stood in the doorway, his flashlight illuminated the Bible on the driver's seat, then scanned the interior. Willie prayed the bus didn't smell like pot.

The officer backed out. He shook his head at his partner who handed River their licenses. "Okay, boys. You can go."

As he pulled out onto the freeway, Willie was dismayed to see the cop car pull out directly behind him. It stayed there for what seemed like a long time. When he saw a rest stop ahead he put on his blinker. They didn't follow. With a sigh of relief, Willie told River the coast was clear.

River was at the trapdoor before the bus pulled up in front of the well-lit bathrooms. "You girls okay?" He helped Ritta out of the hole.

"Yeah. What happened?"

"Man, you wouldn't believe it. Let's just say it's a damn good thing you two were down there or we'd be on our way to the cop shop."

"Really?" Mazie took his hand and crumpled when she tried to stand. "Goddamn, my legs are asleep."

"Oh, thank God. A bathroom." Ritta started for the door.

Willie put his hand on her shoulder. "Can't go now, Ritta."

"But I'm about to pee my pants."

"Look." As a truck passed by on the freeway, its headlights illuminated the outline of the patrol car pulled over near the exit of the rest stop. Willie pushed Ritta below the windows. "Get down," he whispered hoarsely to Mazie, who had already fallen to her knees.

"Oh, shit." River ducked down too, and looked at Willie. "Now what are we going do?"

"Go to the john. "

"Yeah? Well, go for me, too," Ritta whined.

"There's that bucket that Dora used to throw up in. Piss in it and we'll dump it later. River, let's go." Willie started for the door. "River, come on. Act like everything's cool."

River pulled himself up from the floor and took a deep breath. "Okay, it's cool. Everything's groovy."

"Keep your heads down, girls." Willie whispered hoarsely as he and River walked out.

Afraid that sitting on the bucket would make her too tall to hide, Ritta folded the thin mattress in the hole to one side and placed the bucket in the dark vacant corner of the storage compartment. It wouldn't sit flat, so she felt beneath it and pulled up a small, brown bag, which she ignored until her stream of urine subsided to a relieved trickle. Then she opened the sack. Inside were two sealed cellophane packages. She held them up to the light. "Look, Maze."

"What'cha got?"

"I don't know. I found them down here." She handed a parcel to Mazie. "Would you get me something to wipe with?"

Mazie handed her a paper towel from the kitchen box. "Looks like little dried mushrooms. Why would someone put mush...? I get it. These must be magic mushrooms."

"What do you mean, magic?"

"You know, like psychedelic. Like acid. Say, these must be worth a lot. See how many there are?"

"Yeah, but whose are they?"

"Mine," Willie answered from the doorway. "Actually, I'm just delivering them."

Ritta quickly pulled up her pants. "To who?"

"That's all you need to know. Please, just put them down and forget you ever saw them."

"Okay." Ritta took the cellophane package from Mazie, dropped it into the paper bag with the other one and handed them to Willie.

Mazie screeched, "My, God. You two are going to get us all thrown in jail."

"Be cool, Mazie." Willie leaned into the hole and tucked his sack beneath the pad again.

Patch bounded up the steps. River followed close behind. "The pigs are gone."

"Are you sure?" Ritta peered over the window edge.

"I saw 'em go down the road, but who knows what the fucking pigs will do next." River slid into the driver's seat. "I say we get the hell out of here."

"Amen," Willie agreed.

River started laughing, walked over to Willie and slapped his shoulder. "That was a good one, you fucking preacher."

Willie slapped him back, "Oh, no, Brother Fitz. We're celibate."

Soon both of them collapsed in hysterical, teary-eyed convulsions. Ritta wondered what they thought was so funny. Each time Willie tried to explain what had happened, he couldn't stop laughing.

River wiped the tears from his eyes. "Where's my box, man. I need to get stoned."

"Me, too." Willie handed him the stash box.

Mazie looked incredulously at them. "Are you crazy? Get stoned now? What if they pull us over again?"

Willie looked at her solemnly. "Maze, the Lord provides in mysterious ways, and I belieeeeeve we're out of the lion's den."

"Oh, brother," Mazie replied but she took a long draw off the joint when Willie handed it to her. Ritta did the same.

River sat behind the wheel and started the bus. Willie picked up his guitar and sat on the beanbag. Ritta flopped on the bed and patted the mattress beside her, grinning at Mazie.

Mazie grabbed her sleeping bag and unzipped it, throwing it over Ritta before stretching out beside her. By the time Willie tuned his guitar, Ritta was snuggled comfortably with Mazie. *It's like sleeping with Janey, except Mazie's my size, and feels like a woman.*

In the morning, while the others were still asleep, Ritta quietly scoured the boxes looking for something to eat. Three small red potatoes rolled around the bottom of the depleted kitchen box, but with no oil or onions they wouldn't go very far.

She set up the stove on a flat rock outside and poured water in the kettle for coffee, then remembered the soup in her pack. Laughing, she pulled the familiar red and white can from her possessions. Chicken Noodle Soup. *And spuds. That should make it go far enough to feed all of us.*

As she peeled the skins off the potatoes she thought of home and the many meals she had put together like this one. Janey would bring her whatever she could find in the cupboard and the two of them would experiment with the way everything could go together.

When she thought of Janey, Ritta's hand stopped in mid-peel, the paper thin skin dangled from her knife. *I hope she's all right, I hope she has enough to eat now that I'm not there. I hope the boys are leaving her alone.*

She remembered the day she caught their cousin, Jason, trying to make Janey kiss him. They were in his dad's big barn, near the chute. The nearest thing Ritta could grab to defend her sister was the cattle prod hanging on the wall. She jabbed the knife into the air like she had jabbed the prod at Jason. *He sure did jump when those prongs hit his sorry ass.* She laughed out loud.

River stepped from the bus. "What's so funny?"

"Oh, nothing." She resumed her task. "I'm making breakfast. Are you hungry?"

"Starved. Want some help?"

"No. Thanks." She scored the potatoes and cut them into little squares over a pot half-filled with water.

After the coffee was made, she opened the can and dumped the contents into the potatoes.

River watched her. "What are you making?"

"Food. Want some coffee?"

River scratched his head and took the steaming cup from her.

The others stumbled from the bus and were handed coffee and soup. "What is this, Ritta?" Mazie stirred the conglomeration in her bowl.

"What does it look like? Haven't you ever had soup for breakfast?"

"No. But this is fine. Just fine." Mazie dipped her spoon in, pulled out a limp noodle and slurped it. After a few bites she said, "Actually, it's not bad at all."

An hour later, River pulled the bus into the parking lot of a roadside diner. Mazie looked up from her book. "Trouble?"

"No. Stopping to get something to eat." River stood and stretched, then opened the door for Patch. "Just hit the tire, dog. Don't wonder off."

"Where the hell are we?" Mazie put the book down and looked out the window.

"Vacaville. Home of the State Prison."

"Great. I always wanted to see the wonders of California."

As they walked towards the little restaurant, Ritta suddenly stopped and grabbed Mazie's arm. "What is that?"

"What?"

She pointed to the palm trees in front of the cafe. "Those."

Mazie laughed. "You never seen a picture of a palm tree, girl?"

"Palm trees? I thought they only grew in places like Hawaii?"

"Well, they grow in California, too. There's probably a whole bunch of weird plants here that you and I've never seen before." She patted Ritta's arm. "Come on. Let's go eat."

They joined River and Willie at a booth. River pointed out the window at their bus parked at the edge of the lot and laughed. "Look at Patch, doing his guard dog routine." The retriever sat proudly in the driver's seat.

A skinny waitress in a starched red apron poured coffee as she asked them, "What'll it be?"

They ordered pie. While they waited, a shiny black and white Vacaville Police car pulled up in the corner of the lot.

"Damn. Here we go again." Ritta nudged Mazie. "Let's wait in the bathroom until these pigs leave."

Mazie started to protest until Ritta took her hand and led her down the corridor. Before they had locked the door marked "Ladies," two men in blue, night sticks swinging by their sides, stepped into the foyer.

Willie nodded at the officers as they walked passed. One of them returned the gesture. River stared out the window, afraid the smirk on his face would be noticed.

One of the policemen shouted, "Hey, Gladys. Got any coffee back there?"

The skinny waitress hustled out from the kitchen carrying four pieces of assorted pies. She plopped them down in front of Willie and River before hurrying over to take the policeman's thermos. "Is that all I can do for you, Jimmy?" she chirped flirtatiously.

"You can tell me when you get off tonight."

"Same time as last night, sugar." She leaned over the counter and talked in soft cooing tones to Jimmy. His partner sat down at a nearby booth and picked up a newspaper from the bench seat.

"Great," Willie whispered to River.

Ritta and Mazie each took a turn on the toilet, then slowly washed their hands. Ritta stood in front of the large mirror and told Mazie's reflection, "First I can't go to the bathroom because the cops are after me. Now I can't leave one." She made a wrinkled face and stuck out her tongue.

In the mirror, Mazie grimaced back, then pulled down on her cheeks until the roundness of her eyeballs were exposed.

Ritta laughed. "I can top that." She pushed up on her nose while making grunting sounds.

Mazie looked mischievously into the mirror. Without warning, she lifted her shirt, exposing one breast briefly before snapping the material down. Ritta dropped her gruesome expression for an incredulous one. Then, not to be outdone, she raised her own shirt up to her shoulders and turned to face her companion.

Mazie deliberately raised her shirt again. Ritta stared at Mazie's high, upward pointing breasts and looked in the mirror at her heavy, round ones. She turned again to her friend. "Look how different we are."

Mazie slowly closed the gap of distance between them, until their nipples touched. Ritta had never felt anything so soft, so wonderful.

Warmth spread from every place Mazie's fingers traveled; along her ribs, to the small of her back. Ritta's hand touched the dark, soft skin of Mazie's breasts like velvet against her own.

Mazie bent down, her lips teasing Ritta's collar bone then traveled slowly towards the nipple that stretched towards her mouth. Ritta felt a delicious ache deep inside and thought, this is it. This is what Dora was talking about. Pain in pleasure.

Mazie stopped. Just as Ritta thought she would fall to the floor, a hand embraced the back of her head, another held her crotch. She wanted to push into the fingers, engulf them. They kissed hard, teeth bumped her lip.

A knock on the door startled them apart. Ritta sheepishly tucked in her shirt and said, "Just a minute."

Willie whispered through the door. "Coast is clear."

Flustered, Ritta followed Mazie out the door.

Willie met them in the foyer and pointed to the pay phone in the corner. "Why don't you call Jody and get directions. I need to know what exit to take."

"Sure, Willie," Ritta replied, then looked at River as he came out of the cafe, groaning. "What's the matter with you?"

"I had to eat your pie. I don't even like banana cream."

"You ate my pie?"

"Had to. Sorry you had to sit in the bathroom all this time."

"Oh, it wasn't so bad." Ritta looked at Mazie, who gave her a wink before walking off. Ritta smiled, then checked the coin return of the pay phone. She chuckled out loud when she found a dime there. After searching through the deep pockets of her army fatigues she found the piece of paper with Jody's phone number.

She stared at the numbers and the coin in her hand. What am I going to say? Hi, I'm wanted by the police but your mother said I could stay with you? She reached for the pouch around her neck and looked again at the number written in Gert's strong hand. Feeling braver, she dropped the dime in the phone. It slid back to the coin return. Picking it up again, she stared at it for a moment then put it in her mouth, coating it with saliva before dropping it in the slot again. This time it worked. She dialed the number. After she fumbled the requested coins down the slots, a man answered.

"Hello. Is Jody there?"

Soon a brusque "Hello" filled Ritta's ear. A female voice, not very lady-like.

"My name is Ritta and your mother—"

"Ritta, Thank God! Mom and I have been so worried. We expected you here days ago. Are you all right?"

"I'm okay. The bus goes slow and we had to stop in Oregon."

"Where are you now?"

"Vacaville, at some little cafe off the freeway. I need directions."

***

Through downtown Berkeley, Ritta watched another foreign world pass by the open door of the bus. She leaned onto the railing as they slowly made their way down the congested street. Mazie stood next to her. When the bus turned sharply, Mazie held her around the waist and didn't let go. It made Ritta feel good.

Wherever she looked there were young people. Some dressed like they were pretending to be Indians; long fringes on buckskin, moccasins, and beads. Most wore faded jeans whose bottoms flared out, sweeping the sidewalk and hiding their feet. Everywhere bright splashes of color mixed into the pattern of the street. Music faded in and out as the bus crept along. Painted vans and cars dotted the road, some more outrageous than the bus had been. And hair—long and flowing, braided or curly, nearly everyone she saw had lots of hair.

Mazie pointed to a huddle of people sharing a joint in a doorway. One of them had skin darker than hers and an afro that went past his shoulders. Mazie shook her fist out the open window. "Right on, Bro!" The dark man turned around in time to see them and held his fist high in response.

A few blocks further, Ritta noticed two women holding hands. One wore tight jeans and a halter top, the other a light, flowing dress. They stood at a street corner waiting for the light to change. When they kissed each other like lovers, Ritta felt her cheeks warm and stared at them until the bus turned the corner. She felt Mazie's arm around her become a little tighter.

Several turns later River said from the back seat, "Here's the street. Look for 1294 and a half." Willie slowed the bus in front of a shingled bungalow painted light green, its wide front porch littered with dying house plants and beer cans. On one of the pillars were tacked the brass numbers 1294. A small poster of a crimson fist surrounded with the words RED POWER hung in the front window. Willie turned down the cross street and pulled over just as the side door opened, and a woman that had to be Jody came out to greet them.

She looked like her pictures, only stronger and possessing more of the beauty that comes from maturing. Ritta thought Jody looks like her dad, but has Gert's spirit.

Jody strode up to the door just as Willie opened it. "I've been waiting for days. Hi, Preacher. Got my Bible?"

"I surely do, my child." He handed her the leather-clad book from the dashboard as he stepped onto the sidewalk. "Somewhere back there, we got a box for you, too. Hey, is that Hendrix I hear?"

Jody listened for a moment. "Probably." She tucked the Bible under her arm. Patch hopped off the steps, Ritta right behind him. Jody asked, "Hey, ol' dog. What happened to you?" She squatted to look into his eyes, then gave him a good rub on his chest.

"He was broken and now he's patched."

"And you're Ritta." Jody stood and extended her hand. Ritta put Gert's box down and grasped Jody's hand around the thumb. Jody laughed. "Right on."

"Hi, Jody. I'm M—"

"Amazing Mazie. I heard about you, too."

"You look just like your pictures." Mazie leaned on the door railing.

"Except now I pluck my eyebrows. Where's everyone else?"

Willie said, "We left Dora at our friend's commune in Oregon. She wasn't feeling like she wanted to travel another two thousand miles."

"'Cause you knocked her up." River followed Mazie out the door, his stash box in hand. Willie grinned sheepishly and shrugged as all three young women glared at him.

"Well, come on in." Jody led the way to the house.

"Don't you live in the apartment?" Mazie asked.

"I sleep there but we all share the space upstairs. Come meet Bear."

The music was so loud by the time they reached the front door, Ritta had her hands over her ears. Jody walked over to the record player and lowered the volume, then swept the newspapers off a ratty couch onto the green striped shag carpet. She offered them a seat.

"Thanks," Ritta mouthed silently. Jody nodded.

Through a curtained doorway stepped a big man in a pair of faded Levis. His black hair grew low on his overhanging forehead and hung straight to his shoulders. His short, wide nose filled the space between prominent cheekbones. Marking his naked chest was a still-raw scar over his left ribs. "What happened to my sounds?" Sheepishly, he ran his hand through his hair, pulling it away from his deep-set eyes. "Oh. Company. Hi. I'm Wilbur. But my friends call me Bear."

Jody pointing at each person. "Ritta, Mazie, Brook, and the preacher. I'm sorry. Mom told me but I can't remember your name."

"Willie. Hi, Bear."

River grasped Bear's hand. "I'm River. Nice to meet you."

Jody giggled. "Oh, I'm sorry. I was close though. And this is Patch."

Bear scratched the dog on his head. "This is a good dog."

"Yes, you are a good dog." Jody patted him on the back. Patch wagged his tail until he wobbled. Walking towards the kitchen, Jody asked, "Anybody hungry?"

The others were quick to say no, but Ritta followed her to the fridge and peered over her shoulder when Jody opened the door. There were three cans of Dr. Pepper on one shelf and a few pieces of dried out Oscar Meyer bologna on another, its "stay-sealed" package curled open. Jody grabbed the lunch meat and some margarine from a cubicle in the door. "Far out. Let's go downstairs. I have some bread."

In the living room, Willie handed a lit joint to Ritta and said, "We're going to take off after we finish this."

Ritta was stunned. "So soon?"

River told her gently, "We have a ways to go to drop Mazie in L.A."

"Dora's waiting, too," Willie added.

Mazie wrote something on a piece of paper. "Here." She thrust it at Ritta. "My brother's address. Let's go get your stuff."

In the bus, tears filled Ritta's eyes. Be brave. Be brave.

Mazie broke the silence. "I wish you could come with me to Alvin's. But he'd shit if I showed up with another mouth to feed."

"It's okay, Mazie. I'll be all right here." She almost believed it. Shouldering her pack, she looked around the bus now so familiar, and remembered how strange it had seemed when it crept up the hill towards her.

"Mazie, it's only been eight days."

"I know. I'll miss you, sugar."

Mazie's arms wrapped around her. She put her mouth on Mazie's and let herself be lost in the ebb and flow of their lips until the sound of footsteps coming into the bus tore them apart.

"Got everything?" Willie asked, a little too cheerfully.

"I think so." Ritta stepped onto the sidewalk, dropped her pack and knelt beside Patch. No longer able to hold back her tears, she buried her head in his fur while Patch stood stoically.

"Ritta?"

River's voice from above made her pull herself together. "Okay," she said, knowing she had to let them go.

"Ritta," he began again. "I want you to keep Patch. He's more your dog than mine now anyway. I just asked Jody and she said it would be cool."

Ritta looked up. River stood next to the half empty bag of dog food and held Patch's bowl. She jumped up and hugged him. "Oh, River. Thank you. Thank you for everything."

He whispered quietly in her ear, "Be safe, sweetie. Stay away from the pigs."

"You, too." She let him go.

River knelt down to the dog. "Take good care of her, boy." After rubbing Patch's ears one last time, River stood and took the steps into the bus in one long stride.

Willie started the engine. Ritta waved as the bus grew smaller in the distance. They were really gone.

She sat on the grass with an arm around Patch and looked up and down the long row of houses, their small gardens of unfamiliar plants around lush mowed lawns. She closed her eyes and faced the sun, hot and glistening through her tears. A breeze cooled her wet cheeks. She licked her salty upper lip.

When she heard soft footfalls on the grass behind her Ritta wiped her face with her sleeve.

"Still want a sandwich?"

Ritta nodded and took the soft white bread without looking up. She forced a bite around the lump in her throat and tore off a piece of meat for Patch. He took it gently from her fingers, then dropped it on the ground to inspect the morsel before he ate it.

When Jody sat down a few feet away, Patch ambled over to her. She pulled off the desiccated edge of the bologna, leaving the still soft center between the bread, and offered it to him. The dog sat and looked at Ritta. She laughed. "Good dog. You can have it." Patch took it from Jody and wolfed it down.

A jet flew overhead. Its mechanical scream made Ritta shudder, and reminded her of the jets that flew over the reservation on their way back to the military base near home. Home. I'm a long way from home.

When they finished eating, Jody stood and hoisted Ritta's pack on her shoulder. "Come on, let's get you settled before the meeting."

"Meeting?"

"At the Center. There'll be food."

Ritta followed Jody down a steep flight of roughly hewn stone steps to the apartment. She stood at the doorway, peering into a long narrow room. Jody went inside and turned around. "The landlady told me this apartment was originally built for an old woman by her sadistic son-in-law. I believe her."

On the wall opposite the door was a small sink, a square of countertop and miniature versions of a stove and refrigerator. Past the fridge were a couple of steep narrow steps up and a short doorway covered with strands of large wooden beads. A red pseudo-Persian runner covered the floor of the living room, surrounded on one side by books crammed into shelves made from concrete blocks and old wooden planks. A davenport took up the rest of the room, leaving just enough space to walk in front of it, all lit by diffused sunlight through a narrow window below the ceiling.

Jody threw the pack on the brown naugahyde davenport and turned to Ritta standing in the doorway. "Come on in. I think we'll both fit."

"Oh, it's so cute. Is it all yours?"

Jody laughed. "Yeah, all mine. Come look at this. It's so freaky."

She led Ritta up, then down the little steps through the beads, like a stile over the short concrete foundation wall. Jody turned on a light bulb that hung over the bed. In the far corner of the low, wide room stood a white metal shower stall. Near it, on a large square platform sixteen inches high, was a gleaming white toilet with a fuzzy red lid cover. "We call it 'the throne.' Have you ever seen anything like it?"

Ritta shook her head. "What a funny place for a toilet."

"Bear tells me since we are in the basement they had to build it this way to get it to flush. Still, it doesn't work very good."

"Hey, it's a real john."

"I know. I remember when all Mom and I used was the outhouse. I must have been ten or so when she decided to get indoor plumbing."

"Back home we have an inside toilet. But it never got hooked up." Ritta sat on the bed and bounced a little.

"You're kidding?"

"No. Lots of houses are that way. Sometimes Mom's friends drag it into the kitchen for another chair. Even used it for a toilet once. After that, I taped the lid shut."

Jody sat on the throne. "Why would someone put a toilet in your house and not hook it up?"

"I don't know. After we moved in this government man came around with a bunch of questions. He asked me if I liked not having to use an outhouse. When I showed him the toilet wasn't connected, he just crossed out 'indoor plumbing' on his little form and wrote 'inside toilet' instead. I guess that was good enough."

"You're kidding?" Jody repeated. Ritta shook her head no.

They heard the whine of a distressed dog and both jumped up at once. Patch stood at the top of the stairs, anxiously looking down the crooked stone steps. "Come on," Ritta coaxed from the bottom landing. Patch took a tentative hop-step and hesitated again. Ritta climbed the stairs and placed her hand on the scruff of his neck. "Call him, Jody."

"Come on, Patch. You can do it!"

He took a few steps, carefully placing his back leg, getting quicker with each one. They heaped praise on him, then led him back up the stairs to come down again. This time he did it alone. Ritta tried to get him to go down the two concrete steps into the kitchen, but Patch balked and wouldn't be persuaded.

Jody suggested, "Let's put a blanket out here on the landing. He'll be okay. There really isn't much room inside for another body, anyway."

Ritta agreed and soon Patch was comfortable by the kitchen door, bedded down on the cool stones with food and water nearby.

The Rock

Ritta climbed into Bear's Dodge van through the front passenger door, pausing a moment to look at the assortment of branches, feathers and pine cones arranged on the dash before she crawled to the seat in the back. Inside, it was apparent from the mangled mechanisms why the sliding side door wouldn't work.

Bear leaned towards the floorboard to connect some bare wires that started the engine. Ritta patted the back seat. "Here, Patch." The dog jumped into the front and over the engine hump to sit by her side.

Jody climbed into the passenger seat and told Bear, "We gotta pick up Peter."

"Hokey-dokey. Is he at his mother's?"

"Yeah. Do you remember where it is?"

"Think so. What's on the agenda tonight?"

"Alcatraz. Again. Think it will ever happen?"

Bear shrugged his massive shoulders.

"What's Alcatraz?" Ritta asked from the back.

"The Rock," Bear said flatly. Ritta waited for him to elaborate. When he didn't, Jody turned to her and explained, "It's an island in the bay. A long time ago it was a fort, then a federal prison where they kept men like Al Capone and Machine Gun Kelly."

Ritta had never heard of either one of them, but thought they sounded real bad.

Jody continued, "Indians in the Bay Area have been talking about Alcatraz for a long time. A few Sioux actually claimed it in '64 but they were on the island only a few hours before Uncle Sam forced them off."

Ritta got excited. "Sioux? Really? How'd they do that?"

Bear stopped for a light and turned around to look at Ritta. "You Sioux?"

"I'm Oglala."

"Ever hear of the treaty of 1868?"

In her mind she could see Lawrence and Agnes, sitting around the table in his cabin after dinner. The memory brought a tightness to her chest. "Our Treaty. It promised that *Paha Sapa* would always be ours."

Bear smiled at her. "It also said that non-reservation Indians could reclaim abandoned government posts. So these guys charted a boat, landed on the island and said, 'This is ours'."

"Were they killed?"

"No. Too many reporters around. That's the difference between the Bay Area and the reservations. The liberals here won't let Uncle Sam get away with the shit they do back on the Rez."

She thought of Agnes. "Too bad there aren't any liberals in South Dakota."

After they had driven a long way, Bear asked Jody, "Is this the street?"

"Yeah, turn here. There he is, on the porch."

"He's sweet on you, *innet*?"

"Oh, he is not." Jody punched Bear playfully on his bicep before moving into the back. "Scootch over, dogface." Patch moved to the floor at Ritta's feet.

A small man with wire-rim glasses, his thin blond hair pulled into a straggly ponytail, put the papers he had been reading in a briefcase and made his way to the van. Jody told Ritta, "Peter's a real sympathizer with the Red Power movement. It helps that he's a graduate law student, too."

"What's the Red Power movement?"

"An idea whose time has come," Bear said with a grin, then introduced Ritta to Peter.

Peter offered his hand. Ritta clasped it, and felt like she could crush his thin bones if she weren't careful. He seemed bird-like, and even bobbed his head when he talked to Bear about some meeting. Ritta watched the two men, and understood that Bear trusted this little wren of a man.

Soon she caught a glimpse of blue water and leaned over the engine well between the front seats, staring at the bridge ahead. "Is that the famous bridge?"

Peter answered, "The Golden Gate? No, it's just the Bay Bridge. Golden Gate is over there. Why don't you sit up here so you can see. I'll trade you places."

They twisted around each other on top of the metal engine hump and Ritta slid into the front seat. When she looked back to thank him, she could tell that Jody wasn't too happy with the situation. Peter however, looked very pleased.

The evening fog was rolling in. Ritta thought it beautiful, the way the city sat in a cloud on the blue-gray water. In her mind she soared high above it, only the steel girders of the bridge marred her daydream.

Traffic became thicker and Bear seemed more intent on weaving around the cars. Ritta gripped the cushioned handle of the door as she looked out her window at the meager few inches separating her from the next speeding car, and wondered if maybe she should have stayed in the back.

Peter asked, "Ritta, where you from?"

Glad for the distraction she turned towards him. "South Dakota."

"Lakota or Dakota?"

Ritta smiled and nodded. "Lakota. Where are your people from?"

Peter blushed. "I'm the progeny of those Europeans that believed in Manifest Destiny."

Ritta laughed. "I'm sorry."

"No, I'm sorry."

By the time they pulled up in front of the Indian Center on Valencia Street, Ritta and Peter were friends.

Inside, the muffled sound of drumming came from a nearby room. Bear said, "See ya later," and headed off in that direction, his arm already moving in time to the beat.

Middle-aged women arranged food on a table covered with plastic cloth. A group of children ran around, whooping and shooting suction-tipped arrows from plastic bows. Others sat quietly in a corner looking at a big picture book. Men in work clothes pored over papers on another table, their voices full of concern. Ritta was amazed at the array of Indian people gathered in the large hall and wondered how many tribes were represented. But what surprised her most was everyone seemed sober.

Before he joined the men with the important-looking papers, Peter told her, "Have fun, Ritta. You're among friends."

Two little kids came running up to Patch and asked her if they could pet him.

"Sure. She knelt down beside the dog. "But be careful he doesn't lick you to death."

"What happened to his leg?" the little boy solemnly asked.

"It was broke so bad a doctor had to cut if off."

"My daddy was sleepin' and a train cut off his leg. He bleeded to death."

"That's too bad."

"It's okay. I got a new one now. He's nicer. This is my sister."

"How d'ya do. My name is Ritta." She offered her hand and small fingers reached out for it.

"My name is Mary," said the little girl with long braids, her coal black eyes full of shyness.

Jody touched Ritta's shoulder. "I'm going to see if I can help get dinner ready."

Ritta watched Jody's long-legged stride towards the kitchen until the little boy pulled her sleeve. "Wanna play warriors?"

"I should go help the grown-ups with the food." The boy's cheerfulness disappeared from his face. He brightened again when she told him, "But catch me later, and we'll count some *coup*."

They ate dinner sitting at the long rows of tables. Ritta and Bear went back twice for extra helpings. Mary and her brother, Alan, sat with Patch on the floor, taking turns petting the dog's head and feeding him small morsels from their plates. When most people finished eating the meeting began. Talk turned quickly to Alcatraz.

"If the U.S. government couldn't afford to keep it going, what makes us think we can," said a man from a nearby table.

A woman stood up, cradling a sleeping baby in her arms. "Since when has the U.S. Government ever managed anything well? If we don't do it soon we may never get another opportunity. Some other millionaire will buy it and our chance for a real cultural center will be gone."

Many people nodded in agreement with her. Jody whispered to Ritta, "A rich man named Hunt wanted to buy the island and build a space museum. The newspapers ran ads with these little coupons that you could fill out and complain about it to the city fathers. We passed out hundreds of them."

"We have a right to Alcatraz," a pock-marked elderly man said. "My people died there as slaves when they would no longer work for the missionaries. They were taken there and left with no food or water. When it became a fort, our Fathers died in the dungeons. My Grandmother tells me this is so."

After a long silence the man who had protested earlier asked, "And how are we to survive there with no water? On land that won't grow food?"

"If we can live on reservations we can live on Alcatraz," another woman said. "It's time we do something."

Ritta felt a tugging on her shirtsleeve. Alan stood by her side. "Wanna play now?"

Ritta smiled and turned to Jody. "I have a promise to keep."

In the hallway they played an elaborate game of tag, each person 'it' and able to get a point every time they snuck up and touched another. It was a game she had never tired of as a child. After a rowdy half hour, Mary was worn out and started to cry.

Later, when Jody came to get her, Ritta was sitting in a corner of the drum room, with five little children and the dog gathered around her, telling stories that Agnes had told to her.

On the way home, Ritta started to fall asleep in the van, but her head bobbed with every big bump and woke her, until Jody put her arm behind it. She was still half-asleep going down the steps that led to the apartment.

Jody gently shoved her onto the davenport. "Go to bed. I'll take care of Patch."

Ritta took off her clothes and crawled into her blanket on the couch. It seemed strange that everything should be still, she was so used to sleeping in the bus with its never-ending drone and vibration.

When she woke, Jody was running water in the kitchen. The early sun came softly through the high window, sending a shaft of light over her. Dust floated like glitter in the golden air. Patch heard her stir and managed the steps down into the apartment. "Patch, good dog. You came in." Her praise was all the dog needed for reward, but she patted the blanket beside her and he jumped up.

"Did you let that dog on my couch?" Jody turned around, carrying two mugs of steaming coffee.

Ritta and Patch froze, like they had just been caught doing something wrong. When Jody laughed, they relaxed. Jody handed her a mug. "Sleep well?"

"I must have. I dreamt I was on the bus all night." She remembered the feel of Mazie's arms holding her in the dream and tried to dispel the fog of loneliness that crept over her. "How did you sleep?"

Jody laughed a little. "Not very good." She sat down by Ritta's feet.

"Oh. Why?"

"I worried all night about my class today."

"You go to school in the summer?" Ritta propped her pillow up on the wall.

"Yeah, Mondays and Wednesdays. I got to work tonight, too."

"At the Indian restaurant."

Jody laughed. "What else did Mom tell you?"

"She said I'd like you." Ritta leaned back, clutching her cup.

"She told me the same thing about you." Jody smiled.

"Could I get a job, too?"

"What do you know how to do?"

Ritta stared into her coffee. "Nothin'."

Jody patted her leg. "Hey, we all had to learn everything we know. I'm sure you can get a job somewhere. I'll ask my boss. How far did you get in school, Ritta?"

"I was a sophomore last year."

"How old are you?"

"Fifteen. I'll be sixteen next month."

Jody looked surprised. "Oh my god, you are just a kid."

Ritta swirled the dark liquid inside the mug. "Not any more."

Jody wondered about those words all the way to class. There was little question what Ritta had meant when she said them.

Mom told me she'd been raped, to be careful with her. But I don't know what to do. How can I help her when all I want to do is hold her, touch her? She is just a kid, for christ sake.

She laughed and wondered if her mother would have been so anxious to

140

send Ritta to her if she'd known her daughter was a dyke. Or had she always known? I'm not so different now than I was before. Just smarter. And no longer isolated.

Jody thought again about what those men had done to Ritta, and prayed she could do the right thing by her.

After Jody left, Ritta did the breakfast dishes. She looked out the window, a rectangle of bleakness too high to reveal any landmarks. Fog, what Jody had called "the Bay blanket," had rolled in, obscuring the morning sunshine and any warmth. She and Patch tried to go for a walk, but it soon started to rain, soaking through the Army coat and chilling her to the bone. They returned shortly, glad for the coziness of the room at the bottom of the stone steps. When she couldn't find anything else to do, she sat on the couch and stared at the books on the shelf. They seemed to stare back at her.

The walls closed in as the clouds grew darker. She swung her legs up and put her head on the hard armrest. Patch snored softly from the kitchen floor a few feet away. When she closed her eyes the view from her and Janey's bedroom filled her head, and she could see down the hillside and beyond, to Agnes' place.

Agnes. What have they done to her? What did they do to me?

The men had held her down. She couldn't get free no matter how hard she kicked and screamed. She felt the man's skin beneath her nails as she tore at his face. Felt their hands pulling her apart before the blow took her memory away. She remembered the pistol coming towards her head and hearing the smack it made as the metal hit the bones beside her ear. Tears spilled over the newly-healed flesh.

I know what they did. What River tried to do.

She felt the stabbing pain she had when River put his hard thing there. Maybe her head didn't remember what those men had done, but her body did. And it wouldn't let River do it, no matter how sweet he had been.

The pain didn't go away. She thought of River's thing. Like a rounded smooth stick wrapped in the jackrabbit hides Lawrence used to tan with the fur off. Leather so thin you could almost see through it.

River didn't want to hurt her. Even Dora said it was wonderful, that it hurt good. Dora should know, she and Willie did it enough.

It had hurt bad. But it didn't hurt before he put it in. It felt good, like when Mazie's soft breasts touched her and they kissed. The ache that she had when Mazie's fingers touched her happened again as she slid her hand beneath the zipper of her jeans. A part of herself seemed to watch her body lift towards her fingers. She heard herself gasp as they searched inside and found a place she could call her own, surprised at how warm and wet she was, how good it felt.

When the bass beat of rock and roll pounded through the ceiling she realized Bear must be home. Patch licked her face as she stretched on the davenport, her feet hanging over the edge a few inches. She scratched his ears. "Got to go outside?"

The dog turned for the door. Ritta sat up and smelled her sticky fingers. She went to put on her coat but it was still wet, a puddle of water on the floor below the hooks. Jody's gold and royal blue letterman's jacket hung on the next peg. It was warm and heavy. She fingered the RL on the front made from little loops of yarn, and wondered if Jody would mind if she wore it.

The late morning sun escaped from the gray clouds as Ritta and the dog walked around the block. Patch lifted his stump to remark every spot he had hit earlier. Ritta wrapped Jody's jacket around her and stopped to watch the rolling clouds, thinking how different it was from back home. The rains should have stopped by now. The grass will be turning gold and the sage more silvery.

She turned her face to the sun hoping for its heat, but felt only a fine layer of mist like cold perspiration on her cheeks. "Come on, dog. Let's go back."

When she walked into the apartment she noticed a pile of books on the couch. "Jody?"

"Yeah, I'm changing clothes." Jody came through the clanking beads, tucking a white tailored shirt into a tight black skirt. "Goddamn, I hate wearing this."

Ritta looked at the long, strong legs below the hem line. "Looks good on you."

"Well, I fail to see what having good legs has to do with my ability as a waitress." She smoothed the skirt over her hips. "Well, maybe it does help in the tips department." She brushed her short black hair with a few furious strokes while looking at Ritta. "That jacket looks good on you."

"Sorry. Mine got wet and Patch had to go."

"That's all right. I left it home 'cause I didn't want it anymore."

"Your mom gave me a bunch of your clothes. If you want them back, I'll—"

"I didn't want any of that stuff." Jody took a step closer to Ritta and pulled the jacket closed in the front. "Keep it."

Ritta grinned. "You mean it?"

"Sure. I remember how cold I was my first year here. The dampness soaks right through. You'll need something wool."

Jody put her feet into low black shoes, their heels worn down to a slant. "Sorry I have to go in so early. On Mondays I help Rosie with the prep work."

Ritta tried to hide her disappointment by petting the dog at her feet.

"I'll ask my boss if he has any openings. We have a lot of turnover. Will you be all right here till tonight?"

Ritta stood up. "Sure."

Jody went into her room and returned with a light sweater thrown over her arm. "Gotta go. Bear and the rest of them are upstairs. Go on up and introduce yourself to the other guys. They were up the mountains this weekend. If they get too noisy, just take the broom handle and hit the ceiling a few times. They know what it means." Jody had her hand on the doorknob when she turned back to Ritta. "I'll bring something home for dinner. See you around ten."

Ritta did a small circle in the living room. She sat down and stared at the books. Scanning the titles did nothing for her mood since she couldn't pronounce over half of the words. Then her gaze came across a little paperback tucked in the corner of the shelf. *Stranger In A Strange Land*. That's me. She pulled the book from its place and studied the tattered cover with a picture of two faces, a man and a woman, merged at the back, the word "grok" above their ears. She opened to the first page and leaned back on the couch.

When Patch scratched at the door several hours later, she took the book and sat on the step in the weak, waning sunlight, unable to put it down.

Later, when her stomach grumbled, she went to the kitchen, took two pieces of Wonder bread from the blue-checked bag, tore off the crusts and fed them to the dog. Then she sprinkled the bread with sugar from the bowl on the counter, folded each in half and rolled them into tight balls. She sat on the bedroom steps and read while she ate, oblivious to the pounding beat of the stereo above her. She was still there when Jody came home at ten-thirty.

"What'cha reading?" Jody put two foil-covered plates on the counter.

Ritta turned the book over.

"Ah, one of my favorites. How do you like it?"

"I grok it." They both laughed.

Jody stabbed a fork into the middle of the food and handed a plate to Ritta before sitting down beside her on the step. "Dig in, before it gets any colder."

Ritta looked at the unfamiliar yellow food. It smelled strange, spicy. She took a small bite. It was good. "What tribe does this come from?"

"What tribe?" Jody looked perplexed. "What tribe? Oh, no. Not our kind of Indian. Eastern Indian, you know, from India. It's called chicken curry."

Ritta's cheeks burned. "Oh."

Jody placed her hand over Ritta's. "It's okay."

"I gotta lot to learn," Ritta mumbled.

"I did too, when I first got here." Jody chuckled a little. "I still do. There is so much to know."

"But you're so smart. All those books."

"And there's a million more to study. Mom used to tell me that when you quit learning, you're dead. I think she's right."

"Your mom is pretty smart, too."

"And so are you, Ritta. What do you want to be?"

"Be?"

"Yeah. Like, I'm studying to be a lawyer. Bear's going to be an engineer, if he can keep his ass in school."

"I don't know."

"Well, for starters, how about a dishwasher. Down at the restaurant they need one for the weekends. Ever have a job before?"

Ritta shook her head. "There are no jobs back home. Unless you work for the BIA and they don't hire girls."

"Well, India House does and you're it."

Ritta let go a whoop and holler. Jody smiled. "I told Sebastian you were sixteen. We'll worry about a work permit and all that stuff later. You can go in with me on Friday. Till then, I think we should get you some more books. That one doesn't look like it will last you the night."

She finished it hours after Jody folded down the davenport so it became twice its original size, filling the living room. It had a trough in the middle that Ritta soon learned to avoid, but Patch didn't seem to mind it. After closing the book thoughtfully, she wrapped her arms around the dog and lay awake for a long time, thinking about God and Man in ways she was sure the nuns back home never considered.

The next morning Ritta woke up when Patch jumped off the end of the davenport. Jody told him not to go far as she let him out the door, then picked up two coffee cups steaming on the counter and brought her one. Ritta leaned back on the wall and held the hot cup in a corner of the blanket on her lap.

Jody sat on the bedroom steps. "Let's hitch into the City today. Looks like it's going to be nice. We could go through Golden Gate Park and hang out on the coast."

Ritta sat straight up. "The coast? You mean see the ocean?"

"That's usually where the coast is."

"I've never seen the ocean."

"You're going to love it," Jody promised. "I'll make some breakfast and we'll go."

Ritta tucked her nose towards her armpit. "Can I take a shower first?"

"Please do," Jody replied, too quickly.

Ritta tossed a pillow at her from across the small room, narrowly missing the cup in her hand.

By ten-thirty they were walking out the door. Patch followed expectantly. Ritta stopped. "Jody, is it all right if he comes, too?"

"Sure, it will help us get rides."

They walked a few blocks, then turned on Shattuck. Jody went into a small corner market and came out with a piece of cardboard. She took a marker from her pack and wrote 'G G Park' on it. They stood on the street, Jody waving the cardboard, and soon a pickup stopped for them. Ritta hesitated to climb in, remembering, a shudder of fear cold along her spine.

"What's wrong?" Jody asked.

"Nothin'. Come on, Patch." Ritta helped the dog onto the open tailgate, then closed it behind him before putting her foot on the bumper and getting in. Soon they were on the long bridge crossing the Bay. Ritta tucked her hair into the letterman's jacket and marveled at the beauty of the water and the City. Before she saw this one, she hadn't thought a city could be pretty, but San Francisco sure looked fine. Its tall buildings glistened in the sunlight and the water around it was deep blue. She was happy, having conquered the moment of fear crawling into the bed of the truck. She had her dog, Jody for a friend and a job she started on Friday. A real job.

The pickup halted at a stop sign at the corner of Masonic and Haight. Jody banged the top of the cab before jumping off the side of the truck. "Hey dude, thanks." Ritta followed and opened the tailgate for Patch. He jumped out as she stared at the tall, brightly painted houses all connected to one another. She slipped the metal hooks back into the catches on the tailgate, then waved at the man's face that stared at her from the side mirror. "Thanks." The driver waved back.

She tried to take in all there was to see, and still keep up with Jody and Patch as they walked along the steep sidewalk. Music poured from an open window, a woman's voice sang a sad song about the war. A little farther down the street, screaming guitars, like on Bear's records, drowned out the peace song.

Ritta threw back her head and twirled, keeping the light blue sky in the middle of the whirl. She felt like she had stepped into the cardboard kaleidoscope she had as a kid, and was turning it around and around until all the colors blurred.

Jody stood at the intersection. "Hey, Ritta. Come on."

A barefoot, grubby man with bleary eyes sat on the sidewalk. "Hey, sister. Can you spare some change? I haven't eaten for days."

Ritta's hand dug in her pocket. Jody pulled her down the street. "You got so much money you want to give it away?"

"But he was hungry."

"Did you ask him when his last fix was?"

"Fix?"

"You know, like heroin. Ever hear of heroin?"

Ritta stopped and shook her head. Jody tucked Ritta's arm in the crook of her elbow and resumed walking. "It's a drug. A bad drug that's addicting and makes people crazy. The city is a dangerous place, Ritta."

"So's the Rez, Jody."

"You don't have junkies on the Rez."

"No, but we got drunks. Lots and lots of drunks."

They walked in silence for half a block when Ritta skipped a little bit. She walked backwards in front of Jody, grinning. "I have a job. A real job."

"Yeah. Well, we better see about getting you back to high school or you'll be a dishwasher for a long time. Let's cross here and walk through the park."

They sat under a tall palm. Ritta felt the trunk. "It looks like a skinny, giant pine cone, all closed up."

Jody handed Ritta an apple from her pack. She took a big bite then spit it out in her hand and passed it to the dog.

"Smell the ocean?" Jody asked.

Ritta filled her lungs with the salty air. A whiff of something familiar floated by on the unseen currents. "I smell pot."

"You've smoked marijuana?"

Ritta nodded. "River and Willie were always toking. Have you tried it?"

"Yeah. I have to be careful with my wind, you know, running track. I've eaten it."

"Eaten it? You mean, just eat it?"

"No, no. Brownies, you cook it in brownies."

"What's that like?"

Jody smiled and shrugged. "It was pretty far out."

Ritta looked around cautiously, then said softly, "Willie had some psychotic mushrooms."

Jody laughed so hard she rolled backwards onto the grass.

"What's so funny?"

Jody sat up and dried her eyes. "Psychedelic."

"Yeah. What is that?"

After looking thoughtful for a minute Jody said, "Come on. I'll show you."

They left the park and stopped on the corner while Jody peered one direction, then the other. "This way," she said, leading them half a block before she stood in front of The Far aHead Shop, its narrow door covered with bright pictures. "Found it. Are you ready?"

Ritta nodded and Jody turned the knob. Tinny sounding brass bells hung from the door, their tinkling mingled with music from inside. Ritta recognized it as a song Willie had played on his guitar. She hoped he and Dora were still happy.

The walls of the long dark room, originally a breezeway between the two adjoining buildings, were covered in colorful pictures. Some glowed eerily. Ritta peered in until Jody took her arm and they entered, like Alices through the looking glass.

"Smells like the commune." Ritta wrinkled her nose.

"What?"

"That smell. What is it?"

"Patchouli. Where did you smell it before?"

Ritta laughed. "At this place we stopped at in Oregon. The whole house stunk of it." Ritta reached for Patch, his muzzle right below her hand. She scratched his ears as she looked around.

Jody motioned her over. "Look at this one." She pointed to a poster of a Black man playing an electric guitar, his hair swirled around him in garish glowing colors. "Hendrix."

"Why is his hair like that?"

"It's an afro."

"No. I mean the picture. Why does it shine like that?"

"Oh, it's fluorescent paint. It lights up under a black light." Jody pointed to the small light fixture above them that glowed purple. "Cool, huh."

"*Han.*"

From the back of the room, a woman's voice shouted, "A dog!" Ritta and Patch stood ready to bolt when a skinny woman in a tight, red velvet jumpsuit came out behind the counter. "Far out, man. I haven't seen a doggy in so long." Her bright yellow hair frizzed out over thin shoulders. Around her neck hung multiple chains and amulets. On the tip of her nose rested dark, wire-rimmed glasses, useless in the dim light. Patch allowed himself to be petted but tucked his tail.

Jody asked the woman if she still had a strobe. The blond stood, gave them both a measured look, then motioned them through a curtained doorway into the back. The room smelled smoky, a mingling of incense, pot and cigarettes. It had no furniture except for two big, orange pillows on a filthy rug, an overflowing ashtray between them. The walls and ceiling were plastered with colored posters.

The woman turned out the lights and plunged them into total darkness for a moment before the black light warmed up and colors danced off the walls. Ritta looked at Jody. Her white t-shirt glowed violet. Jody smiled and the eerie, amethyst glow of her normally pearl white teeth made Ritta grab her own mouth in astonishment.

Suddenly, with a click, the room jumped into staccato. As the strobe pulsed an oscillating rhythm onto their retinas, Ritta nearly fell over. A bizarre-looking Jody grabbed her in three distinct motions and held her until her equilibrium had compensated.

The invisible sound of electric guitar bounced loudly off the walls. Jody shouted close to Ritta's ear, "Isn't it freaky? It's supposed to be like this if you take a psychedelic drug."

"It's the strangest thing I've ever seen."

A woman's voice started singing about a white room with black curtains.

Jody smiled again and swung Ritta around. The walls spun in a ratcheting motion. Jody pulled her faster and faster, until they both fell into a heap on the pillows, laughing and rolling over each other.

The blond poked her head through the curtain, letting light from the store into the room like a beam of sanity. She shouted over the music, "Had enough strobe?"

Jody yelled back, "Yeah, thanks. Leave the black light on, please."

"Groovy."

When the jarring mind assault ended, Ritta lay back and stared at the ceiling. In the center, huge hand-painted letters in glowing colors spelled, "War is not healthy."

"For children and other living things," Jody said as she put her head on the pillow next to Ritta's.

"What?"

"War is not healthy for children and other living things. That's how the whole saying goes. Sure isn't good for those dudes that get sent there. Like Bear's brother. Lost his leg, poor guy."

"Is he going to be okay?"

"He'll get a prosthesis, you know, an artificial limb. But he lost more than that in 'Nam."

"What do you mean?"

Jody stared at the ceiling. "He said that the Vietnamese reminded him of his own people. He felt like he was killing his folks. Said the Vietcong just want to farm and be left alone. He's been a mess ever since he got home." Jody sat up. "I don't know that anyone can heal those wounds. You can teach them how to walk with a wooden leg, but how do you make them want to go on living? It's a terrible thing, this war. Bear calls it the colorful war, the white man telling the black man to kill the yellow man to protect land he stole from the red man." Jody held out her hand to Ritta. "Come on. Let's go."

"Can I buy one of these pictures?"

"A poster? Sure. Which one?"

"Is there one that says about war not being healthy for kids?"

"I'm sure there is."

The blond sat behind the glass display case full of colorful pipes and little carved wooden boxes, plus a lot of things Ritta had no idea what they were. While the woman went to get the poster, Ritta wondered if River had ever seen a store like this. She hoped so.

Outside Jody took her hand. "Are you hungry?" When Ritta nodded she said, "Let's get to Seal Rock."

"Okay. How do we get there?"

"Watch." Jody's hitchhiker's thumb pointed north. Less than a minute later they were piling into the back seat of a yellow, flower-powered Beetle.

148

Patch squeezed in the middle.

Ritta put her arm around the dog and watched eagerly for the ocean. When they topped the hill she saw it. "Oh my god. Look, Patch. Isn't it beautiful?" Mesmerized, Ritta stared out the side window as they headed up the coast.

Jody told the driver they wanted out at the Sutro Baths. The car stopped on a hill overlooking a small cove protected on each side by cliffs sloping down to the ocean. Between them and the green frothy surf were the water-filled ruins of the old bathhouse. Two small islands stood guard in the bay like ineffectual soldiers, the damage done.

Ritta stepped from the backseat of the car and walked towards the water, drawn by the magnificence of it. Jody thanked the driver, shouldered her pack and skipped down the steep path to catch up with Ritta.

"Jody, what is this place?"

"What's left of the Sutro Baths. It used to be this huge building where people came to play and swim in ocean water and eat fancy dinners and stuff. All that's left are remains of the pools and that restaurant up there, the Cliff House."

Below them, a scattering of people strolled along concrete edges laid out in a several rectangles, one huge, and a large circular area; all filled with brackish dark water. The ocean crashed on the farthest wall. Seabirds outnumbered the humans. Thick-spined plants hugged the hillside along the path, blooming frothy pinks and whites.

Patch loped ahead, turning around to check on them whenever the steep path leveled off a little. When they reached the bottom he turned toward the only edge of the largest pool not contained in concrete, lapping the foul water once. A group of seagulls cursed him and flew away, the tips of their wings clapping.

Jody called him. "Here, dogface. I got some." She poured a steady trickle of water from a canteen into her palm as he licked it up.

Ritta stepped up onto the knee high foundation, following the narrow path around the curve of the large circular pool, until it butted into a rectangular structure the size of a small house. Graffitied inside walls divided it into a deep-celled grid. She turned to Jody. "What was this?"

"I think they must have filtered the water through those compartments somehow. I never could make sense of how everything was laid out."

Jody screwed the lid back on the canteen and wiped her hand on her jeans before climbing on the foundation to join Ritta. Patch followed along side. They continued down the eighteen inch thick stem wall towards the ocean. Patch went as far as he could on the ground, until the wall veered towards the edge where the rocky cliff met sea. There he made a valiant leap onto the concrete. Jody caught him before he fell to the other side. He followed them carefully down the end of the manmade embankment where it created one side of a small pool, shallow enough to see the bottom.

Ritta watched as the surf rolled up the rocky shore and splashed its topmost crest harmlessly into the pool. When Jody reached her, Ritta was taking off her basketball shoes. "What are you doing?"

"I'm going down there. Come on."

Jody shook her head before she cautiously sat down on the crumbling concrete and undid her laces. Ritta turned and lowered herself down, dropping the last few inches onto the rocks that held back the sea. She rolled up her pants, pushed them up past her knees, and stuck her feet into the tingling cold water. Jody followed. They both sat on the rocks, feet dangling. Patch watched over them from the wall.

Large birds flew low between them and the small sentinel island. "Jody, look! They're huge. What are they?"

"Pelicans, I think. Yeah. Pelicans."

As she watched them a calmness washed over Ritta, like the waves surging on the rocks. Something loosened its grip on her as she turned around to look out over the rolling water and the nearby island. She felt herself become empty and let the ocean fill her back up again. "Thanks for bringing me here, Jody. I feel good here."

"Mmm, me too."

Ritta dipped her hand into the water and sucked her fingers. "It really is salty!"

A breaker came crashing up the rocks, threatening to douse them. They both shrieked and crowded against the wall. The wave just touched Ritta's hip as it dumped its crest into the pool. Jody took her hand and pulled her wordlessly up to the wall. They sat facing the ocean. Ritta loved the sound of it, the motion that never ceased. It sounds like thunder from under the water.

After the third threatening breaker came near their feet Jody stood up. "We should go. The tide could be coming in."

"How do you know when the tide is going to be coming in or out?"

"Look in a tide book, I guess. They tell you how high it will get and everything."

"What if you don't have one. The old people didn't have books."

Jody shook her head, "I don't know. Probably the phase of the moon. I don't want to find out the hard way. Let's go."

"Where?"

"There's a tunnel right up there I want to take you through. Then we should go to the Cliff House, to get some food." Jody pointed to the restaurant on the hill across the cove from them.

"Can we come back here, someday soon?"

Jody smiled. "Sure. You can come here anytime you want."

After eating a bowl of chowder at the restaurant and counting the pelicans they spotted from the big windows overlooking the ocean, Jody led her down some stairs and to the left, into a little building tucked beneath the restaurant, the Musée Mécanique.

Inside were a myriad of early arcade games and mechanical fortune tellers, a piano that played by itself, and miniature musical bands encased in antique cabinets, even a baseball game where all the players moved; all lined up one after the other in tight rows. Most required nickels to operate. Jody found the attendant and got change for two dollars. She held out Ritta's hand and filled it with coins.

Ritta giggled every time she dropped a nickel into a slot to test her strength or watch a stuffed monkey play a hurdy gurdy. When she was almost out of money Jody took her arm and led her down the aisle to an ornate solid oak cabinet with a black viewfinder in the center. A gilded crank stuck out the side, like an old Victrola's. Above, the sign warned "For Adults Only. Passion of Paradise, 3D Artistic Figure Study."

"What's this?"

Jody snickered. "Watch." She put a coin down the slot. Ritta put her eyes into the fitted mask. Jody took her hand and placed it on the crank.

"When you're ready, turn."

Slowly her eyes focused on the image of two women, dressed in slinky sheer material that did little to cover their small beautiful breasts. As she turned the crank the picture dropped and another slightly different one appeared, then another until it seemed as if the two women moved in jerky motions, offering each other chocolates. Suddenly the scene changed to a bedroom, one nearly bare beauty kneeling on the bed, the other standing with a hairbrush playfully held high over the buttocks of the kneeling woman. Before the brush met its target the picture went dark.

Feeling her cheeks flush Ritta asked Jody, "Are there more of these…?"

"Peep shows? Yeah."

They searched for all of them, interspersed between the other arcade games in the final row. 'See What a Belly Dancer Does On Her Day Off' had a '20s flapper disrobing behind a screen then stepping into a claw foot bathtub, dropping her towel at a judicious moment. 'At A Lady's Dressing Table' showed a woman, breasts bare, coyly admiring her reflection in the mirror.

Jody laughed. "Oo la la. Pretty risqué for their day."

"I got to bring Maze here, she'd like it a lot." Ritta wondered how her friend was, and if Mazie was missing her as much as she was missing Mazie.

Jody said, "One more."

In front of 'Scenes From A Burlesque Show', Jody took Ritta's hand. "I have just one nickel left. Think we can share the view?"

Ritta nodded and put her right eye in the mask, next to Jody's face. Ritta hardly noticed the pictures at all, with Jody so near, the skin of her hand so warm.

Outside Patch was waiting patiently. They walked to the edge of the balcony that hung over the sea, trying to avoid the families that posed along the banister for photographs. As she braided her hair, which felt stiff from the salty mist, Ritta watched the birds coming and going between the islands.

Jody ran her hand down Ritta's braid. "Beautiful hair. I could never stand to grow mine out. Been thinking of getting it cut even shorter. Easier to run."

"I like to run."

"Oh yeah? Wanna race?"

Patch barked, then tried to follow as they took off. Halfway to the Bath's parking lot Jody was the clear leader only because Ritta waited for the dog to catch up a bit closer before she sprinted. Jody waited for a break in traffic to turn right. Ritta and Patch followed her uphill towards two great stone lions resting regally on waist high blocks, guarding a small overgrown road.

Jody perched herself in front of the left lion, her hips nestled between his front and rear legs, her arm over his tousled mane. "This is where old man Sutro lived, who built the baths."

"Oh my god. It's beautiful. Or was."

Vandals had left their mark on nearly every remaining building and statue among the once magnificent gardens, now so badly overgrown Ritta could only imagine how lush it had been when cared for. Someone had broken the bow on the statue Jody called Diana the Huntress, though she still stood firm and proud. They walked past the ruined buildings to the balustrade at the edge of the hill. Jody put her arm around Ritta to point out Golden Gate Park, hemmed in by the city and shrouded in mist. She was so close and felt so good to be near, Ritta wanted to kiss her.

Jody dropped her arm. "We should be getting home."

Ritta liked her dishwashing job. It was hard and made her sweat till her shirt stuck to her back and rivulets trickled down her side, but the warm kitchen was a happy place. Sebastian made it so. She liked watching the man cook, his roundness draped in a clean apron. The soft sing-song of his voice spilled into the white-tiled alcove where she worked, to be heard sporadically above the clang and hiss of the dishwashing machine. It seemed to Ritta the busier they were, the happier was Sebastian. On hectic Saturday nights his smooth brown face lit up with a smile and he would almost hop around the kitchen, ordering Rosie, the backup cook, to do things she most likely had already started.

Rosie often brought her hot chai, which Ritta let cool on the window sill until the only heat left in it was the spicy bite soothed by milk. She'd drink it on her break, sitting on the back step with Patch, who waited patiently for the end of her shift.

Rosie was from the Philippines; her father, an American soldier. Sometimes, when Ritta helped her clean the kitchen at the end of the shift, they talked about being "half-whites" as Rosie called it. They compared mothers, both were Christian. Rosie's mother had worked hard her entire life, so Rosie could move to the United States when she was old enough. Her mother refused to leave with her. "She said, 'Go to America, where your American blood will help you.' Poor Momma didn't know here I am just another 'gook'."

Sebastian didn't hire white students. He said they got enough breaks. He expected his help to move on and tried to pay them well enough to stay in school so they could. In turn, a large part of his clientele used to work at India House. They loved their old boss as much as his current employees did. It was common for them to shout their greetings through the small opening above the stove. Sebastian would answer back, asking about their careers, spouses, or babies, and cooked their meals as if they were family.

Within a week of starting her job, Ritta was taking a GED class at the high school, two nights a week. Sometimes, she and Patch walked to the university and explored the campus before meeting Jody after her classes. On the days Jody didn't go to school, they studied together, sitting on the big porch, drinking coffee.

Ritta read until her head swam and the words tumbled together. When Jody caught her with her nose a few inches above a book, she insisted Ritta get her sight checked. Now Ritta had glasses that made her look older. They also helped hide the red mark on her temple and the small divot left in her cheekbone.

For fun, they drank beer on the weekends with Bear and the guys that constantly moved in and out of the upstairs. Sometimes they drove to the Center in San Francisco or went to local pow-wows, where Bear would drum. Ritta enjoyed those times most of all. The talk was often of Red Power or of the War. They went to demonstrations, and once crossed the Bay Bridge with thousands of people, joining tens of thousands more. Ritta understood for the first time what 'Power to the People' meant. Her heart felt big in her chest when she raised her voice with the masses around her, shouting "What do we want? Peace! When do we want it? Now!"

Jody started back to school full-time in the fall. Gone were their unhurried mornings together. Ritta took to wandering the streets, and often hitchhiked across the bridge to the City. She and Patch became a familiar sight along certain street corners, sometimes getting rides from the same people more than once.

Ritta loved going into San Francisco, walking around the Haight where the hippies hung out. She and Patch often went back to the places they had gone that first day in the city. One day she went back to the abandoned estate on the hill above the Baths and sat for hours in the fall sunshine. She told one of the lion guards her secret—how much she wanted Jody to touch her.

Remnants of the great garden were still blooming. She picked a stem of soft purple flowers near the base of Diana and rubbed it along her cheek. She imagined the statue of the huntress was Jody. Something about the way her head was tilted, like Jody's before she made one of her wry comments. Closing her eyes to the sun, Ritta yearned for the time they had spent together.

Early one October morning, Bear came down the stone steps and knocked on their door. When Ritta opened it, the kitchen filled with his bulk and anxiety.

Jody came through the curtains, beads clattering behind her. "What's wrong, Bear?"

"The Center. It's been torched." He stumbled to the davenport. "Burned. Down to the ground."

Ritta clutched her sickening stomach. "Anyone hurt?"

"No." Bear looked at Jody sorrowfully. "Our drum was there."

Jody slumped to the floor. "And Minnie's beadwork, and all the other beautiful things in the gift store."

Ritta wanted to cry. Who would do such a thing?

The fire that burned the Center had been extinguished, but the deed started a wildfire of indignation, inflaming the community that relied heavily on the Center's activities. It spread through the Bay area's Indian population which, thanks to the BIA's ill-run Relocation Program, was swelling daily with people from the reservations, people that often found themselves stranded without steady jobs and little of the promised government assistance.

Wherever they met, the talk was of Alcatraz. Leaders of the different Indian organizations argued at more meetings, trying to work out a plan to make the island and its deteriorating facilities their new Cultural Center.

One night after work, Bear's van was parked behind the restaurant when Ritta and Jody walked out the back. He opened the passenger door for them. "Pile in."

They crossed the Bay Bridge. Bear kept driving, down the Embarcadero, down Lombard Street, to a little deserted road that led past the old fort and under the end of the Golden Gate Bridge.

The lighthouse on Alcatraz blinked in the distance. Bear pulled a warm bottle of Hamms out from under the seat, opened it with the magnetic church key stuck to the dash. They passed the beer around until it was gone.

Bear belched and opened his door, mumbling something about a leak and disappeared in the darkness. Ritta looked out the window after him. "I wonder how much he's had to drink tonight."

"No more than usual," Jody answered. "Come on, let's walk."

They headed down to the water. The half moon's silvery reflection became an illusionary pathway between them and the island, pulling them towards it.

Bear's deep voice shouted from behind them, "We're going to take you, Rock. You belonged to us once and we're going to get you back."

Ritta trilled the *waiaglata*. The clear shrill sound carried on the wind across the bay to be lost among the buoy bells and foghorns.

They stared at the island for a long time, as intent on getting there as generations of prisoners had been to get off.

One busy Saturday night several weeks later, Bear came in to the restaurant with a big smile on his face. He ordered a plate of curry, but wouldn't tell Jody what was up. When she brought out his food, she didn't put it down but made sure he smelled it. "Tell me what the shit-eating grin is for and I'll give it to you."

"Tomorrow is the day."

"To take the island?"

Bear nodded, his fork in hand and his eyes on the food as she put the plate down on the counter in front of him.

Jody shook her head, "It's a foolish thing to do. They aren't going to let a bunch of Indians take Federal land. Someone could get hurt."

Bear pointed his fork at her. "The media is with us on this one, Jody-girl. Uncle Sam won't be gettin' away with any shit here. It will be on the national news, I betcha."

Jody went back to the dishwashing room first chance she got. "Bear's here. Said tomorrow is the day."

Ritta wiped her face with her sleeve. "What day?"

"To take the Rock."

"Oh, shit, Jody. We got to work."

"You really want to go?"

Ritta looked at her pleadingly. "I really want to go."

"Okay, I'll go talk to Sebastian."

It didn't take much to convince the boss to let her and Ritta have the day off. She knew how Sebastian's mind worked. Soon, she returned to the tiled alcove, triumphant. "We both got it off."

"How did you manage that?"

"I reminded him it was Gandhi who encouraged peaceful civil disobedience."

November ninth dawned bright. Ritta woke up next to Jody and rubbed her eyes. Fuzziness clouded her head like the fog usually visible out the small window above the bed. Bits and pieces of the previous night's happenings came to her like a dream as she rolled out from under Jody's arm and tip-toed to the throne to empty her beer-deluged bladder—the party upstairs, the white chick who sold hits off a chunk of hash as big as her fist for a buck.

A friend of Bear's had brought a drum. The deep beat reverberated through the house, grounding the rock and roll that blared from the speakers. Some guy had tried to kiss her in the kitchen, his sour beer-breath in her face. Jody came in and shoved him. "Leave her alone, Wayne."

The big, full-blood Navajo sneered at Jody. "What's it to you, track star?"

"She's my sister."

"I didn't know you had a sister."

"You do, now, asshole. Why don't you go play warriors with the rest of the boys?"

The big man walked out of the kitchen with nothing more than a mean scowl towards Jody, who didn't seem to notice. She opened the fridge, grabbed two cans of beer and took Ritta by the hand. "Let's go home."

Downstairs, they turned on the radio in Jody's bedroom, adding to the noise from above them. Jody lit some candles and turned off the overhead light. She handed Ritta the beers and they sat cross-legged on the bed. From her pocket, Jody removed a little brass pipe and a tiny square of tin foil.

"What's this?" Ritta put the unopened beers on the floor.

Jody carefully unwrapped the crumbles of hash. "I bought it. Don't tell anyone. My coach would kill me."

"Why would I tell anyone?" Ritta took a hit as Jody held a farmer's match over the glowing coal. Harsh smoke filled her lungs. Her chest spasmed as she tried to hold it in.

"That's what I love about you, Ritta."

Ritta almost choked and had to let the smoke go in a sharp exhale. As the cloud around her cleared Ritta felt warm all over. She said she loves me! Her heart thumped hard in her chest as she passed the pipe to Jody, who pulled the smoke curling off the bowl into her nostrils and handed it back.

As Ritta exhaled again, the room changed. Things slowed down, got warmer, softer. Jody offered her the hash again. She shook her head and closed her eyes, feeling her body float as if she were in water. When she heard Jody exhale and place the pipe on the chair beside the bed, Ritta asked, "What is it you love about me?"

Jody's voice was close and quiet. "Everything."

When Ritta opened her eyes, Jody's face was inches away, propped on a triangle of bent arm, her brown eyes intensely close. Her hand brushed Ritta's cheek softly, like butterfly wings on her skin. Ritta caught the tip of one finger in her mouth and held it before she noticed the bewildered expression on the face above her.

Jody smiled and said, "I've often wondered if you want to kiss me as much as I do you." Her voice was low and rich.

"I thought you would hate me if I did."

Jody's face came closer, her breath warm on Ritta's cheek. "You're so young. I shouldn't do this."

Ritta put her hand behind Jody's head. "I'm old enough to know what I want."

Jody's lips nearly touched hers. "And what do you want?"

"This."

Their bodies chastely apart, the taste and feel of Jody's warm lips was enough. Softly they explored, venturing to Ritta's eyebrow, then her earlobe before kissing her lips again. Ritta opened, taking Jody's tongue into the hunger of her mouth. Her body rose and closed the gap between them.

Jody pulled away, sitting upright in the bed, as if suddenly coming to her senses, or out of them. She pulled her fingers through her short black hair and grasped it tight on the crown. "I can't do this."

Ritta sat up. Her heart pounded. She felt that ache again.

"I need a beer." Jody reached over Ritta's legs. "You want one?"

"Okay." Ritta propped the pillow between her and the wall and let the warm beer drown her passion. They drank in silence. Jody guzzled hers and blew out the candle on her side of the bed. She pulled off her jeans and used the toilet.

Ritta finished her beer in the soft glow of the remaining candle and wondered if she should stay or get up and sleep with Patch on the couch.

Jody took the pipe from the chair, pinched another piece of hash into the bowl and lit it with a match struck along the concrete wall. The flame left a brief, arched crimson trace. She handed the pipe to Ritta. "Please stay."

Ritta smiled and took the offering. Beneath the covers, Jody's arms curled around her and pulled her close. Ritta fell asleep, happy enough just to be held. She'd figure the rest out later.

Bear knocked on their door just as Ritta opened it to let Patch out. Jody stuffed the day pack with food and extra clothes. Ritta made sure Patch had fresh water and hugged him. "Sorry, boy. You got to stay today." As they walked to the van, she wondered if Bear was as hung-over as he looked.

Ritta curled up in the back seat and fell asleep before they were to the bridge. Jody woke her when they reached the pier. Seeing the throng of people, some in their finest pow wow clothes, lifted Ritta's spirits. Bear joined the young men gathered around the new drum covered with blankets to protect it from the salt air. Ritta and Jody migrated towards a few familiar people standing on the dock.

Ritta fingered the fringed deerskin dress adorned with elk teeth that

Minnie, a elderly friend from the Center, was wearing. "This is beautiful."

"Thank you." Minnie pointed to the moccasins on her feet. "I was up half the night finishing these." Ritta knelt down to look at the fine beadwork.

"Sure are lots of people here. Who are the guys in the suits?" Jody asked.

Minnie smiled. Soft wrinkles echoed her grin. "Reporters. Most of the TV stations have people here. Newspapers, too. My friend Adam called them."

Beefy men stood by cameras set on huge tripods, adjusting lenses or milling with their counterparts, checking notes and looking nervously at their watches.

Minnie looked out over the bay, her smile vanished. Ritta asked, "What's wrong?"

"The boats that were supposed to take us didn't show up. Adam is trying to find others. If we don't pull this off, it won't look good."

Ritta noticed a handsome man, a headband tight around his forehead, walk over to the reporters and ask them to gather on the dock. The air was thick with anticipation as people crowded around. When he had everyone's attention the man squared his broad shoulders and unrolled a scrolled paper.

His voice was clear and carried well as he read:

"*To the Great White Father and All His People. We, the Native Americans, reclaim this land known as Alcatraz Island in the name of all American Indians by right of discovery. We wish to be fair and honorable in our dealings with the Caucasian inhabitants of this land, and hereby offer the following treaty: We will purchase said Alcatraz Island for twenty-four dollars in glass beads and red cloth, a precedent set by the white man about three-hundred years ago. We know that twenty-four dollars in trade goods for these sixteen acres is more than was paid when Manhattan Island was sold, but we know that land values have risen over the years. Our offer of one dollar and twenty-four cents per acre is greater than the forty-seven cents per acre the white men are now paying the California Indians for their land. We will give to the inhabitants of this land a portion for their own, to be held in trust by the American Indian Government—for as long as the sun shall rise and the rivers go down to the sea—to be administered by the Bureau of Caucasian Affairs, the BCA.*"

The Indians roared with laughter. A few reporters got the joke a moment later and laughed politely.

"*We will further guide the inhabitants in the proper way of living. We will offer them our religion, our education, our life-ways, in order to help them achieve our level of civilization and thus raise them, and all their white brothers, up from their savage and unhappy state. We offer this treaty in good faith and wish to be fair and honorable in our dealings with all white men.*"

The crowd cheered. Even the reporters seemed to be enjoying it. The man waited till the crowd was ready to listen again before continuing.

"*We feel this so-called Alcatraz Island is more than suitable as an Indian*

Reservation, as determined by the white man's own standards. By this we mean that this place resembles most Indian reservations, in that it is isolated from modern facilities, and without adequate means of transportation. It has no fresh running water. The sanitation facilities are inadequate. There are no oil or mineral rights. There is no industry and so unemployment is very great. There are no health care facilities. The soil is rocky and non-productive and the land does not support game. There are no educational facilities. The population has always been held as prisoners and kept dependent upon others."

Bear came over and stood between Jody and Ritta at the edge of the crowd. He nodded politely to Minnie.

"Who is he?" Ritta asked.

"Richard Oakes. He's a Mohawk, goes to San Francisco State. Charismatic, isn't he?"

"I'd follow him even if he wasn't leading."

Richard continued, detailing what the Indians would do with the island; their plans for a spiritual center and museum, desalination plants and a traveling school. The people looked at each other, nodding their hope and encouragement.

Jody scoffed, "I'll believe it when I see it. Where's the money going to come from?"

"Come on, Jod." Bear looked down on her, crossing his arms over his chest.

Ritta whispered, "Yeah. Lighten up."

When the young man had finished reading the proclamation he turned and looked out to the bay. No boats. He looked questioningly at the group of older men standing apart on the dock. One of them shrugged helplessly back.

Richard smiled like a live TV host and announced it was time for the drumming. Bear looked startled as a man grabbed his arm and led him to join the others pounding on the drum in front of the cameras. When they started the fourth song the cameras stopped rolling and people began to look at their watches again.

Minnie said, "I'm going to find out what was up with the boat." She scurried off.

Jody shook her head. "I knew it. I knew it."

Ritta was worried, too. "What do you think's wrong?"

"Who knows. Maybe the Feds got wind and confiscated the boat. Sure looks like we're running on Indian time."

The crowd milled around with the nervous expectancy of ducks on a pond. A baby cried and three mothers turned to comfort it. Jody overheard one of the camera men grumble about the delay to a reporter, who said, "At least we aren't sitting in a boat by the island like those fellows from Reuters. I'd be seasick by now."

Minnie came running up to Ritta and Jody, panting with excitement. "Look! Adam found us a boat." She pointed to an old-fashioned ship with three masts, docking gracefully nearby. Below the ship's Canadian flag, a man in a white ruffled shirt, tight pants and knee high boots stood at the bow, his long blond hair blowing in the breeze.

"You're kidding," Jody said, shaking her head.

Minnie had a hold of Ritta's arm, pulling her towards the ship. "Come on, Jody," Minnie called back to her. They joined the throng of people walking up the ramp to the well-varnished deck of the *Monte Cristo*. Ritta ran her hand over the smooth, dark wood railing and shiny brass tie downs.

They crowded aboard, along with the reporters and cameramen. Even some bystanders came along for the ride. Ritta watched as Minnie's friend Adam made his way through the mob, politely asking those who weren't Indian or media to leave. He conversed with the Captain again, who shook his head as he counted people from his vantage point on the bow. Adam walked through the crowd for the second time, seeming a bit more exasperated as he asked the older people and those with small children to leave the ship, explaining, "We can only take fifty people and are asking everyone who can't swim well to wait on shore."

Minnie gripped the brass rail. "I never learned to swim and I'm feeling sick, anyway." She turned to Ritta. "You should go, and wear my dress."

"Oh, Minnie. I'd love too. Are you sure?"

"Yes. At least a part of me will make it to the Rock." Minnie led Ritta through the throng to the bow where the astonished-looking Captain stood. Minnie had to ask him twice if there was someplace on board they could change clothes. He looked at her, dazed, but finally nodded and led them to the door of his quarters and asked them to be quick. In the tiny, luxurious cabin Ritta exchanged her jeans and t-shirt for the darkly-tanned dress adorned with elk teeth sewn in rows and the solidly beaded moccasins that adjusted to fit her feet. The dress was snug, but comfortable, and weighed more than Ritta had expected it to. She pulled the beaded pouch from next to her skin and let it hang outside for the first time. She grasped it for a moment and thought of how proud Agnes would be of them.

Minnie quickly donned the unbecoming baggy pants and frayed shirt. Ritta laughed a little, then apologized.

"I've worn worse, dear," Minnie replied. "And I can tell these are clean. Besides, it's worth it to see you like this." She turned Ritta in a small circle. "Beautiful." Minnie ran her fingers through Ritta's hair and braided it, tying it with ribbons she took from her handbag. Ritta kissed Minnie's wrinkled cheek before they walked out on deck. A reporter snapped Ritta's picture as they squeezed through the crowd to where Jody waited.

"I'd say you got the better part of the deal," Jody told Ritta as she looked her over.

"Me, too. Thank you, Minnie. I'll be very careful." Ritta ran her fingers over the dress.

Minnie laughed. "These are pow wow clothes, dear. Shake it if you get the chance."

A man in a headdress asked Jody if she would leave. He looked at Ritta. "You can stay."

Jody shot him an angry look as he walked off. Then she hugged Ritta and whispered in her ear, "Be careful, little sister."

"Don't worry about me."

"Yeah, right. You're just sailing in a hundred year old boat to overtake a Federal prison with a bunch of idealistic Indians." She turned to Minnie. "And she tells me not to worry."

Minnie smiled. "She'll be fine. Let's go." They left amid the disappointed elders and vociferous children, angry at being left behind.

The crew on the ship loosened the lines and unfurled the sails. A small cannon was fired off the bow, its thunderous boom announcing their departure. Small boats loaded with reporters and television crews surrounded the *Monte Cristo* as it tacked regally into the waters of the bay.

The ship rocked on the waves for a full minute as the wind filled the square sails, popping the canvas. The crew couldn't possibly hear the captain's commands over the excitement on deck, but the ship shifted on course. Ritta gripped the rail at the stern and shivered as they started towards the island. She watched Jody and Minnie grow smaller on the dock, then the dock itself shrink away as the choppy blue water separated them. The ship's timbers groaned. She felt it through the moccasins as her toes gripped the deck. She was grateful for Bear's strong arm around her and followed him when he said, "Come on. I gotta drum."

The drum was set up on the roof of the Captain's quarters. Several men stood around it. When Bear arrived they started with a warrior's song that she recognized from listening to them practice at the Center before it burned down. The rousing beat made her heart soar with pride at being part of this. She looked over the bay to the small island and wondered how the first sailors that crossed the ocean felt, having sighted land after months at sea. *If they had come only as explorers and not as conquerors, I wonder how different our history would be?* She remembered Mazie saying once that in other colonized countries the Europeans eventually left. Here they practiced genocide.

Ritta held onto the rail as the ship lifted with each wave and dropped, leaving her stomach to sink a moment later. From her vantage point on the roof she could make out an official looking boat coming towards them at full speed. She pointed to it at the same time the others noticed it. Adam shouted over the drumming for everyone to wave. The Coast Guard patrolmen smiled and waved back before changing their course.

Ritta sighed relief, then turned towards the island. Several small boats waited for their arrival near the wharf. Soon they were close enough to the rocky shore to see mounds of rusted equipment strewn along the bank. She could make out many buildings. Some were beautiful, but most looked deserted and dilapidated, except the lighthouse, standing purposefully on the knoll. High chain link fences, topped with many strands of loosely rolled barb wire, seemed to surround the island. Then she noticed the huge concrete building that sat at the topmost part. That must be where they kept the prisoners. Her heart felt heavy for them.

Dozens of birds flew over her head, soaring on the stiff ocean breeze that made her glad for the long sleeves of buckskin covering her arms. The weak winter sun felt good on her face as she watched the birds land on the dock. Their nests and long trails of white droppings decorated the large rectangular building closest to the shore.

As they sailed past the wharf, the drumming stopped. Bear came over to her side and said, "The Captain won't dock. That's as close as were going to get." His eyes wistfully searched the island as if longing could propel him across the water.

She thought of how far they had come, how much they wanted it to be theirs. She opened her mouth to try to console Bear when she heard, "Let's get it on!" Then a splash and a great cheer. Richard was in the water, swimming towards the island. Ritta turned to Bear, but he was already gone. She scanned the crowd on the deck and saw him tearing the shoes from his feet. He looked up at her and waved, shouting words she couldn't hear over the hoopla. She could only wave back.

Bear climbed the railing, his massive chest expanding as he filled his lungs before pushing away from the ship in an ungraceful dive. Ritta held her breath until he surfaced. Despite his strength, the tide pushed against him. The island was still out of reach.

Adam's voice blared through a bullhorn. "No more Indians are to jump overboard. Captain's orders." Another loud splash sounded in response as a third man dove head first. The crowd urged him to the shore.

The ship tacked around the point. Ritta watched the swimmers struggle against the tide that pushed them farther away from the island. The reporters' boats headed for them as they surrendered to the ocean and treaded water. She watched a small man next to Adam take off his shoes and shirt and dive quietly into the water. Her eyes grew big as he swam closer to the shore. The tide on this side of the island assisted, instead of defeating, him. When he stood up on the rocky bank the drum sounded his victory amid great whooping and trilling. A woman Ritta didn't know hugged her and they cried. She heard the Captain order the *Monte Cristo* away from the island, "Before any more crazy Indians jump ship."

As the island grew smaller, Adam yelled through the bullhorn, "Have we done enough?"

"No!" the crowd shouted.

"Do you want to go back and take Alcatraz? Really take it next time?"

The people hollered, stamped their feet, beat the drum, whooped out, shouting, "Yes! Yes!"

When they docked, Ritta hurried over to Bear and Jody. "God, Bear, you look so cold." He shivered, despite the heavy wool blanket wrapped around his shoulders.

Jody shook her head. "At least his teeth quit chattering."

Ritta wrapped her arms around his huge, huddled frame. "You were incredible."

"Incredibly stupid," Jody mumbled.

Minnie emerged from the crowd and pulled them over to a concession stand. She told them to order lunch, it was already paid for.

After deciding what they wanted, Ritta and Minnie went to the restroom to exchange clothes. When they returned, their hamburgers with the 'works' were up. Jody thanked Minnie for the meal.

"Oh, I didn't pay for it. This is on Adam."

Bear scanned the throng of people till he saw Adam and tipped his Coke in appreciation. The older man smiled weakly.

Jody started in on Bear the minute they got in the van. "Great takeover," she said with a humph. "Never thought I'd see the day when Indians would hire Columbus and the 'Santa Maria' to take us to the promised land."

"Lay off, Jody," Bear laughed. "We did pretty good." He turned to Ritta. "Did you see the way Richard jumped in there?"

"You got closer to the Island than he did, man." Ritta slugged his arm.

Jody snorted. "You looked like a bunch of nincompoops, jumping into the Bay."

"At least someone made it." Bear replied.

"Big fucking deal. One Indian made it ashore. Boy, that will make a lasting impression on the world."

By the time they got off the Bay Bridge, Bear was hunched sullenly over the van's steering wheel and stayed that way until they pulled up at the house. He slammed the van's door so hard the vehicle rocked on its bad shocks. He stood in the middle of the yard and bellowed, "Goddamn you, Jody. Everyone can't be as perfect as you are. Sometimes you got to do what you got to do."

Jody sat in the passenger seat, looking at her fingernails, until he stomped into the house. Ritta sat glued to the back seat, trying to be invisible.

Jody said placidly, "Let's go in. Patch is probably wondering where we've been all day."

"How can you be so calm? I never seen a dude that pissed off not hit someone."

Jody snorted. "Bear would never hit me. He wouldn't dare. Unlike most men, Bear can control his temper. I push him so he knows where his limits are. You'll see. He'll be fine before dinner. Besides, I'm right. That's what really ticked him off. It was a media circus that will have the world laughing at the ineptness of Indians again."

"We're going back to really take the island, tonight."

"Well, we won't be there. I told Sebastian we'd be at work if it was a fiasco. And it was. I knew it would be."

When they walked into the apartment, Patch rose stiffly from the davenport to greet them. Jody went to her room. Ritta had started to change into her work clothes when someone pounded on the open door. She turned, holding her shirt over her exposed bra. Bear stood on the threshold. Ritta heard his anger, spewing beneath the surface of his words.

"I'm going to the meeting. Are you coming with me?"

Jody came through the beads and stood silently with her arms crossed.

Ritta looked at Jody, then back to Bear. She wanted to go. The exhilaration of the afternoon was still with her. But the expression on Jody's face stopped her. She had to live with Jody. And keep her job. She shook her head sadly, hoping he would understand.

Bear's eyes, full of malice, glared at Jody. He turned and took the stone steps three at a time. Ritta called out after him, "Good luck!"

* * *

The winds of November blew through the barn, despite the mud and rags Lawrence had stuffed in the cracks. Ice crystallized on his blankets in the early morning, the ashes from last night's fire cold in the stove.

The filly snorted, her warm breath visible as it shot from her quivering nostrils. She pawed at the wall that separated her from the human, insisting he rise and toss her a flake of hay. The sound of her hoof striking the wood cut through the arctic air like a rifle shot, but wasn't enough to roust the man from his surrender to the cold.

The filly was far from succumbing to the weather. She only wanted her breakfast and the companionship she had grown accustomed to. Before noon, she kicked the paddock door into splinters and headed to the hilltop where the winter sun was bright, if not warm. The frozen grass crunched beneath her hooves where the bitter wind blew the dry powdery snow away.

Bill Thomas saw her there from the road as he headed to his barn for another load of hay. He stopped and got out to lock his hubs before turning down the snow-filled ruts that led to Lawrence's place. He knew something was wrong when he noticed the makeshift chimney wasn't smoking.

The filly followed the truck, smelling something to eat. Down the draw where the snow became deeper, she slowed and walked in the tracks behind the pickup. When Bill stepped out of the truck, she nuzzled her nose beneath his arm. He threw some loose hay from the bed of the truck on the glistening crust of snow. The filly snatched a mouthful, then threw back her head several times, softly nickering.

Walking towards the barn, his footfalls paused briefly on the hard surface of snow until the weight of his step broke the crust with a thud that echoed in the biting air. The buckles of his overboots jingled as he pulled his legs out of the knee-deep drift. His chest ached with a frigid grip of air as he slid the barn door open.

A shaft of brilliant sunlight cut the dark paddock into halves. He entered the dimness, gave his eyes a few seconds to adjust before he walked to the stove and put a gloved hand on the cold cast iron. When he saw the huddled lump of blankets atop the bed made of hay bales, he started pulling the thick leather from his stiff fingers and moved with a speed that belied his trepidation. Pulling back the layers of tattered wool confirmed his fear. Lawrence's face looked peaceful, despite the coolness of the wrinkled skin against Bill's fingers. He searched for a pulse. When he felt the sluggish beat he looked to the rafters and asked, "Dear God, now what do I do with him?"

The bright slice of sunlight darkened as the filly stepped into the doorway. Bill ignored her as he pondered how to get Lawrence, a man half again his size and about as dead as weight could get, to his pickup. The filly snorted and walked up to him, then pawed at the ground near his feet.

Bill looked at the horse, then to the man lying curled in a ball on the blanket-covered bales of hay. He searched the paddock for a lead rope and found one near a barrel of oats, then returned to pour a generous amount of grain on the dirt floor by Lawrence's side. The filly buried her nose in it as Bill hoisted Lawrence's body onto her back.

He enticed her with the rest of the of the oats, rattling the can briskly as he led her outside, shielding his eyes from the brilliant glare of sun. She stood as he wrestled Lawrence onto the seat of his truck. Bill led the filly back to her stall, poured the remaining oats on the ground and patted her rump. "I'll be back to feed you this evening."

Before Bill had driven halfway home, Lawrence's body began to quiver. When he pulled down the lane to his two-story farmhouse the tremors were so violent Bill had to push his arm over Lawrence to keep him on the seat.

His wife, a small and sinewy woman, met him at the door. Between the two of them, they got Lawrence into their son's bedroom and wrapped him in blankets. Bill wanted to take him into the living room, where the coal stove was, but Nora was cautious of warming him too quickly. Bill heeded her in this, as in most things. He stoked the stove up good before heading out to finish feeding his cows.

* * *

After work, Jody and Ritta walked home without talking. When they reached the house, Jody suggested they watch the late news on the television upstairs.

Ritta thought it seemed too quiet without Bear. Jody fiddled with the dials on the TV until there was a resemblance of a face on the screen. As she adjusted the foil-wrapped antennas the gender of the face and the movement of lips became clearer. She and Ritta slumped on the tattered couch, until the boyishly handsome reporter started with, "A group of Indians sailed across the Bay to Alcatraz Island today, to claim the Federal property for their own." The picture changed to Richard Oakes reading the proclamation on the wharf, then the crowd as the cameraman panned their faces.

Ritta grabbed Jody's arm, "Look, there we are! There's Minnie."

The camera closed in on Richard's movie-star handsome face as he told the world the Indians would "purchase said Alcatraz Island for twenty-four dollars in glass beads and red cloth." The scene shifted to the ship sailing across the Bay, then to the swimmers jumping in the water. A brief close-up of Bear being hauled out of the bay by a television crew caused Jody to snort. The reporter continued, "One Indian made it to the shore of Alcatraz to claim the island for Indians of all tribes." The faint sound of drums across the water accompanied the picture of the small Eskimo man standing on the shore, waving his arms in victory. "The Indians plan a Center for Native American studies, a spiritual center, a training school, and a museum on the island. Federal officials decline to comment on the offer. Next, we'll take a look at the school districts plans to increase enrollment—"

Jody shut off the TV. "Not as bad as I anticipated. They could have really laughed it up. We'll have to get the paper in the morning."

"You do care, don't you?"

"Of course I do. I'm Indian, too. But you know what it's like being a half-breed. I have a foot in two worlds and I'm not welcome in either."

"At least you weren't raised on the Rez like I was. Your Mom—"

"My Mom kept us secluded. I wonder if she hadn't had an Indian baby if she would have gone back to town to live after my dad died. She tried to keep me from all the bigots she grew up with, and in doing so robbed me of my dad's culture as well as her own. We survived, just like you did, doing what we had to do. At least you had your people, you had elders to teach you."

"I did." A shadow of pain passed over Ritta for an instant, then she brightened. "Wait till you meet Lawrence, Jody. He knows how to talk to the animals, he's the best horse trainer back home. Even *wasicu* want his horses."

"Do you miss the Rez?"

Ritta thought for a moment. "There's a hole here," she touched her chest,

166

"where my heart should be, but it's back home with my sister and Lawrence. Back in the hills, in *Paha Sapa*." She reached for Jody's hand. "Someday I want you to go home with me. I'll show you what Agnes taught me, the plants that heal and how to call the hawks. We'll ride Lawrence's horses and race the wind."

Jody laughed. "I used to race the wind. That's how I got to Bezerkeley." She looked in Ritta's eyes and said, "Someday. We'll both go home. But right now we'd better get to sleep. I have an early class tomorrow."

Downstairs, Ritta folded out the davenport and made her bed. Jody called out, "Good night," from the other room. Ritta slept with her dog.

Bear didn't come home the next day. Ritta waited for him until she had to get ready for work, hoping it was a good sign. As she and Patch walked the blocks to the restaurant, she passed a newspaper stand. There in bold head-lines were the words, 'Indians Invade Alcatraz: U.S. Plans Counterattack.' They had reached the island last night! She dropped a coin into the newsboy's hand and read the paper as she walked.

She stopped and shouted, "Yes!" when she read that fourteen Indians hid on the island, successfully avoiding the authorities. This would make Jody proud of them, especially since three of the invading force were women.

The evening news reported the Indians peacefully left the island after promises of negotiations.

"Big fucking deal," Jody said. "More of the white man's promises. What do you want to bet nothing comes out of it?"

As the days passed, Ritta had to admit Jody was right. The Board of Supervisors for the City rejected the plan to turn Alcatraz into a space muse-um, but nothing was said about the Indians' offer. The issue died in the media as the horrifying pictures of the massacre at My Lai shocked a war-hardened public.

The rift between Jody and Ritta grew a little wider everyday as the week passed. Jody needed to study hard and Ritta was growing bored with the slow pace of her GED classes. Most days, she and Patch hitchhiked into the City to hang around the Haight.

Bear became more despondent. He skipped most of his classes and often didn't come home. When he did, he carefully avoided Jody. One afternoon he hinted to Ritta that something big was going to happen.

He looked at her hard. "We got to do something, Ritta. The island belongs to us. It's ours by treaty. The world is watching and now is the time for us to take it back. Our women and children deserve to live on our land, safely."

Ritta gulped. *He knows what happened to me.* "What are you going to do?"

"You just watch the news. We're really going to take it this time." He grabbed the canvas duffel bag he had come home to pack and slung it over his shoulder.

"Wait. I'll be right back." Ritta ran into the apartment and returned with the strand of tobacco ties from her backpack. She knotted the string around the strap of his duffel bag. At the door he kissed her lightly on the lips.

Ritta looked beyond the dented van and the long row of houses. "Thanks."

"For the kiss?"

"No." She slugged his arm. "For not letting me know you knew what happened back home."

"But now you do."

"That's all right. Someday, I'll tell you about Agnes."

"I'd like that." His grin filled his face.

"She'd be proud of you, Bear. I am, too."

Bear folded his arms around her and held her until she could hear nothing but the beat of his heart. Then he let her go and quickly walked towards his van. Before he opened the door he pointed to the rear bumper. "Like my new sticker?"

Ritta ran out to the street to read it. "Custer Died For Your Sins." She laughed, then threw back her head and made the *waiaglata*.

Later that night, Jody led Bear into the alcove where Ritta was pushing a tray of glasses into the machine to be sterilized. It startled her to see them standing in the doorway to the steamy room. "Hi, Bear. What are you doing here?" She wiped the perspiration from her forehead with a dishtowel.

Ritta knew Jody wasn't about to leave, even though Bear glared at her. She just stood there looking smug, like she so often did. He turned to Ritta. "We are gathering to take the island tonight. I'm looking for as many people as we can get together. Join us."

"I can't leave work, Bear."

"We won't be going until late. We're suppose to meet on the wharf at some bar. I could pick you up after work."

Jody folded her arms and leaned on the door jamb.

"How long would we be gone?" Ritta asked him.

Bear shook his head. "This is it, damn it. This is the big one we've been waiting for. I don't know how long, maybe we'll just stay until the government pigs kick us off."

"Bear, I have my GED class tomorrow. And what about work? I can't just leave."

Jody smiled.

Ritta wanted to go, more than anything, and was angry at herself for not having the guts to walk out the back door with him. He left without her, stopping to rub Patch on his head. Ritta heard him tell the dog, "We'll show 'em. They'll be sorry they weren't there."

The morning paper's headlines filled the front page, 'Third Time's a Charm for Indians of All Tribes.' Ritta closed her eyes and felt the salty air on her cheeks, heard the seagulls cry above her. She wanted to feel the island beneath her feet, but could only imagine how it would be to stand on the Rock and look over the bay to the City. Her heart was with Bear and the others.

All day she felt she was in a fog as thick as the "Bay Blanket." She wanted so badly to be on the Rock with them, yet her haunting fear was that the government would do something awful to punish Bear and the others for making a stand, doing what they believed in. She carried the newspaper with her all day, as if holding it would somehow keep her in touch with them.

Jody brought more papers home that afternoon. She and Ritta pored over them before they got ready for work, clipping out the articles and pictures. They raced home after their shift to watch the news. The reporter touched lightly on the occupation, giving a good history of the previous attempts. Jody turned off the TV. "I'll be damned. The press is actually being supportive. Somebody has friends in high places."

As the week went by, they started to collect the underground newspapers too, which were more fun to read. Ritta bought an old photo album at a second hand store and they pasted those articles next to the mainstream press reports, laughing at the discrepancies. The most informative and hopeful were the burgeoning Indian newspapers, *The Renegade*, *Warpath*, and *Akwesasne Notes*. Late night news showed the Coast Guard trying to enforce a blockade around the island, to the musical accompaniment of Cavalry bugle calls.

One night, as Ritta put more clippings in the album, Jody thumbed through *Good Times*, her favorite hippie newspaper. "Listen to this, Ritta. 'The Indian, first father of this land, has returned to claim the soil. He has made his first appearance on Alcatraz Island. He has chosen a spot that the United States government really doesn't want.'" Jody threw the paper down on the table. "Shit, you'd think that all Indians were male."

"Well, it's better than calling us 'Injuns'." Ritta held up a UPI headline: 'Paleface makum war—Injuns holding firm to claim on Alcatraz.' She put two fingers behind her head and hopped around on one foot then the other, patting her mouth to make a woo-woo sound. Patch looked up from his nap in the corner as Jody started to beat the kitchen counter in a trite BOOM, boom, boom, boom, BOOM boom, boom, boom.

Ritta covered her mouth and made the *waiaglata*. The trill echoed off the walls until it filled the small room.

"How do you do that?" Jody asked.

"Just make a high sound and let the back of your tongue go like this." She opened her mouth and showed Jody, but when Jody tried it they both started laughing so hard they collapsed on the rug.

"You sound like a sick turkey."

"Okay, okay." Jody sat up on her knees. "Let me try it again." She pulled her cheeks down in a valiant attempt to make a straight face and took a breath. She warbled her tongue against her palate until the laughter overcame her again.

"Much better. Just make it faster, and a little higher. Like this." Ritta made the sound, clear and precise. Jody joined in, adjusting her tone until it came close to Ritta's. Patch stood up, his ears alert. When he hobbled past them, Ritta noticed the burly, smiling man standing in the doorway.

"Bear!" Ritta jumped up and waited for Patch to received a rub on the head before she hugged Bear. He grabbed her and swayed from side to side like the great beast he was named for. Ritta smelled his unwashed body and the hint of salty ocean as the coarseness of his wool shirt rubbed her cheek. "Are you okay?"

Bear nodded, then kissed her head.

Jody stood alone in the middle of the living room. "How's it going, Bear?"

"Great." He let Ritta loose, draping a heavy arm over her shoulder. "I came to pick you girls up. Tomorrow's Thanksgiving and we are having a feast on our land."

Ritta put an arm around his back. A tremor of excitement shivered through her.

"You mean on the island?" Jody asked.

"Yeah. There's lots of folks already there. I got sent ashore for more supplies. This rich dude is taking me back in the morning on his yacht. I asked him to save room for two more."

Jody stared at Bear. Ritta heard the offer for reconciliation in his words and hoped Jody could, too. He smiled a little. Ritta held her breath in anticipation.

Jody pursed her lips. "Hmm. The restaurant is closed tomorrow. Nobody wants to eat curry on Thanksgiving. Even in Berkeley."

"You'll go?" Ritta asked.

"Yeah, sure." Jody grinned. "Why not?"

Bear gripped Ritta around her shoulders. "Far out!" He bent down to the dog. "You can come, too, old man. I'll feed you turkey."

"What should we bring?" Jody asked.

"Warm clothes. Some water. We have to be on the dock by nine. If I'm not here by eight, come upstairs and wake me up." He kissed Ritta on the top of her head again. "Oh, and bring that sound you were making."

Thanksgiving

Ritta dozed in the backseat of Bear's van until the tires began to hum on the long metal span that crossed the bay. "Hey, Patch. You ready to get on a boat?"

His tongue washed across her face. She wiped it on her sleeve. "What's it like, Bear?"

"What, the Rock?"

"Yeah. What's it like?"

"Cold and windy. And kind of spooky. You can feel sorrow in the place even though we've smudged most of the buildings. But I think the island is glad for our company."

Jody turned in her seat to face him. "What do you mean?"

"I don't know. It's just a feeling. Like when you're in the cellblock and people are drumming you can feel it all over the place. Like a heartbeat."

Jody's brows crossed her forehead. "What are you doing in the cellblock?"

"Sleeping. I had to tie the door open before I could fall asleep the first night. But it's all right."

Ritta leaned on the engine casing between the front seats. "How many people are there?"

"A lot. Maybe seventy or so. People come and go now the blockade is over. My friends in the yacht ran it three times in the past two weeks. Lots of boats did."

"But how do you all eat? What do you do all day long?" Jody asked.

Bear smiled. "We get enough food. Like all that stuff behind you there. People give us donations and money. I tell you, Jody, this is really something. Wait till you see."

"But what do you do?"

"We work. It takes a lot to just live there, hauling water from the barge and feeding all the people that come. It's not a party, if that's what you mean. There's no alcohol or drugs."

Jody laughed. "You can't tell me you guys have been out on the island for three weeks with no booze."

"I am. I haven't had one beer since I got there. Some people bring hard stuff in their water jugs, but if we catch them with it we pour it out. It won't work if we're drunk. Some white people unloaded a few cases of beer with the food and Richard told them to take it right back to the mainland. No booze. No dope." He looked at Jody suspiciously, "You didn't bring any weed, did you?"

"Who, me? You know I can't do that shit." Jody turned to Ritta when Bear wasn't looking and winked. Ritta shook her head.

They parked on Fisherman's Wharf, amid the large, bustling crowd, mostly Indians, some dressed in their finest. Excited children swarmed around adults huddled in striped blankets or heavy coats waiting for someone to take them across the Bay. Ritta noticed a flock of pelicans landing on an empty rowboat tied at the far end of the dock. She took it as a good sign.

A blond man greeted Bear and graciously shook Jody and Ritta's hands. Bear introduced him as, "Jim Cain, my pirate friend."

The young man bowed. "My craft awaits you." His arm swept towards a sleek, white boat tied at the dock. Several people appeared on the deck. Jim called to them, "Come on, everybody. Let's get this tub loaded up." Bear opened the back doors to the van.

Ritta nudged Jody's arm. "Look who's here." She pointed discreetly at a skinny woman in high, lace-up boots, several sheer scarves around her neck.

"The chick from the head shop. Oh, my God." Jody snickered.

As everyone else formed a line to pass the cargo from the van to the boat, the woman walked over to Patch. "A doggy! I just love animals." She petted Patch neatly on his head until the cargo was loaded, then walked over to Ritta and Jody.

Ritta thought for a moment that the woman floated, the way her scarves and hair streamed in the wind. Her dilated pupils peered over her dark, round glasses, and she stuck out her hand. "I'm Abbey. You two must be Indians."

Jody snorted, turned her back, and walked towards the front of the van. Ritta shook the outstretched frail, white hand. "I'm Ritta. You work in the place that sells posters, with the strange lights."

"You've been to my shop? Groovy. I think this is so far out, what your people are doing. Like, power to the people, man. Where's Jim?" The woman drifted off.

Jody handed Ritta the pack, then circled her index finger next to her ear. Ritta laughed, knowing Jody was right—Abbey was a little odd.

Out on the bay, salt spray stung Ritta's face as she gripped the chrome railing of the bow. Patch struggled to keep standing on his three legs between her and Jody. When he stumbled, Ritta sat down and put her arm around him and leaned back against the cockpit.

Jody looked down at her. "Exhilarating, isn't it?" She turned her face back to the spray.

Halfway to the island, Abbey came out to the bow and slid down the wall beside Ritta, her face a pale shade of gray beneath the yellow, frizzy hair.

"Are you all right, Abbey?"

"I don't feel so good. Jim sent me out to see if the fresh air would help. I get sick every time we go out on this damn boat." She closed her eyes and leaned her head back. The sunshine did little to improve her color. When the vessel rode the next large swell, Abbey pitched to the edge of the boat, leaned her head under the railing and heaved her breakfast into the ocean. Afraid she was going overboard, Ritta grabbed her by the waist.

Jody looked down at the woman and muttered, "Jesus Christ!" before she walked away.

Patch nervously tried to stand. Ritta told him, "Sit. Stay. Good dog." She reached around Abbey's face and gathered up the yellow strands of hair to keep it out of the next wave of vomit. After Abbey spit the last of it out to sea and sat up, Ritta handed her a handkerchief to wipe off her face.

"Thanks," Abbey said weakly, handing back the cloth.

"Keep it."

A few bouts of dry heaves later, the boat docked on the island. Ritta and Patch stood with the others on deck, impatiently waiting their turn. She remembered seeing the large, two-story building before, but not the huge sign mounted on the outside wall. "*United States Penitentiary-only government boats permitted-others must keep off two-hundred yards.*"

Large red letters scrawled around the sign declared, "*Indians welcome—Indian Land.*" Ritta smiled and knelt down to rub Patch on his chest, where he liked it the most.

Jody squeezed through the crowd and stood next to them. "Your friend really lost her cookies."

"She just got sick because of the ocean."

"She still looks puny." Jody nodded towards a bench on the dock where Abbey sat holding her head with her elbows resting on her knees. Jim stood over her, watching the passengers file off his boat.

Bear whistled and motioned for them to join the line forming to unload the cargo. They hoisted cases of canned food and toilet paper, blankets, and coolers onto the dock. When the last box was unloaded, Bear turned to Ritta and Jody. "Come on. Let me show you our island."

He led them up a steep, wide concrete path, past a large arched doorway through a tunnel of once-white bricks, turned mossy green by a century of dank air. Bear stopped at one of the narrow windows in the old guardhouse, pretending to fire at imaginary enemies approaching the dock. The window Ritta looked out framed a large, graceful sailboat.

A group of traditional dancers gathered outside, chanting songs in the sunshine. Bells on one man's knee-high moccasins caught Ritta's attention. When she noticed the dancer looking back at her, his smile bright and disarming, she quickly turned away. He stroked Patch's head before the dog followed Ritta up the lane past a cluster of buildings and overgrown gardens.

It felt like a small village; the mission-style chapel, officer's club and dilapidated barracks, separated from the sea by a tall, chain link fence topped with broken barb-wire that hung in wicked, rusting coils. The few strands still taut hummed a tuneless refrain with every gust of wind. Seagulls circled low overhead, squalling.

Behind them, a great cheer sounded from the dock. Bear turned around. "Must be the turkey dinner some restaurant is bringing us. Yeah, see? Bratskellers, there on the boxes."

"You mean us? All of us?" Jody asked.

"You eat, too. Don't you?" Bear teased, then headed back up the road.

"But why would a fancy restaurant cook us dinner?"

"Hey, we've been on the news all over the world. We're famous, *innet*."

Ritta looked at Jody who grinned back at her as they followed Bear up the steep lane. Around the bend, an old green pickup truck headed slowly towards them. It came to a stop beside Bear.

The driver extended his right arm out the window. "*Hau, Mato.*"

Bear clasped the driver's outstretched hand. "Good to see you, Moses. Thought you'd be on the road by now."

The man's braids draped over the chest pockets of his denim jacket. His dark eyes met Ritta's and didn't turn away as he answered Bear. "Haven't gone yet. My ride has a job on the tree crew for a few more days. We're leaving next week. *Ina* waits for me."

Ritta looked down and felt her face get warm. She knew the young man was Lakota and thought he was very good looking. Bear stepped aside and introduced them. "My friends, Ritta and Jody."

Ritta glanced up. "*Hau.*" She liked his teeth, they were nice and even.

Moses leaned out the window a little closer to her. "*Niye Lakota iya hwo?*"

His words felt good and she was glad she could reply that she knew a little Lakota. "*Han, cikala Lakota wowaglaka.*"

Moses asked, "*Nituktetanhan hwo.*"

Ritta had to think for a moment, the meaning of his words drifting slowly through her mind. "I live in Berkeley now. You?"

Moses nodded approvingly. "My family lives near Timber Lake. On the Cheyenne. Know where it is?"

"*Han.* My brothers played basketball there once."

"Me, too. What's their names?"

"Henry and Jake Baker."

"Nope. Don't know them." He looked at her for what seemed a long

174

time. She couldn't think of anything more to say and shrugged.

Finally Moses said, "Hey, did you hear about the survey? They polled all the Indians and only fifteen percent thought the U.S. should get out of 'Nam. The other eighty-five percent thought the U.S. should get out of America."

Everyone laughed. Bear punched Moses on the shoulder. "Good one. Where you headed?"

"Down to the dock. Where else? It's an island, *innet*? I got to get another load. Some fancy restaurant is bringing us dinner."

"It's here. They're unloading it right now." Bear motioned to the dock.

"Catch you later." As Moses let the old truck coast he stuck his head out the window and waved at Ritta. "We talk more, *han*?"

"*Waste*," she replied and waved as he drove off.

"What does that mean?" Jody asked.

"Good. *Waste* to hear Lakota again. My ears like it, but my tongue can't say very much."

"Didn't you grow up speaking it?"

"Oh, no. My mother doesn't know the old words. But Agnes and Lawrence spoke it all the time to each other. I just picked some of it up."

Jody put her arm around Ritta's shoulder. "There you go, getting home-sick again. Let's go look at the cell blocks."

Ritta laughed. "That should be fun."

"Yeah, come on. I'll show you mine." Bear took their hands and pulled them up the hill.

The imposing three-story high concrete block prison sat perched on top of the island like an abandoned castle. Rusty iron bars covered huge rows of windows dotted with broken panes. It was the largest building Ritta had ever seen. Above the front door a plaster eagle perched on a shield of red stripes and blue stars, surrounded by cornucopias spilling brightly colored fruit. Someone had painted 'free' in the stripes. Inside, Bear pointed up to a proud red fist painted over an archway. Then he showed them a small room. "There's the Warden's office and here's the bunker where they kept all the ammo. We use it for storage." He led them past a glassed-in room marked 'Control Center', with panels of instruments and hundreds of hooks for keys.

Bear ducked into the next doorway. "This is the visitor's room. How would you like to talk to your sweetie through those?" Old, broken telephones hung beside four small, extra thick windows, green prison cells on the other side distorted through the glass. A stack of more supplies lined the other wall.

Jody picked up one of the receivers and said in a high soprano, "Oh, Al. The children and I miss you so much."

Bear picked up another phone. "Don't worry, darlin'. Me and the boys are fixin' to bust out of this joint." Then he held the receiver like a machine gun. "Rat-t-t-t-t-t-t-t-t-t. No one escapes the Rock."

"Let's hope not, or we're all in trouble," Jody said as they walked into the main block.

Rows of cells, even the bars painted sickly green, stood three tiers high. Down the hallways voices echoed. Footsteps pounded the long corridors, up metal stairs, through the caged catwalks that lined the outside walls. In the distance, a cell door squeaked and clanged shut. A child began to cry.

"This way." Bear led them down an aisle flanked on one side by massive windows, opaque with years of dirt. The colors of the water and the city across the bay appeared mosaic through the broken panes. Ritta stuck her fist through the bars over the windows to clean a small peephole in the grime on one of the lower corners. The sight made her sad for the prisoners who had looked out at such beautiful freedom from the cages behind her.

The weak winter sunlight created a shadowy grid on the floor's concrete squares, barred windows on one side and barred doors on the other. Ritta fought the panic tight in her throat from being surrounded by so much cold steel and concrete.

Bear led them between the library's empty shelves and into 'D' block, pointing out the six double-doored isolation cells before leading them up the metal circular stairs to the top tier. There he entered cell thirty-four, indistinguishable from the others until Ritta noticed the leather belt, cinched around the bars of the open door and the bars of the wall behind it.

The cell stank of mildew. A dark red, wool blanket covered the cot lining one wall. At the back was a small, rust-stained sink, a concrete toilet base covered with a scrap of warped plywood, and a small shelf in the corner.

Ritta sat with Patch on the thin lumpy mattress. She held the dog close and stroked his fur as she looked around the close walls, painted green halfway up and splotched where paint peeled in different colored layers. Taped to one blistering wall was a poster—the red fist that had always covered Bear's window at home. Funny, she hadn't noticed it missing. "When did you take the poster, Bear?"

"One night when I went home. You girls were at work. It was during the blockade so I had to come back the same night."

Jody picked up an eight-by-ten photograph from the small shelf. She looked at it for a moment, then smiled. "I remember this day. When we went into the City for the peace march. Who took it?"

Ritta reached for the photo. It captured the three of them amid a sea of other protesters. Bear was in the center with Jody and Ritta on either side, their right fists raised in the air, the same determined expression on their faces.

"A lady was here, a photographer from Germany. She recognized me from this picture she had taken that day. Next time she came out, she gave me that."

Jody took the photo and replaced it on the shelf. "Why this cell, Bear?"

He pointed out the window. "Look."

Through the broken panes directly across from the cell were the ochre arches of the Golden Gate Bridge.

"Remember the night we stood below the bridge and looked at Alcatraz? Now I sit and look there, remembering how hard we worked to get here. And I think of you two." Bear suddenly looked embarrassed. "Let's go see what's going on."

They walked arm in arm down the corridors, Bear in the middle. When they entered the exercise yard full of people, many heads turned to look at them.

Bear beamed. "Welcome to the biggest coup since Custer."

He let go with a fierce whoop. Other men joined in until the sound echoed off the high walls surrounding the exercise yard. Someone started beating a drum. After kissing both his companions on the top of their heads, Bear turned to leave. They didn't have to ask where he was going.

Ritta and Jody walked down the concrete steps that formed the foundation of the huge building, each nearly as wide as a sidewalk and two feet above the next, gravitating to the tables piled with food at the bottom. After snatching a few carrot and celery sticks from a platter, they asked a woman what they could do to help. She pointed silently to several white people in tall chef's hats, carving turkeys and setting out square pans of prepared food.

Jody asked the tallest one, "Need any help?"

"No, I think we got it," he replied with a smile.

"Thank you, this is great," Ritta told the man, but his attention was already somewhere else. Ritta snitched a piece of skin from a turkey carcass and slipped it to the waiting dog.

Jody took Ritta's hand and together they hopped-skipped across the cracked concrete of the exercise yard under a light blue sky. The wall around them rebuffed some of the ocean breeze. The wind picked up the drum beat and carried it away to the far reaches of the island and beyond.

Ritta stood for a minute with her eyes closed, feeling the gruesome place shed some of its sorrow in the beating of the drum. Jody bumped her arm gently and she was surprised when she opened her eyes that they were wet with tears. The wind blew them away, too. Jody handed her a pipe, a sacred pipe, smoke curling from its bowl in a momentary respite of calm air. Ritta felt the warmth of the wood, burnished with decades of careful handling. She offered the smoke to the sky, then to the earth and the four directions before she took the mouthpiece between her lips and drew in the blessed smoke. She remembered Lawrence's words about the pipe, how it bridges the physical world and spiritual world, binding us to our relatives. She sent her thoughts to Agnes when she exhaled. As she handed the pipe to an elder by her side she mumbled the words Agnes had taught her, *Mitakuye Oyasin*. We are all related. The man nodded in approval. It made her feel good to be praying openly, on Indian land.

They stood in the circle of people moving to the beat of the drum and watched as the pipe was passed to all who wished to partake. Many people began to dance. Ritta watched the man with the bells on his moccasins who had smiled at her earlier whirl to the drumbeat. He was a good dancer.

After the song, Bear walked by with his fellow drummers. "Ritta, Jody, come on, grub's ready." Ritta told Patch to stay, then joined the others in the line for dinner.

A touch on her arm made her turn to see Minnie, escorted by a proud-looking youngster to the front of the line. Minnie waved and called to her, "I have something for you, dear. Don't leave until I catch up with you."

Ritta marveled at the array of food displayed on the tables. Beside the turkey and trimmings were potluck dishes, mounds of fry bread and lots of pies. She heaped her plate high, knowing it was more than she could possibly eat.

She followed Jody, Bear, and his friends to one of the lower wide steps. She and Jody sat, leaning against each other's backs, and ate. Moses soon joined them. He stood on the step above Ritta. "Can I sit here?"

She liked the way he smiled at her. "Sure." She ignored Jody's elbow in her ribs. When she had eaten about half of the food heaped on her plate she got up the nerve to ask, "How long you been on the island, Moses?"

"Off and on since the beginning. I was supposed to go back home before now, my mother is not well. But I got another job offer, trimmin' trees. Then I heard that Richard was looking for Indians to take the island. I couldn't pass that up." He stopped grinning at Ritta long enough to eat some turkey. "How did you girls get here?" he asked with his mouth full.

"I'm staying with Jody in her apartment. Bear lives upstairs. We were on the boat when we first tried to take the island."

"You mean the day Bear decided to go swimming?" Moses spoke loud enough for Bear to hear.

"Hey, man, I'm from an inland tribe."

Ritta asked, "Were you on the first boat?"

"No. I didn't get word until later. I got here that night though, when we hid overnight. That was a gas, sneaking around this place, following the feds and reporters like ghosts. It would take more than an army to find us."

Jody turned to Moses. "You were damn lucky they didn't send the Army. Where would you have hidden then?"

Bear laughed. "The island took them in. Swallowed them until they wanted to step out."

"Where did you hide?" Ritta asked.

Moses put his plate down on the ground, placed Ritta's food beside it and took her by the hand. "Come on. I'll show you."

He pulled her up, leaving an unsuspecting Jody tipping backwards. "Hey, where are you going?" Jody yelled, trying to stand up.

Bear put his hand on Jody's shoulder. "Let her go."

Patch followed Ritta. Halfway across the compound he looked behind him to see if Jody was coming. Bear still held her back.

Moses opened the heavy iron gate in the high wall that surrounded them. He reminded Ritta so much of home, like he could of been one of Henry's friends.

Moses asked, "How did you get to San Francisco?"

"On a bus."

"I walked into that one. Okay. Grayhound?"

"Church of the Reverent Brethren."

"*Wan?*"

Ritta laughed. "It's a long story." She let the railing slide under her hands as she went down the steep incline of cement stairs through the encroaching vegetation. Huge, glossy leaves brushed against her legs.

Moses followed close behind. "I listen good. *Mis anoghopton waste.*"

"I bet you do. Have you ever seen leaves this big?" She pulled one off and waved it like a flag, sprinkling drops of water over her and the dog that hopped down the narrow stairs in front of her.

Moses shook his head. "Nothing back home grows like this."

Ritta stopped and looked out over the bay and the silver city beyond. Sunlight glistened off the water. Sailboats swooped and turned in imitation of the sea gulls above them. "Nothing here is like back home."

"Do you miss it, Ritta?"

At the bottom of the stairs she propped the giant leaf on the outside wall of a small building. "Don't you?"

"There's no jobs there, nothing to do. Had no job here, though, until I started tree trimming with Scott. But I miss my folks. And the prairie."

"*Han.* Sometimes I miss the prairie so much I hitchhike to Seal Rock to see the ocean. Does that make sense?"

Mosses nodded. "Sure. It's the open space. The waves roll like grass in the wind." He looked out over the bay. "You could go back with us. Scott wouldn't mind another passenger. He's got a van. Lots of room."

Ritta walked into the small three-sided alcove that opened to the stairs. She looked into a closed-off room through a window and sadly shook her head. "I can't go back. Not now. Maybe never."

"Why?"

Ritta leaned against the concrete wall. "Don't ask."

Moses reclined his back on the wall next to her and pulled his braids forward. He was about her size, strongly built but lean. She felt the hard muscles of his arm through her shirt. He looked into her eyes, then she felt him look at the scar on her cheek, before she turned away.

After a moment he said, "Nice to be out of the wind. Hard to believe it's winter, though. I'd trade this weather any day for snow and brr-fucking cold, wouldn't you?"

"Brr-fucking cold?"

"You know, when you walk out the door in the morning and it hits you so hard all you can say is, 'Brr. Fucking cold.'"

Ritta threw back her head and laughed. "I know what that's like. My sister and I called those 'Days of the False Sun', 'cause the sun is so bright but it's not warm. Could be that cold at home now. I heard it's an early winter."

"Probably is. I got to go home though. *Ina* has the consumption. It's real bad now. She wants to see me."

"I'm sorry."

"Me, too. I will miss her."

Ritta thought of Agnes. What I wouldn't give to see her again, to see Lawrence. Lawrence! She pushed herself off the wall. "Moses. Would you do me a huge favor when you get back to the Rez?"

"Probably." He grinned.

"Could you take a letter to a friend?"

"As in hand-deliver?"

She nodded.

"I could do that."

"Thanks. Now show me where else you hid."

He snickered. "Bear was right when he said the island has bowels. It's a spooky place. I don't want to scare you."

"Patch will protect me. Won't you, dog?"

A wagging tail was all the answer she needed.

"Where did you get him?"

"A friend gave him to me."

"Okay, okay. I'll quit asking questions."

"*Waste.*"

Isolated in the Bay, without fresh water or edible plants, Alcatraz had been used for punishment since the earliest missionaries imprisoned recalcitrant Indians on its shore. With nothing to eat, except the eggs of birds during nesting season, the unfortunate souls soon amended their ways to the Christian lifestyle forced upon them. Or died on the rocky island.

Military prisoners built the fort, beginning in 1853. The cannon casemates and the sally port, moat and drawbridge, the dungeon deep beneath the cell block remain; remnants of an outpost that was never attacked.

By 1912, the largest reinforced concrete building in the world housed the Army's convicts on the island, surrounded by the buildings necessary to maintain the post; barracks, chapel, P.X.—built in charming mission style and beautifully landscaped with soil hauled from nearby Angel Island.

During the Great Depression, the prison was transferred to the Federal government. The most feared and incorrigible convicts in the country were caged in its five-by-nine cells. Those who broke the rules lived on 'D' block, some locked in total darkness for months at a time. Escaping the island for the ravages of the sea was not often attempted.

The spirits of those men held captive whispered to Ritta as she followed Moses through the cellblock. She shuddered. Patch touched his nose to her hand. She stroked his ears. He whined when they reached the chest-high cement wall built around three sides of a rectangular hole in the floor. Ritta leaned over to look. From the opening in the short wall a stairwell descended into darkness.

Moses started down. Halfway, he paused and lit his Zippo lighter. "Coming?"

By the light of the flame she saw red splotches on the peeling concrete of the entryway. Cold, musty air wafted up from beyond the wooden door that hung open at the very bottom. The flame flickered. Her foot touched the first worn step. Incredible sadness seemed to surround her. It crept up the stairs like an unseen fog, swirling with grief and madness.

She stopped. "No."

"What's the matter? Afraid of a few ghosts?"

"*Han.*" Ritta turned her head towards Patch standing a few feet away. "See. Even the dog has the good sense not to bother this place. Let's go."

"I wouldn't let anything happen to you." He took a cigarette from his shirt pocket and lit it with the flame.

"What makes you think you can protect me from something you don't understand?" She started back and kept on going, following the sound of the drum until she recognized the door that led outside.

In the exercise yard the weak sunlight felt good. Smoke of burning sweet-grass traveled on the breeze. She saw Jody wave at her from a group standing next to the drum circle. She and Patch maneuvered down the treacherously steep steps. There's stairs everywhere on this island, stairs and concrete. She crossed the compound to join Jody.

"Where's your friend."

"Talking to ghosts."

"What?"

"Never mind." Ritta looked up and saw Moses at the top of the stairs. He walked in the other direction.

Later, she danced in the circle next to Minnie. Ritta looked again at the new beaded moccasins on her feet, a present from her companion. She squeezed the older woman's arm. "They're beautiful, Minnie. *Pilamayaya.*"

Moses fell into step beside them. "*Hau.* Seen any more ghosts?"

Ritta ignored him.

"I'm sorry." He silently danced with them halfway around, as if trying to find the right words.

Ritta, her arm linked with Minnie's as they did the toe-step toe-step to the drumbeat, was searching for something to say, too. She looked down at his small, neat cowboy boots matching her rhythm on the blacktop.

"See my new—"

"If you want—" They both spoke at the same time, then laughed.

"Go ahead," he told her.

She blushed. Minnie danced at her side, politely oblivious to their conversation. Ritta pointed to her feet. "Like my new moccasins? Minnie made them for me."

Moses looked at the beaded design, a cross pointing in the four directions of the wind, and seemed impressed. "They are very beautiful. You are fortunate to have such talented friends."

Minnie graciously bowed her head.

After dancing another full circle in silence, Moses cleared his throat. "I might be leaving next week. If you like, I could stop by your place this weekend, for that letter. If you still want me to do that for you."

"I do. What day?"

"Saturday?"

"I have to work."

"Let me pick you up afterwards. We can go to a late movie or do something else."

Minnie squeezed her arm. When Ritta looked at her, Minnie gave a sly, discreet nod and wink. It was all the encouragement she needed. "Okay," Ritta replied, then wondered immediately how she was going to tell Jody.

"Okay. Great. See you then." Moses grinned and started to dance away from her.

"Wait. Don't you want to know where I work?"

"I do. India House. Bear told me." Moses started to dance backwards.

"Did he tell you what time I get off?"

"*Han.* Ten."

Ritta laughed as the people behind Moses scattered to get out of his way. "Well, he's wrong. The restaurant closes at ten. I have to stay until ten-thirty or eleven."

"I'll wait." Moses turned around just in time to avoid colliding with an elder in a feather headdress who chanted with his eyes closed.

She wrote, *Dear Lawrence,* then chomped on the pencil. *If you get this letter you will already know I am all right. I am in Berkeley, California and I'm staying with Amos' daughter, Jody. You would like her. I do.* She remembered the fight they had last night and erased the *I do.* Damn, she thought, putting another round of teeth marks on the yellow wood. She has no right telling me what to do. I don't need a mother.

I am working at the Indian restaurant where Jody works but it's not our kind of Indian. The boss is real nice, though. I do the dishes. Two nights a week I go to this class that teaches me high school stuff. Some day I want to go to college.

A bunch of our people here took over this island called Alcatraz where there used to be a prison. We had Thanksgiving on Indian land, right in the middle of the bay. Can you dig it? (That's the way they talk here.) Today in the newspaper this Senator here said that he hopes there aren't a rash of these occupations because if you came down to it somebody is likely to claim the whole United States. Maybe we can get back Paha Sapa, too. Wouldn't it be something, to just claim the Black Hills and take it back?

I miss you and Janey so much. I miss the prairie, too. The ocean is a lot like the prairie, but it's water. Do you know what I mean? It's usually wet and gray here. But it's a lot warmer than back home.

There are lots of good people here from many tribes. My friend Minnie made me a pair of moccasins with beautiful beadwork. Most of the people here did the government's Relocation program like Uncle Benny. But there aren't many jobs for Indians here. I'm real lucky to have my dishwashing job. No wonder Uncle Benny came back to the Rez.

I have a dog now. His name is Patch and he's my best friend. He only has three legs but he gets around real good. Sometimes we go into the city, San Francisco, and visit the ocean. I like the ocean a lot.

I know in my heart that Agnes is dead. How can that be? I hope that you and High Tail are fine. I miss you very much. Ritta

She reread the letter then remembered she wanted to ask him something else.

I lost the round stone you gave me. Does this mean I can't come home again?

Usually Saturday nights went by quickly, but this one dragged on. The pile of dishes seemed endless as she scraped plates with her pink platex gloves and dropped them into the sink of scalding soapy water. God, I don't want to do this forever. She shoved a plastic-coated rack full of glasses into the stainless steel machine. A great billow of steam escaped when another rack rolled out the front through strips of rubber-coated canvas. She swung an empty one up to the counter from underneath to fill it before unloading the already dry dishes from the front onto the waiting cart.

Rosie came in for clean plates, wiping the sweat from her brow with an embroidered handkerchief she kept tucked into her bosom. "Take a break now? I cook you some chicken."

"No thanks, Rosie. I want to finish early tonight." Ritta looked up in time to see Jody scowling at her from the pick-up counter, within hearing range. What is her trip, man? Ritta shoved the waiting loaded rack into the machine. Who does she think she is? A tear rolled down Ritta's cheek. She raised her arm to wipe it away on her damp t-shirt.

When the last load was finally through and the little room hosed down, she peeled off the gloves, washed her hands and splashed some water on her face. Rosie came to the doorway. "A man is here for you, Ritta. Says he wait outside."

Ritta reached for a clean dish towel. "Thanks, Rosie. Where's Jody?"

"She go home without you."

Ritta ran a hand over her braids, combing the ends with her fingertips. She took the letterman's jacket down from the hook by the back door, checked the pocket to make sure her letter was still there, and threw it over her shoulder. As she opened the back door, Rosie called out after her, "You be careful, Ritta. Remember, you a nice girl."

Ritta slammed the door. What bullshit did Jody tell her, anyway?

"Hey, Ritta!"

She turned to see a large, blue pick-up parked at the edge of the alley. White-lettered advertising on the door proclaimed 'Hoodson's Landscape and Tree Surgery'. The door swung open, inside the cab was dark. Walking down the alley, she wished she hadn't left Patch home.

When she grabbed the edge around the door and swung herself onto the seat she could tell Moses had been drinking. The whole truck reeked with it. He smiled. "Wanna beer?"

"Okay."

He handed her a Hamms before starting the engine. She popped the ring, pulled it open and put the flip top into the can.

"Shouldn't do that. This dude in 'Nam got one caught in his throat that way."

"Shouldn't guzzle your beer. Besides, they're nasty things for the animals. Patch has cut his paws many times on them, down at the beach."

"Should have seen what it did to this poor fucker. They gave him a Purple Heart for it." He took the beer from between his legs and finished it. As he turned the corner, he tossed the can out the window and into the back of the truck.

Ritta laughed. "You've had practice."

"I've missed a few times."

The beer seemed to go to her head soon after it hit her stomach. She regretted not eating dinner. "Where are we going?"

"I thought maybe we could go downtown and see a movie or drive to the beach. What do you want to do?"

"I'm hungry. But I always love to see the ocean." She finished the beer and tossed it, without looking, into the bed.

"How late can I keep you out?" He had a twinkle in his eye.

She sat up straighter in the seat. "I don't have a keeper."

"I can dig it. Then I have a plan." He drove downtown to a little cafe that stayed open all night. After parking in front he hurried to help her out of the truck.

She refused his hand and jumped from the high cab. "Groovin' truck."

"Yeah, belongs to my roommate's boss. Well, he's my boss too, when there's enough work."

"He just lets you use it?"

"Oh, yeah. He won't care. Just as long as Scotty has it back by morning." He held the cafe door open for her.

"You don't have to do that, you know."

"Do what?"

"Treat me like a lady. I'm a liberated woman."

He smiled.

The waitress led them to a booth by the window. "Coffee?" They nodded before looking at the menu. She returned with the pot and turned over two of the cups, filling them with a practiced slosh. They both ordered burgers and fries. Moses took a pack of Marlboros from his jacket pocket. When he offered her one, she took it. Flipping the silver lighter's top back with a snap of his thumb he lit the cigarette in her mouth.

She tried hard not to cough. Back home, she had gotten to where she even wanted a smoke sometimes, when her brothers had some to share. But now her head was spinning and the black coffee did little to make her stomach feel better. She managed to smoke half of it before Moses said he was going to the john. As soon as he left, she crushed the cigarette out in the ashtray.

The waitress brought their food before he returned. Ritta doused ketchup on her fries and on the top of the meat patty. She thought of Dora and her strange food. When Moses sat back down she asked him, "You ever have tofu?"

"Toe—what?"

"Tofu. It's soybean curd. White squeaky stuff."

"What do you do with it?"

"Eat it."

"Guess not. Where did you have that?" He poured a pool of ketchup on his plate.

"On the bus."

"Not the Greyhound."

She laughed. "I got a ride with these hippies when I left the Rez. They were great. We became good friends."

"Is that how you got the dog?"

"Yep. River gave him to me."

"River?"

She told him about River and Dora and everyone on the bus. About Gert and her little horses, and how she got to Jody's. The waitress came to take the plates and refilled their coffee cups twice before Ritta was through. When the waitress asked if that would be all, Moses surprised Ritta by ordering pie. "Want a piece?"

"Okay." She looked to the waitress. "Do you have banana cream?"

"Sure do. One banana cream and one apple, coming up."

"Now, tell me about you." Ritta leaned into the corner of the booth and put her feet up on the seat. It began to rain outside. Droplets slid down the glass behind her.

"Not much to tell. My folks have grazing units on the Rez. We ran a hundred head of rehab cattle on it till my old man pissed off the committee. They started taking our cattle and not paying us. I got real mad one night and punched a guy right in his office. It didn't make things any better, that's for damn sure. So Dad decided I better get off the Rez until things cool off."

"And have they?"

"Enough for me to go home to see my *Ina*. I hope."

The waitress put the pie in front of them, took the ticket out of her pocket and tallied the bill. After she put it on the table and walked away, Moses looked at Ritta. "What about your family? I know you got brothers. Any sisters?"

A smile lit up Ritta's face. "Janey. She's eleven. No, she's twelve now."

Moses reached over the table and placed his hands around hers. "How old are you, Ritta?"

"Sixteen." She said it in a whisper, like it was a secret.

Moses gulped. "Why did you leave the Rez? You can tell me."

"They killed Agnes. I saw them."

The tears welled up in her eyes but didn't spill over as she continued. "They raped me. I didn't know what they had done then, but now I know. They're looking for me, so I can't go back."

"Who's 'they', Ritta?"

"Tribal Police."

Moses slammed his fist on the table. Quietly, he asked, "Who's Agnes?"

"My *Unci*. Not my real grandma, but she was teaching me the old ways.

She knew all the plants and the prayers. Now she's gone." Ritta looked up at him, her eyes overflowing. She whispered, "I think I killed one of them. I pushed him out of the truck and he hit his head on a rock. They're still looking for me."

Moses reached over and wiped her tears with his fingertips. "Let's get out of here." She nodded.

He put his arm around her after paying the bill. As they walked out into the rainy night she was glad for the comfort. He drove in silence until they came to the Bay. Rain obscured all but the brightest lights of the City across the water. He pulled a cigarette from his pack and offered one to her. When she nodded, he lit one and handed it to her before lighting his own. She rolled down her window and blew the smoke into the wet night. He reached under the seat and pulled the last two warm beers out by the plastic ring. Without asking, he opened her one.

They sat in silence, watching the blur of lights through the sheets of water running down the windshield. Moses tried to roll down his window to throw the can in the back, but the rain blew in his side so he quickly rolled it up. Ritta laughed, then took the can and expertly tossed it out her open window into the bed with a clatter.

"Damn, you're good."

"Here, finish mine." She handed him the half-full beer. He guzzled it, then handed her back the empty and belched.

"Damn, you're bad," she said as the last can rattled into the back.

"I am. I'm a bad-ass mean muther-fuckin' Red Man." His palm struck the steering-wheel with a thud and made Ritta jump. "Me and the others, it's high time we did something, act like braves instead of sittin' around on our asses."

Ritta didn't know whether to be frightened or proud. He looked at her, sitting wide-eyed with her back next to the door, and apologized.

"Hey, man. That's okay. I'd just hate to be the *wasicu* that got in your way."

"Damn right." He laughed as he started up the truck to take her home. When they pulled up outside the house, Ritta noticed the basement's lights were on. She took the letter from her jacket pocket. "Are you sure you want to deliver this for me?"

"Yeah. Who does it go to?"

"Uncle Lawrence. Here. I'll put the directions to his place on the back of the envelope. It's not too hard to find. It might be snowed in, though."

"That's all right. I'll make sure he gets it. I promise."

She looked up from the map she was drawing. He leaned over and kissed her on the cheek. "I'm going to make it so you can go home, Ritta." His words were starting to slur.

"Promise me you won't tell anyone but Lawrence that you know where I am. Promise." She clutched the envelope to her chest.

"I would never ever do anything to hurt you. Do you trust me?"

"I guess I have to, don't I."

"If you wan' that letter dee-livered."

She handed him the envelope, then opened the door and jumped out. "Bye, Moses. Have a safe trip."

Jody just made it back to the davenport as Ritta walked in the door. She saw Ritta notice the wet footprints on the kitchen floor. Ritta hung her coat up on the hook and stooped to pet Patch, who waited patiently by the sink.

Jody asked, without a trace of sarcasm, "How was your date?"

"It wasn't a date."

"What was it then? Where did you go?"

"We went out to eat, then down to the Bay."

"Sounds like a date to me. Did you make out?" As much as she hated hearing it, her sharp tongue could no longer be disguised.

"No, we didn't."

All her jealousy, her guilt for wanting Ritta so damn bad, boiled inside, churning her gut. "I saw him kiss you, goddamn it."

"What's it to you?" Ritta slammed down her fist on the counter. "You aren't my mother."

Jody stood up and screamed, "I don't want to be your mother! Get out. Just get out!" She ran through the beads into the bedroom and flung herself down on the bed.

Ritta took her pack that was tucked behind the davenport and stuffed her schoolbooks and her new moccasins into the gap on top. She picked up Patch's food bowl and the bag of Dog Chow from the cupboard and told him, "Let's go."

The key to the upstairs was hidden under the dead spider plant on the porch.

In the days that followed, they stepped around each other like two wild animals skirting the other's territory. Ritta claimed Bear's empty bedroom upstairs and the dishwashing alcove at work. She didn't join the others in the booth next to the kitchen door for breaks, and even ate her dinner in the small alcove, sharing whatever she had with Patch. She made him a bed under the sink with an old coat she found in the alley.

One night, when Ritta was asleep with Patch sprawled beside her, Bear came home. Patch barked, as startled as Bear was when he turned on the light. Ritta bolted upright in bed until she saw who it was, then she covered her eyes with her arms and flopped back down on the pillow.

"You and Jody fighting?"

"I don't need her telling me what to do," Ritta mumbled from under her elbow. "Jesus, would you shut off the light."

Bear flipped the switch and sat down on the corner of the bed, nudging the dog over. He pulled off his boots and lay back, his feet still on the floor. "Well, if you stay here be expecting company. We're going to use this place for our base in Berkeley."

"What do you mean, base?"

"For donation drop-offs. A place for people to stay when they come to town for stuff. Things like that."

Ritta sat up and brushed the loose hair from her face. "Can I help? I mean, wouldn't it be better if someone was here most of the time?"

"Yeah. I suppose it would. Sure. Can you pay some rent? I came up with some of it but I lost my grant for being gone so much."

"I get paid Monday. And I ain't giving it to Jody."

"So, what are you two hassling about?"

"She wants to tell me what to do, boss me around. I ain't into it. You got a cigarette?"

"Since when did you start smoking?"

Ritta shrugged. "Off and on."

Ritta sat up and reached for the tin can ashtray beside the bed. Bear fished in his coat pocket for his pack, shook out two and handed one to Ritta. "She's jealous, man."

"Of what? She can do everything better than I can."

Bear laughed. "Not that way. Jealous of Moses. Jealous of me."

Ritta thought about that, remembering the night with the hash, the night Jody didn't want her. She took a long drag and leaned her head on the wall. A minute later, she heard Bear snore. She took the cigarette from between his fingers and tamped it out on the side of the can. After putting hers out, she nudged him, "Bear, get under the covers. I'll sleep on the floor."

"I'll sleep on the floor," Bear mumbled.

"No way, man. It's your bed." She stood up, pulling the t-shirt over her underwear.

"You can stay. I promise I won't bother you."

"Bear, you could never bother me."

Bear chuckled. "Wanna bet? But I won't."

Ritta lay back in the bed, near the edge of the mattress, watching as Bear took off his shirt. His smooth, broad chest glowed in the light from the street lamp. He stretched out on his back beside her, his hands on top of the blanket. She listened to his breathing, matching her own to its rhythm. Finally, she asked timidly, "Bear, would you hold me?"

He snored. A deep rumbling snore, like a freight train traveled inside the cavern of his chest. Ritta remembered hearing it before, through the ceiling. She and Jody use to laugh at the sound of it. She picked up her pillow and pulled the top blanket off.

"Come on, Patch. Let's go sleep on the couch."

* * *

Moses negotiated his dad's pickup out of the barn and pushed against the fierce wind to open the truck's door. When he got out, unfettered arctic gusts propelled him towards the building, then tore the big wooden door out of his hands, slamming it shut.

The road was slick with ice, blown clear of snow in the open and drifted in the places that weren't. Gray sky hooded the mottled prairie, slivers of bronze crop stubble lay bare between ever-changing dunes of snow. He drove slowly, lulled by the circular clatter of the tire chains. Getting there was what mattered, not when.

He'd been home three days, listening to *Ina* cough and hack blood. She refused to return to the sanitarium and his father didn't have the heart to force her back to the nightmare of the 'Sioux San.' Moses had loaded all the coal buckets and stacked them next to the stove before he kissed his mother good-bye and left.

He checked his Levi jacket again for Ritta's letter, folded behind his cigarettes in the pocket. The denim and his worn insulated flannel shirt weren't enough to ward off the frigid air that filled the cab, despite the whining heater. Before plowing through the next deep drift, he stopped and dropped the transmission into 4-low, then searched for the wool blanket his father always kept behind the seat.

Thinking of Ritta warmed him more than the blanket. He remembered how she looked dancing on the Rock, her steps proud in her beaded moccasins. We were all proud on Alcatraz. We did it. And they're still there, without me. "And look where in the fuck I am," he said out loud, staring across the wind-swept prairie dotted with *wasicu* farms.

Crossing the invisible line from state to reservation land, the road once again filled with drifts. He stopped at a small cafe for a bowl of soup and coffee. While he waited, he pulled Ritta's envelope from his pocket and studied the map. When the waitress set the cup down in front of him, he asked her, "How do I get to Highway 41 from here?

"It's down the road. Who you lookin' for?"

"An old man named Lawrence."

"Lawrence? I heard he don't live there no more."

"Do you know where I can find him? It's important."

"You might call Bill Thomas. He's a rancher that runs some cows next to Lawrence's place. Maybe he knows."

Moses tried to look up the number in the phone book, but the tattered remaining pages didn't include the T's. He climbed back in the pickup and headed down the road. The wind had stopped while he ate lunch. The remaining clouds broke up and dissipated before he'd gone a mile. Moses squinted from the sky's brilliant blue, even though the sun was behind him. At the next stop sign, he rummaged through the glove box until he found a scratched pair of sunglasses and bent the frames a little straighter before putting them on. He lit another cigarette and rolled down the window an inch to let the smoke escape, no longer caring about the bitter cold air blowing in the gap as he searched for the road that marked the beginning of Ritta's map.

When he found it, the rest was easy. He admired Ritta's small square printing and lucid directions. The lane was where the map said it should be. Moses turned into the ruts with some difficulty since they had been made by vehicles entering from the other direction. He stopped at the top of the incline, suddenly not so sure he was in the right place. Ritta's carefully drawn stick house had no counterpart in reality. Icy furrows led to a barn then circled around to return up the hill. He continued in the tracks, intending to return to the road until he noticed the smoke from a chimney, cobbled together from gallon tin cans. He stopped the truck in front of the barn. The door slid open.

A thin old man leaned on a cane inside the barn. Moses walked around the front of his truck and tipped his hat. "I'm looking for Lawrence."

"Found him."

"I've a letter for you." Moses looked around the hills before continuing, "From Ritta."

Lawrence nodded and motioned for Moses to follow him into the barn. Moses walked slowly beside him, then indicated the bandaged foot the old man kept pointed in the air, walking on the heel only. "What happened?"

Lawrence led him through a narrow door into the stall separated from the rest of the barn with scraps of lumber. Hay bales insulated the outside walls, stacked around a square window covered with plastic that let in the only light. On the small wood stove a coffee pot perked. Its aroma filled the almost warm room. Lawrence plopped down on a twin bed and put his foot on a pile of pillows before he answered, "Frostbite. Where did you see Ritta? Is she safe?"

Moses placed the envelope in Lawrence's leathery hand, reluctantly giving up the only piece of Ritta he had. "She's safe and well. I met her on Alcatraz."

"Sit down." Lawrence pointed to a padded rocking chair next to the stove. "Pour some of that coffee, there."

Moses looked around the stack of wooden crates in the corner, choosing a cup with an unbroken handle. He turned, about to ask the old man if he wanted some, then decided not to disturb him.

Lawrence sat on the edge of his bed, with the letter held in the diffused sunlight. His brow furrowed deeply as his finger pointed to each word he deciphered. Moses noticed the cup on the bale next to the bed, wrapped the pot's hot handle with a towel and walked over to pour the old man's cup full, then sat down in the rickety chair with his coffee, waiting for the grounds to sink to the bottom before drinking it. He looked around the ramshackle place and thought of his own home, which wasn't much better. Why do we have to live like this?

It was one of the lessons he had learned in California—Indians were the poorest of the poor. Even the Mexicans and Negroes had electricity, can shop where they want to instead of the trading post where everything costs half again as much as it should. He thought of his mother and the tuberculosis that racked her body and struggled again to contain the rage that welled up inside him.

Lawrence folded the letter and put it carefully back in the envelope. "Tell me about this Indian land, this Alcatraz."

Moses leaned forward in the rocker, his elbows on his knees, and told Lawrence of the island prison that someday would be a great cultural center for people of all tribes, and how they took it back from the white man. Lawrence asked, "Do drums beat there?"

"Yes, sir. All the time."

Lawrence smiled. "This is good for my heart to hear. A good place for Ritta to be." Lawrence stood up. "Will you go back to this Alcatraz?"

"As soon as I can."

"Tell her for me that she knows right, Agnes' body lies beneath the stars. Tell her High Tail still calls her name, but she must find her own life where the people are proud, not crumbled like this old man."

"She wants to come home. I told her I would try to clear her name so she could."

"Tell her the man she pushed off the truck didn't die. Too damn bad if you ask me. Lopate has no evidence against her. I believe he has destroyed everything that incriminated himself and the rest of his goons. He can't prove anything against Ritta without getting himself in hot water. But he would try to kill her just the same. Like he killed Agnes."

"But there must be something we can do. How can we let them get away with murder and not do anything?"

They heard the crunch of tires on frozen snow. Lawrence stood and slowly headed towards the door. "Don't speak of her to Bill. He is my good friend but he isn't involved with this."

Lawrence introduced Moses as the son of a friend to the white couple that stepped from the new Chevy truck. The woman carried a basket that held a pot of food, steaming in the cold air.

Moses shook the man's hand and nodded to the skinny woman before he turned to Lawrence standing in the door. "Good-bye, Uncle."

Lawrence held out his hand. Moses grasped it briefly before getting into his dad's truck.

San Francisco

On the gravel shoulder beside the I-80 on-ramp outside Berkeley, Ritta crouched down next to her dog and stuck out her thumb. She hunkered in her Army coat and tipped the old hat over her face a little more as the State Trooper passed by in the line of traffic, thankful for the shapeless, stained Stetson she'd found in Bear's closet. Not only did it keep the rain from going down her neck but she tucked her hair in it, like Gert had done with River's. She knew now when someone picked her up, it wasn't because she looked like a girl.

When nobody stopped she stood and walked towards the freeway, patting her leg for Patch to follow. Her insides still churned with the remnants of the afternoon's fight with Jody.

"Why?" she asked the dripping sky as she turned around and walked the other way. "Why does she think she can boss me around? Why did she get so pissed off when I gave the rent to Bear?" Ritta realized she must look like a crazy person, talking to the gray clouds while she walked up and down. She would never get a ride like that. Turning around to face the oncoming cars she stood with her thumb out, businesslike.

Nobody stopped. Ritta squatted down and put her head on the crook of her bent arm, keeping the other straight, her thumb still looking for a ride. She felt Patch sit beside her, then he lay down. Behind her closed eyes Ritta saw Jody, could feel Jody's arms around her like they were the last night they had slept together. How she wanted those times back, wanted to hear Jody say again, "That's what I love about you."

Her hand reached into the coat and through the buttons on her shirt. Cold fingers cradled her breast. She wished for Jody to touch her like this, pinching the tender nipple.

Tires crunched the gravel. She looked up. A turquoise Thunderbird pulled off a few hundred feet ahead. She and Patch ran for it as the rain started down in earnest. When she reached the passenger side, a large, dark-haired woman rolled down the window and asked, "Where you headed?"

"To Golden Gate Park." Ritta smiled at the flamboyant get-up the woman was wearing. Her tight black troubadour pants were topped by a brightly flowered stretch top that accentuated the woman's pointed breasts with matching blossoms.

"On a day like this? Honey-child, the park is glorious place when the sun is shining. And drearier than a preacher's funeral when it isn't. Get in. Mercy, you're getting wetter by the second. And that poor, sweet dog!" She reached over the seat and took a neatly-folded blanket from the back window. "Here, wrap him up in this and don't let him shake in Louisey's car or she'll have my backside for certain. And take off your coat. Put it in the floor in the back so it won't drip on the leather."

Ritta took off the Army coat, folded it with the wettest part to the inside, and laid it on the back floorboard. She wrapped the blanket around Patch and directed him to sit on the floor of the front seat. Her back was soaked from the downpour before she got in and straddled Patch. The heater was going full bore, and soon the whole car smelled like wet dog.

Ritta leaned forward and kissed Patch on the top of his head. The woman abruptly turned to look at Ritta. It was then Ritta noticed something wasn't right. The woman had a bulge, like an adam's apple, between the brown curls that hung perfectly off her shoulders. And the hands that grasp the steering wheel were much too large and strong to be a woman's, despite the blood-red fingernail polish that covered the pointed nails.

"You're a man!" Ritta gasped.

"And you're a girl!" The 'woman' shrieked. "You hippie children have done it to me, again. Take off your hat, child."

Ritta laughed and removed the wet hat, shaking her hair down. "You sure had me fooled. Why are you dressed like a lady?"

"It's part of my act. Do you like it?"

Ritta smiled and politely nodded. "Are you an actor?"

"Oh, honey. Only when I'm at my 'real' job."

"Oh." Ritta looked out the window and tried to decide what that meant.

"My stage name is Melba. Like the toast. It's my agent's idea. Do you like it?" She took a small tube from the pocketbook by her side, opened it and turned up the waxy colored stick before adjusting the rear-view mirror. With a steady hand on the wheel Melba touched up her lips with two quick wipes, rolled her bottom lip against the top, and blotted them on a tissue already covered with heart-shaped lip prints.

"Yeah," Ritta said. "Melba suits you. What do you do on stage?"

"Oh, honey. Are you old enough to ask that?"

"I'm eighteen," Ritta lied.

"Well then, you're old enough to see the real world. What are you doing tonight?"

Ritta and Patch stood backstage beside the ramp the performers used.

Ritta thought it was a good thing they didn't have steps to climb as shaky as some of them were in their high-heeled shoes. She still wasn't completely sure that all the 'women' singing and dancing on the stage were men, some of them were so beautiful. But most were like Melba. When she looked real close, she could tell.

From where she stood, she saw a small portion of the audience through the haze of smoke lit up by the floor lights. Some men in the crowd threw money and flowers as the dancers left the stage.

Melba walked up behind her. "Enjoying the show?"

"It's fantastic." Ritta turned around and softly wolf-whistled when she saw Melba's sequined blue and silver evening gown, low-cut over padded pectoral muscles that resembled the real thing. White gloves covered Melba's arms to the shoulders. She raised an overly-graceful hand to pat the high-piled hair, revealing a deep, shaved armpit, then smoothed the material over her hip. Ritta had never seen such a dress and couldn't help staring at the way the light shimmered off the small shiny disks. "It's beautiful."

"It's my fav. Watch me knock 'em dead."

A fat, sweaty man on stage shouted, "And here she is. What you've all been waiting for. The incomparable Melba!"

Ritta watched, fascinated, as her new friend swaggered up the ramp and strutted around the perimeter of the stage, almost graceful in three-inch heels. Melba leaned over the edge of the stage, hung her hand from a straight arm and allowed several men in the front row to kiss her gloved fingers. The crowd continued to applaud, a few shrill whistles kept up until Melba took the microphone from the stand at the center. She gestured towards the back where Ritta couldn't see and said in a smooth voice, "Maestro?"

The piano sounded rich and clear in the smoke-filled club. The audience instantly hushed. Melba gave Ritta a wink before turning to the crowd and opening her carefully painted mouth. Out came a clear note, not too high or low. Then Melba sang a beautiful, slow ballad.

The audience appreciated the song with a rousing applause. Melba didn't wait for them to stop before cluing the pianist and they took off with "Frankie and Johnny…" The audience went wild.

After many more songs, Melba threw kisses to the crowd, "Thank you, thank you. And thanks to my favorite piano man, Carl. Come up here, Carl, you hunk of gold. Too bad he's straight, huh boys."

Wolf whistles again filled the club as the tuxedoed pianist—handsome, blond and blushing—joined Melba at the front of the stage. He took a deep bow and they both exited down the ramp to the sound of cheers.

Ritta met Melba at the bottom. "That was wonderful!" Ritta let the sweat-drenched star hug her.

"You're my good luck charm, Ritta."

A stage hand offered Melba a towel and she dabbed at her forehead carefully, staring at the club's owner standing at the microphone. The crowd didn't let up. The rumble of their feet stomping the wooden floor made Melba look upwards and smiled broadly. The announcer finally pointed his cigar at her and said, "Let's see if we can get her back up here for one more little number. Melba?"

Melba handed Ritta the damp towel, took Carl's arm and walked slowly up the ramp. As she thanked her audience, the owner came down and glared at Patch for a moment before turning to Ritta. He took the stogie from his mouth. "Who are you?"

"Melba's good luck charm." Ritta's voice belied her nervousness.

"Well, keep that filthy animal out of the way," he told her as he walked off.

Ritta turned to Patch and whispered, "Look who's calling who a filthy animal."

When Melba finished her third encore number she waved to the crowd and made her final exit. Ritta handed her the towel and they walked down the hallway.

"I have to talk to that horrid man and get paid for this gig. Then you and I should go get some dinner. I'm always starved after one of these shows."

"I'm supposed to keep Patch out of the way. Maybe we should wait outside."

"Nonsense. Oh, hell, there's no point in pushing his buttons, even though I did pack his lousy little club. Here." Melba opened a door to a dingy, narrow room that smelled like stale cigarettes and cheap perfume. "You can wait in the dressing room."

She led Ritta past a row of individual mirrors, each surrounded by a ring of bare light bulbs, and turned the last one on with a flick of a switch at the base. Leaning over a wooden stool, she took a powder puff from the narrow countertop in front of the mirror and patted her face with beige talc. "Oh, the miracle of Mabeline." Melba looked at Ritta in the mirror. "Want to try some? We could hide that nasty mark."

Ritta's fingers covered the cheekbone that still hurt sometimes.

"I'm sorry, dear. I hope whoever did that to you was made to pay."

Ritta nodded and looked down at the floor. "One of them did."

Melba stepped out of her heels. She gently took Ritta by the shoulders, sat her down and took off the hat, carefully placing it on the next stool. Patch made himself comfortable at Ritta's feet as Melba took a brush and pulled Ritta's long hair into a high ponytail.

"Such a world we live in. Full of brutes." Melba opened a jar of soaked pads and cleaned Ritta's face with one, tipping her head back so that Ritta looked up past the fiber-filled, sequined breasts and into hairy nostrils. She closed her eyes. Melba dabbed cold foundation on Ritta's cheeks, chin, and tip of her nose then gently smoothed it over her face. "Don't breathe."

She tried not to, but the powder puff made her sneeze anyway. She heard people come into the dressing room. One of them said, "Great show, Melba."

"Thank you, darling."

"Harry's waiting for you," said another, before blowing a kiss.

"Good, let the pig wait. See you all next time. And take care of that cold, Charlie."

Ritta listened to the door close as Melba drew something over her eyebrows. "What are you doing?"

Melba ran a fingertip across Ritta's brow. "Playing with perfection. Even natural beauties like you and me can use a little help." She fidgeted with something on the counter. "Keep your eyes closed." Melba lightly stroked Ritta's eyelids, then said, "Here, do you know how to apply mascara?" Ritta sat up and looked at the tube in Melba's hand. She shook her head.

"Like this," Melba demonstrated without touching her fake lashes with the wand. "I had better see Harry before he comes looking for me. Pick out a lipstick there in the bag. Maybe the Ruby Mocha?" She pulled on her high heels and left.

Ritta looked in the mirror and laughed. Then she looked closer. The redness was gone from her cheek and her eyes seemed to light up from the trace of color above them. Instead of the garish stage makeup Melba painted on herself, she had just accentuated Ritta's features. Ritta picked up the wand of mascara from the counter, twisted it open and carefully tried to brush it on her lashes, making the same long face Melba had. Clumps of it stuck at the ends, she could see them when she blinked. She took her fingers and pulled them off, deciding that was enough. Rummaging through a little flowered bag of assorted lipsticks, she found 'Ruby Mocha' and rubbed it on. She pulled a tissue from the box on the counter and put the fold between her lips when Melba stormed in.

"Fucking asshole. No, too good of words for that prick. Cock sucker. No. No. Oh shit." Melba looked at Ritta, who stared back at her wide-eyed. "That, that bastard. He wanted me down on my knees, sucking his puny little cock. I probably wouldn't even be able to find it under his fat belly. At least I got my money." Melba waved a fistful of bills before dropping them in her pocketbook and closing it with a snap. She looked at Ritta again and her expression softened. "Why, honey, that Ruby Mocha is the color for you. When you got it, flaunt it, I always say. Let's get out of this joint. We can stop by Louise's flat and change there. I got the key." She opened a cloth bag with wooden handles, held it next to the counter and swept all the various make-up tubes and containers into it, then gathered some clothes hanging on the wall opposite the mirrors.

Ritta pulled her hat on over the pony tail. "Come on, Patch."

Louise's flat was in a seedy apartment building next to an alleyway a few blocks away. "This is it," Melba said cheerfully as she pulled the Thunderbird up to the curb. "Weesey's out of town, that's why I have the car. But maybe she left enough in her fridge we can eat here. I'm sure she won't mind. We can even stay if we want. I've slept many a night on her divan."

Ritta opened the door and swung her leg over Patch as she told him to stay. Someone yelled behind her, "Hey, pretty boy!" She looked across the top of the car at Melba's terrified expression, then turned to see a handful of young white men coming from the dark alley. One of them swung a baseball bat.

"Oh, shit." Melba slammed her door, then stormed around the front of the car. As she stepped up onto the curb, her heel hit the concrete and broke. Melba stumbled as she stepped down and caught herself on the grill of the Thunderbird, tearing the sequined gown.

"Just go bother somebody else." Melba pulled herself upright and walked towards them, clumsy on the broken heel.

One of them darted from the pack and yelled, "Get out a' here, faggot." He swung the bat hard into Melba's back.

Ritta couldn't move. She watched Melba reel, then stand up straight, taller than her attacker but defenseless against the bat as it slammed into the back of her head.

Ritta held onto the car door as Melba fell to the ground, blood seeping from beneath her wig. The sequins of her gown still glistened in the street-light.

"This one ain't no fag. It's a girl."

Patch growled and tried to get past Ritta, but she still gripped the car door in front of her, paralyzed.

The man walked slowly towards her, pointing with something black and rectangular. "I know what to do with a real girl, even if she does wear boys' clothes. What's a matter, Chaquita?" He flipped the switchblade open. "Don't 'cha like me?"

He knocked off the hat and grabbed her ponytail, pulling her head down to the roof of the car. Ritta felt the tip of his blade nick the skin at the hollow of her throat. Patch's low growl deepened.

The man pulled the door from her hands and shoved her up against the back window, his erection hard against her bones. Grabbing his hands around the knife at her throat, she tried to pull the blade away and felt him push harder to compensate.

Patch barked and leapt at the man. Ritta felt her attacker jerk as the dog's teeth sunk into his thigh. The moment his hand around the knife went slack she shoved him away. Too late she realized she still held the knife. It slid cleanly beneath his breastbone.

He looked at her, his mouth a wide silent O before his head bent down to look at the switchblade buried to the hilt in his chest. He fell backwards over the curb.

Ritta glanced at the men peering between Melba's legs. Two others leaned against the building, lighting cigarettes. One rubbed the bulging crotch of his tight jeans and laughed.

Their friend writhed on the sidewalk, grasping his thigh where the dog bit him, the black handle still poking out ludicrously from his shirt, blood seeping around it.

Ritta ran unnoticed to the end of the block. Suddenly aware that Patch wasn't beside her, she turned to urge him to hurry. The sidewalk behind her was empty. She looked back.

The glow of the street lamp near the alley spotlighted the man with the bat. He held it high over Patch as the dog stood over the man who had attacked her. With a calculated, mighty swing the bat came down and struck Patch's skull with a sickening, sharp crack. He collapsed after a pitiful yelp.

Ritta's shriek, muffled behind her hands, made the men's heads turn.

One of them threw down his smoke and started after her, yelling "Fucking bitch." She ran as fast as she could.

She ducked into an unlit doorway in the middle of the block and sat trembling amid the litter in the corner. Inside her, a voice screamed, "I can't just leave. Not this time." As she stood to go back, the alcove was illuminated for an instant with the flashing lights of a cop car. A renewed terror gripped her heart as the walls glowed blue/red, blue/red. She lifted the beaded pouch from beneath her shirt and held it tight as she pulled herself to the edge of the bricks. The police car turned the corner.

She ran the other way, up the hill as if they were after her, looking back at every intersection to make certain no one was. More sirens sounded, getting closer. She turned away from their wail. Blocks later, the long, nearly deserted street became familiar, the corner of Golden Gate Park. With her heart pounding loud in her head, gasping for air, she desperately searched for a place to hide.

Bells jangled across the quiet street. Abbey stood at the door of the Far aHead Shop, keys in the lock. She talked quietly with a man holding a grocery bag with a single rolled-up poster sticking out. Ritta glanced down the street behind her. An ambulance sped through an intersection several blocks away. Holding her aching sides, she hurried across the street.

The man saw Ritta first. Abbey was hunched down, fidgeting with the lock. He tapped Abbey's shoulder.

"Just a minute. I almost got it. Damn key." Abbey stood up, the ring of keys still dangled from the lock.

Ritta tried to catch her breath but couldn't get enough air to say anything.

Abbey turned around abruptly. "Hey. I know you. You're the Indian chick from the boat." She took a step towards Ritta. "What's the matter? What happened?"

Ritta pushed the words past the heaving of her lungs. "Down there. These guys. Hit my dog." She gasped. "Hide me! Please?"

Abbey and her companion exchanged frantic looks. Abbey told him, "You split. I'll take her in the shop."

The key still wouldn't come out, even with the door open. Abbey tugged on it again before giving up. She motioned Ritta inside and shut the door, keys and bells tinkling, then turned the knob on the deadbolt.

Ritta leaned on the wall. Silent tears streamed down her cheeks as Abbey looked outside through a rip in one of the posters lining the window.

"All clear." Abbey took Ritta by the hand and led her to the counter at the back of the room, where the box of Kleenex was. "Tell me what happened." She pulled a tissue out and handed it to Ritta.

Ritta blew her nose and wiped her face. The dark streaks on the Kleenex startled her until she remembered the make-up Melba had painted on her. In a voice barely above a whisper she said, "They hit Melba. And Patch. With a bat. I stabbed one of them with his knife." She looked at Abbey. "I think I killed him."

"Killed who?"

Ritta gripped Abbey's arm. "A white man."

"Who's Melba?" Abbey whispered.

A loud knock at the door made them both jump. The door knob turned. The deadbolt hit metal as whoever was on the other side tried to open the door. The bells clanged furiously.

"Who's there!" Abbey shouted.

"Police. Is everything all right in there?"

Ritta grabbed Abbey's hands in panic. Abbey led her to a life-size poster of Marilyn Monroe with her skirt blowing up in the air. The poster swung open, revealing a large, dark closet. Ritta bolted for the opening and collapsed in the corner behind several boxes. The dim light from the room was obscured with the closing door. She tried to quiet the drumming heartbeat in her chest and listen to the muffled voices.

"What can I do for you, Officer?"

"Are these yours?" Keys jangled.

"Yes, how did you get them out? They were so stuck. I was just trying to find my WD 40 to give them a good spray."

"Shouldn't leave them in the lock, Ma'am. Is this your place of business?"

"I'm the manager. The owner is in India, studying with Rajaneesh Someone or other. I came in late to do some paperwork. Thank you for your concern. May I have my keys, please?"

"Don't want to leave those out here in the lock."

"No, it won't happen again, I assure you. I'll get it fixed right away. Thank you." The door closed and Ritta heard the deadbolt slide shut.

She sat huddled in the dark, her arms around her knees. In the silence, she heard the echoing crack of the bat as it hit Patch's head, and his little cry, over and over again in her head. When Abbey opened the door, Ritta looked up at her. Abbey dropped beside her and held her. Both of them cried until their eyes were red and swollen.

"What am I going to do with you?" Abbey took another Kleenex and wiped the watery streaks of mascara from beneath Ritta's eyes.

"I want to go to Alcatraz. I have friends there."

Abbey brightened. "What a far out idea. Who would think to look for you in a prison? I'll call Jim and he can get the yacht… Oh, shit!"

"What's wrong," Ritta asked.

"Jim's on a run, I forgot. He won't be back until morning."

"On a run?"

"Never mind. You can stay here, in the back room. I'd take you home with me, but I have roommates. The fewer people know where you are the better, don't you think?"

Ritta nodded. She put her head on her knees, suddenly feeling drained.

"Come on. I'll get you a blanket." Abbey pulled on Ritta's hands until she stood up then led her towards the back of the shop.

The room was just like she remembered it, maybe a few more posters had been plastered on the walls. Even in the stark light of the overhead fixture, the room seemed to dance in color. She collapsed on one of the huge pillows, remembering how she and Jody had laughed at each other in the strobe light. The memory added to the ache in her chest.

Abbey brought a heavy crocheted afghan, threw it over Ritta then picked up the smelly ashtray and walked towards the door. "I'll see you in a couple of hours, with breakfast. You'll be all right here. Want me to leave a light on?"

"Uh-huh. Abbey?"

"Yeah." Abbey stopped at the door, sorting through the ashtray.

"Thanks. For being here."

"Funny how things work out, isn't it? You must have good Karma."

"I don't know much about this Karma everyone talks about, but mine must be shitty."

"Well, maybe you just have some stuff to work out." Abbey smiled and held up half a tarry joint. "Want to smoke this with me?"

"Sure." Ritta sat up on the pillow and began to braid her hair.

Abbey sat on the other pillow and removed one of the pendants from around her neck. She opened what looked like a locket. Concealed inside was a small clip that she attached to the roach, lighting it with a wooden match from the box on the floor. She inhaled the smoke through her nose, then passed it to Ritta.

When Ritta exhaled, her shoulders dropped from their tense position by her ears. When she took another toke, she had to put her head on the pillow. Her eyes closed before she blew the smoke out. The drug and weariness slowly dulled the pain around her heart.

Abbey plugged in one of the black lights before she flipped off the overhead and closed the door behind her.

Ritta woke hours later, reaching for Patch and grasping only emptiness. She stared at the psychedelic ceiling as tears streamed into her ears, soaking the hair around her neck before she fell back to sleep.

Abbey awakened her with a light touch on the shoulder. Ritta stirred, then sat up as Abbey lit a candle. Its soft glow obscured the garish walls.

"I brought a pot of Darjeeling tea, some whole wheat toast and a cantaloupe. Ready for breakfast?"

Ritta's stomach rumbled loudly. She laughed a little. "I guess I am."

"Good. Jim will be here in a minute."

"What time is it?" Ritta asked.

"Ah, yes. You have been in the timeless space. I myself have been lost for days in this room. Something about not having windows that discombobulates one. Of course, the acid helped me."

Jim came in and sat cross-legged in front of the breakfast tray. He looked tired, but smiled kindly at Ritta. "Heard you had a rough night."

All Ritta could do was nod.

"What can we do to help?" He poured her some tea.

"Would you take me back to Alcatraz?"

He handed her the cup. As she took it from him, he asked, "Are you sure that's wise? The Feds are watching what goes on out there pretty carefully."

"There I am just another Indian. Besides, the island has bowels. It will hide me."

Jim smiled wearily. "Okay. I can get you there all right. We'll leave after you eat. Then it's up to Bear and the rest of the boys."

Abbey handed her a slice of cantaloupe on a paper towel. "There's toast, too."

Ritta ate hungrily, but the food did nothing to fill the hollowness inside.

Free Alcatraz

In the yacht's cabin, Ritta stared at the rain pouring over the rounded glass window in the early light of dawn. The sound of the motor starting jarred her nerves. She wished she had brought the book she'd been reading. But how was I to know I wouldn't be going home?

She fought off the tears and untied the strips of leather that held her braids, then closed her eyes and unplaited her hair. Slowly, she brushed the wavy tresses with her fingers, comforted by the routine motions. Surrounded by the mantelet of her hair she collapsed on the bed, held her breasts in her palms, and drew herself into a ball.

In her dream she was back on the bus, with Patch asleep beside her. She woke briefly when the yacht's engine stopped, and quickly slid back to sleep to escape the pain in her heart. She woke again to the sound of waves lapping the sides of the boat and a familiar voice whispering, "I can't remember ever seeing her without the old dog."

"Bear?"

He held her tight as the boat rocked. She cried until she couldn't anymore and snuffled. He rubbed the wetness from her cheeks. "You need a snot rag."

Ritta looked around the cabin, noticing for the first time the plush furnishings. Next to the bed, pink tissue stuck out of a built-in wooden cabinet. Bear pulled one out with a flourish, making her laugh a little. Three tissues later she told Bear, "I lost your hat."

"Doesn't matter. What happened?"

"Yesterday, God, it seems so long ago." She shuddered. "I was thumbin' into the city and got a ride from this man I thought was a lady 'cause the way he was dressed." She felt Bear bristle and added, "He, she, was real nice though. He called himself Melba, and we were having a real good time, at this club she worked at. She got up on stage and sang these great songs."

"He took you into a queer club?"

Ritta nodded. "It was fun. I can't think of Melba as a man. You should have seen her, she was beautiful." Ritta stopped, thinking of Melba on the concrete, bleeding.

"Then what happened?"

"We went to this apartment that her friend had, but as we got out of the car these *wasicu* came up and hit Melba with a baseball bat. It all happened so fast. One of the guys came after me and put his knife right here." Ritta showed him the little wound on the hollow of her throat. "Patch must have bit him then 'cause he let go of the knife. I tried to push him away. The knife went into him. It must have been real sharp. I think I killed him, Bear."

Bear put his arm around her. "Sounds like self-defense to me. This isn't the Rez, and we have friends that are good lawyers."

"But the cops are after me already. They'll send me back to the Rez. I know they will."

"We won't let them, Ritta. This is our land and they can't come and take you from it."

Ritta hung her head, wanting to believe him. Bear's fingers brushed the hair from her face. "Then what happened?"

"I ran. I thought Patch was behind me, but he jumped on the guy. This other dude with a bat hit him, right in the head. I heard him cry. It was so horrible." She covered her eyes. Bear's arms went around her and she made herself small in his embrace. "I left him, Bear. I ran away and left him. Just like I left Agnes. He saved me and I left him there to die. Oh, God." Her body shuddered as she sobbed.

Bear stroked her hair. "You did the right thing. What else could you do?"

"I shouldn't have left him. He wouldn't leave me." Ritta flung her head back and raved beseechingly, "My, God. What have I done? What will I do without him?"

Lost in her anguish, her head swayed as Bear shook her shoulders. "Listen to me, Ritta. You did what you had to do." He held her tight and let her cry.

Jim appeared by the bed, with a yellow slicker and a large, matching rain hat. "Sorry, man, but we have to split. I thought maybe she should wear these so if the Feds are watching, you know?"

"Yeah. Thanks." Bear stood up and pulled Ritta. She felt limp until her feet touched the ground. When she supported her own weight, Bear wrapped the raincoat around her, plopped the plastic hat on her head and led her out of the cabin.

The dawn had become another gray, drizzly morning. On deck, Ritta noticed Bear exchange a worried look with Jim and Abbey. She thanked them for all their help. Abbey hugged her.

Ritta tucked herself under Bear's arm as they climbed the hill to the cellblock. He nodded to a few early risers that looked curiously at the feeble slicker-cloaked figure beside him. When they got to his cell, she crawled beneath the red blanket on his lumpy cot. Bear knelt on the floor beside her. She clutched at his hand with her eyes closed. He held it and said he would wait until she fell asleep, "But I need to go talk to the council about you staying here."

When he returned, she was thrashing beneath the blanket, muttering in her sleep. Bear shook her by the shoulder, "Ritta, wake up. You're having a bad dream."

Ritta's weepy eyes opened. "Where's Patch? Where am I?" She glanced around the tiny room then turned back to Bear. "It wasn't a dream, was it?"

Bear shook his head. Ritta lay her head back on the flat pillow, staring blankly at the ceiling.

He lit a short tapered candle stuck in a tin pot-pie dish on the shelf. Then he tied an old sleeping bag over the bars and door. Suddenly, the cell became a small cavern. Light flickered on the peeling, concrete walls. Bear took a long wooden flute from the shelf, sat on the defunct toilet, and started to play a simple melody.

When Ritta heard the low, sweet sound she raised her head. "That's beautiful, Bear. When did you learn to play?"

"I just learned that piece yesterday. A man here, Clyde, is teaching some of us. It's his flute." Bear moved to the cot and handed her the carved instrument. "Have you ever seen one?"

Ritta held the flute with reverence, its patina glowed softly in the candle-light. "It's a courting flute. They have a bird's head at the end."

"Clyde said that's suppose to be a prairie chicken," Bear told her, seeming a little embarrassed.

"Once, at home, I saw some prairie chickens do their mating dance. It's really far out." She ran her finger over the glass eyes embedded into the wood, then tried to place her fingers over the holes.

"Here." Bear put her fingertips in the right order. "Six holes for the six sacred directions. Like this. Now, blow."

Ritta put her lips to the small mouthpiece and blew, but soon gave up and handed the flute back to Bear. He sat cross-legged on the end of the bed and began to play again, embellishing the melody.

Ritta curled up beside him and let the music wash over her, soothing the jangled places in her mind. She drifted into a restful slumber and woke feeling a little stronger.

Bear read a book in the faltering light. The room was warmer, the heat from their bodies and the candle contained in the tiny cell.

"You'll hurt your eyes, reading like that." She chuckled when she realized how much she sounded like Jody.

Bear smiled. "Better than not reading at all. Are you hungry?"

"Yeah. I guess I am," she said, a little surprised. "How long did I sleep?"

"A couple of hours. I'll go to the kitchen and get you something."

"I'll go with you." Ritta swung her legs over the side of the bed and started to stand up until Bear shook his head.

"Can't. I promised to keep you out of sight until the lawyer comes. We thought it would be better that way."

"I have to stay in here? For how long?"

"The lawyer should be here tomorrow or the next day, depending on when he can get away. If you have to piss, there's a honey pot here in the corner." Bear pointed down to a Folger's can with a plastic lid sitting behind to the toilet. "I'll bring you some water and something to eat. Anything else you need?"

"How can I get the rest of my things? Whose going to tell Sebastian I can't come to work?" Ritta dropped her head in her hands. "How did my life get so fucked up again?"

Bear put a hand on her shoulder. "The Great Spirit will take care of you here. It will be all right."

Ritta raised her head. "But Sebastian? I can't just let him think I skipped out. I'm suppose to be at work tonight. And Jody, she'll be worried sick if I don't show up. You know how she gets."

"Yeah, you're right. We got to tell her something. I'll see what I can do. Stay put and I'll be back as soon as I can." Bear pulled the curtain aside and stepped out, tucking it up against the wall again before he left.

Ritta curled her legs underneath her and fought the despair that threatened to overtake her. "I'll get out of this mess, I don't know how but I will," she told the shadowy walls. She pulled the blanket off the bed and wrapped it around her shoulders, stood up and walked to the curtain that hid the world from her. She pulled back the edge, squinted in the light, and looked out the through the broken panes in the wall of windows that faced the bay.

She could hear childish laughter from outside, then the slow pounding of a drum in the distance. A bird flew past the window, its shadow sweeping the sunlit floor. Ritta leaned her head on the hard concrete wall and tried to let her mind soar with the bird. But it wouldn't.

She sat back on the cot, staring at the candle. I wonder how many prisoners have sat here. How many men who killed someone.

Tunkasila, forgive me for the two men I killed. The one I pushed out of the truck back home and now this one.

She could still see his face, staring unbelievingly at her and the knife stuck in him. She knew she'd never forget it. Like she would always remember Patch's feeble cry when the bat hit him.

What could I have done to save him?

Ritta jumped when Bear came through the curtain, a plastic bucket of water in one hand and a tinfoil covered plate in the other. Moving with a hurried purpose, he put the plate in front of her and the bucket in the corner before gathering his jacket and hat off the wall hooks. "They're holding a boat at the dock for me. I'll go tell Jody what's coming down and get your stuff. We thought it would be better this way, fewer people knowing. I'll be back as soon as I can. Depends on when another boat comes out. Anything else you want me to bring you?"

"Everything in my pack. My moccasins, and my glasses and some books. Nothing else that I can think of."

"Someone will bring you dinner." He leaned over and kissed her lightly on the top of her head and grabbed the book he had been reading. Then he was gone, through the curtain with a bright flash of sunlight.

Ritta stared at the darkened opening, still seeing the aftermath of brightness, like having your picture taken with a flashbulb. When her eyes readjusted to the candle, she unwrapped the plate. The grilled cheese sandwich was cold and greasy, the salad limp with no dressing. She took a few bites, not bothering to taste, and continued to stare at the diminishing candle. It started to flicker, drowning in its own wax. Ritta calmed her fear of being left in the dark with the reasoning that Bear must have more candles around somewhere. She stood and picked up the small pie pan, burning her fingers on the hot tin. "Ouch." When she jerked her hand away, the liquid wax extinguished the flame.

The darkness was total except for two tiny bright slivers of light from the top of the drape. She started to walk towards them and banged her knee on the bed frame. "Shit!" She slammed her fist into the mattress. Following the edge of the bed she hobbled to the bars and lifted the curtain.

The setting sun shone brilliantly through the broken panes and muted through the dirty remaining glass. After shielding her blinded eyes until they adjusted, she pulled the bottom corner of the curtain into the bars, leaving the doorway open. In the light, she looked for spare candles on the shelf. Finding none, she realized how few places there were to store things in a prison cell, no nooks and crannies to squirrel things away in. Just four walls, a bed, the tiny shelf, sink and toilet. Standing in the middle, she spread her arms and leaned to touch one wall above the wide, green paint stripe, then the other.

I could go loco, caged up like this. She remembered the feel of the knife as it easily slid beneath his ribs. I killed a *wasicu*. I could go to prison. "Great Spirit, I didn't mean to kill him."

Then the memory of Patch's body lying broken on the sidewalk made an angry tide rise in her like the ocean swell crashing on the rocks below. But that other one, the one that hit my dog, I want to take that knife and stab him.

She fell upon the bed and imagined pounding the blade into the man that held the bat. Again and again. Until finally, it was just a thin mattress beneath her clenched fists. She cried until she fell into the abyss of sleep.

Ritta awoke to the light tapping on the concrete block near her head. In the darkness a voice called out, "Hello. Anyone in there?"

"Who is it?"

"My name is Minnie. I brought you dinner."

"Minnie! It's me."

"Ritta?" Minnie walked into the cell. "What are you doing here, honey? They told me some girl was in trouble."

"Oh, Minnie, I killed a white man."

Ritta told her story in the glow of the flashlight upturned on the shelf. Minnie listened quietly, holding Ritta's trembling hands. When she had finished, Minnie pulled her up off the cot. "Come on."

"I can't leave. Bear told me to stay here."

"Those boys can't keep you here all alone. And in the dark. You done nothing wrong. You come stay with me."

"But—"

"You wanna stay in the dark?"

Ritta looked around at the walls that closed in on her even more with the thought of remaining there. "No, I don't."

"Good, come on." Minnie picked up the plate of food she had brought and the flashlight. Ritta started to follow her friend when she stopped.

"What's the matter?" Minnie asked.

"Bear's going to be mad when he comes back and I'm not here."

"We can leave a note." Minnie pawed through the pile of Bear's belongings on the shelf until she found an old envelope and a pencil, scratching a few words on it. "There. Grab your things."

They walked along the catwalk. Their footfall's clanging echo filled the immense hallway no matter how softly they stepped. Minnie held the flashlight down low.

"Here, hold this, dear." Minnie handed Ritta the plate of food so she could grip the railing down the stairs. At the bottom, Minnie took the edge of the blanket draped over Ritta's shoulders and pulled it up over her head like a hood. As Minnie tucked it beneath her chin, Ritta flinched. Minnie asked, "What's the matter?"

Ritta pulled the blanket aside, exposing her throat. Minnie shined the flashlight close to examine the festering, shallow wound, then shook her head. She took the plate and led the way through the dark corridors of the cellblock.

When they stopped at the door to the exercise yard, Ritta heard the drumming. Minnie turned off the flashlight and said softly, "Just keep your head down."

They went unnoticed behind the group of people huddled around the drum. In the faint glow of moonlight they walked, with arms linked, around the shadowy perimeter of the yard to the back wall. Ritta pushed open the heavy steel gate. Minnie went first, down the steep concrete steps littered with vines and huge leaves withered with the cold.

Ritta remembered when she and Moses had walked down these stairs, during the Thanksgiving celebration. She wondered if he made it home all right, if he'd found Lawrence. She stopped at the bottom. Moist wind blew on her face, leaving a taste of the ocean on her lips. The monstrous bullfrog call of the foghorn sounded close, reverberating through her chest. Stars twinkled through a rent in the low clouds waltzing through the night. The intermittent beam of the lighthouse beacon sparkled on the water. She took a deep breath. The air smelled of freedom.

When they reached the paved roadway, Ritta wanted to run, throw back her head like High Tail and race the wind. She flared her nostrils like the filly would have and sniffed the night air. Wood smoke mingled with the scent of the sea. A gust of wind blew the blanket off her head and her loose hair streamed behind her. Minnie turned and shook a warning finger. Ritta wrapped the wool around her again, sobering with remembrance.

Subdued, she followed Minnie down the road around the lighthouse. The great beam circled overhead silently. They passed the Warden's house where several men were standing on the steps of the still-graceful building, smoking and arguing loudly. Ritta could tell at least a few of the men were high. She wondered if Jody was right, that drugs and alcohol would be their undoing.

The two shadowy figures passed unnoticed. Ritta kept her head down, following Minnie along a rickety metal ramp to the back of the barracks.

"Watch your step, dear. This gets slick here if it's wet." Minnie opened the door to her small apartment and lit two kerosene lanterns. She had brought enough of her things from the mainland to give the place a homey feel. Minnie left a lantern burning in the kitchen, on the ironing board that came out of what looked like a closet. Ritta carried the other through a hallway into the small living room. A brick fireplace in the far corner was full of black ashes. Two folding chairs with small pillows on the seats faced it. She placed the lantern on the mantle.

A large piece of buckskin lay draped over a card table near the front window. Dozens of bead containers were stacked in assorted boxes or sitting open around the work in progress. Ritta felt herself drawn to the skin, running her fingers over the half-completed design. "Minnie, it's incredible."

"I'm glad you like it. You can help me with it. I've been so busy teaching at the school and working in the kitchen I haven't had much time to work on it."

"Teaching?"

Minnie picked up several moccasins by the laces, various beaded patterns in different stages of completion adorned the leather tops. "I teach classes at the school. In beadwork. That's why I am here."

"What school?"

"The Big Rock School, here on the island."

"Oh. Jody said that was a farce, something cooked up for the newspapers."

Minnie laughed. "She would, that girl. Some of what goes on out here is for show. The Council won't let newsmen out anymore who don't say nice things about us. But there is a lot of good happening on this little piece of Indian land. The school is very important. Did you know that a hundred years ago, nineteen Hopi men were put in prison here for trying to stop the government from taking their little children away to a boarding school? Seems kind of ironic, doesn't it, that now we have a school here that teaches Indians to be Indians. We got real teachers, too. And doctors. They come from the mainland. Tomorrow, you see one of them, first thing."

Ritta nodded her head then peeked out the window overlooking the dock. Several men stood around a flaming open barrel, talking and laughing. She saw them pass around a bottle.

Minnie peeked out the other side of the make-shift curtain. "Makes me mad to see these people come with their booze and dope. We worked so hard to get the things we have here."

Ritta's fingers moved to the cut on her throat. It seemed to hurt more.

"Let me see." Minnie turned Ritta towards the lantern. "I have medicine my mother made. It is a good thing to put some on when a wound is poisoned like this." Minnie came back with the jar of thick black salve, a towel, soap and water.

"Do you think I could go to school here?"

"You're Indian and want to learn. Sure, you can go to school here. And you can help me teach my class. So many girls want to know how to bead. Boys, too!" Minnie laughed as she wet a corner of the towel and rubbed it on the soap. "You stay here, with me. We'll have a good time."

Ritta smiled. "It's a deal, Minnie."

* * *

When Bear walked into the restaurant, he saw Jody immediately look behind him. "She's not with me," he told her, knowing she was looking for Ritta.

"Where in the hell is she? Sebastian's ready to have a cow. A sacred one at that. She's two hours late."

Bear noticed how haggard Jody looked. "She's safe."

"What do you mean, 'safe'?" Jody's voice sounded shrill. She glanced around at the customers looking up from their plates at her. "Come in the back." She led Bear into the dishwashing room. Dirty plates were piled up on the counter and stacked high in the sink. From his place by the stove, Sebastian gave them a worried, inquiring look. Jody held up a finger to him, then turned to Bear. "What do you mean?"

Bear turned his back to the kitchen and talked quietly. "She got into a little trouble last night. She might've killed this bastard that pulled a knife on her. She's on The Rock, now."

Jody put her hand to her mouth. "How did she and Patch get to the island?"

"Patch didn't. Ritta saw him get hit in the head with a baseball bat before she ran away. She thinks he might be dead. Somehow, she got to that hippie shop where Jim's girlfriend works. They brought her out early this morning."

Jody leaned against the door frame and closed her eyes. "Poor Ritta."

Bear turned around to see Sebastian watching them nervously. Rosie walked out of the cooler and he called for her to come and take his place at the stove as he headed towards them. "Where is our Ritta? Is she okay?"

"She's all right, Boss. But she won't be in tonight. She sent Bear to work for her."

"Me?" Bear gasped.

Jody patted Bear on his chest. "Please, Bear. We got to get through this shift."

"I pay you under the table and feed you," Sebastian offered.

Bear looked around at the mounds of dirty dishes. "Okay, okay." He pulled off his wool coat. "I can do this."

"Very good." Sebastian patted Bear on the back. "I send Rosie to show you how. Jody, your order's up." The cook headed back to his stove.

"Be right there." Jody waited till he was out of hearing before telling Bear, "Thanks. I'm going to call Peter and have him meet us after work. He'll at least know what to do next."

"The council has a lawyer. Don't worry about it." Bear told her as he rolled up his shirtsleeves.

"Your council's lawyer is going to be watching out for their own Red asses. I want someone to watch out for Ritta's."

Bear watched her walk off and shook his head. She's one smart chick. She's going to be a great lawyer someday.

It was near eleven before Bear joined Peter and Jody in the back booth. His back ached and he moaned as he slid his tired body onto the red naugahyde seat. Sebastian called out to him from the kitchen window, "I fix you something to eat now."

Bear nodded, then said to Jody, "I don't know how she does it?"

"Does what?" Jody asked with a knowing grin. "Wash dishes all evening then want to party all night?"

"Yeah, that."

"Could be 'cause she's used to working, Bear."

He shot her the angriest look he could muster. "Well, I'd work, too, if

212

there was a job for me."

Peter smiled. "Looks like there's a dishwashing job open."

Jody had a mouthful of tea when she laughed, spitting some on the gray-swirled Formica. As she wiped it up with a paper napkin, she said, "Let's hope it's a temporary opening."

Sebastian walked through the swinging kitchen door with a plate of steaming food. Bear recognized it immediately by the aroma as chicken curry. When the plate appeared before him, he had to try hard not to gag and wondered if he'd ever be able to look at curry again, after scraping so much of it into a swirling mass of garbage. "Thanks, Boss."

Sebastian stood at the edge of the table, his hands on his hips. "Now you tell me what happened to my favorite dishwasher."

Bear looked at Jody and Peter for any sign of protest. Peter just shrugged. Jody looked at him and said, "He should know." She turned to Sebastian. "She's hiding in the underground. She was assaulted last night in the Mission district and may have injured one of the men that attacked her with a knife he intended for her."

"Why does she hide?" Sebastian motioned for Bear to slide over and sat down in the booth beside him. "Do we not have rights to protect us in this country?"

The three young people looked at each other. Finally Peter spoke. "Ritta believes the South Dakota police are looking for her, or should I say, the Tribal police. She is very concerned that she will be sent back to the reservation."

"What did she do that these policemen are after her? What are these Tribal police?"

Peter leaned on his elbows and sighed. "By treaty, the reservations are like separate countries. But the Feds never honored most of the treaties, and gave the FBI jurisdiction over some crimes on the reservations, like murder, kidnapping. The major crimes, they call them. The Bureau of Indian Affairs set up the Tribal Police to enforce the rest of the laws. Trouble is, not much gets investigated at all on the ."

Jody looked into her nearly empty tea cup, swirling the leaves in the bottom. "Some of these 'police' did something terrible to Ritta, Sebastian. She's right to be afraid of them."

Sebastian shook his head. "This country. I hear all the time as a child, 'America is a good place. Land of the free' and all that. Now that I come here, I know this country is as divided as India, where some religious sect is always fighting with another."

Peter nodded. "Native Americans don't even have the basic right of religious freedom. It's against the law to be an Indian in this country. Ted Kennedy started an inquiry into the reservations and called it a national tragedy, how America has treated its native people. That's why I started study-ing treaty law."

Bear played with the food on his plate. "Land of the Greed and Home of the Depraved." He looked at Sebastian and tried to explain. "The Feds and some big corporations are stealing thousands of acres from my people, pay-ing twenty-seven cents an acre for land that has always been ours, land that is worth so much more. We have no choice, it's being taken away from us, just like what happened on Ritta's reservation. I heard that more than half of all the coal, oil and uranium in the U.S. is on Indian land. Look what happened in Oklahoma, *innet*. They push us onto land nobody wants until gold or oil is discovered, then they steal it, too." He dropped the fork with a clang. "Anyone want this. I guess I'm not very hungry."

Sebastian took a small roll of bills from his trouser pocket and peeled off two tens. "For dishes. Thank you, Bear. I find someone else to wash dishes tomorrow. When you go back to your island, tell Ritta her job is waiting for her when she is ready. I will keep the bed she made for her dog under the sink until they come back."

Bear glanced up at Jody, who smiled sadly and said to Sebastian, "Thanks, Boss. She'll be glad to hear that."

* * *

In the morning, on the northwest edge of Alcatraz, Ritta stood on the rocks beyond the concrete retaining wall and cast her fishing line again. It felt good to be outside, to shake off some of the dread that had kept her awake most of the night. She stared at the green and gray hills on the far shore, with the famous bridge spanning the mouth of the bay. Behind her was a long building with hundreds of windows reflecting the sun. The cold and impos-ing Industries Building sat on the northernmost point of the island, to her right. She had seen two people when Tony led her down here, but they left as she and Tony climbed out onto the rocks.

Minnie had convinced her she should go outside, that no one could see her from the shore if she stayed on the far side of the island. "There's no sense in moping around over what's been done. That boy was the one doing wrong. Not you. He got what was coming to him, you were just the instrument." Then Minnie introduced her to Tony, who knew the "best-est fishin' place." He was right, too. A freshly caught perch still flapped in the bucket. Tony, who was eleven and didn't say much, watched the fish take its final gasps.

She let the line out farther into the water, ignoring the clamor of seabirds swirling overhead. Crouching down between two rocks by the bucket she told the boy, "It's too bad the fish has to die, isn't it?"

Tony nodded solemnly.

"My *Unci* taught me to thank the plants before I harvest them. She told me of hunters who would ask *Wakan Tanka*, the Great Spirit, to bless the animals they had to kill so the people could live."

The little boy's brown eyes looked at Ritta through the hair hanging down in his face. "Can we thank the fish?"

"Sure." They both looked at the perch. Ritta said, solemnly, "Thank you, Fish. For feeding our people."

Tony leaned over the bucket. "Yeah, thanks, Fish." He touched the still perch before gathering up his pole and casting the line heroically into the sea. Hunkered down, emulating Ritta's posture, he let the line out like she did.

A moment later his pole jerked hard. "I got one. A big 'un." He held the pole with both hands, the reel whining as it spun with the sea creature's rage. Ritta dropped her pole and leapt over the bucket. She caught Tony around his thin waist as the mighty fish pulled him towards the ocean's edge, still holding fast to the pole.

"What do I do? What do I do?"

"Hold on," she told him, bracing her feet on the last rock before the tidewater as she gathered the boy between her arms and grabbed the pole midway with her left hand. She tried to stop the frantic whirling of the reel with her other, the handle slamming into her palm for several revolutions before she grabbed hard enough to stop it. The tip of the rod bent with the force of the fish slamming at the end of the line.

"It's a whale!" Tony hollered.

"At least." Ritta laughed, then shouted over her shoulder, "Help someone! Tony's caught a whale!" The handle to the reel escaped her grip again as the fish plunged. Ritta hauled the pole and boy backwards, wincing when the rocks jabbed her side as she fell. Grabbing the handle just before the spool became empty she reeled in a small bit of slack then held it, feeling the creature struggle in fits and throes.

"Help!" Tony's high clear voice sounded over the crash of waves. "Someone help us!" His arms began to quiver with the strain. He muttered loud enough for Ritta to make out some of the words, "...got to get this fish...please Great Spirit...never ask for anything...feed our people..."

"Tony, move your hands up the pole, there. When I say three, pull back. One, two, THREE!" The top of the pole moved a foot. Ritta quickly dropped the tip down and wound the loose line onto the reel. "Again. One, two, THREE. Keep it up."

On the fourth heave, the sea pulled with them, driving the fish closer to shore. Ritta frantically took up the slack, then lost most of what she'd gained with the outgoing wave. They struggled just to hold the rod firm.

When the next surge crashed on the rocky shore around them, the edge of the tide soaked Ritta's shoes. Twenty feet off shore, the fish vaulted into the air. Tony pointed and cried, "Look! Look!" as the pole whipped in response to the monster's sinewy thrashing.

"Hold on. Don't let go!"

Tony grabbed the rod, his skinny arms swinging in time to the fish's maniacal struggle. The bent tip of the pole splintered apart. Four inches of hollow fiberglass rod twirled around taunt line at the metal eye.

"No!" Ritta watched the tip spiral seaward down the filament.

A strong hand grabbed the rod and lowered it before the line severed on the frayed edge. "Keep the tip down. Point it towards the fish," said a familiar voice.

She laughed when she saw Bear standing above her, reaching for the near-invisible line.

"It's a bass! Wind it up!" he shouted over the crash of incoming tide that swirled cold around her legs and knocked her into the rocks. Bear stepped around her and Tony. She reeled furiously as Bear pulled on the line with one bare hand, then the other.

Ritta yelled in Tony's ear, "We got to move before the next wave." Using the slack from Bear's tug of the line, she and Tony crawled up to the next rock. "Bear!" she shouted. "Get to higher ground."

Bear held the line and scrambled next to them as the tide swept around his knees. He started pulling it in again before the water receded, shouting at her, "Take it up! Take it up!"

Tony and Ritta watched in awe as Bear pulled the monstrous fish closer to shore. Drips of blood-stained water from Bear's clenched fists made darker spots on his wet jeans as the hands grasped, pulled, and released the line in alternating rhythm until the fish was struggling on the rocks ten feet from them.

The line went slack. Bear pulled frantically till the broken end was in his hand. The fish still flopped in a shallow pool of water between the rocks. Tony scrambled down the crags.

"Hey, kid. What are you doing?" Bear shouted.

"Tony, hurry!" Ritta yelled, watching the approaching swell.

Tony tried to pick up the flailing fish as it jerked from side to side in one last frantic attempt to be free. The bass was more than half the size of the boy wrapping his arms around it. A wave crashed into the basalt, submerging Tony and the fish.

"Tony!" Ritta threw the pole behind her, slid off the rocks and tried to stand against the incoming tide. The cold water snatched her breath as it hit her chest. Bear leaped off, lost his footing and came up sputtering as the wave reached its apex. A dark shape floated face-down between them, kicking frantically. Ritta was the first to reach him and grabbed the boy's jeans. She tried to hold him against the tide that threatened to sweep them both away in its pull towards the sea. Then she felt Bear's hand clasp her arm, and another strong clutch around her waist from behind. Bear released her arm to grasp the rocks until the sea relinquished its hold on them. It left the boy sputtering at her feet, his skinny arms still entwined around the bass.

She picked him up and hugged him, the fish between them with its tail thrashing. "Are you all right?" She pushed his wet hair from his face.

"We did it," he said between chattering teeth, struggling to hold the dying bass up with both hands, all his fingers stuck in the fish's gills.

"We sure did. It's a great fish, Tony." Ritta looked around the rocks. "But we lost the poles and the rest of the catch."

Bear scrambled over the rocks towards them, her pole in his hand. "I found this. Now let's get out of here before we all drown."

Ritta and Tony squealed as the tide rushed at them again, their water-logged clothes and shoes weighing them down. Bear pulled Tony and the bass up the concrete embankment just ahead of the encroaching tide.

The wind blasted against them. Ritta pulled her wet pants away from her skin so she could walk better. Bear reached to take the fish from Tony, who reluctantly gave up his trophy. The boy huddled, shivering, under Ritta's arm. She tried to shield him from the wind.

Walking up the crumbling concrete at the edge of the island reminded Ritta of the Sutro Baths and the warm sunny day spent there with Patch and Jody, the day she first saw the ocean. She turned and looked at the sun through a break in the clouds, its rays shooting silver across the water as she said a prayer for Patch. She missed him so much.

Ritta followed Bear up the concrete stairway. So many steps on The Rock. Always climbing down or climbing up. She put her hand under Tony's armpit and, with her hip, lifted and swung him up some broken steps. He laughed through chattering teeth.

Out of nowhere a voice shouted, "Bear!"

Ritta glanced around. Bear looked too, then shrugged at her when he couldn't see anyone either.

"Over here." From one of the hundreds of windows in the long two-story building, a hand waved through a broken pane.

Bear shrugged again and headed towards the building. Ritta and Tony hurried behind him.

At the doorway, Ritta recognized the dancer with the long braids that she had seen on her first trip to the island. He smiled. "Hey, Bear. Great fish."

"Yeah, the boy caught it." Bear turned and pointed to Tony, shuddering beneath Ritta's arm. Tony smiled back with blue lips, his hands clasped tightly over his chest.

"Come in. How'd you get so wet?" The man took off his coat and offered it to Ritta. She turned Tony by his trembling shoulders toward the coat.

"Not an easy catch, *innet*," Bear muttered.

"Hey, man. We gotta get you warm before you catch hypothermia and die. Follow me."

He led them through an immense room that felt empty despite the big dilapidated boilers and pipes. Sun streamed in the wall of windows, making Ritta feel a little warmer. It helped just being out of the wind. "What is this place?"

"The prisoners did laundry here for the military bases. Someday, it may be our University. Who knows? For now, it's where some of us hang our bustles." He led them from one cavernous room into the next. Giant red-striped concrete pillars held up the second story. The building's entire western wall was a long row of ten foot tall windows framed in concrete, each with a hundred small panes of glass. The light patterned the floor, reflecting in small pools of water. Broken glass was scattered everywhere. She turned to Tony and whispered, "Watch where you step."

The man led them to the middle room, where a small alcove had been partitioned off with more glass, perhaps for an office. A small fire burned on the tile floor. Ritta huddled around it and watched the smoke rise and curl before disappearing out a broken pane. Sleeping bags and other bedding were strewn in the corners. The dancers' traditional garb hung on the walls; colorful, beaded shirts and turkey bustles, fringed buckskin and eagle wing fans. The room was otherwise empty except for the ceremonial drum covered with a Hudson Bay blanket with wide green and red stripes.

The man offered some dry clothes and Ritta helped Tony out of his wet things. As she wrung his jeans out, Tony wandered around wearing a dry sweatshirt that hung down to his knees and large socks on his feet, looking at the finery. Bear, wrapped in a tattered blanket, sat on his heels with his back against the wall, talking quietly to the man. Then the dancer said loudly, "Goddamn them. They can't come over here then go back and report just the negative things. What happened to the 'plight of the Indian' stories and all the good things they said about us in the beginning?"

"We got to give them good things to say about us, instead of all this bickering and backstabbing," Bear told him. "The elders on the mainland, we need to include them in our council. We need their support."

"This is our show now, Bear." The other man said. "The old guys, they compromise too easily. They go home each night from their white man jobs to their white man houses and dress up like Indians for pow wows and the press. They don't know what it's like here on Alcatraz, or on the Rez. They're just apples. Red on the outside and white inside."

Bear stood up and met the man's angry gaze. "Those 'old guys' over on the mainland gather the donations that feed us here. They solicit money so we can buy the things we need that aren't donated. If it weren't for those 'old guys' there would be no Indian land on Alcatraz."

Bear tossed off the blanket then stomped to the door and picked up the fish. Ritta stood and motioned Tony to come along. She picked up his wet clothes and shoes, then walked out behind Bear, turning at the door to say, "Thanks. I'll bring your blankets and clothes back later."

When Ritta stopped outside to put Tony on her back, trying to get the blanket to stay around them, Bear turned and grumbled, "Hurry up."

"Mellow out, man," Ritta snapped back, shifting Tony's weight to a more accommodating spot. Bear waited for her to catch up with him, then silently walked up the hill towards the barracks, heedless of the big fish he carried, its tail dragging on the ground.

As Ritta headed for the back of the barracks, Bear told her, "Get some dry clothes on and meet me at the warden's house. Peter and Jody are there."

"What! Jody's here, on the island?" Ritta spun around so fast Tony nearly slipped off.

"I told her she didn't have to come, that we could handle it. But you know Jody…" Bear continued up the hill towards the cellblock.

From her back, Tony shouted at Bear, "Hey, my fish." Ritta winced and covered her ears.

Bear turned around and laughed. "I'll take it to the kitchen. Dinner is on you tonight, my friend."

Ritta put Tony down before he shouted again, "Make sure Minnie sees my fish. Tell her to save the head for me." Bear waved from the top of the hill.

She delivered Tony to his mother and reassured her they weren't as close to drowning as Tony's recounting of the catch made it seem, not really believing it herself. She walked, stiff-legged and bone cold, down the hall to Minnie's apartment. When she opened the door, anxious to get out of the wet, chaffing clothes, she surprised Jody, who bumped the bead-working table. The tinkle of hundreds of beads spilling on the hard floor interrupted the gravid silence between them.

Jody looked down at the still-bouncing dots. She fell to her knees and tried to contain the rolling pinheads of color in the perimeter of her arms. Ritta stood above her, unable to pry the damp pants off her knees enough to kneel down and help. Jody looked up. "What happened to you? Fall in the bay?"

"No. The bay fell on me. I need to change."

"Go. I'll pick these up."

Ritta walked stilted to the small bedroom. She removed some dry clothes from her pack, then pulled back the yellow sheet covering the window to let in the weak, winter sunlight. Below, people milled on the dock, killing time before the boat left. Through the doorway, she heard Jody scoop the beads and pour them back into the containers. She dropped to the thin mattress. As she unzipped her wet pants she asked Jody, "What made you come to The Rock?"

"Bear came to the restaurant last night and told us what happened. I called Peter and he met us after work." Jody laughed. "Bear worked your shift."

"Bear washed dishes? No way."

"It was something to behold, that's for sure."

Ritta cursed softly as she tried to peel the tight jeans from her legs.

"What's the matter?" Jody asked from the other room.

"My clothes are stuck to me."

Jody leaned on the doorjamb, her fists hidden in her pockets. "How did you get so wet?"

"This little kid and I were fishing on the rocks. He caught this huge bass and we kind of fell in." Ritta peeled off her flannel shirt and tossed it on the floor. She was so cold her nipples lifted the cloth of her t-shirt. She shivered as she reached for her zipper.

Jody asked quietly, "Want some help?"

"Yes."

Jody looked surprised.

Ritta flopped back to peel the jeans off her raised hips. She shook a leg at Jody. "Hurry, I'm freezing."

Jody stood at the end of the mattress and pulled a pants leg, exposing the skin of Ritta's thigh, bumpy with goose flesh. The wet denim stopped at her knee and would go no further.

"Here, pull the other one, too." She shook her other leg, a little smile on her bluish lips.

The pants came off with a few more tugs. Ritta watched Jody peruse her legs, felt Jody's eyes on the tendrils of dark hair that escaped the elastic around the top of her thighs. She looked down at her belly; soft, dark hairs showed between her white underwear and the clinging thin cotton shirt. Her breasts ached. She wanted to ask Jody to touch them, to warm her up.

Standing above her, Jody met her gaze, then pointed to the spot on her own neck where the square of tape and gauze covered Ritta's throat. "How's this?" she asked.

"It's okay." Ritta looked away, not wanting to think about that now. She would have to, soon enough. She sat up and rolled the socks to her toes, tossing them on the wet shirt. Jody threw the jeans on top of them.

As Ritta lifted the edge of her t-shirt over her head, Jody walked back into the living room. Ritta could hear her picking up more beads.

Rolling her underwear down the prickly gooseflesh of her legs, Ritta knew the time had come. She needed to face the things she had been hiding from. And Jody was going to be first.

With a blanket from the bed wrapped around her, Ritta grabbed one of her dirty shirts off the floor and squeezed her wet braids with it, then finger combed out the plaits. She reached for Minnie's slippers and put them on over her bright pink toes. The blanket didn't feel warm yet, but did start to dry out her clammy skin. She rubbed the wool over her breasts and arms.

Her legs carried her stiffly to the other room. Jody looked up from the few remaining beads on the floor when Ritta said her name.

"Cute slippers." Jody's voice cut with sarcasm.

Ritta glanced at the red and white knit slippers topped with little pom-poms on her feet. "Jody, what are you afraid of?"

"What do you mean, afraid of?" Jody stood and put the bead container on the table, then turned to look at Ritta.

"With me. What are you afraid of with me?"

"Okay. I'll tell you." Jody's eyes closed for a moment. When she opened them again it seemed her face softened. "I want you. Just like everyone else, I want to take you and make you mine. But I don't want to hurt you. You've been hurt so much. God, I just want to hold you."

Ritta shivered. "Come warm me up."

"Are you sure?"

Yes, yes, the voice inside Ritta screamed. She smiled and nodded. With each deliberate step she took towards Jody, Ritta loved her more. Loved the way she knew what Jody was thinking, knew how Jody saw her this moment. Loved how Jody held her face with open palms and kissed her cool lips. Her cheeks warmed beneath Jody's touch. Ritta shuddered, more from anticipation than cold.

"You're freezing."

"That's what I've been trying to tell you. Will you thaw me out?"

"I don't know. Frigid women don't do much for me."

"I'll show you how frigid I am." Ritta opened the blanket by unfolding her arms, the corners of it held in her fists, framing her naked body. Jody radiated warmth with the blanket wrapped around both of them.

Jody cupped Ritta's breasts. Ritta surrendered and let the sensations push the cold from her. Jody's hands followed the curve of Ritta's backside. She bent to follow with her lips, and nudged the worktable behind her. Beads rained again to the floor. Laughing, they pulled apart, then Ritta took Jody's hand and led her back into the bedroom.

Jody had wanted so badly, for so long, to do just this. Falling down on the mattress with Ritta beside her, tangled in Ritta's hair, their arms reaching for each other, was part of every fantasy Jody had spun since the day Ritta stepped off the bus. Yet feeling Ritta's clammy skin warm beneath her touch was more delicious than any sexual daydream. Her fingers had fondled other breasts, had explored the moist, dark caverns of other women. Jody was suddenly grateful for what those forays had taught her. She thought of all the times she had talked herself out of desiring Ritta. She's just a kid, she's just a kid, had become her daily mantra.

Ritta's eyes begged her to hurry as Jody's fingers fumbled with the buttons, the snaps, the extraneous material that kept them apart. Naked, Ritta's hair spread over the pillow, her arms hugged her breasts.

Jody stood above her. "Ritta, you look like a woman."

"'Bout time you noticed that, Jody." Ritta pulled the covers down and slipped between the sheets.

Jody slid beside her. "Oh, I noticed. I just didn't want to hurt you."

"Dora told me once there is always a little pain in pleasure. Don't be afraid to hurt me that way, Jody. I want you to."

Jody cradled Ritta's breasts in her palms, bent her head and took as much of one as she could in her mouth. Ritta arched against her. All the months of Jody's guilty turmoil melted into the pool of sweetness that filled the palm of her hand as it delved between Ritta's thighs.

Peter pulled the coiled ear piece of his wire-rim glasses over his lobes and looked at the papers. "As far as I can tell, Ritta," he looked up at her over the lenses, "there were never any warrants from South Dakota, only the APB which was never renewed. Officially, the Tribal Police are no longer looking for you."

"That's a relief. What about here, in the city?" Ritta sat on the edge of her chair in the front room of the old warden's house, across from Peter. Richard and three others from the council sat along the wall. She didn't dare look directly at them, but stole a glance at Richard. His expression was stern as he listened intently.

Peter told her, "That's another story. They don't know it's you they are looking for, but looking they are."

Out of the corner of her eye she noticed Richard fold his arms across his chest, his slight "hmmm" audible in the silence. Ritta then looked at Peter. "I didn't do anything wrong."

"I believe you, Ritta." Peter looked at her squarely. "Let's go someplace quiet and talk about it."

One of the men glared at her as she left. Outside, she breathed a little deeper. "They don't want me here, do they?"

Peter shook his head. "No. Not as long as the police are looking for you. Can't say I blame them. These guys have it pretty heavy with the Feds just across the bay spying on them all the time." Peter wrapped his coat tighter around his middle and turned his back to the gusts. "Can we go somewhere warm?"

"Back to Minnie's apartment. Jody's there."

"Do you have any qualms about talking freely in front of Jody?" Peter asked as he followed her quick steps down the hill.

She grinned. "No, none at all."

Ritta heard Jody stir in the bedroom as they came in the door. "That was quick," Jody's voice called after the door shut.

"Ah, Peter's with me."

Jody walked out of the bedroom, tucking her shirt into her jeans. "Good. Hi, Peter."

Peter grinned and pulled off the wire-rims. "Does this mean you two finally got together?"

Astounded, Ritta asked, "You mean, you knew?"

"I knew I didn't stand a chance with Jody once she met you." Peter rubbed the dent his glasses made on the bridge of his nose. "But that's all right. This way I get you both, as friends."

Jody walked over to Peter and hugged his shoulders from behind. He put his hand over hers, on his chest, then asked, "Have you told her?"

"No. Haven't you?"

Ritta got scared. "Told me what? Am I wanted for murder?"

"No," Peter said quietly. Jody dropped her arms and started walking towards Ritta as Peter continued. "But the boy did die. The knife nicked an artery into his heart. He was dead before the ambulance got there."

Jody grabbed Ritta's hand. "But two of the other dudes told the pigs that he had pulled the knife on you, and one admitted they were probably going to rape you. That's why it's not manslaughter. It is a homicide though, until it's proven self-defense. Which won't be a problem if the other victim regains consciousness."

"Melba's alive?"

"Mr. Winston, 'Melba'," Peter shook his head before continuing, "has a concussion and keeps slipping in and out of a coma, but is expected to recover. 'Melba' also has a fractured vertebra and a re-fractured ankle."

Ritta closed her eyes and prayed, *Pilamayaya Tunkasila*, Please Grandfather, let him be alive. "And Patch?"

Jody tightened her grip on Ritta's hand. "We don't know. The police records only say that he was taken to an area veterinarian for treatment."

"Then he could be alive. We've got to find out."

Peter smiled sadly. "The police are most likely watching the vet's office. It would be advisable to turn yourself in. Especially since there are no outstanding warrants. That's your lawyer talking."

"And sound advice it is," Jody added.

"Then let's go! I'll get my pack." Ritta stood up and started towards the bedroom. She stopped and turned to Jody. She could do this, she could do anything if Jody were there. "You'll be with me?"

"Peter will be acting as your attorney. The police may not let me stay with you, but I'll be waiting."

"They won't lock me up?"

Peter perched in the folding chair. "Why don't you tell me everything that happened."

From the Embarcadero they took a taxi to the precinct station. Ritta held Jody's hand and looked out the window at the city. At the bottom of the steps leading into the building she stopped to steel herself, silently wondering if she could do this.

Peter turned to look at her. "Tell them what you told us about that night. You did nothing wrong, except tell Mr. Winston you were eighteen. Don't talk about the Rez, or the Rock, just that night."

After waiting more than an hour in the noisy, bustling lobby, she and Peter were taken into a little room where she told two officers everything, but the names Melba called the club owner. She felt safe with Peter there. He no longer seemed like a little bird, more like a hawk, fiercely protective of her.

A woman knocked on the door and told them the line-up was ready. Ritta turned to Peter. "Can you remember what the man with the bat looked like?"

"I'll never forget."

"Good girl. Let's go pick him out."

From behind the window they assured her the men standing on the other side couldn't see through, she saw him. The one who'd hit Patch and Melba. "That's him. Third one down."

"From the left or right?"

"Left." Her anger burned in her belly. Melba had been kind to her, and now Melba, who Ritta couldn't imagine hurting anyone, was in the hospital because of this man. She looked at him again and realized he wasn't much older than she was, and didn't seem so tough now. In fact he looked scared.

One of the officers nodded. "Thank you, Miss Baker. You'll need to appear in court, but you're free to go."

Ritta stood up when the veterinarian and the policeman came out of the exam room and shook hands. The officer walked over to them. "You can see your dog now, Miss Baker. But don't leave the area. We may want to talk to you again after Mr. Winston regains consciousness."

Jody shook the officer's hand and thanked him for his help. He had been very kind, offering to take them to the clinic. Peter handed the man his card. "She can be reached through the Law School's office. Thank you, Officer."

Before the policeman was out of the clinic, the doctor led them through the swinging door to a wall of stainless steel cages. A middle-aged woman in a light blue smock knelt before one of the lower doors, adjusting the tape around Patch's foreleg. He looked small and pathetic beneath the blankets, his head swathed in tan gauze and white adhesive tape. Eyes closed, his tongue, dry and swollen, hung limp from his mouth.

The assistant looked up at Ritta. "Is he your dog?" When Ritta nodded she finished wrapping the tape around his limb and left.

Ritta fell to her knees before the cage. She put her hand over Patch's chest and felt the faint beating of his heart. Looking at the doctor in his white lab coat standing above her, she was unable to ask the question that burned inside her.

He crouched down on the other side of the open door. "I can't tell you how much brain damage has occurred. Or even if he'll make it. If he were human, we would have a brain scan and other sophisticated tests done but, unless we take him to the Veterinary School at Davis, we have no way of knowing."

Ritta's eyes filled with tears. "Can I stay with him?"

The doctor nodded his head slowly. "Of course. We close at nine. But I'm afraid I'll have to ask your friends to leave." He turned to Peter. "As you can see, we don't have a lot of room back here and we're quite busy. Though you are welcome to sit in the waiting room."

"That's okay," Peter told the doctor. "We'll come back in a little while."

Jody knelt beside Ritta in front of the cage. "Will you be all right?"

Ritta nodded without taking her eyes from Patch. Jody left after squeezing Ritta's shoulder.

Ritta whispered over his bandaged head, "You brave old dog. *Wakan Tanka* sent you to me. You protected me like a warrior." She softly stroked his side. "I'm sorry they hurt you. I wish I could save you, like you saved me." She looked up through watery eyes, past the IV bottle and the bank of polished stainless steel cages the color of thunderheads with a sunlit glint. Ritta closed her eyes and imagined the prairie's wind on her face, heard its howl in her ears. Tears of rain fell down her cheeks as she confronted her storm.

Agnes, I couldn't save you, either. I left you to die like I did this brave dog who has been my friend. She dropped her head down on the blanket beside Patch and wrapped her arm lightly around him.

A thought came to her clearly, but it wasn't in words until she put it into her own. He was glad to die for me, to protect me. As was Agnes. *Hoka Hey.* It is done.

She saw the image of Agnes, sitting outside her cabin door, braiding strands of turnips. The old woman had her best dress on, clean and smoothed of wrinkles, like she was expecting company. A smile was on her face and Ritta knew she was happy. Patch sat at her feet.

Ritta reached under the blanket and put her palm on his ribs. He exhaled for the last time. Her fingers searched for the rhythm of his heart and found the slowing beat, counting two, three, four, as it wound down like a clock that just stopped ticking.

She stood and wiped her face with her hands, then dried them on her pants. Wordlessly, she walked out of the clinic.

The doctor and his assistant looked up from the anesthetized cat on the table. They watched Ritta leave the room, then both turned to the open cage. With a nod of his head, the doctor indicated the assistant should check the dog. She lifted the Retriever's eyelid and pressed her finger on the clouding orb. Nodding, she pulled the blanket over his head.

The Indian People's Army

The wave's slosh on the rocky shore of Alcatraz was the only sound after the engines were cut. In the dark midnight sky, stars glistened as brightly as the lights across the bay, and it seemed to Ritta as if she could travel to them, also. She and Bear had been on the road so often lately, to places she would have never seen but for one protest after another. Last month they had joined the National Indian Youth Council in New Mexico at the Gallup Ceremonial, an 'Indian' show put on for white tourists. This time it was a fishing site along the Washington coast. She laughed to herself when she recalled what one underground newspaper had dubbed them—the Indian People's Army.

Bear must have been one of the first off. He waited for her on the dock, their backpacks and bedrolls beside him, black lumps in the dark. His shoulders slumped with fatigue, he silently walked her to the apartment she shared with Minnie, kissed her forehead, then turned towards the Big House. Inside, Ritta lit the lantern and took her journal from the pack. Using the ironing board for a table she sat on the very top of a chair with her feet on the seat, and wrote:

Got another dose of tear gas yesterday morning. My eyes burned for hours, but the police didn't arrest us and quit with the gas after the reporters showed up. Wish they hadn't been late, I hate that damn stuff. Fish and Game showed up with legal papers but our lawyers had their act together and whammied them with papers, too. So the whole thing goes back to court. But that's how we won the last one. Maybe we'll get this one, too.

Missing Jody. Hopefully, she'll come out soon. I know she's busy with school, work, and gathering donations for us but I wish she would come out more often. She said that Radio Free Alcatraz is a big hit, everyone on the mainland listens to it, and it's broadcast from right here on the Rock!

Two more weeks till my GED exam. Better hit the books. Tomorrow.

The next morning, Bear came to the apartment, his face drawn and haggard. Before she stepped aside to let him in, Ritta asked, "What's wrong?"

"On Saturday, Richard Oake's little girl, Yvonne, fell. She's in the hospital."

"Yvonne? Oh my God. What happened?"

"She fell down the stairwell at the Ira Hayes House. Three stories. Onto concrete. Some are saying it wasn't an accident.'

"What do you mean, not an accident?'

"Rumor is she was pushed."

"Who would push a little kid? Why?" Ritta reeled from the implication. Bear caught her as she stumbled and sat her down on the kitchen chair.

"There's people here who don't like Richard or the way he's always the one the newspapers call our 'leader.' It's getting worse, Ritta. Some of these dudes are getting mean. I saw a bad fight last night. One guy got his nose broke. It was pushed way over to the side of his face."

Tears dropped on the page as Ritta wrote in her journal:

Yvonne died today. She was Janey's age. A dark cloud hangs over us here on the island and in my heart. More people come everyday. Angry people who seem to have no other place to go so they come here. I'm sure they are the ones bringing drugs to our island. A man asked me today if I wanted some heroin, then said I misunderstood him when I got real mad.

Minnie is talking about leaving. If she does, I will go too.

Shortly after returning from another trip to Washington, where they had stood with the people at Ft. Lawton, Ritta was leaving the island again, for good. She crouched next to her backpack and waited among the piles of donated clothes heaped on the dock. Some little girls dug through one of the wet mounds, pulling out fancy party clothes to play dress up. Ritta wondered again at the sensibility of some people. It must make them feel good to know that here on the island we won't be lacking for formal wear.

That morning she had worked her last shift in the kitchen, opening unlabeled tin cans in search of something to feed almost a hundred hungry people. Some of the cans were so badly dented or rusted with age that she was afraid to even smell the contents.

The Big Rock School had closed. They had applied for money to be recognized as a real school but the School Board said it was too unsanitary.

Last time she was out, Jody said the whole island was getting to be a slum. Spray-painted graffiti adorned nearly every building and sign; Ritta's favorite were the cells designated to Nixon, Agnew, Ronald Reagan and Andrew Jackson. But she had to admit, Jody was right. The island was feeling like a place she would rather leave than stay. Groups of angry young men roamed around, ready to wield their particular brand of order. The politics among the different factions were killing them. Ritta was tired of it. Tired of being cold and hungry, too. Tired of the long meetings where nothing was decided anymore.

She tried to remember what it had felt like when she first started to live here, to recall the pride they all had on Thanksgiving. They had done something remarkable, taken an abandoned prison and given their people hope. Alcatraz was their Statue Of Liberty. But then Yvonne died. And the government men had cut the electricity and taken the water barge, saying they were going to repair it but never bringing it back. Then someone torched the buildings.

She and Bear were gone that night. The fires that had been set in the Warden's house and the old post exchange must have been fierce. Four buildings had burned, including part of the lighthouse. There was no water to put the fire out, the barge had been taken two weeks before. Minnie said the flames were still burning in all the heated arguments that followed about who set the fires. The Indians blamed government infiltrators and the government, of course, accused the Indians.

She prayed something better came out of their hopes and dreams than this feeling of despair that crept with the fog around the island. The newspapers were right. Booze, boredom, and bickering was doing them in. She got a bad feeling as she watched some men strip copper from cables they had pulled out of the buildings with the island's truck, when it still ran.

Then she saw Minnie and Bear coming down the slope and ran to help Minnie with her bundles. Bear carried the card table Minnie did her beadwork on and the two lanterns that had served them so well, as long as the kerosene had held out.

"Is that everything, Minnie?" she asked.

"I think so, dear. Are you ready to leave?"

Ritta looked around. Other people were gathering on the dock, most had their belongings with them. Seagulls glided overhead like living fragments of the gray and white sky. The foghorn sounded its mournful warning and she realized how seldom she heard it anymore. Above them, the window of the apartment she had shared with Minnie looked bare without the cheerful yellow sheets they had hung for drapes.

"Yeah, I'm ready."

The boat, a rickety old thing, pulled up to the dock and Ritta got in line with the others to board. She remembered the *Clearwater*, the beautiful boat Credence Clearwater Revival donated to the cause, that someone had sunk. Seemed like everything was being destroyed.

A young voice in the distance yelled her name. Tony ran down the lane, waving a piece of paper, a pack of barking dogs following him. "Don't leave, Ritta."

She picked up the boy as he rushed her and swung him around. "Hey, my main Fisher Man. What's this?" He handed her the crayon drawing of the two of them on the rocks, a huge fish attached to the black line the smaller stick figure held. "Oh, Tony. It's beautiful. Thanks. I would never forget that day but this will help me remember it better."

He buried his head against her shoulder. "Don't go."

"I have to. But your momma has my friend's phone number and she promised me that you two would come visit, soon. I love you, Tony."

"Love you, too."

One of the little girls, dressed in a water-stained peach and cream satin evening gown, came and took Tony's hand. They both waved as the boat backed away from the dock and turned towards the far shore.

August, 1970

Ritta was almost asleep, her head propped against the window of the old Plymouth she and Jody had paid a couple hundred dollars for, in hopes it would make the trip. Endless miles of rolling grassland lulled her back to a time when life was as difficult, but the issues were simpler. Find enough food, a safe place to winter. Bury the old when they die and the warriors when they are killed.

"Shit!" Jody's voice brought her back. Ritta sat up and rubbed her eyes. The windshield was covered with drops of water trailing down the glass.

"It's raining?"

"No. We must have blown a radiator hose."

Ritta felt the humid air coming through the vents, adding to the discomfort of the mid-day Dakota heat. Jody turned off the engine, then had to wrench the steering wheel to get the coasting car onto the gravel shoulder. After she tugged the hand brake, Jody slipped on her sandals, not bothering to buckle them. They flapped on the pavement as Jody walked to the front and lifted the hood. A white cloud escaped amid a hissing sound.

Ritta rubbed her eyes and heard the slap of Jody's footsteps again. The car rocked as Jody moved boxes out of the deep trunk and rummaged around.

Ritta pulled on her shoes and opened the door. She almost stepped on Jody, who was half under the car, sliding a plastic kitchen tub beneath the leaking hose. Jody stood up and clapped the road dust from her hands. "I think I can fix it, but she's too hot to work on now. Let's find some place to get out of this sun."

Ritta scanned the horizon and pointed to a low rock outcropping they had passed a short ways back. Its northern face offered the only shade for miles. Ritta leaned over the front seat to grab the bota bag and the blanket they had slept under last night in Colorado. Jody smacked her rounded buttocks with an easy familiarity.

"Hey, watch it," Ritta threatened.

"I am."

Ritta laughed, then handed Jody the blanket.

"Oh sure, give it to me." Jody rolled it into a ball and tucked it under her arm. They walked for several minutes in comfortable silence, broken only by the clipping rhythm of Jody's loose sandals on the hot asphalt.

Ritta tipped the open bota bag towards Jody's back, pouring a small trickle of water down her thin shirt. Jody wriggled and laughed. Ritta pulled the windband Bear had given her from her pocket and poured a small puddle of water on the cloth. She wiped the sweat from her face, then tied it loosely around her neck.

When they neared the outcropping of rock, Ritta stepped into the long grass off the road. "Let me go first, in case there's any rattlers."

"Oh, great! I'm in sandals and you're talking about snakes?"

Ritta chuckled. "I'll protect you. Don't you have snakes in Montana?"

Jody stopped to fasten her buckles. "Sure. But Roscoe's too high for rattlers. I think that's why Momma stayed there. She was bit by one when she was a little kid, visiting cousins in Miles City. I'm surprised she didn't show you the scars."

"No, she didn't tell us that story. But I'll never forget how she lost her ear."

"Foolish old woman. It will be good to see her again."

Ritta stopped and turned to face Jody. "Have you thought anymore about what we're going to tell her, about us?"

Jody grimaced. "Just three state's worth. Have to decide soon. She's going to meet us at the protest." She exhaled with a snort, then looked into Ritta's eye, placed her palms on Ritta's warm cheeks and said quietly, "I love you more than I ever thought possible. I know we have to be careful on the Rez, here in 'Missionary Land'. But I would like to find a place on this trip we can be together and not have to hide the way we feel. Beside, I think the old girl could handle it."

"I think you're right." Ritta held Jody's fingers to her mouth and kissed the tip of each one. Without a word, Ritta led the way towards the rocks, still grasping her lover's hand.

When they stood in the narrow strip of shade, Ritta slipped the bota bag off her neck and offered it to Jody.

"Christ, it's hot." Jody squeezed a long draught of water into her mouth from the fur-covered pouch. A trickle escaped her lips and ran down her chin. "How in the hell did you talk me into coming here, anyway."

"Me? You're the one who hooked us up with the UNA. Too bad Bear and the others can't come sooner. It's going to be tough taking Sheep Mountain. Mount Rushmore could be harder. We'll need all the bodies we can muster."

"Hey, where's that fearless woman warrior that I know and love?"

Ritta didn't smile. "It's different now that we're really here. I know I've been talking a long time about coming home, but..."

"Still worried that Lopate will be out to get you?"

Ritta unconsciously stroked the scar on her cheek. "Uncle Lawrence said in his letter things are getting worse. But how could I stay away when this is cooking? We've been all over helping other tribes gain back something they had lost. It's time to come home and take our land back. Time to face the bastards here."

"We have to be very careful. We could get killed, you know."

"I don't want to hear that. Tell me again we can make a difference on the Rez." Ritta flopped on the blanket spread out on the flattened grass. She patted the bumpy spot beside her.

Jody sat down. "You can make a difference. Besides, you're not alone this time. Bear and the contingent from Berkeley will be coming soon. And the traditionals, if we can get them to rally. Remember how Lawrence said the elders are so glad you're coming home."

Home. Ritta looked out over miles of undulating hills, yellowed grass, and yellower black-eyed susans. And rounded mounds of silvery green sage, how she had missed it. Far in the distance, a windbreak of ill-formed trees surrounded an old homestead. Above them, clear blue sky went on forever. The sun blasted the earth. Heat radiated upwards in waves, distorting the scenery with ghostly shimmers. The only sound was the relentless chirp of grasshoppers singing their summer song, accompanied by a rapid click, click, click as one spread its ebony wings towards another dusty stage. The only car was their own. No rush hour traffic. No people except the one she loved the most.

Jody pointed to a large bird circling in the distance above them. "It's as beautiful as you said it would be. Stark, and too goddamn hot, but so open. It's going to take some time to get used to, especially after California."

"Kind of frees your soul though, doesn't it?" Ritta lay back on the blanket next to Jody, watching the hawk spiral. She whistled and watched the *wanblee* get larger.

"Yeah. Like being high up in the mountains, where one wrong move and you could die, just from the elements. I never heard of anyone dying just from fog, have you? Maybe that's why there's more people in California than up north."

"No one in their right mind wants to live here in the winter. As hot as it is now, it will be that extremely cold. The winds howl and whip you and make you cry, just like that."

Jody sat upright, indignant. "Now wait a minute, girl. Don't forget where I grew up. Montana gets plenty damn cold."

"Yeah, but you have all those mountains to break the wind. Here it just blows right through 'cause there's nothing to stop it on its way to Nebraska. We used to get so cold all us kids would get under Grandma's old star quilt and huddle all day to keep warm. It was the one time we got along."

Jody snuggled next to Ritta. "If we end up staying, I'll keep you warm."

As their lips touched, the unmistakable shudder of a rattler's warning riveted their attention. On the rock ledge a few feet above them the snake coiled and raised its head.

Ritta's fingers tightened on Jody's hand. "Move real slow. Don't be afraid."

"Oh, sure." Jody whispered hoarsely.

"Real slow. But you got to move." Ritta pulled Jody's hand with tedious slow motion until they were crouched, then standing. Ritta gathered the blanket and bota bag as they backed away, still holding Jody's trembling fingers.

Their pent up fright exploded into a race to see who could get to the road first. Even in her sandals, Jody was the winner. She didn't stop until she was in the Plymouth, sitting on the passenger side, trying to catch her breath, but safe from legless intruders. Ritta slowed before she reached the car, dragging the blanket behind her. She dropped it and leaned over the trunk, her sides heaving, then jerked her hands away from the metal. "Damn, that's hot." She fiddled with the plastic cap on the bota bag, poured some water on her scorched palms then squeezed the bag over her face. The cool liquid ran down her flushed cheeks. Some dribbled into her mouth. Then she saw the *wanblee* swooping silently at the edge of rock. "Look!"

Jody followed her gaze in time to witness the swift demise of the snake as talons bent and lifted it far above its normal realm.

Ritta walked to the open window. "You can come out now."

"No way. Not until dark. There might be more."

Ritta laughed. "You don't even want to wait till dark. Snakes seek warmth after the sun goes down. They'll crawl right into a sleeping bag."

"Oh, shit. Car, you better get us out of here." Jody pounded on the dashboard.

Ritta laughed.

"What, you think it's funny I'm scared?"

Ritta shook her head and stifled her chortles. Jody tried to open the door, then jerked the handle hard when nothing happened. Ritta, her lips plastered shut in a quirky grin, reached through the open window and pulled up the door lock. Jody sheepishly opened the door. Ritta held her mouth to contain the giggles, and watched Jody try harder to be mad. When Jody swung her legs to the road, then quickly bent down to look under the car, Ritta couldn't hold it any longer. Jody finally started laughing too, and soon tears rolled down both their cheeks.

Wiping her eyes on her shirt, Jody walked to the trunk and pulled out her tall boots. She put them on, not bothering with socks, and laced them all the way up before she gathered some tools. Ritta watched her look underneath the car again, as if convincing herself it was safe to concentrate on the task at hand.

"Can I help?"

"No. Yes. Watch for snakes. I think I can get it if there's enough slack in this hose to pull it past the split." Jody ducked under the hood. "Shouldn't be too long before we're ready to roll."

Ritta looked around at the familiar landscape that had filled her heart with longing, and remembered the day she had left her childhood behind. Reaching her hands to the sky, she gave thanks for the road that had brought her back again, and the happiness that filled her heart.

Near dusk, they pulled into Lawrence's place. Ritta was surprised to see a dozen or more elders gathered there to welcome her home, sitting on blanket-covered bales and two rickety chairs, drinking coffee. She looked around for her mom and Janey. Lawrence hugged her, then said, "I didn't tell Mabel you were coming home. We'll go find her tomorrow."

After each of the elders greeted her and Jody, they wanted to know about Alcatraz, hardly believing that a group of unarmed Indian people still held the former prison.

Ritta rubbed High Tail on the forehead and soft horse lips, then let the mare nuzzle her neck. "We can do it here, too," she told them. "We have a right to reclaim the land the government stole. What did they do with it? Drop bombs on it. Then they said no one can live there again. They abandoned it. We have a right to it, and to *Paha Sapa.* Our treaty gives us that right. No one is going to hand it back to us. We must take it, like they took it from us. First by possession, then in the courts when we get the media's attention. There are people all over the world who will stand with us. We just have to make them pay attention."

Headlights turned off the road and down the lane, a rooster tail of dust behind it lit by the lights of the vehicles that followed. Ritta turned to Lawrence, her heart slamming inside her. He reached behind the bale next to him and pulled out a rifle. Several of the elders walked over to stand between Ritta and the truck's blinding headlights.

A voice called from the driver's open window. "Ritta. It's me, Moses."

"Moses!" Ritta rushed to hug him. "How did you know...?"

"Moccasin telegraph." He nodded hello to Lawrence. "Bear got ahold of me a couple days ago. Told me to watch out for you two till he gets here."

Jody shook her head, but smiled warmly and clasped the hand he offered her. "Good to see you, Moses. How many friends did you bring along?"

"'Bout twenty. More will come later. All my *kolas* are coming."

Soon the first fires were lit, the young children fed and bedded down in tents and makeshift shelters. Moses and a few others carried a large drum to the center of camp, then followed Lawrence for more hay bales to arrange around the drum. As they sang *Akicita Olowan,* the warrior's song, Ritta looked at all of them; the elders, her uncle, Moses and his friends who had come from many reservations to join them. She turned to Jody, who was trying to sing the words to the song. Jody took her hand and asked, "What?"

Ritta smiled. "I'm home."

Afterword

In 1958 members of Congress traveled to Pine Ridge reservation to hear testimony from tribal members. This hearing brought about an amendment to bill H.R. 7860 which provided "payments be made to certain members of the Pine Ridge Sioux Tribe of Indians as reimbursement for damages suffered as the result of the establishment of the Pine Ridge aerial gunnery range."

Dewey Beard was ninety-seven years old at the time of the hearing, and told the Congressmen he had fought at the Custer battle, after which he escaped with Sitting Bull into Canada. Later he returned to his homeland, and was with the Big Foot band at Wounded Knee. His wife, daughter, mother and father were killed, he was wounded. Then in 1907, Mr. Dewey and his second wife were allotted land, nine-hundred eighty acres in what became the gunnery range. They had a log cabin, farmed, and ran a hundred head of horses on this land. He was eighty-four when the Army told him he had ten days to move. His son, who had tuberculosis, was not able to help him and Mr. Dewey lost everything, again.

Another tribal member reports, "that at the time of the taking in 1942 he was told by Mr. Van Camp of the Army engineers, that the land would not really be taken away from him. He was assured it was going to be used during the war and would be returned to him afterward. The money he was going to get from the Government, he was told, was not the real price of the land but only for damages done to the land during the war."

One hundred twenty-five families lost their allotments to the gunnery range. Most were compensated a meager amount; this bill awarded $3,500 each to those people, or their heirs, as this was fourteen years later. This was amended by the Secretary of the Interior to "only eighty-three heads of families domiciled on trust lands within the taking area…" The others who lost their land did not have houses built there, so were not compensated, even though those people used the land to gather food or run livestock. In the early 1970's, NASA's instrumentation in space confirmed large deposits of uranium beneath the Sheep Mountain Gunnery Range.

It was this piece of land that the Wounded Knee occupation was supposed to bring to public attention—a fact entirely lost as the armored personnel carriers rolled through the reservation. For a more thorough understanding of the situation, read *In the Spirit of Crazy Horse* by Peter Matthiessen.

Hundreds of Lakota people were assaulted and murdered on the reservation during Tribal Chairman Dick Wilson's "reign of terror." Very few of these brutal incidents were investigated, even though many eye witnesses tried to speak up. The FBI has jurisdiction over "major crimes" committed on reservations. Much controversy still exists over the murder of Anna May Pictou Aquash, a Micmac from Nova Scotia who was part of the occupying AIM force at Wounded Knee.

For an excellent account of Alcatraz, the Red Power Movement, and AIM, read *Like a Hurricane* by Paul Chaat Smith and Robert Allen Warrior. *The Occupation of Alcatraz Island* by Troy R. Johnson and *Alcatraz, Alcatraz* by Adam Fortunate Eagle were also invaluable aids in writing this book.

Recent novels from New Victoria

Talk Show
A novel by Melissa Hartman $10.95
Gossipy, sophisticated and erotic
Nita grew up eclipsed by the fame and drug abuse of Gina Wilde, her rock star mother. Now, after her mother's mysterious death, her aunt, a notorious lesbian talk show host on daytime TV, wants to produce a show about Gina's tempestuous life and that ambivalent mother/daughter relationship.

Callaloo and other Lesbian Love Tales
LaShonda K. Barnett $10.95

These sensually charming stories of women's love across race, age and class are like the aroma of good cooking with that extra special spice.
this book is a vicseral glimpse of Black lesbian lives/a remembering and celebration that we've long waited for!—sharon bridgeforth, *the bulljean stories*

Flight From Chador
a suspense novel by Sigrid Brunel $10.95
Public beheading would be her fate if she failed.
Anouk Trabi, an Egyptian woman pilot schemes to save a German teenaged girl from a forced Islamic marriage. When the American photopher, Karen Jensen, insists on helping, they enter Yemen disguised as Arab husband and veiled wife. But the rigid Islamic laws test them to the limits of their love and power in this death-defying rescue mission.

Send for free catalog:
New Victoria Publishers
PO Box 27 Norwich, VT 05055
or write to our email address: newvic@aol.com
Check out our our web site at: http://www.NewVictoria.com